Sold for Endless Rue

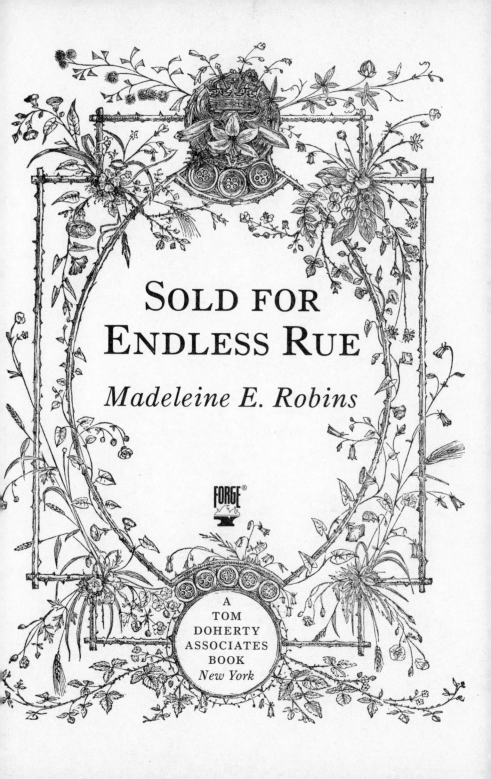

SOLD FOR ENDLESS RUE

Madeleine E. Robins

FORGE®

A
TOM
DOHERTY
ASSOCIATES
BOOK
New York

SOLD FOR ENDLESS RUE

Copyright © 2013 by Madeleine E. Robins

A Forge Book
Published by Tom Doherty Associates, LLC
175 Fifth Avenue
New York, NY 10010

www.tor-forge.com

Forge® is a registered trademark of Tom Doherty Associates, LLC.

ISBN 978-0-7653-0399-8 (hardcover)
ISBN 978-1-4668-0675-7 (e-book)

Forge books may be purchased for educational, business, or promotional use. For information on bulk purchases, please contact Macmillan Corporate and Premium Sales Department at 1-800-221-7945 extension 5442 or write specialmarkets@macmillan.com.

First Edition: May 2013

Printed in the United States of America

0 9 8 7 6 5 4 3 2 1

For Emil and Penny, with love and history

Part I

THE WITCH

Chapter One

The world was all sound: the crack of brush underfoot, her own harsh panting, the whip of the branches as she pushed her way through them, and behind her somewhere a man's guttural cursing. The girl tasted salty blood from a cut below her eye. There would be more blood if Urbo caught her. That thought gave her a burst of strength as she climbed the rocky hill, pushing aside the brush. Then, at the crest, she stopped, stunned. She had never imagined the vista below her. Houses spilled down steeply to a city, thence to a broad bay. She had never seen the ocean before; had she not seen the white curl of waves breaking on the rocks at the harbor's edge, she would not have believed the flat plane of gray to be water. Above, the leaden sky, bleak and still, frayed to mist where it met the water.

Then at the farthest horizon the clouds broke and a shaft of light like a finger touched the sea and made it gold-lined silver. The girl forgot that she was under sentence of death and stood, heedless of runlets of blood on her ankles and feet where thorns had torn at them. Her fisted hands uncurled and her breath quieted.

Then there was a rattle of dirt and pebbles from behind her, and not far behind. The moment was gone. The girl began to clamber down the rocks as fast as she dared, making for what might be a path. If she could reach a cottage, people, someone, might help her. If she could find a church she could beg for sanctuary. If she could reach the sea, she could throw herself in and drown.

The path she found was only a beating-down of scrub grass that threaded among the rocks and wind-shaped trees. Some of the rocks were large enough for a scrawny child to hide behind; others were small enough to cut her feet and send her skidding and sliding down the hill. She barely looked ahead, concentrating on keeping her feet until she reached a boulder that nestled in the curve of the hill. Rounding it, she crouched down and peered back up the way she had come. Despite the cuts on her feet and legs, she saw no blood on the path. Perhaps she had left no trail, but her panting and the drumming of her heart felt loud enough to call any pursuer down upon her. She looked farther, drew back, looked again, weak with terror. Up near the crest of the bluff where she had first broken out of the brush, a man was crouched against the gray sky: Urbo.

Of course. He had promised to deal with her himself if ever she dared run from him. If he caught her there was no chance she could fight him: she was eleven years old, half-starved, nearly at her strength's end. She would have to hide. She turned, began to run and slide, keeping behind the trees and rocks where she could. Twice she almost fell. She came down a steep path in a rush and very nearly slammed into a wall.

The wall was made of white stones, half-again as tall as the girl herself. She could just see the roof of the house within. Crying out, she ran the wall's length, turned the corner, and ran again, looking for a gate or doorway, hoping someone would hear her and come out, even to chase her away. The gate she found at last, but it was barred against entry, and all within seemed ghostly quiet. She turned and ran on.

Next was a stone cottage; a pair of short-nosed brindle

dogs was tied to the gate, and they bayed and snapped at her, drowning out her calls. She went on, expecting at any moment to see Urbo behind her, rounding the corner. There was one more cottage ahead, then a stand of cypress trees. She said a prayer to Saint Margaret as she ran. Here there were no dogs and no gate to speak of. The wall was low enough that she could see into the garden by the door. The first house she had passed looked prosperous but empty. The second, well-tended and well-guarded. This one was small, shabby but neat. The girl went to the door.

A woman's voice called out before she could speak, a voice thick, full of rales. "Carolina? Is that you?"

The girl looked in the door and spoke as loud as she dared. "Help me. Please. I beg you in the name of Christ and all his saints, please please—"

"Who? What?" Although the day was overcast it was a moment before the girl's eyes adjusted to the dim light in the cottage. Past the firepit, where only a few coals glowed, there was a wooden bedstead tucked against the wall, its covers thrown everywhere. From it a woman spoke.

"Who is that?" The old-woman voice again, but the woman was young.

"Auntie, I beg you, don't rise if you're ill—but please, I need a place to hide. A man is chasing me. He's sworn he'll kill me. Please, I'm afraid." Face to face with another human being she could think of no better persuasion than her fear. But this woman was very sick; the cottage stank of illness. "Auntie, you're sick. I don't want to bring trouble to you. Is there a priest who would give me sanctuary? Anyone? He *will* kill me."

"But you're only a child." The woman's voice was a little stronger now. "Not from Salerno, either. Who would hurt you?" She sank back into the pillows again, breathing hard. She was pale as thin new milk and her dark hair was plastered against her head with sweat. "Carolina!" she called again. Then, "No, she hasn't the sense to keep a secret. Here, girl." She hunched her body toward the bed's edge. "You swear that you're not running from the law, your father, or the church?"

The child nodded mutely.

"Well, if you fear your pursuer more than you fear my fever, hide here." She raised up the sheets and made a place for the girl on her far side, by the wall. The girl did not hesitate. Dying from a fever or flux seemed a kinder death than what Urbo had promised her. As carefully as she could, the girl climbed over the sick woman and burrowed down among the damp, rank sheets. The woman pulled the covers over the girl's head and lay back, coughing. "Lie still," she said at last. "You should be safe here, for a time."

The girl lay still. The woman's body gave off heat like a bake-oven through her shift. It was the first time the girl had lain in a bed of any sort for over a year, and for a moment she imagined herself at home, cuddled beside her mother after a terrible dream. Despite the heat in the bed she began to shiver.

"Shhh," the woman murmured. "When my daughter comes, say nothing. Lie still."

The girl did her best. "Aunt, may I pray for you?" she asked. "For whom should I ask a blessing?"

The woman coughed again. The cough was deep and liquid and released a cloud of foul air. "I will be grateful for your prayers if you can say them silently. My name is Sofia. Now hush. Perhaps we both may sleep." Sofia rocked onto her hip to face the door, and the girl curled as close to her as she could, thinking a string of *Aves* for her savior until the prayers lulled her into a doze.

Voices wakened her. There was a child, younger than herself, calling, "Mama! Mama!" Sofia stirred in her sleep, stiffened as she felt the girl tucked against her back, then raised herself up on one elbow.

"Carolina, where have you been?"

"Playing at the fountain, Mama. I met a man."

A man. The girl longed to look, but knew she dared not.

"Did you?" Sofia's voice was weak but calm. She coughed again. "Who, little one?"

Another voice, and the scuff of boots on the hard-packed earth floor. "A traveler, sister."

The girl's heart clutched: she thought surely the room must ring with her fear. It was Urbo, speaking with expansive geniality.

Sofia lifted herself higher, perhaps to mask the way the girl had started behind her. "What do you want, brother? You see I'm not well. My daughter should know better than to bring a stranger home when I'm in this state."

"He's lost his little girl, Mama," the child said.

"I have, sister. A girl of about ten years, red hair, brown eyes. She's likely to be filthy after the chase she's led me." He sounded reasonable. Had the girl not known otherwise she would have trusted him herself. "Ran off to spare herself a hiding."

"Why would you think to find her here?" Sofia coughed again. Pressed against her, the girl could feel Sofia, propped upon her elbow, tremble with effort. "You see that the only child here is my own, brother. I can't ask you to—"

"She has been here, though, hasn't she? Did you send her on?" Urbo wheedled, the voice he used before he raised his fist. He was still across the room: he feared sickness. "She might have slipped in while you were sleeping."

Sofia dropped back onto the bed, breathing rapidly. Her heart beat fast against the girl's cheek. *Please let her not die,* the girl prayed, and pressed herself again her, making herself as small as she could.

"Brother, if you wish to look in this house you're welcome to do it, but then go; I have no strength for talking." Sofia coughed again. "Carolina!"

There was a bump and a shift in the bed as the little girl came to sit beside her mother. Under the sheets the girl could not tell if Urbo was looking about, was deciding to leave, or had left already.

Then a new voice. A man's, deeper than Urbo's, demanding to know what a stranger was doing in his house. The girl could see nothing but knew Urbo must be gauging the newcomer, judging how much of an opponent he would be. If he thought the man not worth fighting, he would become more dangerous, as if he meant to throw his opponent's weakness in his face. She had seen him do it. She tensed in her hiding place.

"You can see there is no child here," the other man was saying. He sounded young, vigorous, and careless, as if he counted Urbo as little threat. "My wife is sick. Look elsewhere for your child."

"Where else would she go?" Urbo challenged.

"All of Salerno lies just down the hill."

Now a third voice broke in. "Nicolo, take this outside, unless you wish to bury Sofia tomorrow. And you, man, can you not see there's sickness here? Do you wish to bring it back to wherever it is you come from?" This was a woman, not young, but forceful and used to being obeyed. "You two men go bristle and preen yourselves in the yard. Leave me to my business. Carolina, I need more water than this. I've come to make physic for your mama."

"All right, grannie. I'll go," Urbo said. "But have *you* seen a child—"

"I'm a midwife, brother. I've seen hundreds of children, but none today. Now: *go*."

Urbo went. His boots scuffed on the doorstep, and the girl heard the rumbling of male voices outside the house, still wary but civil. The little girl, Carolina, left her mother's side and ran off to fetch water. The old woman began to move around the room, rummaging and muttering. Sofia began to cough again.

"Hush, shhhh," the old woman murmured. Sofia rolled onto her back, squashing the girl into the straw pallet. The sheets rustled, there was a pressure of hands as the old woman smoothed them across Sofia's body. The girl braced herself, waiting for discovery.

"Well," the old woman said briskly. "You have a guest. No—" The girl had stiffened and started to rise, but the old woman pushed her back. "If you have not taken the fever by now, an hour more won't hurt you. Lie still, girl. Is that man truly your father?"

"No, grannie," the girl whispered. "He's an evil, evil man, he swore—"

"He's gone now. Lie quiet. Sofia, I'll talk to Nicolo."

The girl lay still, listening to the homely sounds of water poured into a kettle and set on the fire. When little Carolina returned, the nurse woman set her to grinding herbs, and for a time the hidden girl drowsed, confusing the tapping of the mortar and pestle with the beating of Sofia's heart. She woke again when the nurse sat on the bed and raised Sofia up to drink her physic.

"It smells foul," Sofia protested.

The nurse laughed. "If you can care for how it smells, dear one, Death doesn't hold you in his hand. Carolina, is there any honey in the house? No? Then run to Anna's house and borrow some. Quickly!" There was the sound of footfall as the child ran out. "Now you, girl. I told Nico to take the stranger down to the city, so we've some time. Sit up and tell me what's what." The girl sat up, blinking in the light. The healer had lit a lamp and set it near the bed. It smoked, and with the smoke from the fire as well, the cottage was hazy.

When the girl saw the nurse's face she understood at once why Urbo had left so easily. He was superstitious, and the old woman had the face of a witch: wrinkles, bony nose, small dark eyes.

"No, I'm no beauty." The old woman laughed.

The girl blushed. "You're beautifully kind to me. Thank you, grandmother."

The healer clicked her tongue, but was clearly pleased. "You were going to tell me how you come to be tucked into Sofia's bed in this fashion. First, get out and—" She pulled a cloth from her belt, or perhaps it was a scarf. "Wrap your head up in this; that red hair is too remarkable. If anyone asks you, you're my new apprentice. What's your name, girl?"

"Fil-Filipa." It had been more than a year since anyone had used it. "Filipa." She climbed out of the bed, careful not to disturb Sofia, and took the cloth to wrap up her hair. Sofia lay quiet, watching Filipa and the nurse.

"Fetch the mortar where that foolish child has left it." The nurse pointed a long finger toward the hearth. Unlike her fierce features, her hands were well shaped. "Now, Filipa. Why is that foreign brute chasing you through the outskirts of Salerno?"

"He swore he'd kill me," the girl said. She brought the wooden mortar over, but, rather than take it, the nurse pushed it back to her and handed her the pestle, gesturing that she was to grind the gray-green herbs in the bowl.

"Why would a man like that bother to kill a child like you?"

"I ran away. He said if I ran—"

"And how did you come to be with such a man in the first place?" the old woman asked. "Is he some kin to you?"

Filipa scowled. "He's no kin to any human man. He's a brigand, and he killed all my family and destroyed my town."

The old woman looked down her nose. "One man alone destroyed your town?"

Filipa shook her head. The hand holding the pestle shook. "There were many of them, a dozen, then. They fell on our village like dogs, surprised us. Killed all the men—" Her voice was high.

"A dozen men." The old woman looked at Sofia. "Are they with him now?"

"Most of them are gone—some left to join with another band, another one died from a poisoned wound. There were four, and Urbo, when I ran."

"Are they near enough for yon Urbo to bring them back here? When did you escape them? "

"Three days ago." Filipa steadied the mortar in her hand.

"So his mates are some days away. Keep working, girl. Carolina will be back in a moment, and I want to make more of this for us to leave for Sofia."

"Leave?" The girl looked at the woman on the bed; Filipa did not want to leave her, even for the old woman who seemed so matter-of-fact in taking her in. "Can't I stay here?"

"And do what? If your enemy comes back, can Sofia fight him off? If Nicolo tried, well, he's no fighter. No, you'll be safer with me. We shall give you a craft name and say you've been bound to me as an apprentice; if you show some skill, perhaps it will be true. Now." She took the girl's chin in her strong, reddened hand. "What shall I call you? Zenzera, for that hair? No. Artemisia? Too grand for such a scrap as you." She laughed, but her eyes bored deep, as if she were divining in a pool of water. "Laura," she said at last. "For the laurel, which has much magic but a plain appearance. I am Crescia, but you'll call me mistress, is that clear?"

"I will call you saint—"

The old woman gave her chin a final squeeze. "Don't blaspheme, girl. God doesn't laugh at such jests." She turned back to Sofia. "Well, my dear. This is my new apprentice, Laura. She's going to finish grinding the feverfew and mix in some—" She produced a pouch from a basket by her feet. "Some ground betulla, and when Carolina returns we shall add water and honey. You're to drink a cupful every hour until your fever breaks."

Sofia made a face. "And if the fever doesn't break?"

"What a baby you are!" But Nonna Crescia stroked Sofia's forehead. "The fever will break, daughter. You'll be up and chasing after that scatterwit child of yours in a few days. For now, you sleep." She made a pass with her hand over the sick woman's eyes.

Sofia smiled and closed her eyes. Smiling, she slept.

With a great clatter Carolina ran into the house, a clay pot in her hands with a bit of honey in it, and much more on her fingers. She stopped when she saw the older girl, and frowned. Nonna Crescia explained who the stranger was; the child—less than half Filipa's age—edged around the room until she stood on Crescia's other side, and held the honey pot out to her.

"Laura, hot water," the old woman commanded. Filipa did not remember her new name for a moment, and the healer gave her a clout on the shoulder to remind her, but it was a woman's buffet, not the sort of blow she had been used to in Urbo's camp. She dipped hot water and rinsed the honey from the sides of the clay pot and into a bowl. When she had done so, Crescia mixed in the ground herbs and stirred the whole into a gray-green sludge, then added more water until it was a light syrup.

"When your mama wakes, she must drink a cup of this. If the fever doesn't break before noon tomorrow, come and fetch me." Carolina was staring at Filipa. Nonna Crescia took her chin in her hand and turned the child's face to her own. "Do you understand, 'Lina?"

Crescia repeated the instructions. The child nodded.

"Well, then." Crescia reached down to feel by the bed and came up with a stick of polished wood with a knob of stone set at one end. She leaned upon it to rise. She was only half a head taller than her new apprentice. "Come, Laura. You carry the basket."

Filipa—now Laura—picked up the basket, which clacked with jars and vials. The old woman moved slowly to the door and out, her weight as much on the stick as on her own legs. The girl followed after, just as slowly. It was not that she feared Crescia, or disliked pretending to be her apprentice. But what if Urbo had lingered? She was certain no amount of scolding and playing the herbwife would save her or Crescia from death.

At the gate the old woman stopped. "There is no point in being fearful, girl. That bad man has gone down into the city with Nicolo to look for you. Nico has no love for foreigners. He was a boy when the city was sacked a dozen years ago. He'll have the fellow lost and found and turned around, all the time sure they'll find you at the next corner, until the man himself cries off and heads for home."

Laura did not believe it. She feared for Nicolo almost as much as she did for Sofia and Crescia and herself.

"You don't know," she began.

"I know his sort," Crescia said firmly. "A bully. But he won't be so brave away from his men, daughter. One man—I grant you, a big man—one man alone in a city he doesn't know, being escorted by a helpful fellow who may call his neighbors for assistance?" The old woman shrugged and made the threat of no account. Laura was not persuaded. Urbo and his men had needed a scant hour to destroy Villaroscia the year before.

It was nearly dusk. The clouds had lifted, leaving rosy light on the horizon, gilding the eaves of Sofia's house. A breeze wicked around Laura's legs; her tunic barely reached past her knees. Nonna Crescia looked at her. "Don't dawdle."

Laura had run before, when she had terror to drive her. Now it seemed hard even to walk; she limped on her bad right leg and struggled with the basket she carried.

"The first thing is, you must be decently dressed." Crescia led the way through blue shadows, past the houses Laura had passed earlier, and along a path she had not noticed before, up the hill again until they reached a cottage of stone and plaster, circled by a low fence and framed by cypress and olive and orange trees and a cluster of wooden sheds. Nonna Crescia had picked her way up the path, moving as if her stick was all that kept her upright. But once inside the fence she stood erect, tucked the stick under her arm, and moved forward briskly.

"Come, Laura."

The girl stared after her, thinking this must surely be witchcraft.

"Neve, Decoro, Ravanella, Bonta! This is Laura, who will stay with us. Come, my dears!" The old woman stood, hands outstretched, and four white goats bounded out of a shed to greet her. She laughed like a girl, looking over her shoulder at Laura, inviting her to join them. She did, but she was cautious. The animals in Urbo's camp, like the men, had been rough. One of the goats jumped at her and knocked Laura off her feet. It was too much: to be free, and frightened, and tired, and knocked down by a snowy white goat onto her backside in the rocky yard. The goat nuzzled at her ear as Laura sobbed.

"Bonta, you devil!" Crescia pushed the goat aside, pulled Laura to her feet, and guided the girl toward the house, all the while stroking her forehead as she had stroked Sofia's earlier. "Come, girl. You'll have food, and bathe, and I will tend those scratches on your legs, and then you'll sleep. And you may tell me all about it or not, as you please."

Crescia's cottage was larger than it had appeared from the path, a series of square rooms strung together in a line. The first was a workroom with benches and two tables and shelves that held vessels and a fire with a great kettle hung above it. The room was dense with the smell of aromatics; bundles of flowers and grasses hung from the rafters, and garlands of bulbs and roots. Along one wall were jugs and pots of all sizes, some so small they might have only held a grape or a few seeds, some so large they might have held whole melons. Laura looked around her, trying to make sense of what she saw, until Crescia pushed her gently toward the next room. "You may start to learn about all this tomorrow."

Through the square doorway into the next room was another table, and the more usual furnishings of a household: stools, a chair with a back, another firepit with a tripod and kettle; a basket with a spindle and a spool of coarse yarn, a cupboard, a broom. The old woman pushed Laura down onto a stool, took up a basin, filled it with tepid water from the kettle, and put it on the table beside a bowl of gray-green soap.

"Wash," she commanded. She turned her back to poke the banked coals in the fireplace to life.

Laura stared at the healer. It had been more than a year since anyone had cared whether she bathed or not. Crescia turned back, took a cloth, dipped it in water, and scrubbed it across Laura's cheek. "Wash," she repeated.

Laura scrubbed her face, then her hands and arms and finally, when the old woman held out her hand to receive the girl's shift and tunic, at her chest and as much of her back as she could reach. That was not so bad; the welts there were mostly healed. Still, when the old woman saw the marks of whipping across Laura's shoulders she made a noise with her tongue against her teeth, took the cloth from her hand, and gently cleaned the skin around the welts. Laura washed her legs, dabbing at the scratches and scrapes she had got in escaping Urbo. She could not bring herself to unwind the cloth wrapped around her right ankle, fearing what she would see there.

Crescia gave Laura a blanket to wrap herself in, but then pulled it away from her shoulders, smoothed a cool, green-smelling unguent on them, and laid a cloth lightly over it. Then she knelt to inspect the ragged scratches on Laura's leg, and unwound the cloth on her ankle.

"What did this?"

The pain of even the healer's light touch made Laura queasy. "When Urbo—when he and his men came, they leashed the ones of us they didn't kill to their horses, like calves. I tried and tried to get the rope off, but all it did was tear the skin until it rubbed raw."

Crescia pursed her lips and nodded. "You'll have a scar, and lucky it isn't worse inflamed than it is."

"I covered it with the rag," Laura said defensively. "I put spiderweb on to stop the bleeding."

"Did you?" The healer looked up and smiled. Painstakingly the old woman cleaned the sore flesh and then dabbed more of her unguent on it and, at the last, bound it with more cloth. Laura was light-headed by the time it was done.

"Now, clothes." Crescia held out a clean shift.

It dropped to Laura's toes, and the sleeves fell past her fingers.

"Roll up the sleeves, and I'll shorten a tunic for you tonight. Sit, child." Crescia had put a bowl of broth and beans and a piece of bread on the table. Laura's stomach growled, but the old woman had not yet put her own bowl out.

"Eat!" Crescia said. "It's a fasting day for me. Eat, before you perish in front of me."

The girl did. She made herself eat slowly so that she would not be sick and lose all the good of her food. It seemed dreamlike to be clean and full and warm. She felt tears start, but shook her head and stopped them.

"There, now." Crescia had settled in the high-backed chair and was stripping the shells or husks off some beans into a bowl in her lap. "Tell me."

Laura told her of the morning when Urbo's men had come to Villaroscia. Her father was cut down before he could say a word. She told of Mama and her sister Bice, raped and raped again and finally beaten to death by Urbo himself. She told of the months she and the few other survivors had been dragged along with Urbo's band. They had once meant to join the army at Naples, but lawful warfare proved too restrictive for their taste. Urbo sold most of the other captives from Villaroscia, but not Laura. She had no need to tell Crescia of the beatings: she had treated their scars. But Laura told her of Urbo's threats, that when he wanted her compliance he would smile and touch himself, hoisting his privates in a silent threat: *as your mother and Bice, so you.*

"He told me if I ran he would kill me." The bowl before Laura was empty. She had used the crumb of her bread to sop up the last of the broth.

"And still you ran away?"

Laura nodded. She could not explain why she had done so, or why now rather than next month or three months before. Perhaps it had been the scent of the ocean on the air. Perhaps the same good angel that had kept her alive in the months since Mama died had whispered hope in her ear.

"God does everything for a purpose," Crescia said. "Perhaps he meant you to come to me. Now, though, you need sleep." As the healer said the words, Laura knew it was true, although the moment before she had not been sleepy.

Crescia rose—inside the house she did not use the stick at all—and guided the girl into the third room, a small chamber with a narrow bedstead. Laura stepped toward the bed, but Crescia caught her back. "I sleep alone, girl." She looked around the room and seemed to come to a decision. "You'll sleep here."

She pointed to a large chest on the right side of the room. Beyond it was a narrow space just large enough for a pallet. From the chest Crescia drew blankets that she handed to Laura.

"Go." She gave the girl a little push. "Tomorrow we'll make a real bed for you, but tonight I don't think you'll mind the floor. Go on."

Mind? Laura dropped to her knees and took the old woman's skirt in her hands and kissed it. "Thank you, mistress. Thank you for my life."

For a moment it seemed the old woman was moved. Then she snorted and pulled her skirt away. "I'm not the Queen of Heaven, girl! And I'll make you work hard enough to wonder if those thanks were earned. Go, now. Sleep." Without bothering to see whether Laura obeyed or not, Crescia returned to the kitchen.

Laura slept, but woke a while later to see Nonna Crescia's shadow on the wall above her makeshift bed. She was preparing for bed, moving about quietly. Laura heard her pray before she got into her bed, which creaked under her slight weight.

"Sleep!" the old woman commanded. How had she known that Laura was awake?

"Yes, mistress. Good night." A moment later a thought came to Laura and, because she was half-asleep, she gave it voice. "Are you a witch?"

In the darkness the old woman laughed. "I am a healer. You may be too, if you're willing to work. Will that please you?'

The girl was asleep before she could say yes.

Chapter Two

Laura woke screaming in the dark. She did not know where she was, only that the hand that reached her was not Urbo's. She felt herself rocked against a woman's breast, heard a murmur of soothing words, until her screams ebbed into whimpers and then into silent, shuddering breaths. Shortly, lulled by that steady rocking, she slept.

When she woke again she lay still. Where was she? In a house, and the blanket she lay on was clean and sweet smelling. She heard birdsong, saw the rose light of dawn, and felt the coarse-finished wood of the chest beside her. Was this a dream? A good dream? Then she remembered: she was in the healer's house. The thud of her heart slowed a little and she sat up, feeling for the clothes that Crescia had taken from her the night before. Instead she found a neat folded garment and a clay pisspot. As quietly as she could, she used the pot, folded the blankets, and pulled the tunic, a too-large thing of rosy brown wool, over her shift and belted it. Dust motes swirled in the thin morning light.

Laura sidled from the alcove with her back pressed against the wall, hoping not to wake Crescia. The old woman might believe that Urbo was not a threat, but Laura knew better. Her dreams had reminded her. He meant to kill her, and he would not stop until he had done so. She did not want to bring calamity down upon the people who had helped her. She must leave. She turned into the next room, her back still against the wall, wondering if she might find some bread to bring with her.

"Good morning, daughter. Bring the pot out. You may empty it in the ditch behind the goat shed." Crescia's voice came from the workroom. "If you must leave me you may, but surely you'll want to eat first." She went to the fire and stirred something in the pot there. Laura's stomach growled.

"Go on. Empty the pot, then wash your hands and come eat."

Feeling as though she moved in a dream, Laura obeyed. When she returned, Crescia was sitting at the table, pouring milk from a bowl onto porridge. Another bowl, a wooden spoon, and a jar holding a comb of honey were arranged neatly across from her. Laura sat at the table and, with a sense of great daring, broke off a piece of the comb and put it on her tongue. The burst of sweetness made her close her eyes for a moment. The honey tasted like sunlight on rosemary bushes. When she opened her eyes Crescia was watching her.

"Give thanks, child." The old woman bowed her own head and her lips moved silently. Laura said her Our Father in a whisper and crossed herself.

"Now eat." Crescia was smiling.

As she ate, Laura examined the old woman more closely. In the morning light she thought she had been wrong about her age: her hair, which she had thought was white, was more silvery-fair, and her carriage was straight and energetic. The wrinkles seemed fewer than they had the night before, although the warts and bony nose were unchanged.

"I appear different to you this morning? No, I'm not a young woman, but I find it useful to take on the seeming of a greater age than I own. Age confers authority. So, with a few tricks, I look older even than I am, and I meet far fewer arguments. Now, *you*—" She scraped a last morsel of porridge from her bowl. "I imagine you're still afraid of that hulking man."

"Urbo," Laura said, low.

"You think he'll find you if you stay here, and that's why you were skulking off. If you wish to stay, as I proposed last night, I'll show you a few tricks so that, even if the man does come back, he won't know you."

Laura gaped. "Is that possible?"

"We make you look taller and older and darken your hair a little. Believe me, daughter, there is nothing to fear from one lone man. If need comes, I have draughts will make him gentle as a kitten."

Laura almost smiled. The idea of staying here, clean and fed and learning a craft from Crescia, was powerfully attractive. But the woman did not know Urbo as she did; how could she believe that it would be safe? Unless she *was* a witch, as Laura had suspected the night before. Surreptitiously she crossed herself before she took another bite of porridge.

Crescia, finished with her own meal, washed her bowl and spoon, covered the honeycomb with a bit of cloth, and put it up on the shelf. Then she washed her hands with water from the kettle and soft soap from a bowl; the old woman's hands were red from washing. When Laura had finished her porridge, Crescia gestured to her to do likewise.

"Now." The healer was braiding her hair into two plaits. "Brush your hair and braid it. We'll cover it today—where is the scarf I left you? Later we can color it a dull, drab, safe brown." As she spoke she had twisted her own hair into a roll on the top of her head and covered it with a linen veil that she pinned under her chin. When she was done a few tendrils of silvery hair showed about her brow; when Crescia slouched and scowled she was suddenly an old woman.

The transition was so startling that Laura stopped braiding her hair and clapped her hands. "Mistress, is that magic?"

The older woman snorted. "Nothing of the sort. I'll teach you the trick and then you'll know. Now, finish with your hair, daughter. We have work to do."

* * * *

As easily as that, Laura was apprenticed. When she had done the chores Crescia set her, the two of them left the house, each carrying a basket, a pouch, and a small, sharp knife. While they were near other houses Crescia's back was bent and her gait hobbled, but as they followed the hill—in a different direction, Laura was happy to see, from the way she and Urbo had come the day before—the older woman stood straighter and moved with ease.

"Come learn," she told Laura. "This is comfrey. We use the root for ruptures in childbirth, the leaf for soreness of muscles of all sorts." The leaves were veined and hairy and there were small bell-like purple and white flowers in clusters. "This is a most important plant for any healer." She uprooted three of the plants and bound them together to carry with them. "Never take more than you need. Plants are like a town: if you take all the strongest, the babes and old folk die."

They walked and gathered until the sun was high, pulling leaves, cutting plants, carefully stripping bark from a tree, again with the caution that they must not take too much. "The tree needs its bark as you need your skin, daughter." As they went along, Crescia kept up a steady stream of instruction until Laura thought her head would burst from so many new ideas and facts crammed into it all at once.

"Too much?" Crescia asked once, chuckling. "Don't fret, daughter. I think the Queen of Heaven sent you to me: it was high time I was passing all this along. You'll hear everything again, over and over, until you're sick of it or know it well enough to teach to someone else in your turn." And she went back to teaching.

The sun was past its height when they returned to the house. Laura's feet were hot from the sun-warmed rocks she had clambered over, and her legs were sore. Crescia laid their trove out on the table in the workroom and examined it with satisfaction.

"Are you hungry? When we have eaten I will show you what we do with these."

They dined on cold porridge and water, then Crescia took down a large stone mortar and pestle and set Laura to grinding a bunch of herbs that had dried to her satisfaction. The healer tied in bunches the greens they had brought back today and hung them up from pegs that ringed the walls near the ceiling. When Laura had finished the grinding, Crescia pulled down a large fired pot and filled it halfway with oil. "From olives," she told her apprentice.

"This is a favorite potion of mine," she said. "It clears bruises and works miracles with burns of all sorts. I have some left—" She indicated a jug with a broad cork in its mouth. "But if we brew a new batch today, it will take a fortnight to cure. So we give it that time and we will not be without." She took down boxes and jars, scooping dried flowers and leaves into the pot of oil as Laura stirred it. The whole made a fragrant gray-green sludge that Laura regarded with dismay. Crescia laughed.

"When the virtue of all these plants has seeped into the oil we'll strain them out and what will be left will be purest green, a very powerful unguent. Now, hand me—"

What she wanted next Laura was not to learn. A wavering child's voice cried from the yard, "Nonna! Nonna Crescia, come!"

At once Crescia's back stooped and her expression became subtly that of an old woman ignoring the pangs of age. She gestured to the door with her chin and Laura stumbled forward to answer it. Sofia's daughter Carolina stood with her hand raised to knock.

"Come, Nonna! Mama's hot!" the child said. Tears had striped her dirty face, and her hair was a knotty, windblown cloud around her head. "Papa says come! He says she's dy—"

Crescia stopped the word with a hand across the child's

lips. "Don't invite the devil, child." She pressed the finger to her own lips for a moment, then spat. "There. Your mama's fever hasn't broken?"

When the child shook her head vehemently, tears flew. Laura felt them on her arm.

"Very well. Run tell your papa we follow at once."

Carolina pivoted and ran, raising a cloud of dry dirt. When she was gone Crescia straightened and began to give orders: they must fill a basket with packets of powdered herbs and roots, then wash their hands again before they left. Laura would have grabbed at the shelves in her hurry, but the old woman went slowly, deliberate and calm. At last, Crescia leading the way and Laura following after her carrying the basket, they left. The healer walked briskly down the hill toward Sofia's house, her step surer than Laura's. The girl, on unfamiliar terrain and put off balance by the heavy basket, slipped more than once, almost colliding with her mistress. Crescia did not chide, just set Laura back on her feet and continued. Over her shoulder Laura saw the city below, spilling down the hills to the sea.

"Why do you live so far away from the city?" she asked, when she had breath to speak. "Aren't there more people to tend down there?"

Crescia smiled. "There are more people here to tend than you have seen, girl. Beside, the house we live in was my teacher's. Why would I live anywhere else?" She gestured back at the way they had come. "Here are the plants I need, good water, room for the goats. What do I need from the city?"

"Have you ever been there?"

"Of course. It's no more than half-an-hour's walk down to the cathedral, although we have a church here, not far from Sofia and Nico's house—I'll show you today. I go to market from time to time to buy the things I can't find in these hills: gums from the East, spices, compounds I can't make myself. But the city doesn't need me: have you never heard of the Scuola? The medical school of Salerno? The wisdom of the East, and the Greeks and the Jews, all brought together and taught to monks and gentlemen, educated folk. My medicine has the wisdom of these hills, and the woman who taught me; the city is not for me."

Laura's hem snagged on a thorn. "I'd never seen the sea before," she said. "Is it exciting? From up on the hill the city looks full of towers and castles and—it seems very grand."

Crescia shook her head at Laura's foolishness, but smiled. "You may come with me when I next go to market and judge for yourself. I don't know that it's so grand when you're in the middle of it." As the path leveled out, they rounded a cypress tree and saw the cluster of houses Laura had first approached the day before. Crescia's shoulders rounded and her gait slowed. She leaned heavily on her stick. "Remember, now. Your name is Laura. You've been my apprentice for a few weeks. It is better that you watch and help rather than talk."

"Yes, mistress."

"Good girl."

At Sofia's house, Crescia walked in without salutation, Laura in her wake. The sour smell of sickness was thicker today than the day before, mingling with the acrid smoke of the fire just extinguished and the stench of night soil. Little Carolina was sitting on the floor at the foot of the bed, fresh tears on her face. Nico sat on a stool by his wife's head, dabbing at her forehead with a dingy cloth.

"So the fever has not broken yet." Crescia's tone was matter-of-fact, as if this was just what she might have expected. "That cloth won't do her much good, Nico. Find me a tub. I want to bathe her in herbs and cool water. Carolina, sweet, Laura will give you a packet of herbs to grind. Where is your mortar?" Shortly Crescia had given them all tasks.

Nico, having found nothing larger than a basin in which to bathe his wife, had gone to bring more water. Carolina was pounding enthusiastically and inexpertly at the mortar, mashing green-gray leaves into a waxy paste. And Laura and Crescia were stripping Sofia down to nothing, sponging the foul smell of sickness and sweat from her, watching as the water with which they bathed her evaporated on her skin.

"This fever is stronger than I had hoped," Crescia murmured. Laura looked at Carolina, but the child was grinding away, oblivious. "We will do what we can, and pray. Fenugreek and hellebore are specific for quartan fevers; let us see what they do here. There's no sign of a poisoned wound that I can see."

"Is that good?" Laura whispered.

Crescia shrugged. "Who can say? If there was a pustulant wound or a boil, we could drain it and poultice it. Since there's no cause ready to the eye, there must be some hidden evil. We fight the heat in her with fenugreek, which is hot, and hellebore, which is not, in water that is neither hot nor cold, since we want Sofia to be neither too hot nor too cold. And we'll make a salad of pellitory and my namesake, *crescione*, and warm it and see if we can get her to eat a little. They are herbs that bring balance. Balance is what we want, daughter," she crooned as she stroked the dry hair from Sofia's forehead. "Balance will win you back to us."

Nico came with a bucket of water and went to pour it into the kettle.

"Stop! Is the kettle clean?"

He shrugged as if the question made no sense. Yesterday he had been a handsome man, sure of his place in the world. Today he was diminished and anxious. "There was soup in it yesterday," he said. "But we finished it last night. The child was hungry," he added, as if in excuse.

"Never mind, Nico. Have you a second bucket? Good.

Fetch more water. You, Laura! Take the kettle out and scrub it clean. " She pointed to a bundle of dry leaves in the basket they had brought. "Use that to scrub, and a little water. Then bring it back."

Laura lugged the kettle out into the garden and scrubbed until her shoulder ached; rinsed it with a little more water, and returned to the house. She filled it with the water that remained and hung it over the fire.

"Did it matter there had been soup in it? The soup was gone."

"It does. I'll explain it to you later, daughter." Crescia took the mortar back from Carolina, thanked her for a good job, and tossed the pounded leaves into the kettle. Shortly the room was fragrant with a sharp aromatic scent. When Nico returned with the second bucket of water, Crescia had him bring the kettle to the bedside and pour the cold water into the hot. What resulted was a pale green-yellow liquid the temperature of Laura's own skin. Crescia took two cloths from a clean bundle in her basket and instructed Nico and Laura to sponge Sofia with the cooling potion. For her own part, she took a bundle of greens from her basket and a small brass dish and slowly warmed the greens over the fire. Wisps of gray smoke curled from the dish. Crescia let it cool, then attempted to feed the greens to Sofia.

The sick woman gagged. Calmly, almost humorously, Crescia murmured a stream of reassurances as she prized Sofia's teeth apart and pushed a little more of the greens into her mouth. This time Sofia chewed a few bites before her face screwed up in distaste. "I know it's bitter, dear one. But it will make you well." Crescia pushed a little more of the greens into her mouth. "You'll eat it all, then you may sleep."

When Sofia had eaten the last of the greens and the last of the herb wash was applied, Crescia sent Carolina out to play while she and Laura dressed Sofia in her shift and covered her with a sheet again. Nico stood just inside the door, watching anxiously.

"Go work your clay," Crescia said at last. "She's sleeping, and I think the fever is less. I know you're frightened, son, but you can do nothing but pray for her. You may as well do that at your wheel, where you're master. Go on."

Half-reluctant, half-relieved, Nico went. Crescia settled onto the stool at the head of the bed, and Laura, after a moment, sat on the floor at her mistress's feet.

"You asked why we could not use a dirty pot. The blessed saints and the Queen of Heaven with whom they intercede love what is pure, girl. They love cleanliness, and we keep ourselves clean for them. That's why we wash when we change our tasks, before we eat, when we have woken and used the pot: our tithe to the Queen of Heaven. That is what I was taught and what I believe. But also, girl, every substance in the world has a virtue, even soup! But the virtue of soup may work against the power you use to help your patient. So we make sure there is nothing in the pot but what we want there. You understand?"

Laura nodded. It made sense.

Sofia, eyes closed, murmured something and shifted in her sleep. Crescia put a hand to her forehead, then nodded. "I think that's better. What do you think?"

Gingerly Laura put her hand on Sofia's forehead. It was hot, but not with the dry, scorching heat of an hour ago. She nodded.

"Now, go scrub that kettle again. The fountain is farther along the road, by the church. We must make that infusion all over again: the smell drives out evil as much as the cool balances the heat."

When Laura returned she found Crescia hunched over the mortar in her lap, grinding herbs into fine paste. Laura went for more water, filled the kettle, and set it to boil. When it did Crescia passed her the mortar and nodded. Laura tossed the herbs into the kettle and slid it away from the fire.

"This, we'll let cool naturally. Come sit down by me and rest, girl."

When Laura sat, the old woman cupped her chin in her hand and looked into her face. "You have worked hard today, and there will be more work to come. Are you still happy with what you have undertaken to learn?"

Laura nodded. "I want to learn it all," she said. "Will you teach me to read the writing on your jars?"

Crescia laughed. "That's not writing. They're pictures I drew, but I'm not much good at it. I know what I'm reaching for by sight and smell. It would be a fine thing to know how to read as the monks do—perhaps we can ask Fra Fraternus at the church to take you on as his student. He might, even though you're a girl. Each generation learns more, adds more to the craft. If you could read—"

Sofia stirred and kicked at her sheets. Crescia put out her hand to stroke Sofia's forehead. "Hotter than before. I think the crisis must come soon. Help me to roll her over."

Laura stripped the sheets from Sofia, who was shuddering slightly, and helped Crescia to roll their patient onto her stomach.

"Push up her shift." Crescia took a small earthen pot from her basket and peeled away a scrap of fabric from the top. Sofia's flesh was ashen and flaccid, as if it were melting away from the bone. "Now, watch." Crescia scooped up a soft, waxy, gray-brown ointment with two fingers and daubed it on Sofia's shoulder blades, then on the center of her back, then in each dimple at the top of her buttocks. Then she murmured two Our Fathers and a plea to the Queen of Heaven to intercede for the life of her daughter Sofia.

"Now, rub the ointment into her whole back, from the nape"—Crescia pointed with one finger—"to the end of the spine. Rub it in well, girl. Arrogon is a powerful medicine—it should be, for what it costs. Don't waste any."

The ointment melted into Sofia's hot skin. Laura rubbed and rubbed, beyond the point where the arrogon had been absorbed, as if she were rubbing health back into Sofia. When she began to tire Laura glanced at Crescia, who growled, "Go on, girl. You may be tiring, but Sofia is fighting with the devil." Laura continued rubbing with a will.

At last Crescia snapped, "Stop! Do you want to rub her skin off the bone?" Together they pushed Sofia's shift down to her knees again and rolled her onto her back. Crescia rolled back her own sleeve and tested the water in which the fever herbs had been steeping. Then the two of them took up cloths again and began to wash Sofia's face and shoulders, her arms and legs, over and over until there was no more of the solution left.

They waited. Nico returned from his pottery and Carolina from her play, and they sat by the fire, casting glances at the bed. Laura thought she heard Nico humming to his daughter. Carolina grizzled quietly: she was hungry, she was tired, she wanted Mama. Nico put her on his lap and fed her bits of bread.

An hour after nightfall the crisis came. Sofia's restlessness turned to thrashing, her moans to cries and foul language. Laura looked at Crescia anxiously. "Does the devil have her?" she asked.

"Sickness is the devil, girl. It's the devil trying to undermine our faith in God and the Queen of Heaven. But remember that God helps those first who strive in their own behalf. Sofia"—she gestured toward their patient with her chin—"is fighting mightily against the evil that sickens her."

As Sofia struggled, Crescia sent Nico for more water. This time they did not bother to steep herbs in it, only laid wet cloths on Sofia's brow and neck, her breasts and wrists.

"The skin is thin there," Crescia said. "Better to cool the blood." As Laura attended on Sofia, applying wet cloths and removing those that had dried against her feverish skin, Crescia rose, grunting, and went to the fire. She uncovered a pot, shook her head, and bent to put it on the grate to warm.

"Nico, there's porridge here. No reason for you and 'Lina to go hungry."

Nico, with Carolina in his arms, regarded Crescia with blind, miserable eyes. "Sofia?"

"She's fighting. And you need strength for the fight. So eat. And feed your daughter." She put another small pot onto the grate and stood over it.

In a while the scent of warming porridge filled the house, mingling with the smells of herbs and sickness. Crescia returned to the bed with a cup of something steaming. "Anise boiled in milk, a very good sedative." Together they raised Sofia up; Laura settled herself behind the sick woman to support her while Crescia fed her tiny sips of the sleeping draught. By the time she had drunk the whole, Sofia felt a little cooler to Laura's touch. Laura, on the contrary, was drenched with sweat, her own and Sofia's. She slid out from behind the sick woman and helped Crescia settle her on the bed.

"She'll sleep now," Crescia said. She called over her shoulder, "Nico! Go to sleep. We will sit with Sofia tonight."

Laura, looking at Sofia's white, sunken face, said a silent prayer for her recovery.

"Good." Crescia's voice was soft. "Prayer is a powerful tool. We have done everything we can, except to pray. Sit, daughter."

Laura sat and prayed, echoing the words Crescia was murmuring. At last, "We'll be here all night," the old woman said. "I may as well school you a little. Arrogon, which we used before? It's a compound medicine made of many different things. I buy it when I can, but to make it, start with three drams of rosemary, marjoram, and pellitory of Spain and four drams of Cuckoo-pint and rue. These must be crushed but not powdered. Now, take as well three ounces each of bay, sage, and—"

Laura fell asleep with her head on her mistress's knee.

* * * *

Her neck was stiff when she woke, and the cloth she had wrapped around her hair had unwound and fallen across her shoulders. The room was dark but for the glow of embers across the room. When her eyes adjusted to the dark, Laura saw Crescia, asleep with her head thrown back, snoring softly. The snores were echoed from the other end of the room, where Nico and Carolina were curled together on a blanket by the fire. It was Carolina who was snoring.

She turned last to Sofia. The woman lay so still that Laura feared she was dead. She stood, rewrapped the cloth about her telltale hair, and bent over Sofia. She was relieved to feel the butterfly flutter of breath on the finger she held to Sofia's nose. Laura touched the woman's forehead and found it nearly cool again.

"Will she take some water?" Crescia's whisper came from behind her. "Water is the enemy of fever."

Again the two of them lifted Sofia up and held the cup for her. This time she drank more thirstily, half-asleep. Laura would have kept holding the cup to her lips until it was empty, but, "Too much and the fever will fight harder. Let her sleep again," Crescia ordered.

With tenderness, they settled Sofia back in the bed, covered her with sheets, and resumed their places: Crescia on the stool, Laura at her feet.

* * * *

When Laura woke again it was light. Sofia was awake, sitting up in her bed and combing through her tangled, dry hair with her fingers as she took in the visitors asleep at her bedside and her family asleep across the room. Laura raised her head and Sofia started, then leaned forward conspiratorially.

"I do too," Laura whispered back, and went to fetch the pisspot from its place behind the door, to which Sofia had directed her. She helped the sick woman to use the pot, used it herself, and took it outside to empty. When she returned, stepping over Nico and Carolina where they slept, Sofia mimed drinking. Laura brought water but, mindful of Crescia's order earlier, only let Sofia drink half a cup. After that the woman dozed again. Laura thought it was time to wake her mistress.

Crescia listened as Laura recounted with pride the care she had given Sofia. "Ah, mistakes. But you meant well, and there is no great harm done. But urine—particularly the first urine of the day—is a great tool. We use it, the smell and feel and color of it, to tell us things about the sickness we're treating. Never throw out a sick person's piss until you're certain you have learned all you can from it."

Laura hung her head. "Yes, mistress."

"Don't look so miserable, daughter. I hadn't told you, so you didn't know. Next time you *will* know. As for the rest—letting her drink was fine, but had you washed your hands after you used the pot?"

Laura shook her head.

"What did I tell you yesterday? The Queen of Heaven loves cleanliness, and it is she who watches over all that we do. Go wash now, and bring me water to do the same. We wash between chores, after eating, after using the pot. Cleanliness means we don't bring the taste or texture of some other thing to what we're now doing, you understand? It is the most important thing of all. That and prayer."

Laura went to fetch water. She would not forget again.

Chapter Three

Sometime before noon, when Crescia was satisfied that Sofia had passed the crisis, she and Laura bundled the pouches and jars they had brought with them into Crescia's basket, left Nico with instructions for his wife's invalid care, and started back up the hill to Crescia's house. By the time they reached the yard, the goats were frantic with welcome—Neve and Ravanella were sorely in need of milking—and Laura's stomach was growling so loudly it startled Decoro when he nuzzled at her. Crescia laughed and sent Laura off to milk the goats. "You know how to milk a goat, do you? But first wash your hands and say a prayer of thanks to the Queen of Heaven."

When Laura came in with a bowl brimming with goat milk, Crescia had spread out a feast: bread, white goat cheese, a bowl of dark, rich broth, a dish of pale jelly. "From the lemons," Crescia told her. "Put a little on your bread with the cheese. But first, wash—"

Laura was already at the basin, pouring water over her hands.

She tried not to fall upon her food like a wolf or one of Urbo's men, but she had eaten nothing since the night before. "Some of the folk we care for have very little. I don't like to take from them," Crescia had whispered to her when Nico offered to share the porridge with them.

"How can Nico pay you?" Laura asked now, around the corner of a crust smeared with jelly and cheese.

"The jars in the workroom? Nico makes them. Much of what I earn comes in trade; it's why we have fish and meat to eat, and good fresh bread. The baker gives me two loaves a week for a year for the birth of his son. The hunter gives me rabbit or venison, the weaver an ell of cloth. A few can pay in coin—*follari* or *piatstre*. That's useful at the market, but mostly folk here offer what they have. And unlike the great physicians of the city—" Crescia sniffed. "I don't turn anyone away if they can't afford to pay." The look she gave Laura made it plain she expected the girl to do likewise.

After lunch, while Laura cleaned the bowls and put away the cheese and bread, Crescia returned to the fire the pot of oils and herbs she had been preparing the day before. When the pot began to simmer and the scent of green filled the air, Crescia nodded as if pleased.

"Now, we do something about that head of yours."

She sent Laura to gather up sticks and build a fire in a circle of stones behind the house. By the time the fire was burning, Crescia had brought out a small pot that sloshed as she walked. "Set that on to boil," she said. The old woman took from a pocket a bundle of sage and a sheaf of bark. "Walnut bark," she said, and broke bits off the bark and dropped them into the pot one at a time. When the bark was gone she threw in the sage, moved the pot to one side of the fire to slow the boil, and covered it with a wooden lid.

They wound wool, spun from the goats' hair, while they waited. When, by some inscrutable sense of timing, the old woman judged the dye was ready, she pulled the pot off the fire, let it cool, and ordered Laura out of her clothes.

The girl looked at her doubtfully.

"Go on, daughter. The day is mild, there's no one to see but me, and I've already seen all you have to offer. We'll keep the dye away from your shift so."

For the next hour Laura felt like a poppet, pushed this way and that, head back, head up. Crescia grabbed handsful of the warm gray-black sludge at the bottom of the pot, smearing it through Laura's hair until her head was stiff with it.

"Now wait for a while," the old woman said. "The sun feels good today."

As Laura sat on the stool, a rag across her shoulders to keep the dye from her skin, Crescia schooled her in other ways to change her seeming. "For everyday, having other than your own hair will likely serve. Especially—" She took up a twig and used it to dab dye on Laura's eyebrows. "There. But if you meet someone who knew you in your old life, there are tricks that will help convince him you're *like* the girl he knew, but not that girl."

"You have a limp on that side." The old woman pointed to Laura's bandaged ankle. "Learn how to walk without it, and anyone who knew you before will think, 'Filipa has a limp, but this girl does not,' and they'll see Laura, not the girl you were."

"Is it really so simple?"

Crescia shrugged. "People see what they expect to see and expect what their eyes tell them. If you walk on your toes, just a little, they'll come to think you're taller than you are. And if you're fearful, look the person you fear in the eye: it distracts them from looking at the rest of you. Men think a direct gaze must be an honest one."

The old woman went on this way for a while. Laura, well-fed and tired, fought to stay awake.

At last, "Down to the stream," the old woman commanded. There, she poured bowl after bowl of icy water over Laura's head to rinse out the dye.

When she returned to the house Laura was shuddering with cold, but her hair was a damp, dark brown.

* * * *

That evening before they slept, Laura helped Crescia to strain the oil and herb mixture that had been simmering since their return home. The scent that filled the workroom was like the forest under hot sunlight, green and mysterious.

Crescia lined a clay sieve with coarse-woven cloth, had Laura hold the sieve over a large bowl, and poured the warm oil into the sieve, stopping from time to time to let the oil sink through the sludgy sediment into the bowl. By the time all the oil had been poured through, Laura's arms were trembling with the exertion of holding the sieve above the pot.

"That sits for a fortnight. Then we strain it again, into a jug. That much oil will last a three-month at least, unless something bad happens." Crescia covered the bowl and set it in a corner of the room, away from light and commotion.

"Bad?"

"There was a rock fall last year that killed two—God was merciful—and injured half a dozen more. I used this much oil in just a few days."

Chores left the day before were completed now. Laura worked until Crescia put cold porridge and jelly on the table. Then she was almost too tired to eat. When dinner was done and the bowls scraped and washed, Crescia sent her to bed.

"You've made a good start, girl."

*   *   *   *

The nightmares did not cease at once. They came less frequently, though, as Laura came to believe she might be safe. Then, when she had been with Crescia for almost a full moon, Urbo appeared at the gate.

It was not the Urbo who loomed, huge and sinister, in Laura's dreams. The man who stood by the fence, calling to those who lived within, had stooped shoulders. His face was flushed, his eyes red-rimmed.

"Is there a healer here?" he called again.

Laura stood at the door of the goats' shed, frozen. Her mouth filled with the taste of fear.

"You, girl. Is there—" He stopped. "I know you."

Laura rocked forward onto the balls of her feet to look taller. *Don't limp*, she told herself.

"You want my mistress."

Urbo put his hand on the gate and leaned heavily on it, staring at Laura. "I know you," he said again, but with a question this time.

"No, uncle. I don't think so." Her voice came out in a croak of fear, but she kept it low, pleased that it did not shake. "Is someone sick?"

Urbo pulled at the hem of his tunic until he revealed, at the top of his leggings, a dark gash on his thigh, dirty and caked with dried blood. The skin around the wound was tight, shiny, and red.

"I'll fetch my mistress," she said, and turned, remembering to walk without the limp. She did not invite Urbo to follow her, nor did she look back to see if he did. When she entered the house she found Crescia bent over the worktable cutting thin slivers from a knotty root.

"*It's Urbo,*" Laura said, low and urgent, as if to speak his name louder might summon him to the house directly. "He's here. He's got a wound that hasn't healed. It looks awful. And he thinks he knows me."

Crescia straightened up, pushed the knife and root away, and went to the basin. She washed her hands, gesturing with her head to remind Laura to do the same. "Now listen to me: *you are safe here.* Know that. But if that man is ill or hurt, my job is to help him. Can you help *me*? If you can't, go and I'll tend him." She stooped, taking on the character of her older self, and went to the door to summon their visitor into the house.

Laura swallowed hard and followed her.

Urbo at once settled into a chair in the workroom, looking around him with a shadow of his old appraising stare, as if judging what it would take to own what the house held.

"My daughter says you have a putrid wound," Crescia said.

"Your daughter?"

"My daughter-apprentice. Such as I don't marry. Let me see this wound."

With gentle hands she pushed his own away and rolled his legging down from the site of the wound. Seen close, it was even uglier than Laura had thought. Crescia clicked her tongue.

"How did you do this? And when?"

"I went down to the city to look for a runaway slave. Scraped myself on a bit of iron set in a wall. Hardly a wound at all, but—" Urbo shuddered as Crescia touched it and a thin trail of dark yellow pus oozed out.

"There is no blood sign," Crescia said. "That is hopeful."

"*Hopeful?*" Urbo sat straight and glared at the healer with the frightening authority Laura remembered. "What does that mean?"

Crescia shrugged. "Gently, brother. It means if we can cure the ulceration there will be no danger of losing the leg—"

Urbo erupted out of the chair, his face red, his eyes bulging. "Lose the leg? Say that again, hag, and I'll cut your ear off."

Laura, watching the two adults from the corner where she hoped to remain unnoticed, cowered. She knew this Urbo; no matter how ill he might be, she knew this man.

Incredibly, Crescia did not seem afraid. "Calm yourself, brother." She sounded amused. "If you cut my ear off, how likely is it that I will work my medicine at my best? Sit. I have work to do." She put her reddened hand square in Urbo's chest and pushed him back onto the chair. Laura was astonished.

"Laura, fetch me comfrey, oil of violets, and a head of garlic. Then you'll need to pick some violets, fresh, from the south side of the hill. As many as you can hold in two hands. Go on!"

Laura went to the wall and broke a head of garlic from the braid hanging on a peg. She had no way of knowing which

jars held comfrey or oil of violets—the pictures that Crescia
had scratched on the side of the jars might as well have been
in Moorish script for her ability to decipher them.

Crescia boxed her ear so hard that Laura's headcloth was
knocked askew and her braid of dyed-brown hair swung
forward like a whip. "Stupid girl, must I do everything myself? Have you learned nothing in all the months you've
been with me?"

Laura opened her mouth to defend herself, but then realized that Urbo was listening. He always enjoyed watching
someone take a beating. "I'm sorry, mistress."

"Go pick the violets, girl. I can't abide the sight of you."

Laura left. Out of sight of the house she stopped and
vomited up all the fear that had filled her. When she reached
the valley west of Crescia's house where violets grew, her
hands shook as she worked. She gathered only those from
the south side of the hill, filling her apron with three handsful, just to be sure.

Urbo was still seated, his thigh bared, with an odorous
gray poultice on his wound. From the sweat on his forehead
and nose, the sharpness of the garlic was painful. "How
much longer will you keep this foul stuff on me?" he snarled.

Laura remembered at the last moment to float up onto
her toes and manage her limp, before she faced her mistress
again. Crescia smiled.

"Here, mistress." Laura shook the violets out of her apron
onto the table.

"Well, you did that right. Wash, then find a clean mortar
and grind half these flowers into a paste, with as much garlic. Here, brother, this is for you." Crescia handed a cup of
something warm and flowery-smelling to Urbo. "It will ease
the pain."

"I fear no pain." Urbo pushed the cup back at her. "It's
the smell I can't abide."

Crescia nodded and spoke as if she were talking to a child. "Of course, of course, brother. But this will help relax you while your body heals."

Urbo took the cup in both hands and put his nose into it as if he would drink with it. Laura, bent over the mortar grinding violets and garlic, watched sidelong as Urbo drank and pretended to ignore Crescia's ministrations. Every time he shuddered or writhed, Laura remembered her mother and Bice and the other women of her village, writhing under Urbo's weight, then beaten, then raped again. Every time he shuddered, Laura smiled a secret smile and ground harder on the garlic and violets under her pestle.

"That should be ready now," Crescia told her.

Laura brought the mortar to her mistress, who examined the gray paste with satisfaction. "Good. I'll need three strips of linen—in the box topmost on that shelf there. Make sure they're clean."

Laura nodded, took a step toward the shelf, then remembered and went to wash her hands again. Crescia gave a crack of laughter.

"What?" Urbo barked.

"Nothing, brother. Sit back."

When Laura brought the strips of linen, Crescia smeared them with the violet-garlic paste, washed the poultice out of Urbo's wound, and tied the strips tight around his thigh. Urbo grunted and set his teeth, but did not cry out. When it was done, Crescia gave him more of the floral tea and he drank thirstily. Afterward he dozed.

Crescia took Laura out of the house. The sunlight of late afternoon gilded the hillside. The goats bleated fitfully as they grazed in the warm breeze.

"Daughter, that man must stay here tonight so I can satisfy myself that the wound is clearing. If it doesn't, I will have to send him to a chirurgeon in the city, for there is nothing more I can do. If it does, we will send him on his way. I know you hate him—and Jesu knows you have cause. But while he's here and suffering, the Queen of Heaven commands that we care for him tenderly. Can you do it? If not, go spend the night with Sofia."

It was tempting to go, to be away from Urbo, whose very smell set Laura's stomach churning. But neither could she bear to think of Crescia alone with him, if she crossed him.

"I'll stay, mistress," she said now.

Crescia smiled. "Good, daughter. We're not always given to choose to whom we minister. About the blow and hard words earlier—I was playing the bully, you know that. And he saw your good brown hair; by the time he leaves he'll have convinced himself that you're someone other than his runaway. Now, I want you to fetch me wild lettuce—a good double handful. You know what it looks like? Leaf and flowers both. Hurry, now. The sun will be down sooner than later, and I want you home before dark."

"But Urbo—"

"Urbo will sleep until you return. Go now! Look at the roadside by the walls of the houses where folk aren't so careful to pull up weeds."

When Laura returned with an armful of spindly wild lettuce, Urbo was still sleeping. Crescia took up the herb and added one plant to the pot in which she had been warming the floral decoction. She beckoned Laura forward to watch as she pulled off the linen strips she had tied to Urbo's thigh earlier. The man shuddered and shifted in his chair but did not wake.

"What do you see?" Crescia asked.

The girl hesitated. *An ugly mess of pus and blood, and I hope it kills him,* she thought. Crescia cocked an eyebrow as if she had heard the thought. Laura looked more closely.

"There's pus still, but less of it. And it's lighter in color.

The wound is not so puffed up as it was. You washed out the dirt and we can see where the cut was—it's clean, now the dirt is gone. Whatever he cut himself on, it must have been sharp."

Crescia nodded. "Very sharp. In fact, I think Brother Urbo got into a quarrel—in an ale shop, perhaps—and was sliced open for his trouble, but won't admit to it. That may be what saves him; had it been the sort of ragged wound one gets from stumbling into a bit of iron set in a wall, I doubt we could have brought him this far. Heat more water and we'll wash it out again."

As they worked, Laura had several times to turn away as the smell or sight of the wound overwhelmed her. Crescia said nothing, matter-of-factly taking the cloth from her apprentice's hand and continuing to bathe the wound. By and by it smelled less foul; Urbo was stirring from his slumber as Crescia tied a fresh set of linen strips treated with violet and garlic on his leg.

"Are you hungry, brother?" she asked.

Urbo growled something, and Crescia at once set Laura to fetch a clean pisspot. When he had used it, he handed it carelessly to Laura, not looking at her this time.

"Let me see," Crescia commanded. She hobbled to the door to catch the last of the daylight, and turned the pisspot this way and that, inspecting it. She dipped two fingers in, rubbed them together, smelt them, and then—to Laura's horror—licked them. She nodded as if all this had told her something. Blessedly, she did not require that Laura follow suit.

Instead, she offered Urbo broth and bread, and when he growled that meat and ale were more to his liking she laughed at him like a *nonna* with a cranky child. Sulkily, Urbo drank a bowl of broth and then another, broke off some of the coarse bread to sop up the last in the bowl, and looked about him as if he were only now aware of his surroundings.

"What's the hour, auntie?"

"Dark is falling. I'll give you a blanket for your sleep." Crescia did not offer to make up a pallet for Urbo.

"I've slept enough."

Laura, washing the bandages Crescia had removed from Urbo's leg, knew his tone. She turned, anxious. Surely— Crescia was an old woman—surely Urbo did not mean to take her.

"No, brother. You need more sleep if you mean to keep that leg," Crescia said calmly, again as if he were a child. "Now, drink this." She gave him a bowl of the floral decoction in which she had put the lettuce plant, some honey, and a drop of wine.

"Why?" Urbo asked suspiciously.

"Because I said so." Crescia seemed to enjoy teasing the big man. Laura, still with her back to the scene as she bent over the kettle of water warming at the fire, could not bear to turn and watch what happened. "It will help you to have the sleep you say you don't want. It will make morning come faster and allow your body to heal itself. It would not hurt you to say a prayer or two while you're drinking, either."

Urbo did not pray, but he took the bowl this time and drank it down.

As Laura hung the washed strips of linen on a line near the fire he watched her.

Then he beckoned to Crescia. "Your daughter-apprentice." His tone mocked the words. "How long has she been here?"

Crescia looked at Laura as if to invite her answer. "A year? Nearer two. You came to me just after the feast of Saint Margaret, didn't you, girl? Her poor father has four daughters, one for the cloister, one for me, and two he hoped to marry off."

"She looks too young to marry."

Crescia lied baldly. "She's the youngest of the four, and the least comely. Her older sister was wed last fall and is big with child. How old are you now, girl? Fourteen summers?"

Laura coughed the anxiety out of her throat and lied. "Fifteen on Saint Cypriano's day, mistress."

Urbo snorted. "Looks younger than that."

Crescia smiled as if Urbo had said something witty. "Never had a bite to eat until she came to me. Likely she'll be short all her days. But you, brother. Did you ever find your lost slave?"

Urbo shook his head heavily and raised one hand as if to chase away a swarm of unseen insects. "No. I looked all over the city. Never found her."

"What does she look like?" Crescia touched a finger to her lips as she looked at Laura.

"Half the size of your wench, skinny as a bone. Disobedient little bitch."

He yawned.

"Perhaps when your leg is healed you'll find her."

Urbo yawned again, nodded. After a little while he began to snore.

*   *   *   *

Crescia paid no further attention to Urbo. Stepping past him into the middle room she put out bread and cheese and lentil porridge for their supper, and as they ate she talked to Laura of what she had discerned from Urbo's urine.

"He's a sick man, and not just because of his wound. His humors are all heat and choler, and his liver is sick—the urine was dark and sweet. Might be he has the honey sickness. He didn't come to me for these complaints, nor do I feel it is my job to mend him of them—if I could. The leg will likely not kill him, and if he wants to leave in the morning we'll let him."

"But he knows where we are! He could come back. He—"

"Did you not hear him, daughter? He thinks you're like, but not like, his runaway slave. And I gave him an extra something in his drink tonight: the wild lettuce. The syrup is almost as excellent a sedative as syrup of poppy, but generally I don't use the flower except for scrofula—it's chancy stuff, and can empty the mind and make it lose its way. I think that the farther your Urbo gets from this house, the less he'll remember of his stay here. Just that we mended his injury and sent him on his way."

Laura put down her bowl and gawked at her mistress.

"Close your mouth before a hawk roosts in it. Do you think, because we're pledged to heal, that we're pledged to make ourselves targets for the violence of any brigand who comes to our gate? I have no more inclination to be raped in my bed than you do, Laura. Finish your broth."

* * * *

In the morning Laura woke and did her chores—milked Neve and Ravanella, emptied and washed the chamber pot, carried water to the house—while Crescia examined Urbo's wound again. The man slept through her examination this time, his snores thick and gluey. Once they had washed and prayed and broken their fast, Crescia set Laura to taking down the pots from the shelves to see which ones needed refilling. It was a cumbersome chore, for Laura did not yet recognize the aromatics by their scent or appearance. Most herbs, dried and broken, looked very much alike to her. So the girl clambered up on a stool, lifted down a jar, and brought it to Crescia, who would identify it for her and tell her some of its uses. Everything had a use and a story. Laura was certain she would never remember them all.

"If we could read and write as the monks do it would be easier," Crescia agreed. "But as we can't, you'll learn them by sight and scent." She put aside one of the little clay jars to be refilled. "Can you reach the top of that shelf?"

Laura clambered up on the stool and stretched to reach the jars on the top of the shelves. She grasped one, but knocked another off. It fell and smashed on the earthen floor in a puff of ground spice and clay dust. The noise woke Urbo, who shot up, then as quickly sank back into his chair as the pain in his leg struck him.

"What?" he grunted. "Where?"

Laura, balanced on the ball of one foot, very carefully shifted her weight on the stool and slid the jar in her hand along the shelf until she could regain her balance. She felt the hem of her shift skimming the backs of her knees. *He'll see my ankle*, she thought in a panic. The scar that laced around her ankle was mostly healed now but unmistakable. *If he sees it he'll know who I am*. In her anxiety she almost fell off the stool. But when she had climbed down and turned to put the pot on the table, she saw Urbo's eyes, crusted with sleep, half-open and unregarding. Already Crescia was on her feet, back hunched, fetching him her anodyne draught and instructing Laura to bring the pisspot for their guest. When Urbo had used the pot and grudgingly, under Crescia's instructions, washed his hands, the healer had Laura bring him bread and cheese and water. He had a greater appetite for his food today and complained that there was neither ale nor meat. Crescia only shook her head and smiled. When Urbo had finished, Laura took the bowl away and Crescia examined Urbo's wound.

"Come here, girl. I want you to see this." She motioned Laura forward. "See? The pus is whiter, less foul, and the area less swollen. And"—the healer pointed at the end of the wound—"here, the skin is pulling together. You'll have a scar, brother," she said to Urbo. "But I see this is nothing new for you. The knife that cut you—was the blade long or short?"

"Short." Urbo had forgotten his tale of having knocked against a wall. "It was a lucky blow."

"Nearly unlucky for you," Crescia observed. "So, brother, I think you may go about your business today, if you don't walk too far, and if you're returning to your own village. I'll give you a packet of herbs to mix with hot water, for later, when the pain builds up. And before you go we will dress the wound one more time."

Laura ground the last of the violets with more garlic, the paste was smeared again on strips of linen, and the strips bound again round Urbo's thigh. Laura was sent out to find a branch sturdy enough for the man to use as a walking stick; as she left the house she heard Crescia ask him how he planned to pay for her services. Was there no end to her nerve? Laura half-expected to find the old woman laid out on the ground, struck down for her audacity, but when she came back Crescia was holding a coin that glinted silver and reminding her patient to drink the tea she sent off with him. "Twice a day, in hot water. Let it sit and steep for the length of three *Aves*."

Urbo took the branch from Laura, thanked the healer, and started out the door. "Learn well, girl. I wish I had such skills among my men." He studied Laura for a moment. *He knows me*, Laura thought. But then he shrugged and nodded to her, then to Crescia, and limped out of the house.

"That's the end of him," Crescia said. "He's like to throw the medicine I gave him away at the first corner, and if he does not keep that wound clean it may kill him in a month. But that is not our concern. What *is* our concern is the galangal that was in the jar that broke. You must help me to remember to buy more when we go to market."

Chapter Four

Laura worked harder than she had ever imagined. Not mere physical labor either. What Crescia was asking of her was mind work, learning and memorizing the differences between comfrey and foxglove—both had bell-shaped flowers, but foxglove would kill as well as cure—and the properties of an astonishing range of other plants. No one had ever asked anything of her that would have suggested she had a scholar's mind, but Laura thrived.

Her school was the hillside and the workroom. In the one she followed Crescia, seeking grasses, bark, roots, and flowers; in the other she repeated the names and uses of herbs and rhizomes until she could repeat them in her sleep. Crescia began with what she called the dangerous blessings: plants like foxglove and wild lettuce that could poison as easily as cure. She went on to more benign local plants, then to the botanicals from far places that must be traded for, then to minerals and metals, animal substances.

After Urbo left they had some quiet days taken up with what Crescia called "kitchen healing": making potions for rashes, syrups for coughs. The dust of powdered herbs was always in Laura's nostrils: when she sneezed the snot was gritty and gray. She memorized the phases of the moon and the proper prayers to address to Saint Margaret and to Saint Catherine. Her arms grew wiry from grinding and carrying. "It is good to have a quiet time," Crescia said when Laura yearned for more excitement. "When we're needed, we draw on this rest."

Then, within two days, three households were stricken with fever. In the first, three children sickened, their fevers so high it seemed that the water Laura sponged on their fore-heads sizzled in the evening air. Crescia left Laura to help at the first house while she moved back and forth between that and the second cottage and the third, where the illness was not so dire. Laura watched Crescia, taking note of the herbs and powders she prescribed and the physic she brewed. More, she noted, and attempted to copy, the demeanor of calm and kindness that seemed as much a medicine as any Crescia brewed. If the manner sat oddly on a half-grown girl, no one said so to Laura.

The children's fevers had broken, their rashes were fad-ing, and they were choleric and itchy. Crescia was talking with their mother when a boy came for her. His sides were heaving and his voice unsteady. There were dusty tracks of tears on his face.

"My dad's hurt, *nonna*. Come quick! He was cutting wood and he fell and the axe—"

Crescia was on her feet. "What did I say about quiet time?" she murmured to Laura as she packed up her basket. "Keep watch here. I may send for you." She left with the boy.

Before sunset he returned. Laura was smoothing a salve of thistle and goose fat on the children's rashes. "Nonna Crescia needs you to fetch things for her," he told her, but he could not remember what she wanted. Pulled along by the boy's urgency, Laura left the children to their mother's care, washed her hands, and kilted up her skirt so that she could run more quickly up the hill. The boy's home was small enough and rugged enough to make Sofia and Nico's house seem like a rich man's home. Inside, Crescia was standing over a shrouded table. She barely turned.

"You have the bandages and alum?"

"Mistress, he could not remember what you wanted." Laura drew back, anticipating a blow, but none came. Instead, Crescia pushed her headcloth off her brow with a forefinger and stared into the air. "Bring bandages, all that we have. Bring alum, shepherd's purse, sanicle, and wine. And bring my great knife," she added quietly.

The boy had gone round the table to stare, wide-eyed, at the man who lay there, covered with a gory sheet.

Laura left at a run. Crescia's cottage was on the other side of the village, up the hill. By the time she got there and assembled what Crescia had asked for, the light was almost gone. The path, with its stones and ruts, was chancy. Laura trotted as best she could, with Crescia's great knife, a blade nearly long enough to be used as a short sword, held stiffly to one side lest she slip and fall on it.

Crescia barely seemed to have moved since Laura left. Someone had put up rush lights, which left soot in the air and threw off a muddy yellow light. Crescia took the knife from Laura's hand at once and thrust it into the coals of the fire. "Now, the alum, the wine, and the—yes, yes, that's shepherd's purse. Why did you bring this other stuff? Mugwort? Elder? Never mind. Grind the alum, then the shepherd's purse— separately, separately! Go, girl. I must work."

Laura bent over the mortar, grinding the alum into as fine and insubstantial a powder as she could make it before she shook it out onto a clean square of cloth. She cleaned out the mortar and began again, grinding the shepherd's purse. Stealthily she watched as Crescia, still murmuring calm, soothing nothings, fed the man on the table some of the wine Laura had brought. The boy stood at the head of the table, his face averted. His father's head rested against his slight chest. Crescia pulled back the cloth and Laura saw the man's leg, crusted with blood, a rag tied on the thigh above the wound. Crescia dabbed at the leg with a wet cloth, then turned to the fire. When she turned back the knife was in her hand, the blade a dull red from the fire.

"Shut your eyes, little son," she told the boy. Laura looked

down at the mortar and felt her stomach lurch when she realized what Crescia intended. In a moment there was the
stench of burning meat as she cauterized the wound. The
man on the table screamed and fainted; the boy did not
open his eyes, but he swayed.

"Laura! Mix the alum with a little wine." Crescia nodded
toward a bowl. "Quickly. I have sewn up or sealed most of
the wound, but we must dress it." Dressing meant pouring
the sluggish pink alum-wine mixture over the wound and
brushing it to cover with the edge of a cloth. "Now, squeeze
the juice from the sanicle and mix it with the shepherd's
purse. Little son, you must open your eyes now," she said
gently to the boy. "Can you find me a cup and wash it well?
Yes, your papa will sleep for a while now, but we must give
him more medicine while he sleeps."

An hour later, their patient dosed with sanicle and shepherd's purse, the deep slice in his leg dressed loosely, and the
gory sheet exchanged for a clean blanket, Crescia sent Laura
back to the house of the sick children.

When she left the cottage it was full dark, inkiness laced
with darker shadows. Almost, Laura turned back to tell Crescia she was afraid of what might lurk there, but the thought of
disappointing her mistress was as painful as her fear. She
picked her way carefully, starting at rustling in the brush,
her mouth full of bile. When she reached her destination,
she was almost sick with relief.

The children's mother she found cooking gruel; the oldest
of the children was sitting against the wall with the youngest
in her lap, stroking the toddler's head absently. The middle
child, the boy, was still asleep.

"Is all well?" the mother asked. Laura had forgotten her
name.

"Yes, auntie. Nonna Crescia will be back soon. She's
dressed the wound—" Saying the words made Laura's stom-

ach lurch at the remembered smell of burnt flesh. "She's just finishing."

The woman nodded. "You'll take some supper?"

"When my mistress returns, if she wills it."

"Mama!" the oldest girl called. The toddler in her lap was chuckling. "I have a new game for Pira." She ran her finger down her sister's forehead, wiggled it before the child's eyes, then snapped her fingers. At the snap Pira tensed, then giggled.

"Do that again," Laura ordered.

The girl looked to her mother, who nodded. "Do what the healer says, Serama."

Before Laura could take pleasure in being called healer, Serama repeated her game with Pira. Again the baby looked past the finger waggling before her eyes, looked into the darkness of the byre at the other side of the room. When Serama snapped her fingers the baby laughed again, a bubbling chirrup.

The mother looked at Laura anxiously. Laura was only half a dozen years older than Serama, but she was old enough to know something was not right. Was this what it was like to be the healer? To feel this weight of responsibility? Laura wasn't certain of what she was seeing or what to say. She would wait for Crescia.

The old woman hobbled in serenely an hour later, complimenting the mother (her name was Giunia) on the scent of her broth and congratulating Serama and her brother Adeso for sitting up for their supper.

Then she took Laura aside. "What is it?"

"How did—"

"You wear your worry like a mask. You must learn to let only the concern show. Fear is for the moments when you're alone and can't sicken your patients with it. Now, what worries you?"

"The baby. I don't think—I think—"

Crescia's lips twitched. "Which is it, daughter?"

"She doesn't see," Laura got out. "Serama was playing with her, but the baby didn't see. Could it be a passing thing? Perhaps—"

Crescia's expression did not change. "Let me look at her."

Murmuring something comfortable to the older children, Crescia bent and took up the baby, who was awake, burbling quietly on the pallet. She went and sat on a stool by the fireplace, Pira in her lap, her voice a singsong ripple under the snap of the fire. After a while she called Giunia to her. Laura watched the two women fearfully. In a moment the mother covered her own mouth with her fist, hard.

Serama peered around Laura, trying to see what her mother was doing with the baby. Instinctively Laura distracted her, asking a question about what went into the broth.

The bells for compline were drifting up from the city's churches when Crescia led Laura from the house. "I want my own bed, and that poor woman needs time to recall that God and the Queen of Heaven have given her back her children, who were in the arms of the angels only last night. I don't doubt when her man comes home they'll weep again, but they don't need us for that."

As they climbed the path to Crescia's cottage Laura heard a soft clink.

"Coins?" she asked. She had never seen Crescia take hard money from a neighbor before.

The old woman nodded. "Bretald works as a mason in the city; they have little to trade. It hurt to take it from them with the news we had to give tonight."

"Then why take it?"

"People value what comes at a cost. And how can I help them if they don't value what I do? Half of any cure lies in the faith that people bring with them. That's a lesson for you, daughter: always make sure you're paid, somehow, in some way. It lets all keep their pride and their faith."

Another of Crescia's rules. Unlike the lessons on plants and preparation, these rules had dozens of conditions and variations. Laura had learned to nod and look as if they made sense to her. She did not think Crescia was fooled.

In the morning, when the goats had been watered, brushed, and let out to graze, Laura went to replenish the shepherd's purse and thistle they had used. She was following the path from the house, turning to climb the hill, when she was stopped by a man in fine hose and a tunic of dark-dyed wool, with low leather boots and a smart round cap. She had never seen anyone so finely dressed.

"Are you the midwife's girl?" he asked.

Shy before so great a gentleman, Laura only nodded.

"My master's wife—her time came early. You must bring her. The midwife." His voice trembled and Laura realized that, despite his finery, he was a very young man and he was afraid. That freed her tongue.

"Where do I bring her?" She was already turning her back on the hillside.

"The house of Dino di Pietre. She'll know."

Laura started up the path, but not quickly enough to please the youth.

"Run!" He shoved her in the direction of Crescia's house. Laura caught her balance and walked on with dignity—until she had turned the corner out of his sight, when she picked up her skirts and ran.

The house of Dino di Pietre was one she had passed before, large and well kept, with a stable yard to one side and a gated wall facing the road. Laura followed Crescia, carrying as always the larger of the baskets that the old woman had filled with jars and packets and bits of stuff.

They were met at the gate by an old, rheumy-eyed man

with a long thin nose and sparse hair who wore the same
color tunic and hose as the boy who had found Laura on the
hill.

"Master bid me welcome you," the old man said, all but
yanking Crescia into the yard, and Laura after her. "Beatricia is—"

A scream echoed across the yard; two chickens started
and clucked furiously. The old man swiveled, looking upward, led the way into the house. Like Crescia's cottage it
was broken into chambers, but here there were many rooms,
some of them up a short staircase. The house was grander
than any Laura had been in, and she would have liked to
look her fill: the floors were made of wood and there were
hangings of painted linen on the walls. But Crescia was moving as quickly as Laura had ever seen her, stopping only a
moment to greet a heavyset man with the stamp of fear on
his face, who sat on a stool in the hallway.

"How early has the baby come?" Crescia asked.

"I think . . . a month or more." The man looked powerful
and helpless.

Crescia shook her head as if despairing of someone's care-
lessness. "We'll do what God permits," she said, and pulled
Laura behind her into the birthing room.

It was an odd-shaped chamber, a rounded rectangle. The
large curtained bed stood against the far wall. Several chests
were set against a sidewall to serve as cupboards and, now,
as seats for two older women who sat praying loudly. A fourth
woman, a servant older and more hardened, Laura thought,
stood over the laboring woman, clucking as if disapproval of
the woman's suffering might help her.

The wife was only half a dozen years older than Laura
herself. She lay, sweating and miserable, in a damp shift, on
damp, disordered sheets. Crescia shook her head again and
clicked her tongue with displeasure.

"She's been shriven. We did what we could to make her comfortable," the tirewoman at the bedside said. "We thought it might keep the baby from coming so early."

Another shriek from the woman on the bed suggested that it had not. One of the women seated against the wall buried her face in her hands and wailed in sympathy or horror.

Crescia began to bustle. "You, bring a bath, fill it with hot water and put in as much mallow, fenugreek, and barley as you have—at least a handful of each. We'll put her in that and it should ease her a bit. And you—" She turned to the seated women. "If you can't be helpful, at least be of good cheer. If you can't do that, leave." Without waiting for a response, Crescia went to the bed and wiped her patient's forehead. "Now, daughter, there is no need to make such ado. Crescia is here and will aid you. Women have struggled and brought joy into the world and so will you." As she soothed the laboring woman, Crescia was examining her hands, her feet, running a hand over her belly. The two older women had already left the room.

"Laura, quick. Check this room to make sure there are no knotted ribbons or bands to keep the womb tight. Her color is high but not feverish." She stroked the woman's hair. "Now, daughter. I want you to hold this in your left hand." From one of the pouches that dangled from her belt Crescia produced a plum-sized, polished piece of rosy jasper. "It will help to ease your difficulty."

The woman smiled wanly. "Thank you, *nonna*." Her voice was a hoarse whisper. "But he comes too early. Can't you—"

"Shhhh, daughter. Do you question the will of God? If this baby is to be born now, it is to be born now." Crescia smiled. "We're here to help you. Laura, go see that the kitchen has the herbs I asked for."

What they lacked Laura supplied from the stores in Crescia's basket. When the tub arrived, brought to the door by two powerful-looking men in what she realized was the house livery, Laura stirred in the herbs until the room was humid with fragrant air. She and Crescia helped Beatricia, the mother, into the tub, still in her shift. The fine cloth belled around her as the mother sighed and leaned against the side of the tub.

Beatricia di Pietre lay in the water until it was too cool to be soothing, then went back to the bed Laura had made fresh for her. Her labor seemed to have slowed. Laura wondered if perhaps the pains would cease entirely until the baby was more ready. But in the late afternoon the pains began again. This time Crescia had ready a mixture of laurel oil and fenugreek that they rubbed into the belly and back, the legs and pudendum. Laura had never seen the sex of a woman before, and to see it now, ruddy and swollen, damp with sweat and fragrant with oil, was terrifying and exalting. "Watch me," Crescia said each time she rubbed or manipulated or examined. Once she even insisted that Laura put her hand into the mother's vagina to see if she could feel the hard surface of the baby's skull. She could not.

"Something is holding that baby inside," Crescia murmured. "Feel the belly and tell me what you can divine."

Me? What I can divine? I know nothing! Laura trembled but, obedient, she rubbed a little oil on her hands and ran them gingerly over the mother's belly. She tried to imagine a baby in the shape under her palms, tried so hard that she lost sight in her mind of where the mother was. "Here." She ran a finger along one shuddering curve of belly. "The head is . . . here? Here is the back and here the feet?" She opened her eyes. Crescia nodded, grim.

"That is the head," she agreed. Laura heard dismay, and when she looked down at her hands she saw that the head rounded out the left of Beatricia's belly and the back lay across the bottom where it blocked the mouth of the womb.

The mother arched in another contraction, her face taut with pain.

Crescia waited until the contraction ended. "It seems this child of yours wants you to remember his birthing day! I will need to do a little work to help him come into the world." She smiled beautifully at the mother, as if she feared nothing for her or her child, and went to wash her hands.

"Now, pour a little oil." Crescia held out her hands to catch the drops of oil Laura poured out. "Not too much." She rubbed her hands together until they glistened dully in the light from the high, narrow window, then turned to the tire-woman who waited by the door. "I need more light. Bring a lamp. Bring two." She was curt. "I must see what I'm doing."

With the lamp held high over her shoulder, Crescia knelt and had Laura pull her sleeves as far back as they would go. Then she began to pat and rub, massaging the baby's head downward and the buttocks upward within the dome of Beatricia's belly.

Beatricia moaned.

"Hold her," Crescia ordered the servants. "Not you with the lamp, you stay where you are."

She worked more, making subtle little changes in the baby's position. The room was silent except for Beatricia's whimpers and the spit of wax as the candles burned lower. After a very long time she told Laura to feel the mother's belly again. "What do you think? Has the babe moved?"

Laura oiled her hands and ran them over Beatricia's belly. "Yes. The head is lower. Still not—" Crescia leaned forward to make one more manipulation. Beatricia moaned. Laura felt for the feet, followed down to the back, which now seemed to her to lie against the side of the womb rather than across the bottom. "I think—I think that's better, mistress. The head is down."

"Blessed Saint Margaret." Crescia sank back to sit on one

of the chests, looking as exhausted as the mother herself. She nodded to the tirewoman at the head of the bed. "You can let her go now. Go and pray for her." She took the lamp from the woman by the foot of the bed. Both servants looked happy to be dismissed.

Crescia washed her hands again and shook her sleeves down. "Now we wait," she said softly. "Perhaps we can all sleep a little." She sat by the head of the bed, stroking Beatricia's hair. The contractions still rippled visibly across the flesh of her belly, but they were not so strong now, and her pallor had lightened a bit. Beatricia closed her eyes and leaned into the hand stroking her head.

Laura tidied what she could, then sat on one of the chests until Crescia sent her to the kitchen to bring a kettle of hot water to steep another posset. The stool on which Dino di Pietre had waited was empty. When Laura returned with the kettle she found Beatricia bowed in a powerful contraction and the period of quiet over.

"The baby is coming. Get a blanket ready, and oil." Crescia turned to Beatricia and smiled confidently. "All right, daughter. The time is now. You're tired, I know, but you must use all your strength and push. Laura, hold her—no, sit behind her. Let her lean on you."

Laura half-sat behind the mother, bracing her as she began to push. This time Beatricia did not scream, did not cry out. She pressed her lips together as if pressing her screams downward to push the baby out. After a moment, at Crescia's urging, she stopped. Then began again.

On the fifth push Crescia made a brief sound of satisfaction. "Once more, daughter."

On the sixth push the baby was born, slithering out into Crescia's hands. Beatricia lay back panting. Laura could see what the mother did not: the baby was the color of a black grape, unmoving, the cord looped around its neck. Crescia took the cloth she had ready and rubbed the baby all over, but it did not move or cry out and its smell was foul. Crescia took a drop of oil and drew a cross on the baby's forehead, then turned her head and spat.

"My baby. Is it a boy or girl?"

Crescia shook her head, then smiled at Beatricia. "A girl. Next time a boy, yes? Now you must give us the afterbirth, daughter. Laura, take the child away to be made clean."

She handed the corpse to Laura, tilted her head in a silent direction to take the body from the room.

Outside there was a crowd: the female attendants had returned, and shadow-eyed Dino di Pietre. They were like a grove of poplar, still and trembling. No words came to Laura. After a moment she offered the linen-wrapped corpse to the man and shook her head.

"What happened?"

"The cord," Laura began. One of the women started to wail.

"Hush, fool," the man said. "Does my wife know?"

Laura shook her head. "My mistress blessed the baby, but you'll want—" She looked over her shoulder, longing to be away from the grief of these adults who looked at her as if she knew what must be done.

Dino di Pietre looked at the tiny bundle in his arms. "Thank you," he said at last. "Does the healer need anything else?"

"Time. And prayers for your wife." As if in punctuation there was a cry from within, not so sharp as the earlier cries had been. Laura thought the young wife sounded tired. "I'll go back in," she told Dino, and left him with the dead child.

By midnight the afterbirth had been delivered and Beatricia di Pietre had been cleaned and blessed and lay asleep, ashy and exhausted. Crescia had conferred with the father and the eldest of the attending women, who was Beatricia's

aunt. The healer prescribed broth and honey for a few days,
then red meat and a drink of honey, wine, and balm to glad-
den her spirits. "When she wakes she'll be strong enough to
bear the news. She's healthy," the healer added meaningfully. "You'll have other children."

Laura listened, kept her head down, did the tasks she was
given. She did not know how to meet the eyes of the family.
Crescia moved among them with the same cool kindliness
she had shown Giunia, Pira's mother, or the son of the
woodcutter. When the priest came, Crescia took Laura from
the room and let him talk to Beatricia alone. Healer and apprentice sat in the short hall.

"Will she live?" Laura asked.

"If her spirit does not fail her and God sustains her. She
bled much, but she's young, which is in her favor. She's not
sturdy—well, it is always in the hands of God and His Queen.
We've done what we could." Crescia turned her head and
looked at Laura. "When I sent you for shepherd's purse yesterday you also brought mugwort. Why?"

It took Laura a long time to remember.

"I couldn't recall which jar—I don't yet know its smell."

Crescia nodded without blame. They sat quietly until the
priest left the birthing chamber. "Go give the lady some of
the honey draught. Go now." She pushed Laura toward the
chamber. As Laura went she saw Crescia conferring with
the priest, their heads bent together.

Beatricia was propped against pillows, her face milky-
green in the lamplight. She had covers drawn up to her chin
and looked very small in the midst of the great bed. She did
not look up when Laura entered the room, or speak.

Laura washed her hands, then poured some of Crescia's
draught into a bronze cup. "You must drink this all," she
said, attempting to copy Crescia's firm, gentle tone.

"You were here with the *nonna*," the mother said. Her voice was reedy and hoarse. "You saw it?"

"It?"

"My baby. It died inside me. Fra Fraternus told me. But the *nonna* blessed him, so perhaps God will be kind—"

"Her," Laura corrected. She sat on the edge of the bed and slipped her arm around Beatricia's shoulders, holding the cup to her lips.

Like a child, the woman swallowed obediently until the cup was empty. Then she sank back into the bed. "She. Died inside me. But God will know it was not her fault but mine. I—" Hectic color came to Beatricia's cheeks as she warmed to what she said. "My womb is cursed."

"How can you say so? Has this happened before?"

The flush ebbed a little. Beatricia shook her head. "No. But how else?"

Laura sat next to Beatricia on the bed as she had used to do with Bice when they were small, and took her hand. "I don't know who is to blame. The baby came too early, and was not in her proper place. You might as well blame the baby for being too eager. This—" Laura waved her free hand at the room. "My mother had two stillborn children between my sister and me. Nonna Crescia says you may have other children. So you must rest and get strong so your next baby will be born proper and strong, too."

Beatricia sighed and closed her eyes and, after a little time, fell asleep with her head on Laura's shoulder. After a while Laura slept too, until Crescia came to collect her basket, her stores, and her apprentice.

Chapter Five

The house was empty when Laura woke the next morning. She rose and said her prayers, dressed, and started on her chores: brushing and watering the goats, sweeping the earthen floor, bringing water from the stream behind the house. That done, she cast about for occupation, and was clearing out the few weeds from the garden when Crescia returned. The old woman was walking faster than she usually did. Her mouth was pinched and her cheeks and long nose were red. She was angry. Laura had never seen her so furious.

"Leave that, girl. Wash and make yourself presentable. We're going to the city."

As Laura gathered up the small pile of weeds she had pulled, Crescia seemed to find herself in her anger. She breathed deep, smoothed her hands over the skirt of her tunic three times in a ritual of calming, and reached up to straighten her headcloth. "Braid your hair neatly and put on the new tunic," Crescia instructed in a cooler tone. "When you're dressed, empty the large basket. While we're in Salerno we might as well go to market."

Laura washed her hands and face, rebraided her dyed-brown hair, and took up the basket. Crescia smiled at her with distracted kindness, and Laura felt a twinge of relief: whatever had angered her mistress, it was nothing she had done.

"Are you ready, girl? Wait! Shoes! We don't want the people of Salerno to think you're a shoeless peasant!"

Well, but I am a peasant, Laura thought. She did not say it. She laced on the shoes, an old pair that had belonged to Crescia. They were loose and made picking her way down the path to the city a clumsy business. Laura trailed in Crescia's wake. She wondered what had made her mistress so angry but feared a clout if she asked. They had been walking along the stony path for some time before she gathered up her nerve, but Crescia did not scowl or scold.

"I went back to that house this morning—went to see how the mother was faring. At the door, as I was waiting, a physician from Salerno, one of the young ones fresh from the Scuola and full of his dignity, was being shown out. They'd called him to check my work!" She spat to one side of the road. "He spoke to me as if I were a child or an idiot, and he half my age! He stood there and told Dino that he should keep hedge-witches and quacks away from his wife. As if it had not been me up to my elbows in gore last night, saving the life of that same wife! Then, as I was going, one of the aunts came fluttering after me to make sure I had not taken offense. I think she feared I'd cast spells on the family if I were offended!"

Laura gaped at her mistress. Could a woman who stood up to Urbo be bested by any other man? A prince, perhaps, or the king in Sicily, or the pope. But some lesser man?

Crescia was still speaking, as much to herself as to Laura. "The worst of it is, I might have learned from him and he from me. They know things, those scholars at the Scuola, but they don't know *everything*." Crescia shook her head, but the rage had leaked out with her words.

In silence they trudged down the path. They came to a turning in the road, and, as she had done the first day she saw the sea, Laura stopped. The city was laid out below her, white and gold and red in the glaring sunlight, sloping down to water as blue as the sky it mirrored. There were boats pulled up on the shingle, others swaying and bobbing at anchor, and people as small as ants moving in the streets that ringed the harbor. Houses, more than she had ever seen in

her life, rose in ragged rows up the hill. Turning north to
look back the way they had come, Laura could see the looming presence of the castle of Arechi, who had died long ago
but left his keep to guard the city he had ruled. When she
turned back she noted, in a line between where they stood
and the harbor, a great square tower rising from what looked
like a building large enough to be a town of its own. The cathedral of San Matteo. Crescia had told her of it. In the
shadow of that tower was a market square so busy and filled
with people that it seethed.

At the nearer side of the city, where the land curved westward in a rise of hills, a cluster of towers and galleries shone
creamy white in the sun, ringed round with walls breeched
by streets that led to the heart of the towers. Perhaps a new
home for a duke, Laura thought. The city extended up toward the towers in narrow streets, low houses with tiled
roofs and squares of garden.

"Come along, daughter." Crescia had turned to see why
Laura had paused, then followed her gaze to the cluster of
towers. "Ah. There it is, then. That's the Scuola. The physicians' school. Come, now. I want to reach the city before
sext."

The path widened as they approached the city, with fewer
rocks but more cart ruts. The houses they passed were closer
together. Some were blank-faced and seemed immense, although Crescia said that most were half the size they appeared, since the walls contained gardens and courtyards as
well as dwellings. In between the large houses that were made
of stone or stucco were smaller ones made of wood. They
passed a yard where a smith, tunic off and belly hanging over
his belt, was hammering with slow, deliberate blows at a
piece of iron, and Laura jumped at the prodigious hiss and
burst of steam when he thrust the iron into a crock of water.

She wanted to see the cathedral. The great stone tower

loomed over the city, and it seemed impossible to her that something so tall had been built by men. But Crescia urged her along through a crowd that got denser as they went. The smells were different here than in the hills: the salt of the sea, the scents of sweat, wine, fish, and ordure. The press of the crowd pushed them toward the market square. Here the smells changed again: fish and grain and the blood of freshly slaughtered poultry, the sharp green scent of mint, a whiff of honey, the salty scent of leather, and the ropy smell of newly dyed flax. Tables shaded by tents were thronged by men and women hefting fruit and sniffing greens, fingering fish in osier baskets. Farther down the way at a dyer's stall bright skeins of yarn hung from poles, and a cobbler worked under an arched rack from which dangled shoes and belts and pouches. Laura had never imagined such abundance.

Crescia's tug on her sleeve brought Laura back to herself. "Don't gawk, daughter. Keep your eyes open, your mouth shut, and watch for light fingers. I have very little coin to spend and I mean to spend it well and not lose what we buy." Crescia took her wrist and pulled her toward the near side of the square, where the tables and baskets were piled with produce. Laura pushed past the people around her until she could see what lay on the first table. She recognized some plants from her mistress's garden; others she had never seen before. The tall, bony farmer with the liquid cough recognized Crescia.

"I've fresh mugwort for you today. Good stock, too. And that mix of mints you like, too, mother." He plucked at the sleeve of Crescia's gown. "Good for all sorts of women's problems, or so my wife tells me."

"Your wife hasn't a thought in her head that you didn't put there," Crescia said, but agreeably. The man laughed and coughed.

"Who's this, then?" He nodded toward Laura.

"My apprentice. High time I had someone to do the hard work."

The man laughed again. "If I could find a likely boy I'd have me a 'prentice too, but these—" His gesture included all the boys playing and chasing among the stalls. "Not one doesn't want to be a soldier of the king and break heads."

"More likely they shall have their own broken." As if by some signal Crescia and the man bent over the table, examining herbs he put out for her. Laura watched them, trying to discern why one sheaf of pennyroyal was better than another, why the mugwort that seemed fresh and plentiful Crescia disdained to buy.

"Smell it!" Crescia ordered, putting a sprig of the debated mugwort under Laura's nose.

It was sharp and green and a little spicy, with a faint mustiness. Laura attempted to tell her mistress what she smelled.

The gaunt farmer gave a bark of laughter. "She's got a good nose, your apprentice girl. I kept it in water, but it was picked a six-night ago."

Crescia nodded at Laura approvingly. After they left the table they examined other wares, although Crescia bought only a little of what was on offer. She was on friendly terms with many of the sellers, who greeted her by name or called her mother. When they had wound through the entire market and Crescia had allowed Laura to marvel at the troupe of boys tumbling for the crowd, they sat by the fountain and ate bread and cheese Crescia had wrapped for them and gnawed at the small wrinkled apples left from last autumn's stock.

"Now to the 'pothecary," Crescia said when they were done.

"More stalls?"

"No, daughter. Up the hill to the spice shops. That's where they sell things we can't grow or find for ourselves."

Laura followed her mistress, holding tight to her basket

and wishing she dared take hold of Crescia's sleeve to make sure she did not get lost. As they climbed the sloping street, the press thinned out and Laura was able to walk almost at Crescia's side, looking around her with amazement. There were people in clothes far finer than Dino di Pietre's: Men wore long robes of fine brown and blue and green. Even the monks who passed them seemed to have cleaner, finer habits and neatly shaved tonsures. The women wore headdresses of folded and starched linen and robes with beads or fur at the neck and wrists. Some were carried through the streets in curtained chairs. Laura was so taken up with looking that she was startled when they stopped their progress. They were almost at the towers of the medical school.

Crescia turned into a narrower street, almost an alley. They passed several shadowed doorways before Crescia guided them through an arch, down a short hall, and into a square room. "Now, you hush and keep your eyes open," Crescia told her before she turned to greet the man seated behind a high table.

The farmer in the market had been tall and thin, ruddy from sun and wind. This man was short and round and might never have seen the sun at all. His eyes, which were large and round, blinked and teared as he regarded his visitors. He wore a robe of deep green wool, trimmed with fur at the neck, and a cap, also with fur trim. Since he appeared to have no hair other than his heavy white eyebrows, the effect of the cap (and his thin-lipped, pursed mouth) was to make him look like a wealthy turtle. Laura looked upward at the dust motes swimming in shafts of sunlight from the high windows and tried not to giggle.

"Good day, Lot," Crescia said. She took a leather purse from her sleeve and shook it slightly. At the clink of the coins the apothecary's already protuberant eyes bulged further, and he leaned forward.

"Crescia." He sounded cautiously welcoming. "What can my unworthy shop provide for you today?"

"Spikenard. One dram. Two roots of jenever and one of galangal. Have you any—"

"Wait! Wait!" The old man's voice was high and reedy. "One thing at a time. A dram of spikenard." He turned to a tall cupboard behind him, fitted with dozens of small drawers. The old man stood so close to the cupboard his nose was almost pressing against it, his head tilted to one side as he peered at one drawer, then another, his hands palsied as he brought down a drawer and took from it a small vial. He unstopped the vial and offered it to Crescia, who took it without comment, sniffed, considered, and nodded. She passed the vial to Laura.

"What do you think, daughter?"

Laura sniffed at the vial, which released an intense aromatic scent. "It is—it's a soothing oil?"

Crescia nodded. "Among its other uses. Now, Lot. Jenever and galangal?"

The apothecary took the vial back from Laura, stopped it again, and put it aside. He returned the drawer to its place in the cupboard and again peered at the shelves.

"Here." He brought down another drawer and produced a long, knobby light brown root. "Only one jenever here." He turned his head and called, "Natalia! Have we more jenever?"

From a doorway to the far left of the cupboard a woman's voice, younger by far than the man's, answered, "Wait!" There was a rustling, and then the woman herself looked round the door. "No, no more. I expect more when the— Oh! Crescia! Good day, *nonna.*" The woman came out from the room beyond, short, round, and smiling. Lot's daughter, Laura thought. She had a child on her hip, sucking a finger and twirling a lock of his hair. There was something strange about his face, his eyes were slanted and his features oddly flat. He was large and too old to be carried around in such a fashion.

"Good day, Natalia." Crescia leaned forward toward the child. "Pambo, this is Laura, my apprentice. Can you say hello to her?"

The boy smiled around his finger but said nothing. Natalia shifted him on her hip. "He doesn't speak." Her voice was resigned. "He hears, but—" She shrugged.

"When God wills it, he'll speak. Until then, say your prayers and love your son." Crescia turned back to Lot. "What about the galangal?"

Already Lot had produced a second long root, paler than the gingerroot and with the dried leaves of two offshoots depending from it. "I don't charge you for the leaves."

"That's just as well, they're of no use to me," Crescia said. "Have you camphor?"

Lot put the two rhizomes aside with the vial of spikenard and turned again to the cupboard. The woman Natalia smiled at Laura and went back to the other room.

After what seemed to Laura a very long time spent with his eye to the cupboard, pulling drawers ajar and peering in, Lot shook his head. "No camphor."

"This will do, then." Crescia unknotted the string on her purse as bells—first one deep-throated musical one, then others in smaller, tinnier voices, tolled for mid-afternoon prayers. Laura wanted to leave the dusty shop and go outside in the sun to listen to them, but by the time Crescia's purchases had been added to the basket the bells were silent again.

They left the apothecary's shop to blink in the lemony afternoon light. Crescia turned them left, down the street they had come on, thence down another street and another until Laura could not see even the tallest tower of the medical school behind them. Looking down the hill, she saw the square tower of the duomo and the market square and the harbor. They paused for a moment as if Crescia was deciding her route.

"Mistress?"

"Yes, girl?"

"That boy."

"Pambo? He's one of the Queen of Heaven's children, that one. He was born that way."

"Born what way?"

"A natural. A simpleton. But a loving heart, he has. Still, it's a shame. Lot and Natalia have but the one child."

Laura was so surprised that the round-faced, cheerful Natalia could be the wife of dour Lot, whom she had thought must be her father, that she forgot about Pambo.

Crescia guided them east and south, on a street that ringed the harbor, until they stopped at a chapel. It was a small, dusty, plaster-and-wood box with a tiny bell tower and single wooden door; it reminded Laura of the church in Villaroscia, where she was born. The old woman led them around to the side of the church, to an adjoining building that was little more than a shack. There was a wooden bench by the door. Crescia pointed to it: "Wait here, daughter."

Laura sat. Her feet, in the ill-fitting, unaccustomed shoes, hurt. She rubbed them as she looked around. A few people passed on the street, about their own business and uninterested in a scrawny girl waiting outside the church. Most were dressed as she and Crescia were, in shifts and tunics of hemp or linen, girded with leather or flax. Few were dressed as grandly as those she had seen near the school. Laura clutched the basket to her lest some city thief try to steal its contents.

At last Crescia came to fetch her. "I had to wait until he had finished the prayers. Straighten yourself! Shake the dust from your skirt. I want you to appear to advantage, daughter."

Laura felt a pang of unease. The only reason she could imagine that Crescia would bring her to the city and want her to appear her best was that the old woman meant to send her away, sell her or apprentice her to someone else. She rose and shook and smoothed and patted herself into presentability, but her hands were clumsy. She followed her mistress into the shack, trying not to betray her anxiety.

The room they entered was big enough to hold a cot at its rear, a brazier, a table, two stools, and a stocky monk in black robes. He looked like an ogre from a children's tale: broad, barrel chested, graying tonsure, small dark eyes under flying gray brows, and a large, deeply pocked nose that overwhelmed every other feature. When he looked at her, Laura saw only that nose, shadowing his round, stubbled chin. When he gestured at her to sit on the stool by the desk, the nose seemed to point the way.

"Fra Bruncio, this is Laura, my apprentice." Laura heard "my apprentice" with relief. That did not sound as if Crescia meant to send her away. She bowed to the friar, both from respect and so that the adults would not see her smile.

The monk rose, not much taller on his feet than sitting, and took Laura's chin in his hand, turning her face one way and then the other. Her eyes were level with his brow. "Is she a good student for you?" His voice was startlingly high and musical.

"She is. That is why I brought her."

"Very well, girl. Let us see what you can do." The monk took up a slate from the table, cleaned it with the edge of his sleeve, and then drew something on it with a small, crumbling white chalk stone. "Can you copy this?"

Laura took the chalk stone and copied the shape, like an arrow's tip with a line across it. The monk nodded and had her copy another shape, then another. They played this game for a while, until the monk wiped the slate clean again.

"Now, draw every shape you have made since we began," he ordered.

The game made no sense to Laura, but she was determined to win it. She put the chalk to the slate and carefully traced the shapes again.

The monk grunted and nodded. "Good. She *is* clever. Very well. I'll take her on."

Laura stood up from the stool in alarm. "No! Mistress, what have I done? Please, I'll do better. Don't—" She faltered, reaching a hand to Crescia. The old woman and the monk looked at her without comprehension.

"What are you talking about?" Crescia peered at her as if to discern an illness.

"If the girl doesn't *want* to learn . . . ?" Fra Bruncio's eyebrows met about his prodigious nose in a scowl.

Laura didn't know whether to shake or nod her head. "I *do* want to learn," she said. "Please, mistress, I want to learn everything. Only don't send me away!"

"Away? What do you mean?" Crescia asked.

And Fra Bruncio said, "What use would *I* have for a girl?"

"Laura, I am not sending you away. I'd thought to arrange for you to learn to read and write as the monks do."

Laura was for a moment so consumed with relief that she could not make sense of what Crescia was telling her. "Read? How can I?"

"By coming down from the hills every morning to study with me, then climbing back up the hill to help your mistress," Fra Bruncio said. "We'll see which benefits more from the exercise, your brains or your legs. Crescia, you had not told her what you intended?"

Crescia laid a hand on Laura's shoulder, as warm as an embrace. "I wanted to make certain that you would take her before I let her hopes rise, brother."

Laura found her voice. "I can learn to read?"

"And write." The monk seemed to be amused.

"And then you'll write on the jars and never mistake mugwort for shepherd's purse again," Crescia said dryly.

By the time they left Fra Bruncio the lemony sunlight had grown tawny. Laura followed Crescia up the hill in silence, too overwhelmed by the sights of the day and her own extraordinary fortune to chatter as she might have done. As they went, Crescia pointed out the landmarks by which Laura might find her way home after her lesson. "Tomorrow I will bring you down so that you can learn the path there. After that—" The healer looked at her sideways. "You'll be on your own. You must be careful not to talk to strangers; you're not a woman yet, but there are men on the roads who would not let that interfere with their pleasures. Straight to Fra Bruncio's and straight home. And all the tasks you have done before this will still be yours, and there will be studying to do as well. Now you're used to the idea, is it something you want?"

Laura nodded vigorously.

"Good, daughter. You please me."

"But mistress, why today?"

"Today? What do you mean?"

Laura paused to put the thought together. "When you came home this morning you were angry. Then we went to the city. Did you always mean to do this, or was it only today . . ." She did not ask, *When your anger is gone will I cease to have these lessons?*

Crescia stopped. "Pardon me, girl. My anger at that pompous fool this morning moved me to act. It must have confused you." The old woman shifted as if her back hurt. "I'd been thinking for some time that if you had the knack of it you might add to our store of knowledge. I can't afford to send you to a convent as the rich men do their daughters, but I *can* pay a poor monk for lessons, so yesterday I asked

Fra Fraternus to suggest someone. Now Fra Bruncio and I
have come to an agreement, and your job is to keep your
eyes open and learn all you may."

Laura promised solemnly that she would do so and they
continued up the hill, stopping once more when Crescia
spied an oak apple on the low branch of a tree and sent Laura
climbing to bring it down. "There, you see what you find
when you keep your eyes open, daughter?" She put the gall
in the basket as Laura unkilted her skirts. They continued
up the path.

*   *   *   *

Laura had believed, in the first year as Crescia's apprentice,
that she had worked hard: fetching, grinding, grating, carrying, learning all the time. She had risen with the sun and
drowsed over supper at nightfall, washing her hands so
many times in the course of a day that they grew as rough
and red as Crescia's own. Now she rose and worked, ran
down the hill to study with Fra Bruncio between the bells
for prime and terce, then ran back up the hill again to do her
work. After dark she sat by the brazier scratching letters on
her slate. She was always hungry, although Crescia's table
was plain but plentiful, and it seemed to Laura that her body
was growing as fast as her brains were filling. By the time her
name day came in late summer she had grown by inches and
filled out. And she knew all the letters and had begun to use
them to learn a new language.

"Why don't we read what we speak?" she asked Fra
Bruncio.

He snorted as if the question were ridiculous. "Latin is
the language of learning. Even barbarian foreigners know it,
and write their letters and laws in it. They save their own
language for bawdy poems and tall tales. Are you a barbarian foreigner?"

Laura shook her head.

"Then you learn Latin." Fra Bruncio was a very different sort of teacher from Crescia. He believed that a slap or a smack on the wrist was a great aid to learning and did not much care whether Laura understood the why of what she learned so long as she had it fixed in her mind. He was more generous in his praise than Crescia was, but at the same time told her he did not expect much from a woman child. Laura felt more pleasure in her mistress's rare smiles than in Fra Bruncio's sarcastic commendation.

She became used to rising with declensions in her head, murmuring verbs as she milked the goats and brushed them, reciting psalms as she worked in the garden or ranged over the hill seeking madder or starwort. No matter if she had been up through the night with Crescia at a birthing, when the bell of the duomo rang for prime Laura was expected to be at her studies with a clear mind. Somehow, she was.

Often, trudging up the hill after her lesson, she thought of her mother and Bice and herself, two years before. None of them would have recognized the girl she had become, and more, they would have all disapproved of the freedom Crescia gave her, perhaps mistrusted her new learning and skills. Laura missed the fading memory of her family, but she did not miss the child who had followed cravenly in Urbo's shadow for more than a year. She had a new name, a home, and a calling of her own. The nightmares had faded. She could imagine a future without fear.

Chapter Six

It was spring before Fra Bruncio gave Laura anything more challenging than psalms to read in Latin. By then she had begun to label the stock of dried herbs, spices, roots, and simples on Crescia's shelves, writing in a painstaking block hand in chalk or charcoal on the unglazed clay jars. Laura offered to teach Crescia so that she could read them as well. Her apprentice's learning delighted the healer, but, after an afternoon spent bent over Laura's slate, Crescia pronounced herself too old to learn such a skill. "You'll be the learned one for both of us, daughter."

Spring was busy. Ravanella had a pair of kids; one Crescia sold in the market in Salerno; the other they loosed to graze with her mother, with the promise of roast kid and kidskin shoes at midsummer. Herbs flowered and were collected, dried, and brewed into simples to keep on hand. The days were so full of work and learning that Laura rarely had time to remember the time before she came to Crescia.

Latin, she found, was a language with rules as strict as any Crescia had about cleanliness or the mixing of unguents. It had never occurred to her before that the language she and Crescia and the folk around them spoke had rules; now, as she learned the grammar of Latin, she attempted to apply the rules to her everyday speech. Latin had a word for everything, sometimes more than one, and each time Laura learned a new word—particularly for one of the botanicals—she rewrote the label on the jar. Crescia nodded when Laura told her the Latin names, but continued to call for mallow rather than *altea* and hyssop rather than *ysopus*. By the time her second autumn with Crescia drew in, Laura had attended at seven birthings, fetching, carrying, observing, sometimes helping to hold or pull or move the mother as she labored. After that harrowing first time, once a mother had died. The rest of the childbeds had been as uneventful as such things could be. Two of the children died in their first year; Laura thought she would never forget the coarse, terrible sound of the mother's cries when she saw her infant, seeming-healthy a day before, lying still in Crescia's hands. But most often midwifery was joyful work. Laura fetched and carried too when the healer was called to help with sickness or injury. When they were summoned it was now she who assembled the basket of supplies to bring along for an injury, a fever, an abscess, or a rash.

And every day but Sunday Laura laced up her shoes, tied a kerchief around her hair—long since permitted to return to its original shade—and ran down the hill to Fra Bruncio for a lesson.

On the morning of Saint Hermione's feast, Laura woke alone in the house. Crescia had stayed the night with a young mother and her new baby, halfway down to the city. "If I'm not home by dawn say your prayers, do your chores, and go to the brother for your lesson." So Laura dressed and washed and fed the goats, ate bread and berries and tidied and swept the house, then set off for Salerno.

The monk was in a mood. He had Laura read pages of ecclesiastic script and demanded she tell him the sense of it. She could read Latin aloud swiftly now, but what she was reading now made no sense to her. It was all "kind greetings" from this holy one to that, followed by instructions and admonitions and names that Laura did not know. By the time the sun was high and Fra Bruncio had let her go for the day, her eyes were tired, her ears burned from the monk's slaps, and her head buzzed with information that seemed, at the least, useless.

She let her eyes adjust to the autumn sunlight outside Fra Bruncio's door, blinking and feeling the midday heat warm her stiff shoulders. Then Laura trotted up the street and out of the city, arriving breathless at the branching of paths that led, on the left, to Crescia's house. There she dropped in the shade of an oak tree, exhilarated by her exertion. She took a moment to retie the scarf on her head, listening to the buzz of bees hovering around a late-blooming amaranth. Then she lay back, eyes closed, smelling the familiar scents of the hills: dust, crushed grass, the sun baking the leaves of a myrtle tree nearby. Above her, when she opened her eyes, she saw something in the join of two boughs. It was a wasp gall, a big one of the sort that Crescia prized. Laura gauged the height of the lowermost bough, looked about for gall wasps and saw none, and finally took off her shoes and kilted her skirts up.

The lower bough dipped close enough to the ground that Laura could swing up onto it. Then it was a matter of edging along the bough to the join and examining the gall. It was almost a hand's breadth wide and firmly fixed to the bough. Laura took her knife from the pocket that swung from her waist and prized and cut at the gall until it began to loosen from the bough. When it fell at last it left a white scar on the bough, but no wasps emerged. Very pleased with herself, Laura shifted her weight forward and slid off the bough, landing in a crouch by the gall. She inspected it one more time for wasps and, assured that she would not be stung, tucked it under her arm, and started on the path homeward, listing the remedies of which oak gall was a constituent.

Someone was waiting at the gate, which meant Crescia was not yet home. Laura settled the gall into the crook of her arm and continued toward the house, ready to greet the man and ask his business. She did not recognize him, but Crescia's skill was known beyond their village and strangers were not unusual. She called a greeting and walked more briskly.

When she got near enough to see him she stumbled and hurriedly righted herself: the man at the gate was Urbo.

He was changed from the man who had destroyed her village and her family. His powerful belly was sunken and his arms withered. His dark, vigorous hair was lank and salted with gray, and his beard was almost white. His eyes, though, were the same: full of malice and a sense of deadly power. Only the downturn in the corners of his mouth suggested his bewilderment at the weakness that had overtaken him. He was sick.

Laura swallowed bile. She was no longer the child who had run from him. She was a healer's apprentice, she could read and write in Latin. More to the point, she had grown more than a handspan since she'd fled his camp, put on flesh. She was a different person. Why should he see the scared child who lingered inside her? Best to act as though he were just another passerby.

"Good day, uncle," she said.

"Where's the old woman lives here?" Urbo did not bother wasting charm on a barely fledged girl. "The healer. Where is she?"

"My mistress was called to a lying-in last night and is not returned yet. May I help you until she returns?" Close to, Laura saw he was favoring his left leg. The skin over his cheekbones was taut and flushed, and his eyes bloodshot. "You're hurt."

"How d'you know that?"

Laura lowered her eyes. Urbo's belligerence did not disguise his fear and his need. "My mistress has taught me to know such things. Will you wait for her, or will you let me help you?" She stepped around him and through the gate, where the goats clustered around her, bleating and butting against her legs, craving attention.

"You can heal a sore foot?"

"I can begin to. Time is the great healer; I'm only her handmaiden," she quoted Crescia. Urbo nodded. Perhaps he really was just another sick man. "Come in, then."

Urbo followed her into the yard and at once the goats surrounded him. Laura shooed them away, but not fast enough. Bonta butted at Urbo, trod on his foot, and the man screamed with pain. He wheeled around on one leg, swearing, his fist sweeping before him, and caught Laura a blow at the side of her head that knocked her to the ground. Dizzy, with a taste of blood in her mouth, she scrabbled to her knees to rise, but could not. Urbo had his hand on her shoulder, pressing down heavily. His blow had knocked the cloth from her head, and her hair, red as berries, hung in a plait across her shoulder.

"*You?*" Urbo peered at Laura's face, blinked, looked again. "Let me see your leg."

Laura resisted. He reached with his free hand, fumbled, took her right foot, and raised it until he could see the scar circling her ankle. He grunted.

"All this time it was you. That old witch magicked you somehow. Or me." His hands had not lost all their strength. He squeezed Laura's shoulder until she cried out. "First you'll tend to my foot like a good healer girl. Then I'll settle our score." Urbo ran his free hand over his loose belly and down to his privates, the old threat that had so terrified Laura. "You, then the old witch for cozening me. Take me into your hovel, little bitch." He jerked Laura toward the cottage. "I made you a promise the day I killed your mama. I'll keep it tonight."

He would rape her until she died.

Laura's legs barely held her. Urbo's hand was tight as a strap around her arm. The goats followed after, waiting for the handful of leaves or grass Laura usually brought for them. They bleated and would have crowded around them, but Urbo swore again and they backed away. At the door Urbo pushed Laura before him into the cottage. The house was quiet, the fire banked as Laura had left it that morning.

"My mistress is at a birthing," Laura said again.

Urbo wiped a line of sweat from his upper lip. He was gray and wheezing. "Don't worry about your mistress." He said the last two words with derision. "I'll do for her later. You get to work now." He sat carefully on the stool by the fire and looked around him at the orderly workroom. "And bring me something to eat."

Without comment Laura went into the next room and returned with a slice of bread, some cheese, and a handful of late berries. She put the bowl on the table near Urbo's elbow.

"What kind of muck is this? Is this what you eat? And where's to drink?" He looked around him as if for a cask of wine or ale. "What's in that?" He pointed to a large clay pot covered with oiled linen.

"It's an unguent for burns. We drink water, most days. Or goat's milk."

Urbo spat, then shoved a thumb-sized piece of cheese into his mouth. "Then bring water, if it's all you have. Jesu, I've a thirst could drain a river." He leaned over and tugged at his boot. "Saint Peter's balls! What did that devil-goat of yours do to me?" The pain did not make Urbo more careful in pulling off his boot; when it came at last he roared. A smell of pus and putrefaction filled the room.

Laura felt her training take over. "Let me look."

Low on the leg, just above the ankle, a carbuncle almost the width of her palm glistened redly. Laura did not touch it; it must be exquisitely painful.

"Bring me water," Urbo said again. "Then tell me what sort of magic your witch has for a sore like that."

Laura dipped out water into a horn cup and put it on the

table. "We make a warm poultice to draw out the pus. And give you a draught to help with the pain."

"Like the muck I drank the last time? There'll be none of that, little bitch. I've a plan for tonight, and I won't be tricked into sleeping. Draw out the pus; that sounds like the thing to do. But none of that—what was it?"

"Wild lettuce," Laura murmured.

Urbo grabbed her braid, pulling her face to his. "No wild lettuce." His breath was foul with a fruity sweetness like the smell of rotting apples. Crescia had said she thought he had the honey sickness. "No draughts."

"It will hurt to drain the carbuncle," she protested. "With-out something to ease the pain—"

"What am I, an old woman? Find another way."

Laura thought for a moment, then brought down a pot of salve from the shelf and pushed it across the table to Urbo. "This might help." She was certain it would not. "Spread some on the sore."

The man stuck two dirty fingers into the pot—Crescia would throw the rest out, Laura thought—and took a gob of salve which he dabbed on the carbuncle. She saw the pain rip through him.

"Peter's balls!" He swung around to clout Laura, but she had danced out of his range.

"There's pus and poison under the skin," she told him. "As long as it's there you'll get sicker and sicker. What you need is a warm poultice, but it will hurt as much as that salve does."

"Find another way." Urbo was panting.

"There isn't any. For the pain I might . . ." An idea came to her. "No wild lettuce, I promise. But I can make a differ-ent tea to relax the muscles and take away some of the pain. Then I could poultice the carbuncle and drain it."

"I won't sleep?"

"No, you—"

"Do it!" he roared. "*Now*, by Sebastian's prick. Where's the damned old woman?"

"She'll come, she'll come!" Laura stirred up the fire and dipped water into the kettle. She washed her hands, took down the comfrey and rosemary from the shelves, and put a measure of each in a beaker. "See, I'm starting the tea, then I'll make the poultice." She put the kettle on the fire and, while it heated, cut more bread for Urbo, poured him more water, and stayed just outside the range of his arm. In a mortar she put a measure each of fenugreek, flaxseed, and mallow and ground them quickly. When the water had boiled she dipped a measure into the beaker and let the tea steep. Then she made a paste of the fenugreek mixture and spread it on clean cloth.

"Drink," she said, and pushed the beaker toward Urbo. The man looked at the beaker suspiciously. "None of that piss you gave me last time."

Laura shook her head. "Only comfrey and rosemary, I swear it."

Urbo grinned at the fear in her voice, reached for the beaker, and tossed the whole brew down as if it were ale, swearing afterward that he might as well have been drinking piss. "How long until it works?"

"Soon. But I must put the poultice on now, while it's hot. It will hurt."

She knelt at Urbo's feet again, sickened by the glistening blisters of the carbuncle, and as gingerly as she could put the warm poultice on.

Not gently enough. Urbo reared back, screaming, and kicked at Laura with his good leg, knocking her backward into the wall. Her head rang and she opened her eyes to see the man curled forward as if protecting his pain like a laboring woman, cursing the wound, Laura, and God with a steady stream of profanity. Laura put her hand up and wiped a trickle of blood from her lip.

"You God-cursed whore, what have you done to me?"

"I said it would hurt." She pressed back against the wall. The poultice had stayed in its place, held there by the gummy herbal paste. "When it cools I will—" She looked more closely. "Already it's working." A thin trail of creamy yellow pus, followed by more of a darker yellow, trickled from under the poultice. "See? One of the blisters is draining."

Urbo raised his head, his eyes more bloodshot than before, and looked down.

"Working. Learned something from the old witch, did you? Perhaps I've misthought, little bitch. P'raps I should keep you alive. Show you your place, yes. Then bring you back to camp to be useful."

The brief moment of pride Laura had felt vanished. Her throat filled with acid. *Never.* Better she die now. Or that he did.

"I'll need to take the poultice off soon and put on fresh," she told him. "You'll want more tea."

Again Laura put comfrey and rosemary in the beaker. Murmuring the prayer to Saint Catherine that asked for a good outcome for her work, she took two foxglove flowers, crushed them, and added them to the beaker. As before, she added water. "Do you want some honey to sweeten it this time?"

"I'm no woman to need the brew sweetened." He scowled.

While the tea steeped Laura made a fresh poultice. When it was ready she pushed the beaker toward Urbo. "Drink it before I change the poultice."

Urbo tilted the beaker back and swallowed the whole.

Laura knelt again at his feet. "This will hurt," she reminded him. It was not easy to get the cooling poultice off. Urbo yelled, then gritted his teeth and sank back.

"When is that piss-water going to take the pain?"

"Soon." Laura had no idea. Crescia had never used more than the tiniest bit of foxglove as a remedy for racing heartbeat, always in combination with other medicines. She had told Laura that foxglove was virulently poisonous, but beyond that Laura knew nothing. "I hope soon," she added to herself. If it took long enough for Urbo to realize that she had poisoned him, she would certainly die.

"Do I need more?" Urbo pushed the beaker across the table.

"No, no. That should be enough. Now I'll put this on."

As carefully as she could she applied the poultice. He groaned and scowled, but did not strike her this time. Again there was a seep of pus from under the linen.

"That's enough for now. You should rest."

He laughed. "Save my strength for my work tonight. I thought you were dead in a ditch somewhere, little bitch. You should have stayed in camp."

"Will you bring me back?"

The man groaned and shuddered and laughed. "Mayhap. Mayhap only that braid, to show I found my kill. I don't know what enchantment you and the old woman used on me when I left you here last time. I thought that girl was years older and dark haired."

"Not enchantment." Laura thought he was sweating more heavily. "We dyed my hair. I walked on my toes to seem taller."

"Witchcraft." He shook his head. "Don't think I'd be fooled by that, d'you? More water."

Laura poured more water.

Urbo emptied the horn cup, gestured for more, drank it down, and was silent. Laura leaned against the shelves, as far away from Urbo's fists as she could get. He was between her and the door, and Crescia might return at any moment and be captured. Laura was sure that her mistress could not out-run Urbo, even with his injury. She watched him for some sign that the foxglove was having an effect; he seemed paler, and a muscle in his forehead spasmed.

"*Deo*, my mouth's dry as rock. More water."

She dipped the last of the water into his cup and Urbo drank it down. He blinked. "My head hurts." He squinted at Laura. "Did you do something to the medicine?"

"I wouldn't know how," she lied. *Please, Saint Catherine, Saint Margaret, Blessed Queen of Heaven, let me have done it right. Let him die.* "All my mistress has taught me are simples, remedies. To do ill is a far longer study, very complex." She looked down as if to say with her eyes that she did not have the wit to study anything.

Urbo chuckled heavily. He was breathing slowly, squinting. "Christ, I say my head hurts. Have you no remedy for that?" He had forgotten her mistress. "My head and—" He ran one hand around the stubble on his jaw and across his chest. "Hurts," he said again thickly. He leaned forward. "What did you do?" Urbo's head dropped down close to his chest. A powerful convulsion went through his whole body, and he toppled to the floor.

Laura did not stay to see what happened next. She dodged one out-flung hand and ran for the door.

She sat at the far end of the goat pen with Bonta and Neve guarding her while the sun slid farther and farther along the arc of sky. There was no noise from the house. Laura thought she should go back and see whether Urbo still lived, but she was afraid. She stayed surrounded by the goats, comforted by their warmth and smell and affectionate nudges. After a while she heard someone on the path to the cottage. Crescia.

Laura got to her feet and ran to stop the old woman. "Mistress! Don't. It's not safe."

Crescia put out a hand to steady Laura and took in the

sight of her apprentice. "You look as if you rolled down the hill, girl. And you smell as if you've been sleeping with the goats. The Queen of Hea—"

"Mistress, *please*."

Any humor vanished from the old woman's face. "What has happened?"

In as few words as possible, Laura told her.

"And is he dead?"

Laura looked down, ashamed. "I think so. I didn't—I couldn't stay. I was afraid that you'd come back before he was gone and he might hurt you."

"And foxglove was your only recourse? You might have dosed him to sleep. There was no need to kill—"

"There *was*." Laura stamped her foot. "You weren't there. *You don't know*. He said he'd kill you if you tried again to out-think him. You, mistress, rape and—"

Crescia slapped her.

Laura stared at her teacher, unbelieving. A tear edged down over the stinging welt on her cheek.

"*Do not make me your reason for taking a life*," Crescia said, low.

They watched each other in silence. The buzzing of insects, the settling bleats of the goats in their shed, the breeze stirring the rosemary in the garden and releasing its scent filled Laura's ears.

"I'm sorry, mistress. I was afraid. I did not see how making him sleep now, then go away, would keep us—me—safe. You saw him twice. I lived in his camp for a year. I know what he's like, and even if he did not kill me he would have killed you and taken me back to physic his men and to fuck."

Crescia pushed away the tear-trail on Laura's cheek with a gentle finger. "Forgive me, daughter. You were there. You know him better than I. I would not ask you to go willing to whoredom. Not everyone has the stuff of saints, to face a bad death. Now we must clean up the mess your Urbo has undoubtedly made of our workshop."

After the subtle, warm sounds of life outside the cottage, the workroom was doubly still. The table, kicked out of its place by Urbo, stood on two legs, leaning against the shelves. The fire in the brazier was low. The cup from which Urbo had drunk the poisoned tea lay close to the embers, and the beaker had fallen and broken into shards of rosy clay. In the center of the mess was Urbo, curled on the floor, his face pinched in fear and pain. One hand reached to the door, fingers clawed. The other grasped at his chest. To Laura's horror, Crescia bent, fingered the damp earth by Urbo's body, and licked her thumb thoughtfully. "The honey sickness," she said absently. "No wonder he had such a carbuncle." She looked at Urbo's ankle, examining the poultice Laura had tied there. "Fenugreek and mallow?"

"And flaxseed." Laura wondered that Crescia could bear to handle the body. In her life Urbo had been a devil; who knew what sort of evil might yet live in those bones, that clawed hand.

"You did well with the carbuncle, daughter. Now, fetch the cart and hitch Bonta to it."

Laura stared. The cart? The goats?

"Unless you want to get rid of this Urbo by letting him rot away under our feet—a useful lesson, perhaps, but not one I want to live with—we must do something with the body. Get the cart, daughter."

The cart was a wooden box less than the span of Laura's arms, square with wooden wheels and a tongue that could be pulled, as Laura did when she collected something too large to carry in a basket or drag to the workroom, or hitched to one of the goats. It was rickety, built by one of their neighbors in payment for his father's last illness, but, if it rattled as it rolled, still it rolled. Laura hitched Bonta to the cart and led him back to the house.

Crescia had closed Urbo's eyes and straightened his limbs. The death stiffness had not yet set in; the body could be moved. Laura followed Crescia's direction, grasping Urbo's feet and dragging him toward the cottage door. Crescia came to help, and they pulled him outside. Urbo might be diminished from the man he had been, but he was still tall and heavy, and they were still an old woman and a girl.

The sun was a rim of light behind the rise when they got Urbo's body into the wagon and covered it with a blanket. Crescia set out in the lead, westward toward the cliffs, with Laura guiding Bonta behind her. When they reached the bluff they tugged and wrestled the body out of the cart, rolled and pulled it through the stony scrub to the cliff's edge, and shoved it over. It bounced and rolled and fell toward the sea.

Laura did not wait to see where the body landed or if the sea took it. She turned away, feeling ill.

"He was dying," Crescia said. "A very sick man can lose his footing and fall to his death. Come, now. It's getting chilly."

Home in the cottage, Laura went wordlessly about cleaning up the signs of Urbo's presence, sweeping the floor, righting the table and stools, returning the herbs to their places on the shelves, sweeping up the shards of the broken clay beaker.

Crescia, all the while, sat and spun Ravanella's fine gray hair into thread. When Laura was finished she said, "Rest a moment, child."

Laura sank down to sit at her mistress's feet. "Mistress? What else could I have done ?"

Crescia shook her head. "I don't know, daughter. I wasn't there, as you say. And we'll never know. Perhaps if we had tricked him again he would have come back again. Perhaps he wouldn't have lived to return—he was a sick man. But rage is like love, child. It can do things that surprise us. Urbo is gone. His pain is at an end."

A last fear filled Laura. "What do I tell the priest?"

"At confession? The truth, if you expect to be shriven. A man tried to kill you and you defended yourself. God knows it already. You're only telling a man."

"But will God forgive me? Such a sin!"

"The priest will give you penance and absolve you. And not God nor his Son nor the gracious Queen of Heaven will judge you ill if what you tell me of your heart is true."

Laura sighed.

"Now, girl, it has been a long day for both of us, and I see our late guest ate the last of the bread. Put the pot on and make porridge. And let me tell you what happened after you left the lying-in. It will be instructive."

As if there had been no dead man in their workroom an hour before, Crescia talked and Laura set about preparing their supper.

Chapter Seven

SALERNO, AUGUST 1209

In the five years Laura had lived with Crescia, the healer's ageless face had become fine drawn and her skin papery. There was less pretense to the bend of her back and the stiff-ness of her gait. She worked as hard, and as long, as she had always done, but Laura worried for her. "It's only age, which comes to us all, daughter. There's no physic for it."

The two women were preparing to go down to the city on

an errand about which Crescia was stubbornly mysterious. She had dressed in her best gray kirtle and linen headdress and bidden Laura to be likewise careful in her dress. Laura was now slightly taller than than her mistress and far straighter, and years of good plain food had rounded her curves. Still, she would never be tall or plump. Her red hair had darkened to a rosy brown; her skin, which burned easily when she stayed in the sun, was clear and fair; her eyes were dark beneath straight auburn brows. With a new coif and shoes of soft leather she looked, and felt, like a woman nearly grown.

They heard mass at the duomo. After, when the priest was putting away the vessels, Crescia gathered herself and said, "Come, girl. We go to the Scuola."

Laura stopped. "The Scuola?" Crescia did business with apothecaries near the medical school, but Laura had never known her to go to the school itself. These days she spoke of the medicos with derision if she spoke of them at all.

"Have you something in your ear? The Scuola."

Crescia walked slowly up the hill and Laura worried. Was there some ailment her mistress had not spoken of, something she did not trust herself to physic? "Mistress, are you well?"

"Me?" Crescia looked at Laura, surprised. "I'm as well as a woman of my years can expect to be. But my mind is full." She pulled a fold of paper from her sleeve. Laura recognized Fra Bruncio's hand in the letters writ there. "What does this say?"

Laura turned the paper right way round to read it. "Father Anselmo. Superior of the Scuola."

"That's who we want." Crescia looked around her as if the priest might be lurking in a doorway. Laura, who had become used to the bustle of Salerno, saw that her teacher was uneasy so close to the medical school itself.

"Should I ask someone where to find him?"

The old woman nodded. "It's your business we're here about."

It is? This was the first Laura had heard of it. She approached one student, then another. Both brushed past her unseeing; she was too insignificant to notice. A third student took a moment to direct them along a passage between two buildings, up a staircase, and onto a gallery overlooking a garden. They took the stairs slowly, pausing at the top so Crescia could rest.

They admired the order of the garden below them, herbs set out in rows, their leaves stirring in the warm air. When Crescia had caught her breath, they went on, turning into a small, square, windowless chamber with an arched doorway on the far side. A monk sat at a table in front of the door, poring so closely over a scroll that his nose almost brushed the parchment. His mouth turned down as if what he read displeased him. He did not look the sort of man to grant whatever favor Crescia meant to ask. The healer stood in the doorway, silent, as if she feared to interrupt his work. They stood so—Laura and Crescia waiting and the monk ignoring them—until Laura sidled past her mistress.

She bowed. "Your pardon, brother. Are you Father Anselmo?"

Very deliberately the monk put his finger on the parchment to mark his place and looked up. His expression did not change. "The indigent's hospice is in the next building." He jerked his head in the direction from which they had come and looked back at his scroll.

It might be a sin to dislike a man of God, but Laura did not like this one. "Thank you, brother, but we're not ill. Nor indigent. We have business with Father Anselmo."

This time when he looked up the monk seemed to actually see them. "I am Father Anselmo's second, Fra Ranulphus. What's your business?"

Crescia gave the folded paper to Laura; Laura handed it to Fra Ranulphus with another bow. He took it between two fingers as if it were befouled, read it, folded it again, and slid it into his own sleeve. "Which of you is Laura?"

Laura bowed again.

"Wait here."

The moment the monk vanished through the doorway behind his desk. Crescia let out a gusty breath. She straightened her shoulders and looked around her. "This place." She waved a hand. "It makes me feel small. All these learned men."

Laura stared at her teacher. Crescia, who had faced down Urbo and told Adamo the cobbler that if he did not stop beating his wife he would answer to her, who birthed children and closed the eyes of the dying—Crescia frightened by the scholars of the Scuola?

"But they're just like you, healers."

"They're men, and they're learned, and they have power. Remember that, girl."

The monk returned.

"Father Anselmo will see you." His voice was sour. "Come." He turned back without waiting to see if they followed, and led the way through the arched doorway.

"The women, Father."

The monk bowed and left them.

The room they were now in was much larger than the first, warm with sun and filled with papers and scrolls and books, in stacks, on a table, on chairs, even on the floor. By one window, at a smaller desk, a vigorous-looking man with a dark beard and clean-shaven tonsure sat on a high stool. He had work spread before him but, unlike his junior, at once gave his full attention to his visitors.

"Come." He waved them farther in. Crescia and Laura bowed deeply to him; he waved a hand in acknowledgment.

"Will you sit, mother?" He gestured Crescia toward the one chair that held neither paper nor scrolls. Crescia sat. Laura went to stand behind her mistress.

"Your teacher thinks well of you, girl." The priest waved her forward.

Of me? What was she to say to that? Laura still did not understand the purpose of the visit or why it seemed to be about her. "My teacher is kind, Father. I only hope to do credit to his teaching."

"Well spoken. From this—" One of the priest's short fingers stabbed at the fold of paper that lay on the table before him. "It seems you have done so. Our brother Bruncio says that you have learned all the mathematics he can teach and that you are grounded in rhetoric and disputation. He says that your other teacher speaks highly of your skill and dedication."

Laura looked at Crescia, who nodded, her eyes on Father Anselmo.

"The study of medicine is more than bone setting or birthing, however. Those things can be managed by practiced craftsmen, and very important work that is." He cleared his throat. "A physician understands the philosophy of healing, the effect of the stars, the humors, the elements on the human form. He must know the history and knowledge of the ancients and the infidel. There is much to learn. I would not expect you to give yourself airs because you have attended a few births and mopped a few brows."

"No, Father. Of course not." Laura was bewildered.

"Your mistress says you have been her apprentice for five years. She says you're singularly gifted in herb lore. You are deficient in some areas, however: geometry and astronomy in particular. It is unlikely that you will ever become a physician. Unlikely, but not impossible if God wills it."

Laura turned to look at Crescia, whose earlier unease

seemed to have dropped away in Father Anselmo's genial presence. The old woman nodded. "It's all she asks, Father. The chance to attempt it."

Attempt what? Becoming a physician? A member of the Scuola? Was such a thing even possible?

Father Anselmo rose. He was shorter than Laura had expected and moved with a bowlegged sway, brisk and energetic. "Is this a thing you want, girl? Your mistress's desire is clear, but it will be you who does the work. You will have to work hard and long to make up for what others of your age have been studying for years. You will need tuition in geometry, algebra, astronomy, and harmonics. Even if you finish those studies and come here you may find there are teachers who won't admit you to study with them. We have a liberal tradition here, but not every man who teaches or practices here is likewise liberal. A woman with neither wealth nor family is certain to have a difficult time. You must be certain that this is what you want."

He looked at Laura seriously but not unkindly. She felt Crescia's gaze on her.

What do I want?

The answer welled up in Laura with a fierceness that was utterly unexpected. "It *is* what I want," she said. "Father, I ask only to justify my teachers' faith in me. And yours."

Father Anselmo nodded. "It might be easier for you if you took vows. We have some sisters come to us, sent by their houses." He paused. "No? Perhaps your vocation is for medicine alone. We serve God in many different ways." He turned to Crescia. "She will need tuition in mathematics for two or three years at least. I can recommend a tutor, but the cost—"

"I can pay," Crescia interrupted. "I have been saving against this day."

Another surprise. Laura had almost ceased to wonder at them.

"Well enough." The priest sat again and wrote something on the back of Fra Bruncio's letter. "Take this to Carlo Alarabi. He has rooms above the scrivener in the market square. I've asked him to arrange for your tuition."

He offered the note to Laura. She took it unread and gave it to her mistress.

"Thank you, Father." Laura bowed again and then turned to give Crescia her arm. The old woman smiled, murmuring an echo of Laura's thanks.

"*Benedicite.*" Already the priest was returning his attention to the work on his table. They went out past the spare, disapproving monk in the antechamber.

"Why didn't you tell me what you meant to do?" Laura whispered when they had reached the street. "I thought you disliked the medicos?"

"I may dislike *them*, but I don't dislike their knowledge. You'll learn and come back to share it with me." Crescia, now her petition had been met as seriously as she had made it, seemed suddenly brisk and energetic. "As for why I didn't tell you, I didn't know what they'd say. Why get your hopes up?" The same as when they had first gone to Fra Bruncio. Crescia was Crescia.

They found Carlo Alarabi up the stairs in a set of low-ceilinged rooms as tidy as Crescia's cottage and as packed with scrolls and papers as hers was with botanicals. Alarabi was a sharp-featured man with the scars of smallpox and sharp, down-turned brown eyes. He was gaunt and dark, like a figure carved in wood, and when he read Father Anselmo's note, then turned it over to read what Fra Bruncio had written, his body curved over the paper protectively.

He returned the paper to Crescia. Laura listened as they negotiated the terms of Laura's study, so quickly and sharply it seemed to her they were speaking a foreign language. When they had settled he added his opinion that Laura's work would be for nothing. "There aren't many women at the Scuola these days, not like in Trocta's day. Is that what you want, girl? To be our new Trocta?"

Laura, with no idea who or what Trocta was, nodded. Crescia paid three copper *follari* into Carlo Alarabi's hand. They left with a tightly furled scroll under Laura's arm.

"Read as much of it as you can and come back in a five-day. We'll see what sense you can make of it."

* * * *

"Well." They were walking up the hill. Crescia was pleased. "That was a good morning's work."

Laura followed Crescia along the path, as meek as a Greek slave. It wasn't until they reached their own gate and the goats were bleating a welcome that she found her voice.

"What is Trocta, mistress?"

"Trocta?" The old woman snorted. "A day of surprises for you and that's all you can find to ask? Trocta was a teacher at the Scuola a hundred years ago. A famous physician, and a wife and a mother."

A woman a physician and a teacher. A famous one.

She thought of something else. "Am I still to study with Fra Bruncio? How can I, when Ser Alarabi—and how can I help you if I am in Salerno all day?"

Crescia rapped her on the chin with two fingers, a sharp tap that made Laura's skin sting. "Do you think we're fools, Fra Bruncio and I? Do you think we never spoke of all this? It was he who first told me you had talent as a scholar. We have had this plotted for a year or more."

Laura thought of the frequency of her tutor's blows, meant to spur her memory. "I thought he didn't like me."

"Like you?" Crescia sniffed. "He's an old monk with no patience. You're a young girl. It would be a miracle if you did not annoy him, child, but he's wise enough to see that you're a smart girl and may bring him credit. See that you do."

"I will." Laura was swimming in a sea of new ideas. "Mistress?"

"Yes, daughter."

They were at the door to the cottage. The breeze wicked through the rosemary and mint, the goats bleated, and the bees hummed. The air was hot and sweet.

"Do *you* like me?"

Crescia smiled. "Never doubt it, daughter. Now." She was all business. "Once you have read that book and returned it to Ser Alarabi we can make a plan for your days. For this moment—we have almost no nightshade. Go find what you can. Make sure you get the youngest of the flowers you find."

Laura changed from her good kirtle to the everyday one. Crescia was braiding garlic together and waiting for water to heat in the kettle.

"Shall I bring more water, mistress?"

Crescia looked up; her deft fingers continued the braiding. "Later, daughter."

Laura, barely aware of what she meant to do, hugged Crescia tightly for a moment. "Thank you, mother," she whispered. She fled out the door before she could see if Crescia was pleased or no.

* * * *

Fra Bruncio was grudging in his pleasure at Laura's news. "Now your work really begins. I know old Alarabi; he'll work you hard, girl. Far harder than this old monk has done. You'd best not embarrass him, is all I can say."

When she tried to thank the monk for his help and for the letter, he waved his hand as if dispelling a bad smell in the air. "Get to your studies. You're not a student of the Scuola yet," he reminded her. "Nor are you too far grown for correction."

Laura bent to her Latin.

When she returned to Carlo Alarabi five days later she was filled with questions about the book he had given her. "Some of it I understand—I think. But some of it barely seems possible."

"Tell me what you think you understand," he said. "I will tell you where you are wrong."

He did. By the time she left him Laura felt as if her mind had been stretched and pulled every which way. She felt, too, a keen excitement, as if understanding were possible and just beyond her reach. She would go twice a week to see him, twice a week to work with Fra Bruncio, and spend all other hours helping Crescia and studying. It was exhausting. It was exhilarating.

*   *   *   *

They lost a mother and babe just before the feast of All Saints, a grueling birth that ended in a bath of blood that all Crescia's work could not stanch. The priest came, scowling at Crescia as if the deaths were her fault, and gave the mother the sacrament. Outside the room, the family waited, weeping and praying. Laura, who had been up all night at the childbed, gathered the bloody apron and basket of simples to carry back to the cottage. Her eyes felt gritty and her brain fogged. From down the hill the bells of the duomo tolled for none. She had lost track of time.

"Alarabi!"

Crescia made Laura stop to take off her own stained apron and wash her hands before she set off, running down the hill to the market square and Carlo Alarabi's rooms.

"You're late." Her teacher scowled. "Your hands are dirty. If you have no more respect for—"

"I washed my hands," Laura snapped. She was too tired after the sleepless, fruitless night to keep hold of her temper.

"Not well enough," Alarabi snapped back.

"It's blood, Ser Alarabi. It doesn't wash away so easily."

That took the tutor aback. "You were at a sickbed?"

"A birthing."

"Ahh. A blessed birth." His tone was satirical. "Even so, if you—"

"It was not blessed. The babe was born dead, rotting in his mother's womb, and she bled to death." The muscles in Laura's jaw hurt. She had not wept yet, and did not mean to now, with Alarabi watching. She took a breath, then another, knowing she must apologize. "Your pardon, Ser Alarabi. I had no sleep, and it was a hard night."

"And you find geometry beside the point this morning. I did not realize you were already attending at births."

"Since I was a girl." Laura did not think of how that might sound to a man of Alarabi's years. "Since my mistress took me in and made me her apprentice."

"And now you hope to be a physician."

"I *mean* to be."

He nodded thoughtfully. He sat on the stool at his writing desk, his shoulders stooped, his head thrust forward like a bird of prey. "You mean to be. So you have work to do, and for that work mathematics is not beside the point. It is a study that trains your mind to derive answers."

"What good is it to know the length of the hypotenuse when I have a patient who—"

"Listen." Alarabi took up a slate, wiped it clean with the edge of his sleeve, and scratched something on it with a piece of soft chalk. "You derive for sickness the same way you derive the length of the hypoteneuse. Say you're called to the house of a man who is ill. You do not at first recognize his sickness, only some symptoms. Let us give each symptom a name. Fever is A, rash is B . . ." He raised an eyebrow at her, encouraging her to continue.

"Pain is C? And . . . rapid pulse is D and excess of bile is E, and, yes, I see we can assign symbols to symptoms, but—"

"Well, let us say that your patient has A plus B plus D. Solve for the illness."

"But is there pain?"

"Your equation includes only A, B, and D. Solve the problem."

"It might be scarlet fever. It might be a dozen other things."

Alarabi shrugged. "It's not an exact analogy, but perhaps you see where I am tending with it."

"It's a tool," she said thoughtfully. Laura's gaze went to her hands and the circles of rusty red under her nails. "I had thought it was just one more obstacle to climb. I am sorry, Ser Alarabi. I will go wash my hands again."

Alarabi nodded. "No learning should be an obstacle, least of all my beautiful numbers. Me, I was meant to study astronomy to help my father, an astrologer in Parma. I came here and saw the beautiful dances of numbers and gave my heart to them."

"What did your father say?"

A cold, closed look passed over the mathematician's face. "He died. A robbery—or a client who did not like his predictions." He put a finger on the slate on the table. "So here we are, and you will learn to make the numbers dance. Back to work. You have a long way to go before they will dance for you."

* * * *

Laura came to study the mathematician as she had watched Crescia. From Alarabi she learned, unconsciously, to project confidence in matters of intellectual rigor even when, in her heart, she was unsure. He had a way of sweeping into a room that made her forget his bony, ugly looks and notice only the drama and importance of his presence. The one time Laura tried to sweep into his room in just that way, Alarabi laughed heartily.

"Until you're as old as I am, girl, an air like that will only make you look like a kitten playing at lion."

* * * *

Three winters and four summers passed before Laura and Crescia returned to the Scuola. Laura had reached her woman's height; she was half a head taller than her mistress, but still thin as she had been as a child. She had stopped wearing her hair down in a maiden's braid; today she wore a linen headdress folded and pinned to her coif as Crescia did and a gown of green wool she had bought from the weaver and sewn herself. She carried letters from Carlo Alarabi and Fra Bruncio attesting to her accomplishments in mathematics and astronomy, rhetoric and logic. Now when they walked through the upper city it was Crescia who followed Laura; the old woman was still ill at ease among the crowd of students and physicians in the school.

The tall, dour monk still guarded the Superior's office. His nostrils twitched as if the women smelled of the stable or midden, and he tried to send them away. Laura, now used to dealing with Carlo Alarabi's moods and tempers, did not falter. Respectfully but firmly she repeated: she had business with Father Anselmo. She offered the letters to prove it. If she thought the praise of her teachers might convince the monk to accord her some respect she was wrong. If anything, he seemed more displeased. But he did rise and speak to the Superior. When he returned to invite them into the office he was scowling.

"So, scholar girl," Father Anselmo greeted her. "You have prospered in your studies." He invited Crescia to sit. Laura knew a little more of the world now; a man of Father Anselmo's importance need not be mannerly to a peasant healer and her apprentice, but he was. It gave her hope.

"I have worked hard, Father." She must walk a line, Crescia had told her, between modesty and arrogance. *Men may be arrogant; women can't. But don't be so modest that he forgets you're standing before him!* Laura continued, "And my teachers have been generous and patient."

"Ser Alarabi patient?" Anselmo chuckled. "If he was, it is because you made it worth his while. He says you're gifted. That old algebraist would not say such a thing unless it was so. And you have kept up your work with your other teacher, Fra . . . ?"

"Fra Bruncio."

"Our Fra Bruncio. He too is pleased with you. I must ask again: you truly want to study medicine?" He looked at Laura as if he would see into her heart; his mouth crooked into a smile. "You do. I could wish you an easier road, girl. Even with a history of women students. The workings of man's body are a mystery too strong for some women. Those that stay find that the men they study with are not always kind. Even nuns sent from their houses to study here are often overwhelmed."

"I am willing to chance that, Father. If you permit me."

He waved a hand. "It is not for me to permit—you must talk to the lecturers and gain their permission. But some will be more persuadable than others, and if you prove your ability, others will be readier to take you. Don't attend more than one or two *studia* at first. It will be different from the way you learned with your tutors; now you'll be with other students, listening and talking. I would say—" He smiled at her. "I would say that you will like it."

He turned to Crescia. "You live in the hills? Lectures usually are held just after prime, and the day is long. Will the distance be a problem for her?"

Laura would have said there would be no problem, but Crescia forestalled her.

"She'll live in the house of Lot, the apothecary, and his wife. It is arranged, whenever the girl starts her studies."

Laura stared at her mistress. Again Crescia kept secrets.

"Very sensible. Also, girl—" Father Anselmo hesitated. "I hope you will take care for your safety, particularly outside the Scuola. Salerno is a seaport. There are foreigners and cutpurses in any city. Sadly, students are allowed more license than I would like, or than they sometimes know how to handle. Some of them are not—well, not all of them are monks, or even mannerly. A woman alone . . ." He let the words drift away to nothing, as if the threat spoke for itself.

Laura, who had spent half a dozen years trotting the streets of Salerno unaccompanied, parrying the half-serious suggestions of wine-soaked loungers and judging when a step to the left or the right was the safer path, shook her head. "I'm not afraid—" she began.

"Don't be foolish, girl." Crescia turned back to the priest. "Lot's son Pambo will be her escort," she said. "The boy is simple, but he's big. No one will trouble her."

"You've thought the matter through, mother. And the fees?"

"She has some coin she has earned. What she can't pay I will." Crescia put her hand on the purse that hung from her belt as if she would count out coins now.

"You don't pay me, mother! The lecturers set their own fees. Now, girl, was I you, I would start with Magister Paolo's *studia* on Aristotle. The Greek is the father of much of the healer's art; he will inform all your studies. And perhaps anatomy? I will give you a note to Fra Ambrigliano, who lecturers to the anatomy *studia*."

From his office, Father Anselmo escorted them to the gallery, pausing to tell Fra Ranulphus that Laura would be entering into tuition at the Scuola. The gaunt monk kept his opinion to himself and bowed to his superior.

Then they were walking down the hill from the Scuola to the market. Laura's head and hands buzzed with anxiety and excitement. She had a dozen questions. When had Crescia arranged for her to stay at Lot's shop? How could she afford board and room with the fees for the *studia* to pay as well? How would Crescia manage without her?

"I still have some secrets, daughter." Crescia's smile was sly. "You'll be worked hard, don't fear. You earn your place at Lot's by doing for him what you do for me: grinding and preparing and fetching and carrying. The old man—" Crescia lowered her voice, although there was no one but Laura to hear her. "His eyesight is waning. Natalia has been fearing for their livelihood. So you do them a service acting as his assistant, and they do you a service by keeping you."

"But I don't need that great gawk Pambo following after me like a dog."

Crescia shook her head. "I say you do. Have a little sense, or allow me to have some for you. You're old enough to wife, and it's past time that you had someone to escort you. There are men who won't hesitate to take by force what you'll not give them willingly. Those of us who serve the Queen of Heaven—we have gambled until now with your safety and your chastity. Pambo is a big boy, likely to make even the meanest rogue take thought before he accosts you."

"But I've never had trouble." As she said it, Laura realized that more than once she had escaped a bad situation by luck and wit.

"Then you have been lucky, but you can't plan to be lucky forever. And another reason to have an attendant, girl: some of those men, the students and physicians both, will want to treat you like a peasant girl from the hills—"

"I *am*—"

Crescia shook her head. "No. You are a woman of learning. You're a midwife. You've had more experience than some of the fellows you'll find yourself among, and they won't like you for it. Having an attendant will give you . . ." The old woman paused for the right word. "Consequence. The same way a neat gown and clean linen will make them treat you better. The greater your consequence, the harder for them to question your ability."

Laura gave in and accepted that Pambo would be her companion. It was hard to argue anything when her thoughts were already on the Scuola.

*   *   *   *

Laura rose at first light and made her way to the lectures on Aristotle and anatomy with Pambo following her, wiping sleep from his eyes. The early rising was no hardship for her, but some students who had spent the night carousing found the early morning lectures a hardship they suffered through, bleary and sweating. Laura loved the lectures. She felt as if the lecturers were pouring knowledge from a ewer directly into her mind. It was strong drink; no other tempted her.

The *studia* were a different matter. Laura had been Crescia's only pupil, and Fra Bruncio's. She had not shared her lessons with any of Carlo Alarabi's other students. A *studium*, where a dozen or so students met to discuss the lectures and readings, should have been exciting. But the men talked fast and interrupted one another. None appeared willing to entertain the opinions of a woman. Laura felt like a ghost in the room; the two other women, both nuns, kept their counsel and held their tongues, while she was bursting to add to the discussion. On the few occasions when she forced her way into the discussion, she was punished with pranks that she schooled herself to ignore. One fellow passed a scroll to her that, when she unrolled it, had a pig's phallus inside. Another man followed her so closely through the halls of the school that the heels of her shoes bore the marks of his toes; it wasn't until Pambo turned around and glared down at him that the fellow fled.

At last Laura found her voice. She arrived early for her *studium*, took a seat near the center of the room, and bided her time until most of the group had arrived but few were seated. Then, speaking as if she were continuing a discussion with another student, she said loudly, "I know Aristotle says that the organs of generation in women are lesser than those of men, but I don't understand his reasoning. Looking at the womb—"

All heads turned toward her. "When have *you* looked upon a womb, *magistra?*" a richly dressed man about her own age drawled.

"In the course of delivery, *magister*." She did not rise to his sarcasm. "The womb makes a case for the fetus and nurtures it for nine months. The phallus, in contrast, contains only semen—"

"Only semen?" The same fellow, sounding incredulous. "The philosopher tells us that semen carries the form of humanity itself; the uterus contributes only the brute matter."

"It's a worthy point, though," another man said thoughtfully. "Why should the philosopher consider the uterus, which nurtures the fetus until it is born, a lesser organ than the phallus?"

The first man scowled as if it were his own manhood under question. "As well to say that the dirt that nurtures the seed is greater than the seed itself—or the hand that plants it."

"If you're using your hand, Renalte, you're not planting anything." This from another student, a loose-limbed, foppish fellow who frequently snored through the lectures. He made a ribald gesture with one hand.

There was general laughter; even Renalte joined. The discussion continued, but now when Laura spoke she was accorded attention.

*   *   *   *

When she returned to Lot's house in the afternoons, Laura went to work at once, grinding and mixing medicines for Natalia to sell while Lot sat on a high stool, giving orders, observing with his rheumy eyes, and consulting with customers. He would call to Laura or Natalia to bring out this remedy or that in his high, reedy voice while Pambo washed the crockery, vials, and jars or swept the workroom. Lot did a brisk business in love philters and cosmetics. Laura learned to make them too.

Several times a week she worked at the hospice, the Scuola's clinic for the poor. By the time she fell onto her pallet each night—a narrow straw-filled mattress set behind the desk in the shop, with the shelves and drawers towering over her as she slept—Laura was exhausted. She ate moderately, worked hard, slept deeply, and rose every morning giving thanks for the chance to do it all again.

* * * *

On a gray, misty day, when she had been a student at the Scuola for more than a year, Laura emerged from a lecture on *res sex non-naturales*, the six non-natural factors in sickness and health, and stood blinking in soft light, seeking Pambo's familiar face. She did not see him until the boy came pelting around a corner, eyes wide, as if he were in terror of his life.

"The man!" He gasped, bent over, his dark hair falling over his brow, his cap long lost. "Sick man!"

"What sick man?"

A few of Laura's fellows stopped to listen, curious.

"The dark man." He wiggled his fingers before his own face. "Man with the holes."

Holes? The pits of smallpox. "Carlo Alarabi?" Pambo had come with her more than once to visit her old tutor.

"Said to bring Laura." Pambo's sides heaved like bellows. "Sick. Very sick."

Laura took Pambo's elbow. "At his rooms? Take me to him."

They started down the street, slower than Laura wanted in deference to Pambo's clear exhaustion. She could not help but ask questions, but the boy could only repeat that Ser Alarabi was sick. Pambo was fearful of sick people and did not like to look at or talk to them.

When they reached the tutor's rooms, Laura forgot her dignity and ran up the stairs. Pambo stayed below, still panting.

Carlo Alarabi sat at his desk, his head in his long-fingered hands. It had been months since her last visit. The algebraist had always been thin, but now he was skeletal, the skin over his cheekbones taut and yellow, his humors disastrously out of balance. His smile bared teeth from which the gums receded, more a grimace of pain than an expression of pleasure.

"Well, there you are." The words were evenly spaced, laid down like bricks by a mason.

Laura went to his side at once, kneeling beside him and taking his hand. His pulse was weak and hectic. "*Magister*, how long have you been this way?"

"Stupidly weak and aching?" He shrugged and grimaced again. "Months, I suppose. Not every hour, but enough of them. Today—I have a student coming soon, and I don't want to greet him this way. Give me a powder to set me right."

Laura closed her eyes on her anger: sick for months and told no one, here in the greatest center of medicine in the world. "I can't prescribe until I know what the matter is. Let me examine you."

She took his pulse again, felt for fever, of which there was none, and looked into his eyes, pale yellow and bloodshot.

"I need a sample of urine."

Alarabi shook his head. "I don't know that I can—" He looked away.

"I can leave," Laura offered.

"No, no. It's not—I have pain when I make water."

She nodded. "How bad a pain?"

He smiled grimly. "How hot is the sun? It is important? Then I will try for you."

Laura left the room and went down the stairs to where Pambo crouched, drawing pictures in the dirt with a stick. Before she set her foot on the bottom step she heard a cry of pain that turned her knees to water. She ran back up again.

Carlo Alarabi stood, leaning on his desk with both hands, his body sagging between his arms. A flask stood on the desk with an inch of cloudy brownish urine with strands of blood suspended in it.

"I am sorry for my weakness," he said after a moment. He could not summon a smile.

She wanted to scold him as she would a child, tell him not to be foolish. "Making noise is a way to discharge the energy of pain," she told him. "We see this all the time."

"We?" The ghost of her tutor's humor was in the word. He had straightened out and was looking at her, daring her to be solicitous.

"We," she said. Carlo Alarabi did not need a student he could bully and tease, he needed a healer. If what she saw in his demeanor and what his urine told her was accurate, he needed a healer more experienced than she.

"I must fetch one of my teachers," she said. "I'm only a student."

Alarabi raised a satirical eyebrow. "My brightest algebra-ist cannot solve for a simple diagnosis? Old man plus bloody piss, over pain and weakness, multiplied by yellow bile and a bad star—" He chuckled. The chuckle turned into a spasm of coughing.

Laura put her arm around her tutor's shoulders and guided him to a chair with carved arms and back.

"Keep your strength, *magister*. There's no need to show off for a girl." She noted that when he sat it was gingerly, as if wary of pain in his back or hips.

When she pulled up the hem of his robe to examine his feet, Alarabi scowled and attempted to push it down again.

"Your brightest algebraist requires information before she can solve the equation," she told him briskly.

"It is not fitting," Alarabi said. "A woman—"

"When you're my patient, I am not a woman. If that doesn't suit you, let me fetch one of my masters. Either that, or let me do my work."

His mouth quirked into a smile. "Bully." But he dropped his hand and let her raise his robe a few inches. His ankles and legs were swollen and rough, a dark sullen red. Hydropsy, pain, weakness, thick bloody urine. An excess of black bile, suffered to go on far too long. Her heart fell. She let the hem of his robe drop.

"There are remedies we may try," she said cautiously, hoping her tone did not give away her dismay. With the illness so established, only prayer was likely to save her teacher now. He must have read it in her face.

"All men die, girl. If the equation has no solution—"

"We don't know that."

Carlo Alarabi shrugged. "You may try to cure me, but more important, can you give me something for the pain? I have students coming." He shifted in his chair and his face paled. "There. I cannot teach geometry when my body distracts me this way."

Laura thought, nodded, and went downstairs again to find Pambo sitting in the doorway, humming to himself and drawing in the dirt.

"You must run home. Tell them I need—" She collected her wits. "I need wheat for poulticing and a good measure of hieralogodion. Lot's best tea for pain. Say it all back to me."

"Wheat, heeralogody, pain tea."

"Good boy." She could only hope he'd remember it all. "Go, fast as you can. I'll bring the payment home when I come."

Pambo trotted off and Laura returned to her tutor.

"Let me write to your student and tell him you're indisposed."

Alarabi shook his head vehemently and was seized by a pain that made him double forward in his chair. "Without students I have no money to pay my healer," he said at last. His voice was thin.

"No money for wine and books," Laura teased. Gently she eased Alarabi to his feet and supported him toward the bed that stood in the room's farthest corner. So close to the man she could smell illness coming off him, sour and sweet like rotting fruit. Briskly, so that neither of them would have time for embarrassment, she stripped off his robe, left him in his shift, and helped him to bed, where he sank, exhausted, eyes shut. As she was drawing the blanket up her teacher's narrow chest Laura heard a noise behind her.

"Pardon, Ser Carlo. I had no idea you were—" The voice was young and male and mocking. "*Occupied.*"

Laura felt herself take on Crescia's most severe manner. She turned, smoothing the sleeves of her robe over her wrists. "Ser Alarabi is sick. I am his physician."

The boy, fair and ruddy-cheeked, blushed and swept off his cap and bowed. "Your pardon, *medica*. I didn't realize."

"No, I suppose you did not. We must hope Ser Alarabi is well enough to meet with you next time, but for now, as you see—" She gestured toward the bed.

"Is it catching?" The boy backed toward the stair. Pambo appeared behind him with a basket, and there was a moment's confusion as the two dodged back and forth in each other's way. The student pushed past Pambo and hurtled down the stairs and Pambo held his basket out at arm's length.

"You brought it all? Very good. Stir up the fire and fetch water, Pambo. We'll need to draw off the pain."

Soon there was hot water in which to steep the herbs of Lot's anodyne. Laura roused Alarabi from a doze and gave him the cup. The algebraist winced at the odor but drank it down, as obedient as a child. Next, Laura took a tarry bar of hieralogodion the size of her thumb, measured in as much honey and a pinch of salt, and stirred hot water into the whole until it was dissolved.

Before she gave it to her teacher, Laura went again to the stairway and called to Pambo, who had got away as soon as he could. When she asked him to fetch a physician from the Scuola to attend on Ser Alarabi Pambo's face crumpled with anxiety. This was more than he could manage.

"All right, then. Go home and tell your mama that we need a medico here."

Pambo nodded, relieved. "For the man—" Again his fingers played over his face to indicate the scars.

"That's right. Good boy."

Laura went back to Alarabi's bed. "Now, master, I have another dreadful potion for you to swallow." She gave him the hieralogodion mixture in a small cup and stood over him as he drank the dark, sticky stuff.

When Natalia arrived with a short, beetle-faced man with somber dark robes and an important air, Laura had just placed a poultice of hot grain on Carlo Alarabi's belly while the mathematician swore colorfully at her. The physician scowled at Laura and pushed past her brusquely. Carlo Alarabi held up a narrow hand and muttered something, and the physician turned back to her. "You're a student at the Scuola? This is your handiwork?"

Laura bowed. "Yes, *magister*. The most recent urine is

here." She pointed to the flask on the table. "I've given him hieralogodion with honey and salt to reduce the black bile, and the poultice to ease his discomfort."

The physician nodded and took the flask to the window, holding it up to the afternoon light. "How long have you had blood in your piss?" The algebraist shrugged. "What other complaints?"

Carlo Alarabi repeated what he had told Laura in a voice gravelly with fatigue. The physician nodded several times, rubbing the side of his jaw with one hand as if to do so was an aid to thought. Finally he stepped away from the bed and pulled Laura to one side.

"Hieralogodion may help, but I doubt it. Have you cast his horoscope?" When Laura shook her head he scowled and spoke quietly. "The man appears to be dying." He picked up the flask, swirled it around a few times to set the threads of blood in the urine dancing, and held it to the light. "I'll consult the stars, but for now it seems that all that can be done is to keep him quiet and ease his pain."

Carlo Alarabi called, "How long?"

Laura and the physician froze, looking at each other. "You'll be up in a day or two," the medico assured him. "Give him hope; there may yet be a miracle, and the truth would only scare him," he muttered to Laura from the side of his mouth. "Ser Alarabi, what day were you born?"

Alarabi ignored the question. "How long do I have to live?"

The physician looked grave. "That is for God to know."

He stayed a little longer, collecting his fee, advising Laura to apply poultices to the belly and give Carlo Alarabi poppy and mandrake to help with the pain. When he left and Natalia had gone down to instruct Pambo to bring more water, Carlo Alarabi shook his head. "Pompous fool. I only want to know—" A sigh juddered through him. "I only want to know how much longer I may teach."

Laura brought a stool to the side of the bed and sat, holding her tutor's hand. "Did the tea help with the pain?"

He nodded. "A little. No, girl, don't look that way. A little is a great deal to me right now. I can think—more clearly, anyway."

"All right then, master. If the tea helps, you may take it as often as you like. And you may teach—" She turned her palms upward in a gesture that said she did not know. "You may teach as long as you may teach. I don't think," she said, lower. "I don't think it will be very long."

Alarabi nodded again, more decisively. "I have matters to set in order. That fool, Damiano? The boy you sent away? He can barely add, let alone understand true mathematics. If I'm not to be the one to beat them into him, I must find some other willing fool to undertake it."

Laura stayed with her tutor for another hour until he fell into a doze. Natalia had left to return to Lot and the shop. Laura was surprised, when she left Alarabi's room, to find Pambo still sitting at the base of the stairs, staring into the gloom. She tapped him lightly on the shoulder. The boy came out of his reverie, and they went home to the apothecary shop.

*　*　*　*

Every day after the lectures and *studia* had met and adjourned, Laura went to check on her tutor. The painkilling draughts worked almost too well; the man was determined to work as long as he could, and he did, far longer than Laura thought was wise. "What can I do? Drive myself to death? That's already in hand. Let me do what I can to finish my work." So every day she made it her business to sit with Alarabi, see to his medicines, make sure he took some food. He taught for almost two months before the sickness started to corrupt his mind. When she arrived one afternoon, Laura found him sitting by the window, tears running down his face, his mouth working soundlessly.

She stayed with him after that, returning to Lot's only once during the day to wash and eat. When she was with Alarabi, she fed him, worried about his sleep, slept herself sitting in the chair by the table. The night when his last breath rattled through his parched yellow lips she was sitting with Carlo Alarabi, his long-fingered hand cold in one of her own, saying prayers for his swift journey to God. Laura prayed to the Queen of Heaven to intercede on behalf of the curt, bullying, demanding teacher who had taught her how to reason.

Chapter Eight

After Alarabi's death the nightmares, almost forgotten, returned. She had lost flesh in the last month of his sickness and slept little. When her tutor was buried, she returned to Lot's house and worked and slept, waking cold and whimpering in the night. Melancholy settled on her, and not all the physic in Lot's shop seemed to lift it. Natalia, frightened by Laura's haggard appearance, sent word to Crescia, and the old woman appeared one morning to bring Laura home to the hillside.

It was late summer, and many of the students had returned home to help with the harvest or supervise it. "School can wait," Crescia told her. "Natalia says half your fellows are gone home now. You come for a month, breathe some good air, eat well, and sleep, dear girl."

In the first days she did little but sleep, eat, wind wool, and braid garlic and onion. Crescia set her to sit outside with the sun warming her shoulders and baking the chill from her bones. When she was stronger, Laura spent some afternoons in the hills seeking plants to replenish Crescia's store, enjoying her freedom, out of the city, unaccompanied and able to drop etiquette. The gauntness of her face began to soften and the nightmares receded again.

Laura told her mistress about the school, trying to share what she learned. Crescia listened when Laura spoke of astral charts and Aristotle and Galen and the heathen medicines of Avicenna, but she was not impressed. "This is what the medicos give themselves airs about?" She shook her head. "Don't try to teach me, girl. I'm too old. The Queen of Heaven's kept me and the ones I help in her hands. This is for you, this knowledge. When you come back to stay you'll use it; no one will dare put on airs with you." So Laura told her stories of the school instead and made her mistress laugh at the story of Fra Ambrigliano dissecting a boar in the kitchen of the chapter house while the cook complained, the spitboy hooted, and the students watched, grave.

*   *   *   *

When Laura returned to the *studia*, some of her fellows seemed surprised. "We thought you'd given up," one said. "Gone home to marry and have some fat babies."

Laura did not return his smile. "I was tending a sick man, one of my family."

"And cured him, of course." He said it like a joke.

"No." She turned away.

While she had been in the hills, a quartan fever had settled on the city; those who worked at the hospice were busier than ever, and busyness seemed to be her best specific against sadness. She was there several days out of the week, accompanied always by Pambo, who sat drawing figures in the dust with a willow twig or staring incuriously at the exotic strangers who came and went, waiting for Laura to emerge from the school.

Late one afternoon she heard an ado in the yard outside the hospice, and Pambo's voice raised in agitation. She could not immediately excuse herself, and when she did get away she found Pambo crouched in the far corner of the court-yard, his face covered with snot and tears. He tried to tell her what had happened, but, as always happened with Pambo, his urgency outstripped his words. "Wan my mam," he sniveled. "Wan my mam. Wan my house."

Laura still had patients to see. "Soon, soon," she crooned to him as comfortingly as she could. Pambo's sense of time was not like her own. "I'll get you a sweet on the way home," she promised. That brought a smile of pleasure to the boy's tear-mucked face. "Sit just a little longer, Pambo."

She meant to be quick for the boy's sake, but she was de-layed once, then again. It was twilight before she washed her hands the last time and emerged to look for Pambo.

He was gone.

Laura cursed him. He had nothing to do but wait for her, and he had failed of that. She did not doubt she would find him at home, eating fish gruel and bread at Natalia's knee. But he had left her with no escort through the streets, and night was drawing on. At the school, where she was marked as a talented student, she felt safe. But she had lost the knack of walking through Salerno unaccompanied. Foreigners— Arabs, knights traveling to the Holy Land, merchants, sailors—all saw a lone woman as fair game. Many Salernitan men did too.

It was not yet dark, and less than a quarter hour's walk to the apothecary's house. She did not want to spend the night at the hospice; she had studying and work to finish at Lot's. Laura took down the tail of her veil, which she had pinned up to be out of her way as she worked, and pulled it across her face, hoping the sign of modesty would be enough to ward away trouble. She started for home, thinking of the things she would like to say to Pambo as she went. As much as she could, she stayed to well-traveled streets, but as she neared the market the streets were empty of their daytime activity. When she crossed from the street leading from the market square to one that would take her down to the apothecary's shop, her jaw tightened. The end of the street was crossed by a man's shadow. Was he lurking there for some evil purpose? Laura turned to go another way and found her route blocked.

Blessed Saint Catherine. Laura stepped to the side to let the man pass. He stepped with her and forward a little, forcing her farther into the street. Walls rose steeply on either side without windows. If she cried for help, would anyone hear her? She heard footsteps behind her; the man who had been lurking at the street's end had come forward now to join the game.

"Let me pass, friend." She kept her voice steady. "I am a *medica* at the Scuola, and I'm needed there."

The man who had blocked her retreat grinned and said something incomprehensible to the man at the end of the street. Foreigners. In the last light of day she saw the shine of mail at his collar. A knight headed to the Holy Land? A mercenary hired to guard a foreign merchant? She did not dare presume that an appeal to God or His Son would save her. "Pardon," she said, and stepped to her left, trying to push past.

He raised an arm to block her. His clothes were rusty with road dust; he had several days' accumulation of dark stubble on his jaw and a scar that ran from behind one ear down his neck to disappear into the collar of his mail. His eyes were hungry. *Rape*, Laura thought. She did not think he or the other man would kill her. Just take what they wanted and go on their way.

"Sister!" From the street behind the foreigner, a man's voice came, clear and confident. "I thought I had lost you! You walk too fast."

It was a man from one of her *studia*, a tall fellow with dark hair. Matteo, she thought his name was.

The man before her scowled and said something she did not understand. The man behind Laura came close; she could feel his presence like a pricking in her shoulder blades. She pressed her back against a wall so that she could see both of the foreigners.

Matteo walked easily toward them as if he perceived no threat. "Your husband will have my head if I do not get you home in time for prayers."

The two foreigners watched him approach, poised to attack or run, she could not tell which. The one who had been behind her was tall and heavy; he wore no mail, but had a brutal cast to his face and a very large sword at his hip. The new man appeared unconcerned. He said something in the same incomprehensible language that made both men step back.

Matteo took advantage of that to reach for Laura and take her arm, drawing her toward him. "Come, sister. It is time you were home with your family." He put her hand on his arm and led her away from the foreigners, talking all the while about her imagined husband and children.

When they had left the strangers a street's length behind them, he stopped and bowed to her. "Pardon my familiarity, *magistra*, but I thought you would find it permissible. I am Matteo di Sette; we attend some of the same *studia*. Where may I take you?"

Laura gave him directions to Lot's house. "I am Laura. Thank you. I had begun to be afraid."

"I can imagine. A woman so clever at the study of medicine should know better than to walk the streets of the city alone." He did not sound critical; it was as if he invited her to tell him what had happened.

"My page was taken ill."

SOLD FOR ENDLESS RUE

"Page? The simpleton I see walking with you?"

He watched her? Not just in *studium*, but elsewhere? She flushed. "Pambo isn't clever," she agreed. "But he's large, and most of the time that is all that is needed."

Matteo laughed. "I suppose so. When he's there. But where are your brothers, your father, your uncles, that they let you walk through Salerno with only one large simpleton to guard you?"

She ignored the question. "I stay at Pambo's house while I study. Which is how he comes to be my escort." In the cooling evening air Laura was suddenly aware of Matteo di Sette's warmth and his height. She barely came to his shoulder. His hair was dark and curled around his head, and he wore a silver palmer's pin in his collar. His clothes were good; she thought he might be a mercer's son, someone prosperous enough to have sent his son on a pilgrimage to the Holy Land. The arm upon which her fingers rested was muscular.

That thought made her flush again.

"You must let me be your brother when you have need of one," he said. "If ever your—Pambo? If he proves insufficient to the task, call on me."

When they reached the apothecary's shop Matteo's eyebrows rose. "Is this fellow honest? Some 'pothecaries chalk their powders to swell the volume and their profit."

"Not here. Lot's honest, and we're careful to make no mistakes."

"We?"

"I assist the apothecary, until I am permitted to practice as a physician."

"A clever arrangement for you both."

"It is."

"But you must make sure your page stays with you, Magistra Laura. I can't be everywhere watching for you."

"I will. And thank you for your kindness."

"It is my pleasure." Matteo di Sette took her hand in his own warm one and swept her a deep bow, as one might to a courtier or contessa. "I will see you in *studia*." He left her.

In Natalia's kitchen Pambo was waiting, a welt on his jaw in the shape of his mother's palm.

"Sorry," he said, and ducked his head.

Natalia, her own face red from the heat of the fire, was ladling out a bowl of soup rich with fava and greens and tiny dumplings. "I told him he ain't to leave you, not ever, no matter if someone does try to make him drink a bowl of piss." She handed the bowl of soup to her son. "It ain't safe for a young woman alone in this town. You hear me, Pambo?"

The boy bent over his supper, nodding as he ate.

*   *   *   *

From that evening, Matteo di Sette seemed to have a word or a smile for Laura each time their paths crossed. Recalling these meetings later, she might drift into daydreams. She had read of love; the Roman poets she read with Fra Bruncio were voluble on the subject. The monk had been more interested in the craft of the poetry than its subject. "It is better to marry than to burn," he had said curtly, as if that ended the subject there. "The life of the body is a distraction to a person of solemn purpose"

Crescia had said much the same thing. "The Queen of Heaven loves purity, daughter. Purity of purpose most of all. A healer cannot give her whole heart to easing pain when she's distracted."

Laura said nothing to anyone, but watched Matteo when he was unaware. He smiled easily, was liked by the other students, and carried lightness and ease like charms.

He was open in his admiration of Laura, although it was her skill and wit he commended and nothing more personal. Just once, she thought, she would like to hear him say something about her eyes or her brow, as the Roman poets did about their loves. Which was foolish. He was the son of a wealthy merchant, the sort of man who might dine with governors and princes. He spoke languages beyond the Salernitan dialect, Latin, and the smattering of Greek and Arabic most students picked up in their studies. The language in which he had warned away her attackers, he told her, was the language of the English. He also spoke some German, enough to trade with. His clothes were of rich stuff and handsomely made, and, in addition to the silver pin in his collar, he wore a silver ring on his right hand. Laura had little conversation that was not related to medicine, herbs, or midwifery. She doubted she would ever dine with governors or travel far from Salerno.

She could not stop thinking of Matteo di Sette's hands.

* * * *

She had been studying all day in the Scuola's library. When she could not read without her eyes burning, Laura returned the scrolls to their keeper and stepped blinking into white sunlight. The air was startlingly warm after the shadowy cool of the library, and Laura stood by the door enjoying it, slipping her slate into a net bag hung from her belt. Then she called to Pambo, who sat dozing by a horse trough. She wanted to walk: down to the market and back at least, to stretch out muscles cramped by sitting.

"Shall we see if the baker has any little breads?" she asked Pambo. He nodded and grinned. They had bought their rolls and were strolling through the market as they ate when someone hailed her. "Good afternoon, *medica*."

Matteo di Sette, light gleaming on his dark hair as it might on a raven's wing, leaned easily against a stall canopy, eating an apple.

"Good afternoon." Fearing she seemed unfriendly, she smiled.

"Looking for your dinner?"

She shook her head. "Taking a little exercise before I return for the *studium*."

"The *studium* on diagnosis? A sober topic for so beautiful a day."

"An *important* topic."

Matteo shook his head, mocking her. "So earnest! Don't you ever dance? Or sing? Gather flowers on the hills, just for their beauty? I think I would like to see you laugh." He pushed himself off from the canopy and tossed away the apple core.

Laura flushed. "I laugh. And I've picked flowers and lain in the grass to feel the sun on my face. When I was a child. Now—"

"Now you're a grown woman and a very serious *medica*." He was teasing her. "I wish that serious *medica* would take a holiday. The cyclamen are blooming on the hills; they have no medical use I know of, but I would take you to pick some, just for the uncommon sight of the serious Medica Laura with a handful of posies. Can't you take one day? The *studium* will meet again."

At his words she was tempted, filled with longing to walk in the sun and smell the grass, hear the distant bleat of goats, watch a hawk circle overhead. Most of her day was spent looking down, at books, at patients, at the slate on which she took notes, at the ground before her as she walked demurely through Salerno. How wonderful to look *up*.

"I must ask his mother if Pambo can come," she said.

"Your shadow? If you need him, by all means."

An hour later, her veil pinned back so that she could feel the breeze on her face, Laura was walking toward the hills with Matteo, with Pambo trailing behind them. The boy seemed wary of Matteo, but he was wary of most folk until he knew them. Free from the necessity to walk decorously, Laura reclaimed the long strides of her girlhood. Matteo said, laughing, that he could barely keep up with her, and Pambo maintained a dogged pace half a dozen steps behind. They climbed past the hamlet where Nico and Sofia lived and onto a broad, grassy slope where, as Matteo had said, the cyclamen reached their rosy petals toward the sun. The air was soft and green.

Pambo spied a goat a dozen paces farther up and ran to make friends. The goat, wary of the lumbering boy, trotted farther up the hill and Pambo followed, bleating at the animal.

"I see he's found a friend." Matteo dropped to sit on the grass and, pulling his cap from his head, tilted his face toward the sun. After a moment Laura sat beside him, closed her eyes, soaked in the warmth of the sun. They did not speak for a while, and when they did it was about flowers. Laura had seen courting couples sit so on the hillside when she was a girl. *Am I one such?* She heard Pambo talking to the goat nearby.

She did not know she had fallen asleep until she woke, her head pillowed on her arm. When she opened her eyes she saw Matteo di Sette lounging near her, watching her with an expression that sent a pang of feeling through her, so powerful it made her eyes close again. When she opened them he was sitting upright, holding a few cyclamen out to her. "They're very delicate tasting," he said.

"I know." Laura sat up and took one of the flowers. Before she could nibble at the dusky pink petals Matteo leaned forward and kissed her. His lips were warm and gentle. When he moved his mouth from hers he ran a thoughtful finger along her jaw. "Very delicate," he said again.

Then he leaned away from her as if the kiss had never happened. Laura, frozen by a dozen competing sensations, did not move until Pambo trotted down the hill, the goat beside him.

"I name him Bruno," he said, pointing to the animal, which was neither brown nor male.

"Did you?" Laura cleared her throat. "Look at where the sun sits. We must get back to the city before Natalia worries."

Matteo got to his feet, brushed grass and flower stems from his cotte, and offered a hand to Laura. She took it just long enough to get to her feet, then let him go. So slight a touch made her feel light-headed. Did he feel the same? He must: he had kissed her.

"You return to your apothecary and I to—" He sighed. "To my father's table. He has important guests tonight and wants his sons in attendance."

As they walked down the hill toward the city he told her about his family. He was the youngest of three sons and two daughters. The middle brother was meant for the church, and the eldest was worked in their father's business. "Father thought it would be useful to have a medico in the family. My only other choice is to turn to trading as Ghibilo has. Marry a fat merchant's daughter and fill the family's coffers."

"You can fill them as a medico, surely."

"Perhaps. I don't have your gifts, though. I don't know if I'd rather be an adequate healer or an adequate trader."

"What does your heart say?"

"If I followed my own heart," he began, low. Then stopped. They had reached Nico's potting shed. Carolina had begun to help her father there; she waved incuriously at the passersby without recognizing Laura.

"Did you always want to be a healer?" he asked when they had passed the houses.

"I was adopted by a healer, and she raised me up and sent me to be schooled."

"So it is duty for you, too?"

She was surprised. "No, fortune. God led me to my mistress and my calling. If I have talent, it is God-given, but I love what we do. To ease sickness and pain?" She shrugged. "Why would I want to do anything else?"

"No fat husband?"

"Not a fat one! A *medica* must set an example of moderation. Physicians may marry," she reminded him. Was he hinting something to her? "I would have to hire someone else to keep the house; I learned more healing skills than householding."

They were on the edge of the city. Pambo had bid farewell to the goat and was a pace or two behind them. *Perhaps I should not have said that. Perhaps he thought I was presuming, thinking that kiss meant something it did not.* With each step back toward the city, Laura's anxiety grew. She had begun to watch the path at her feet.

"Look up, *medica*!" His voice scattered her thoughts. "Didn't our visit to the hills do you some good? You have that pinched look again." He held his arm out for her to take, as he had done in the street that other night. "Look up!"

She put her hand on his sleeve and smiled up at him.

*   *   *   *

It was not a far thing, from one stolen kiss on a hillside to more kisses stolen in the shadow of the Scuola itself. In lectures and *studia* and at the hospice, she and Matteo ignored each other; she was too aware that losing the reputation of virtue would be disastrous. To practice medicine she must have a commendation of her character from a priest. Were it known that Laura di Crescia gave kisses to a fellow student in the alley behind the hospice, she would lose the recommendation, and her work would be for nothing. She would return to Crescia without the title of physician that both she and the healer coveted. Every time she stole away with Matteo she swore it would be the last. Then he would ask her again to walk in the hills.

Pambo grew used to Matteo's presence and less wary.

Without thought, Laura kept them to the southern paths, away from Crescia's cottage, so that she and Matteo could sit, hands clasped, exchanging kisses. They began to speak of a future in which they were physicians, of the ills they might cure and the wealth and fame they might earn. Laura had always meant to take her learning home to Crescia; now she imagined herself in a Salernitan house with cool mosaic floors and an arched veranda. "With your skill you will surely have noble clients," Matteo teased her. "You will dress in silk and fur."

She had grown comfortable with his teasing. "What will you wear?"

"Silk too, of course. The two of us, famous physicians in the most famous city for physicians in the world." He leaned to kiss her. "I should like to see it."

On their few perfect afternoons in the hills they talked like this, and the more they did, the more Laura came to believe it possible: a real house, servants, silken clothes, and Matteo di Sette beside her. Summer was drawing in, the light was as clear and golden as honey; insects hummed in the fields, and the feverish heat of the hot months was tempered with a breeze from the sea. In the spring, with God's grace, Laura would be examined and given permission to practice as a physician.

On an afternoon when sickness seemed to have taken a holiday and a dozy quiet lay over the city, Matteo found Laura at the Scuola.

"Come away. You've been all morning at lectures in musty halls. Come breathe sweet air with me."

She had work to do and a *studium* to prepare, but the thought of breeze and downy grass beneath her, and Matteo's kisses on her lips, was too powerful to resist. She called to Pambo, "Do you want to visit the goats?"

He jumped up, delighted, ungainly, grinning. His cap fell into the street. When he picked it up and slapped it against

his thigh he raised a dust that made an elderly physician
scowl at him in passing.

"Bruno!" Pambo said happily. He took his place at Laura's
elbow, beaming. They began the climb, and when they reached
the meadow they favored, Pambo pointed farther up, to a
cluster of goats. "Bruno!" The goats were used to the boy
now and barely stirred when he trotted up to join them.

Laura sat with Matteo in the cup of the hill, shielded
from the sight of casual observers. They talked, and Matteo
traced the line of veins on the back of her hand; his touch
made Laura sigh. When words ran out he kissed her, a gentle seeking touch of his lips that made her feel as if her bones
were melting inside her. His next kiss was less gentle, more
urgent. Laura felt her own urgency rise, the touch of his
hand at her throat tracing like flame, hot. When she pulled
away Matteo groaned and she felt an answering pang.

"Please," he murmured. He drew her close again and kissed
her just at the point where her veil covered her jaw. The mol-
ten feeling seemed to capture her core. She had no will to do
anything but touch his face and feel the burr of masculine
skin under her fingers, the pulse under his jaw. When his
hand found her breast through her kirtle she shuddered.
She could not think clearly—or did not want to. *This is why
a man and his wife share glances full of secrets. This is the mystery.* Matteo's hands traced her body; his mouth was on hers
and she felt drunk with kissing. But they were not yet married. From far away she recalled the reasons why they must
not do—

"No, Matteo. Beloved, no." Her lips were against his brow.
"We mustn't."

He did not answer her. His hands became more insistent,
pushing aside the skirt of her gown, pushing up her shift.
Parting her legs.

"No," she said again, warring with her body, which said *yes.*

"It will be good, sweet," he murmured. He kissed her jaw again. "It will, just—"

She felt pain as he entered her, a sobering, sharp pang that made her panic. She tried to push him away, but he was atop her, heavy, moving in a way that was both delicious and terrifying. She could not make him stop. When she pushed at him he pushed himself deeper into her, over and over. Heat spread from her sex until her whole body was filled with fire and she pushed back. Then he groaned deep in his throat and of his own accord rolled away from her, reaching as an afterthought, to pull her skirts back over her legs.

Laura rolled to one side, shaking. Her body still yearned, unsatisfied and tense with anxiety. Without his touch she recalled every reason not to let him do what he had done: her reputation, their standing at the Scuola, the anger of his family if they discovered that she didn't come to the marriage a virgin. She curled in on herself, arms around her belly, feeling tears seep in the corners of her eyes.

"Laura?" She felt his finger trace her cheekbone and flick away a tear. "Laura." Her veil had come unpinned, and his finger wound around one of the auburn curls near her ear. He sounded happy. When she opened her eyes he was smiling down on her, haloed by the sun like an angel. He leaned down to kiss the corner of her mouth. "The boy is coming back. We must right ourselves."

They walked back to the city at a decorous pace with Pambo bounding along between them. Twice Laura looked sidelong at Matteo and felt that sudden pang of sweetness in her center, the blood rushing to her cheeks. He walked with the air of a man sure of himself, pleased, proud. He had made her his own. When he looked at her she forgot to worry about Crescia or his family or the masters at the Scuola. She was his and he, in turn, was her own.

Chapter Nine

G od organized man's body," Fra Ambrogliano told his students. "The sight of it should inspire in you the profoundest awe."

They stood over the body of a wiry, wasted old man, ready to explore the mysteries of anatomy. The monk invited one of the students to make the first incision into the belly. The other students, their sleeves pinned back and wearing sailcloth aprons, craned over the table, marveling one by one at the branching of veins and arteries, the wiry red muscles, the organs safely packed into the cage of the ribs. Human dissection was unusual; it was a privilege to attend one. The old man had died, Ambrogliano told them, of an excess of yellow bile that had corrupted his liver and caused tumors to form, secreting insalubrious pus and poisoning healthy tissue.

"What might have been done to reduce the bile?" the monk asked. He sat, kinglike, on a raised chair, overseeing the dissection without laying a hand to it. Each student had his turn to make cuts and display muscle, fat, and blood vessels. When her turn came Laura worked with complete attention. At the back of the group, Matteo stood with a distinct look of dismay; he was gone before it was his turn.

Afterward, when they were washed up and the unfortunate man's remains had been removed for burial, Matteo rejoined the class, sidling close to Laura to murmur an invitation to walk in the hills later, "to take the taste of *that* from our mouths." Laura had much to do, but never had the heart to say no when Matteo asked.

"Do you never study?" she teased him later.

"I'd have a hard time studying anything after a morning in the dissection hall. That poor devil—how you kept from vomiting, craned over him that way!"

It had been so fascinating that she had not, after a first instinctive stab of pity, felt anything but curiosity. Glancing sideways at her lover, she realized that disgust was the only feeling the morning had inspired in him. Disgust for her? Did he think her unwomanly?

"It was difficult," she lied. She had never lied to him before. "I had to remind myself that what we learn now we will use to save other poor devils."

"I suppose. But Saint Luke's ox, I never thought it would be so—"

"What would be?"

"Medicine! The blood, the stinks. Even the sick. I'm not a saint like you, dear one. Don't you ever want to say, 'For the love of Christ, go home and purge yourself, and next time don't drink'?"

"I do tell them that, when they're well enough to hear it. But some sicknesses are visited by God, not the patient. No amount of abstemiousness would help."

"I wonder you can do it." He sounded sour.

"Matteo?" She looked at him closely. "Doesn't this work please you?"

He shook his head. "I thought it would, but it's difficult. I haven't your goodness, *carissima*." He took her hand and, after a look around, raised it to his lips.

She was no saint. They would surely send Pambo off after the goats as soon as they reached the meadow. Now it felt important to her to help Matteo to his right path. "I'm a little further along in my training than you," she said fairly. "In spring I'll be examined. You have another year, and in that time—"

Again he shook his head. "I don't know, Laura. When my

father said I should be a healer, I liked the idea of knowing the secrets of life. It felt important. But the more I learn, the more it seems to me that a physician is just another servant to be summoned at any hour to slave for his betters."

"A servant?" This was so far from Laura's idea of medicine that it made no sense to her. "God's servant. Physicians are scholars of the body who know things even princes and bishops can't—"

"Yes, yes." He waved his hand, making it of no account. "If it was only bishops and princes we treat, that might be different. But why must I care for every gouty old man or rheumy grandmother who asks? Do I want such responsibility?"

This was much more than a moment's dissatisfaction. "Beloved, do you wish to stop your study?"

"If it wasn't my father's will, I would quit it tomorrow. I don't have the patience for it. Another year of study for what? It feels womanish to be so concerned with sickness and bodies." He stopped and turned to her. "I disappoint you."

"No, no. Never!" Even as she touched him Laura felt a cold sadness. She had thought they were as alike as two people could be, that they both sought knowledge and the chance to ease suffering. It was an occupation, but also a calling; she had thought Matteo felt that as she did.

She extended her hand, and he took it in his own, square and warm.

"If I left the Scuola and returned to trading, would you think less of me?"

"No, no," she said again. It was too open here to stroke his cheek or kiss him. "Whatever you do will be for the best. But would your father permit you to do it? He ordained you should study medicine."

"Sometimes I think he regrets the idea. If I talk to him—"

"Then that's what you must do."

"Even if it shows me a failure?"

"Do you mean to be a failure?" she teased. "Why not be a success, you as a merchant and me as a *medica*? And a happy couple in our own ways."

"We will," he said fiercely. "We *will* be happy."

When they reached the hollow in the lea and Pambo had been encouraged to caper up the hill after the goats, Matteo took her almost with anger, driving his cock like a pestle with herself as the mortar, grinding his choler to dust.

They returned to Salerno and parted near the marketplace. Laura thought her lover was easier in his mind. He had made the decision against medicine. She had hidden her disappointment and given him the courage to speak to his father. When they parted, standing near in the shadow of the duomo, she dared not kiss him or touch his hand reassuringly. Laura only smiled and told him Saint Luke would help him find his proper way. Matteo's returning smile, as he took his leave, promised her his heart forever.

From that day Matteo was no longer at *studia* or lectures. If he wished to see her he would find her outside the Scuola and entreat her to walk up in the hills with him. These occasions were rare: Matteo was studying his father's business, learning to gauge the weight and worth of stuffs from the East, fingering silk and Persian brocade. He brought her a length of green silk, a fine white veil, golden thread, all of which thrilled her with their beauty and for none of which had she any use. He spoke of traveling north to trade, or east to negotiate with silk weavers, of the money to be made importing spices. He spoke of the give-and-take of bargaining with deep pleasure. It was exotic to Laura, who had been told at the Scuola that a physician should never appear concerned by money lest his authority be sullied.

Taught by Crescia, she knew that patients had more faith in a service paid for, but haggling over price seemed undignified.

It was the first time she felt they were truly on different paths, but not the last. More and more Laura felt that she and Matteo were becoming separate, joined only by the blood and humor that mingled when they came together on the mountainside.

*   *   *   *

She had been invited again to the anatomist's hall to examine the organs of a woman, a prostitute who had been cut down in the street by a sailor. Rather than outrage decency by displaying the entire corpse to his mostly male students, Fra Ambrogliano's assistant displayed, one at a time, a breast, the uterus, the liver, the heart while the monk lectured. "The heart is smaller than in a man, as befits her weaker state. The womb—you see where it was perforated by the blows of the knife? Yes. The womb, unused for the purpose for which God created it, is collapsed upon itself. Most of you will never have to view such things," he added, as if this were the preferable thing.

Laura took the flensed breast in her hand. It looked like a flower: a ring of yellow fat, blue veins converging on the center, other structures she did not recognize. She was going to ask what they were, but a sudden nausea overcame her and she was forced to drop the breast into the copper bowl from which she had taken it and run for the door. She managed not to be sick inside; when she had done, she wiped her face and returned to face the curious glances of her fellow students. Never, even when she had just begun to study at the Scuola, had she so disgraced herself. She managed to ignore her nausea for the rest of the lecture. When the class was over she returned at once to Lot's house, cleaned herself, made up a draught of ginger and salt, and drank it down. Perhaps she had taken a sickness from one of the patients who came to the hospice, but this should set her right.

For the rest of the day and into the night as she worked, Laura felt well. The simple had quelled her nausea. But the next morning she felt, again, the churning, sour nausea. This time there was no cause, no human organ in her hand to make her feel queasy. She was at a lecture, listening to Father Ranulphus himself discussing the organ of veneration and its location in the brain, when the same upwelling of bile struck her. She left the hall with undignified speed.

She was within months of becoming a physician, recognized by the Scuola Medicina and licensed by the Bishop of Salerno. She had spent years at Crescia's heel, learning practical aspects of women's medicine that even some medicos of Salerno might not know. She was not one to avoid a truth. When she counted backward to her courses she was certain: she was carrying Matteo's child.

Again she returned to the apothecary's, and again she mixed a simple, this one a specific against morning sickness. As she worked, then waited for the physic to take effect, she thought of what she must do. Tell Matteo first. They would have to marry before the pregnancy became obvious, for her studies and licensing as a physician depended in vital part upon character. In the hills, in her own village of Villaroscia, brides often came to the altar with swollen bellies, but here in Salerno, among merchants and priests and nobles, virginity was a crucial token. She did not doubt the men of the church, even those who were sympathetic to her, would regard anticipation of the marriage bed grounds to deny her petition to practice.

How soon could they wed? He would have to tell his family, and she would meet them at last. Matteo's father would likely regret that she brought no excellent property with her, but she brought a skill and potential for wealth; surely that would be enough.

She must tell Crescia. She owed her mistress everything; would the old woman feel abandoned when Laura chose to live in the city with her husband instead of returning to the hillside? Perhaps she could go once or twice a week to help Crescia even after she wed. But she was going ahead of herself. First she must tell Matteo.

She knew where the Sette warehouse was, near the docks in the harbor. When Lot had gone for his dinner and left Laura to mind the shop, she wrote a note out to Matteo. Pambo stumbled in after his meal, ready for occupation, and Laura sent him to deliver it. "To Matteo and no one else."

It took him a long time to return.

"Did you find the place?" she asked him. "Was he there?"

Pambo held the note out at arm's length. "No. No Matteo."

Laura quieted her impatience with the boy and set him to grinding galangal. When Lot returned she was filling vials with a clear red syrup of rose and cinnamon. When she finished she took off her apron, washed her hands, and excused herself. "I have an errand I must do. For the Scuola." Lot never questioned such errands. Laura gestured to Pambo, who was happy to put down the pestle and follow her.

The sun was behind the clouds; the city looked silver-gray, there was water in the air, and the breeze from the harbor reminded her that autumn was nearly upon them. *A spring baby*, she thought. She made her way past the fish barrows and rope makers, the sailmaker's workshop and the first of the great warehouses, thinking of carrying the baby in her arms, of teaching her all she knew, of combing out hair as raven dark as Matteo's.

At the Sette warehouse she was directed to a man like enough to Matteo to prove their relation, older but not old enough to be his father. His mouth was drawn down and he

had the harried distracted air of a man thinking of too many
things at once.

"Yes?"

Laura cloaked herself in the authority of the Scuola. Her
clothes were good, though not so luxurious as Matteo's or
this man's, and she had learned a thing or two about authority.

"Good evening," she said firmly. "I come from the Scuola
Medicina, and I'm seeking Matteo, of this house."

The man's mouth drew down farther. "My brother is not
here. He sailed up the coast to Pozzuoli three days ago."

Left, and hadn't told her? Laura pursed her lips. "When
does he return?"

"Not until his bride's father is willing to let her travel to
Salerno. Is it something urgent? His health? I can get word
to him if it's needful." He looked as though sending a letter
to his brother was the last thing he wished to do.

Laura's head buzzed. She shook it. Surely he was wrong.
Surely he was making a mistake. Certainly the bride he
spoke of must be his own, not Matteo's.

"I don't wish to be rude, but my parents and brothers are
in Pozzuoli for the wedding and left me behind to deal with
all you see. If the physicians of the Scuola have a reason to
write to my brother, I'll see he gets the letter, but if not—"
He looked at her meaningfully.

"Of course," Laura said. The buzzing in her head was
louder and the world seemed to be withdrawing into mist.
"Thank you, brother." She turned away, moving as slowly as
an old woman, and walked without seeing, determined not
to faint. That was her whole focus: to walk, unseeing, one
foot before the other, until she reached a place where she
could sit and think. No one accosted her, attended by Pambo
as she was, and the few people she noticed drew away from
her as if she bore the mark of death. *Perhaps I do*, she thought.

Why else would Matteo, who had loved her, loved *her*, have so easily left her, gone to Pozzuoli to marry without so much as a word?

When the silver mist cleared from her eyes and the buzzing in her ears ebbed, Laura was filled by a rage as hot and fierce as fever. He had not bothered to lie to her or tell her that it had been his father's will. He had used her like a peasant girl or a whore. Whatever her skill as a physician, it was clear she would never have been worthy to marry into the house of Sette.

"I prattled about the future in which I was a *medica* and he was a great merchant. How comical he must have thought it." She remembered the last time they had lain together on the grass above Salerno, his hands on her breasts, his breath in her ear, and for a moment her treacherous body softened. Then she thought, he had been laughing at her then, even then. All softness deserted her; she would, somehow and someday, revenge herself upon him for holding her so cheap. When she was a physician and cured bishops and princes, when she was wealthy and famed.

And then she remembered that she was with child, that without a husband to legitimize the baby she would be a woman without character, expelled from the Scuola, all her work for naught. A man might love where he pleased, be shriven, and study and work without shame. She must be beyond reproach. There could not be a child.

It was not so difficult a thing to manage.

Laura returned to Lot's shop and to her work, writing out tiny labels for the phials and packets Lot sold. The old man drowsed by the fire; Pambo followed his mother to the kitchen to grind peas into flour, the tapping of the pestle making a counterpoint to the stream of Natalia's chatter. Laura rose from the table and gathered together what she would need: cardamom, stock, myrrh, rue, fenugreek, wormwood, and pennyroyal. She ground them up and mixed them with honey and beeswax until she could form a lozenge the size of her thumb, and put it high on a shelf to cure and dry. The scent of honey reminded her of the scent of sun on the grass above Salerno, but she put that from her mind. She ground up another weight of pennyroyal and put it to steep in a measure of wine and—because she must be certain—added pennyroyal oil as well.

Feeling resolute and relieved, Laura returned to Lot's work. After that she studied, reading on the authority of stars in medicine. It was not until after supper, when the fires in the kitchen and workroom had been banked and Lot, Natalia, and Pambo had retired, that Laura did what she had prepared to do.

First, a quick astrological calculation. The time was as favorable as it could be for such an endeavor. By habit she washed her hands, hearing as she did it her mistress's voice: "The Queen of Heaven loves cleanliness, girl." When this was done, she would be clean again, for always. She took the pessary down from the shelf and inserted it, gritting her teeth against its roughness on tender flesh. She washed her hands again, then strained the wine, added a little water, and drank it down. The bitter, minty taste of the herbs mixed unpleasantly with the tannic burr of the wine, but she finished it in three swallows, washed out the cup, said her prayers, and went to bed.

In the morning Laura felt anxiously at her bedding and shift, but there had been no flux in the night. The pessary had dissolved; she made another and steeped more pennyroyal in wine. She had thought, had hoped, that she might wake in the morning and find the business had been settled while she slept, but it was not to be. It took three more doses of wine before, that evening as she sat at her books, she felt cramping in her belly. Like the physician she was, Laura noted the rash on the inside of her arms, the dizziness that seemed to come and go, and the slow thudding of her heart, and knew her task was almost finished. To be certain, because she must be certain, she took one more dose of pennyroyal wine before they went to bed.

In the darkest part of the night she began to vomit and cramp, then to bleed. The pain was her punishment. Not just her belly but her back and limbs cramped. She thrashed and moaned on her pallet, biting her lip until it bloodied to silence the worst cries. She was alternately cold and hot, her vision blurred. She could not stagger to her feet to go outside to relieve herself; when she used the pot she saw that her urine was bloody too. She had taken too much, she thought distantly. She might die. But no one would know what had happened to her, how stupid she had been to be Matteo di Sette's peasant whore.

When she woke Natalia was bending over her bed, her round face drawn with anxiety. "This is what comes of working day and night at that hospice, making yourself sick." She crossed herself and kept her distance just in case. "What must we do for you?"

It was hard to think, her head still buzzed. What did she want most? *Crescia.* The mere thought of the healer's cottage and her calm presence filled Laura with yearning. *My mistress will know what to do.* Laura felt the stickiness of blood between her legs. Crescia would slow the bleeding. Crescia would soothe her brow with her rough, red hands. "I want to go home," she said. "Back to the hills. Until I feel better."

Natalia nodded and said she would see to it.

Pambo borrowed a mule from a neighbor and with eager clumsiness helped Laura onto it. She almost screamed at the pain that sitting upright on the sturdy, jogging animal caused her. He led it through the streets and to the path to the northern hills, starting by reflex to turn toward the meadow where he and she and Matteo di Sette had spent so many sweet afternoons.

"Up the other way." Laura forced the words out between her teeth. She was almost blind with pain, white with exhaustion, still bleeding. When they reached the gate to Crescia's cottage, Pambo saw the goats and would have gone to play with them at once, but Laura called him back tersely and sent him to look for the healer. When Crescia appeared in the door of the cottage, shaking her reddened, just-washed hands and assuming her healer's demeanor, Laura felt at last that she could give way to her fear and illness.

"Mistress," she said. "Mother."

* * * *

When she woke, Laura lay on the pallet that had been hers for so many years, the sweet-scented hay covered with bedclothes that smelled of sun. For a moment she lay with her eyes closed, imagining herself a child, ready to rise and set about her chores. Then a cramp rippled through her belly and she pulled her knees up, panting.

"Awake? Good, daughter. I want you to drink this."

She had not heard Crescia's step, but when she looked up Laura saw her mistress holding out a dipper of something that steamed. She raised herself on her elbow and drank, as obedient as a child, trying to guess what she was drinking.

"Myrrh, mallow, a little oregano, some laurel." Crescia smiled at her. "This is not the time for studying, dear child, no matter how in that habit you are. Drink, sleep, and regain your strength."

This simple advice Laura followed for almost a week. In the first few days all she did was sleep and drink Crescia's potions and, after two days, eat thin gruel. Crescia was always near, her hands always busy with a task, talking when Laura wished to talk, silent otherwise. When Laura could stay awake longer, Crescia gave her work to do, braiding wreaths of garlic to hang in the workroom, bundling laurel and basil into sheaves, cleaning the roots Crescia meant to dry and store. Whenever she was tired, she could put aside the tray on which she worked and take it up again later.

When at last Crescia permitted her out of her bed, the old woman settled her outside in the sunshine, cloaked against the autumn breeze. Laura sat, talking with the goats that crowded around her, as she had when she was a girl. She had not thought of Matteo when she lay abed, nor of the Scuola. Now she thought of both. She had been a fool, but her foolishness was not known. She would do as she and her mistress had planned: finish her studies at the Scuola and return to the hills to minister to the people there.

*　*　*　*

Crescia had gone to visit a house where a man and his two children lay ill with rash and fever. When she returned to the cottage she washed her hands, then brought a stool and joined Laura where she sat in the sunshine. It was a ten-day since Laura had arrived, and she was healthy enough to sit up all day, although she still tired easily.

Crescia made a show of touching Laura's brow to test for fever, taking her pulse, looking at her eyes as if she were any patient at all. The old woman's roughened fingers lingered fondly on Laura's wrist. The touch was comforting, like a mother's, but her hands were swollen and knobby at the joints, red with constant washing. *I have a lotion will help with that*, Laura thought. *When I'm back in the city I'll make some up for her.*

"No fever. Still pale, but that is to be expected, given the fight your body has had. You must eat flesh when you can get it—not too much. And greens, rabe and *bietola* and cress." Crescia made a little ado of smoothing her skirts, very unlike her usual unfussy way. She looked across the hills and said, "Tomorrow you may return to the city, to your studies."

"I will miss you," Laura said. "I will miss being here. I had forgotten . . ."

Crescia said nothing. Laura realized that her mistress had no work in her hands, no mending or sorting of leaves or cutting up of roots. One of her hands gripped the other hard enough that the knuckles were whitened. At last, with a sigh, the healer turned to look at her apprentice.

"Daughter, tell me what happened."

Laura felt a blush of shame and thought of spinning a tale, but who knew her better than Crescia? If she owed truth to any living being, surely it was to her. Haltingly, full of a bitter sense of her own stupidity, Laura began to talk. She did not blame Matteo in the telling; he had never actually promised her anything. While she lay abed recovering she had recalled every conversation they had ever had. He had spoken of loving her, had spoken of the future, he had never offered marriage. That had been an invention of her own desiring. "He wanted what men want. I was the more fool in that I gave it to him."

"You believed he loved you," Crescia said. "If you were Sofia's daughter, Carolina, and he a farrier or a farmer, you'd have been bundled along to the church with the boy and no more said. The priest would have shriven you and wed you and told you to sin no more."

That was true too. "I am not likely to sin, not ever again. I endangered every thing you raised me to, mistress. I am sorry."

Again Crescia did not deny but nor did she condemn. "You nearly died."

"I did not intend *that*," Laura said quickly.

"I know that, daughter. The Queen of Heaven knows what's in your heart, and she'll intercede with God and His Son for you. I saw you fight to live these past few days. Not even the sternest churchman would say you intended so great a sin as self-murder."

Laura tilted her head back to catch the slanting rays of the sun. She had tears in her eyes, but they did not fall.

"And now what will you do?" Crescia asked.

"Go back to the city and finish my studies. By Eastertide I should be examined. By midsummer, I will be a physician."

"And after?" Crescia turned to look again out into the hills.

"After? Return here, and be a help to you."

"Daughter." Crescia cleared her throat. "You cannot." Her voice was very gentle.

"Can't?" For the second time in a fortnight Laura felt a buzzing in her head. "Mother. Mistress. This is what we have always inten—"

"Daughter, dearest girl, you've learned everything I could teach you about healing, everything the learned men of the city could teach you, but this one thing: everything we do is by grace of the Queen of Heaven."

"I know that. But you yourself said that she knows what was in my heart, that she would intercede for me. Should I not devote myself to the sick to show her my gratitude?"

"You should. You may. But not here. Not with me." Crescia cleared her throat as if she had an old woman's catarrh. "I was raised by my teacher as you were raised by me. I was taught that the Queen of Heaven will have *all* in those that follow her, or none. Chastity—"

"I will never take another man to my bed. I mean now to be as chaste as a saint for the rest of my life."

Crescia would not look at her. She kept her gaze on the hills. "All or nothing, daughter. When I taught you that we must not bring the ashes of one task to kindle the next, what did you think I meant? You can't mingle the carnal life with a life in service to her."

"Because I am no virgin? Even the church takes married women, widows. What if Urbo had raped me when I was a child, as he threatened? I thought you did not blame me—"

"I don't!" Crescia's voice was high and urgent. "Dearest girl, daughter, I don't blame you for loving that man or being fooled by him, or for finding a way out of difficulty. I wish only that you'd come to me sooner and not endangered yourself. What I say now is different. Everything I know of healing begins and ends with the Queen of Heaven and her grace. That grace demands purity. I adopted you, and was adopted myself because I, and my teacher before me, remained chaste. Do you think I never felt a stirring, or that no man ever wanted me? I *chose* to serve her."

"And stay a virgin. Why did you never tell me this?"

"I did. In everything I did it was clear. Should I have spoken more plainly?"

"Yes. *Yes.*" Laura shouted it. "Yes, you should have. You made this another of your secrets! Didn't your teacher speak plainly to you?"

"Daughter, don't excite yourself so—this anger will make you sick again."

Laura turned away, looked, not at the hills but at the close-cropped grass at her feet. When she had regained her temper she asked again, low, "Did your teacher make such a secret of it?"

Crescia shook her head. "I didn't—I didn't mean to make a secret of it. But speaking of such things is hard."

"Hard? I've seen you tell a father, a mother, that the child she labored to bring into the world is dead. How hard to say, you must be chaste or be gone? The Queen of Heaven doesn't ask this of every healer, does she? Of men? Have they no hope of healing because *they* are not chaste?" Laura's emphasis was bitter.

"They serve God in their way and do good—perhaps more good than I do. I don't know." Crescia reached to take her apprentice's hand. Laura pulled away. "But they do not work beside me—"

"—because that would mingle the carnal with the pure." Laura clenched her teeth. She wanted to rage. "Will you tell the priests at the Scuola? Father Ranulphus would be happy to bar another weak woman from the school."

Crescia looked genuinely shocked. "Why would I deprive the world of a good physician? I would never. What happened to you is not Father Ranulphus's business. The church asks if your character is good, and of that I have no doubt. You intended marriage, and if you anticipated the wedding night, you're not the first to do so. But carnality, whatever the intention, breaks the bond between you and Our Queen. So I was taught," she said again. "So I believe."

When Laura spoke again the sun had dropped low enough to gild the distant hills. "You must burn everything I touched this week," she said. "And my pallet. Even my breath may have fouled your simples. I should leave now so that I don't corrupt your house further."

"Don't be silly, child. You're not well yet. We should go in, the sun is almost down. You need to sleep, daughter."

"Not your daughter." Laura was pleased that she had not cried. "Just a peasant girl. A stupid peasant girl who disappointed you and the Queen of Heaven. I hope I do not disappoint my teachers at the Scuola with my peasant stupidity—"

The old woman looked shocked. "Don't blaspheme, girl. You've never disappointed me, don't think it. Nor the teachers at the Scuola either, I expect. Don't speak this crazy way."

Laura got to her feet, pleased that the trembling she felt was not weakness but rage. "Mistress, I was only stupid, not crazy. Now I am better schooled and know my place. I thank you for your care for me. You'll want to be paid. I hope you can wait a few days until I can arrange—"

Again Crescia extended her hand to Laura. It trembled. "Laura, please. Daughter. We must not part in anger. Stay tonight, let us talk."

"I think we have talked enough." Laura shook out her kirtle and pinned her veil in its place. "God protect you, mistress. The Queen of Heaven watch over you and your secrets."

She walked out of Crescia's yard. The goats, expecting a caress or a treat, bleated at her as she went. Laura walked slowly, carefully down the path, aware that she was weak and, as the anger drained from her, inexpressibly tired. *I will not trust hope*, she told herself as she went. She would work, as she had been taught to do. She would be a physician, not to the hillside peasantry but to the wealthy and powerful.

Small, lonely, damaged, Laura picked her way down the rocky hillside where, ten years before, she had come to hide. She would hide no more.

Part II
THE WIFE

Chapter Ten

The house was in the southern part of the city. Agnesa's father had looked for one he deemed suitable nearer his own house, but there were none to be found. "Our city is growing too fast," he complained, smiling broadly. Unfurnished, the house seemed enormous to Agnesa, but Papa assured her it would one day seem small, even crowded. "Indulge your father. Let me give you and Cencio this house, and you can fill it with my grandchildren." He did not say that he relied upon her to produce sons: as Uberto di Marini's only child living, Agnesa knew her duty.

They walked through the house, admiring in turn the kitchen, the solar, the garden in the rear, the mosaic tile on the stairs. Upstairs there were two galleries, one at the front and one overlooking the garden. The rear gallery ran the width of the house and was shaded by a broad tile roof; the columns supporting it were of soft yellow stone carved with leaves and vines. Agnesa ran her fingers over the stone and looked out at the gardens of her soon-to-be neighbors: on the left, flowers and a few cypress trees reaching toward Heaven; on the right, an herbary laid out in neat squares. The sun on thyme and rue sent up sweet scent. "That's the physician's house on that side," Uberto told her. "And Tutilo the lawyer on the other side. He's a widower, so there will be no women in his house for company. All the more reason for you to have good Suora Horicula with you, child."

Agnesa had hoped that marriage would mean that her companion would retire to a convent. She loved the sister; Horicula was kind and devout and devoted to Agnesa, but she was like a long-faced dog, faithful but underfoot. She had come to keep Uberto's house when Agnesa's mother was ailing and had stayed on after she died. It was a sacrifice for Uberto to send Horicula away with Agnesa—unless he was as tired of the old nun's long face as Agnesa was.

"Well, sweet? Do you like it?" Uberto swept out his arm, proud as if he'd built the house himself. Agnesa forgot her dignity as a woman nearly wed. She put her arms around her father's neck as she had done when she was a child and he brought her a treat from the market. "It's a wonderful house, Papa! Thank you! Cencio will thank you—"

Uberto patted her shoulder. "All that boy has to do to show his thanks is to work hard, learn his father's business, and fill you up with a quiverful of babies."

Agnesa shivered happily. She had grown up fearing that she would be married to an old man, a crude or ugly man, but Cencio di Rienzi was twenty to her seventeen, round-faced and handsome and smiling and boyish. The few times she had met him since their betrothal they had both been shy but pleased at the marriage arranged for them. When he took her hand in his own to bow over it she had realized that soon this boy, this *man*, would be licensed to touch every part of her. Since then the thought had returned to her often, unsettlingly.

"Suora Horicula will see to the hiring of servants," her father was saying. "The stocking of pantries, the purchase of other necessaries. Luca says his wife and daughters have sewn your linens as their gift to you, but you will need plate and kitchen ware. And furniture—"

Agnesa took her father's arm. He led her out of the sunlight back into the house, talking enthusiastically of oaken
tables and featherbeds.

* * * *

The joining of two of Salerno's important merchant families
was celebrated on the steps of the duomo on a hot, still day.
Agnesa wore her fair hair loose down her back, confined
only by the virgin's crown of gilt and flowers. She had a new
cotte of green silk and a new linen chemise; she was a little
distracted by the sweat that dampened the soft fabric under
her arms and breasts. It was a relief, when the ceremony was
over, to enter the cool cathedral for their nuptial mass. As
she and Cencio knelt side by side, Agnesa struggled to keep
her mind on God and His Son, not on the man beside her.

Then there was feasting. It seemed that all Salerno came
to her father's house to eat and toast their good fortune and
fecundity. Later, when wine and ale had flowed freely, there
was dancing too. And later still, when Agnesa was half-asleep
with the lateness of the house and the unaccustomed wine,
they were taken to the house that her father had bought, carried up the stairs on the shoulders of her husband's friends,
and put to bed still in their wedding finery. The boys had
laughed and hooted until Cencio chased them out. Then,
consciously, he muttered something about giving her time
to say her prayers. As he left, Suora Horicula edged in behind him.

"Silly brutes." She hissed disapprovingly while she brushed
Agnesa's hair and helped her change from the crushed and
stained silk to an embroidered shift. "Think no one was ever
married before. There, now, *tesora*. Are you ready?" The soft
crepey skin of the sister's jowls shook. "Say your prayers
and don't worry, dear one. This is as God wills." She kissed
Agnesa and scuttled out.

Agnesa knelt and began the paternoster.

Then Cencio returned to her. He had changed into a clean shift and his hair was damp at the collar: he had scrubbed his face and neck. *Such a boy!* Agnesa thought. He looked at her diffidently, as if she might send him away. She smiled a small smile and, after a moment, nodded encouragingly. He would know what to do. He was the man.

Somehow they managed.

*　*　*　*

When they had been married a week, Cencio returned to work at his father's warehouse, where he was learning the differing weights of Cathayan silk and brocades from Arabia, differences in quality, supplies, colors. Each evening when he returned to her, Agnesa asked questions. She had been raised on her father's stories of sailing with a cargo of spice and trade goods; commerce was familiar to her, if mercery was not. All the while she was looking at the way her husband's curling dark hair peaked over his left eye, the curve of his mouth in the corner, the rough shadow of beard on his chin. A week, and already she loved him. She thanked God every morning and night for her luck.

When Cencio was not at home, though, she rattled around the big house looking for occupation. Suora Horicula spoke to the servants and managed the storeroom; she had taught Agnesa to do these things as she grew, but in Uberto di Marini's house she had never quite turned them over to her charge. Even now, in Agnesa's own house, the sister seemed loath to relinquish her responsibilities. The servants knew where the experience and authority lay and went to Horicula before they approached Agnesa with a problem or question. When Agnesa suggested that this should change, the nun smiled and nodded, but nothing changed. "Enjoy your youth, *tesora*. Soon enough there will not be enough hours in the day for all you must do."

Which meant babies. What was she to do until that time?

Agnesa stitched hangings for the walls. She went to mass. She visited friends who had married or welcomed them as visitors. But Bertrissa, the first married, now had a son, and Lomilla was pregnant. Before Agnesa wed they had been very superior and vague about the secrets of the marriage bed. Now they were just as superior about the mysteries of motherhood. *When I am a mother I will not make childless friends feel stupid,* she vowed. Before she married, everyone had told her that marriage would change her. It had and it had not: people still treated her like a child. It was clear that until she had a babe of her own she would not be the equal of other women.

With a will she bent herself to the task of becoming a mother.

It was easy to do. Cencio had been diffident at first, but as he succeeded in pleasing her he became bolder, nuzzling at her breast, kissing her neck and elbows and fingers, encouraging her to do the same to him. In bed they played like children until their laughter rang through the halls of the big house. They made love every night, said their prayers, fell into blameless slumber, and rose to the slanted light of morning at the window.

* * * *

Suora Horicula meant to go to market, and Agnesa intended to go with her. The nun had suggested that her mistress stay at home. "What a bore it will be for you, walking among all those strangers, looking at fish and butter! Would you not rather stay here where it's cool, *tesora*, and rest until afternoon mass?"

No, she had much rather not. So three of them, Agnesa, Suora Horicula, and the page, Giani, went to market. It felt good to walk briskly toward the center of the city, wonderful to move through the market in the cool shadow of the duomo, exciting to see and smell the food and goods spread before them. She watched closely as Suora Horicula bargained for a pot of honey; ran a finger over a large fish, smelled it, and shook her head; ordered flour and half a hundredweight of onions to be delivered to their kitchens. The sister bought lye and tallow and oil and pepper, loading Giani up until he was almost hidden by the bundles in his arms. Then she sent him home.

"Come, 'Nesa. The bells for sext will be ringing soon."

The cathedral was cool, dim, and smoky with incense. Agnesa and the *suora* knelt, listening to the chanted Latin and its antiphons. The voices soared upward with the music.

When mass was done, the two women walked home by a shadier route than they had taken to reach the market. Their path took them a little closer to the harbor; salt breeze soothed the skin and fluttered their headdresses. Looking west to the harbor, Agnesa had an inspiration.

"Let us surprise Cencio with a visit!"

The nun frowned and shook her head. "No, child. A harbor warehouse is no place for women. Beside, *tesora*, your good husband is working." The nun was adamant. "The world of men is different, harder and dirtier, and the harbor is no place for a gently reared girl. What's more, Cencio and his father would not like to see you there. Ask him tonight, child, if you think I'm wrong."

Agnesa was inclined to argue, but the suora would not be persuaded. The street turned uphill away from the harbor. *Child.* That again.

The two women walked the rest of the way in silence. By the time they reached their street, Suora Horicula was redfaced; drops of sweat stood on her upper lip and brow, and her breath was rapid.

"We will rest and have a little lemon water and a wafer," she said.

But Agnesa had not won her point before; she was unwilling to go meekly inside now. "I want to walk up a little farther," she said. "We have lived here almost four months and I still don't know this neighborhood. Come, *suora*." She did not give the nun a chance to refuse. Agnesa walked briskly past her own gate and up the steep street until she reached the stand of poplar that marked its end. When she turned she could see all the houses that surrounded her own, the red and brown tiled roofs of houses farther down the hill, extending clear to the blue of the sea. A breeze stirred damp bits of hair that had escaped her veil. Suora Horicula, coming behind her, was frankly panting, one hand on her hip as she climbed.

As suddenly as Agnesa's petty anger had risen, it was gone. She repented of making her companion climb the hill when she was tired. "Dear sister, you're limping. We'll go home at once. I had no idea how far it was. Take my arm." Suora Horicula's long face was red; sweat was now rolling from the edge of her coif into her eyebrows and down her cheeks.

They went down the hill more easily and more slowly than they had come up it. Suora Horicula leaned heavily on Agnesa's arm, apologizing as they went. To silence her Agnesa made up stories about the owners of the houses they passed: this one was a prince from Persia come to take physic with the medicos at the Scuola; that one was a Sicilian pirate on holiday from his exhausting work. Suora Horicula smiled and shook her head at the nonsense and breathed more easily as they reached the level path.

"I know who some of our neighbors really are," the old woman told her. "Here." She pointed a bent finger at the house they were passing. "This is where Guisto the rice merchant lives. He has a wife only a few years older than you, and they have two little daughters. And this—" She pointed across the street. "That is the house of Betti, the builder. No wife, but his mother and two sisters live with him. Next to Betti's house is another lawyer. I can't recall his name . . ."

The sister had regained her breath, but she still leaned hard on Agnesa's arm and her face was still very red. Agnesa listened with half an ear to what the old woman said, concentrating on supporting Horicula's considerable weight. As they approached their own gate she saw a woman, richly but soberly dressed in a cotte of dark green and a headdress of plain linen, at the door of the physician's house next to their own. Perhaps that was one of his patients. But didn't medicos normally go to their patients? Then perhaps she was the medico's wife. Agnesa nodded to the woman, who smiled and, when she saw that Agnesa meant to enter her own courtyard, spoke.

"You're my new neighbor, yes?"

Agnesa looked at her again. The woman was short and very thin, not elderly but not young. Her skin was pale and slightly freckled, her brows a redding brown. Agnesa saw no ring to show that she was married. The physician's sister, perhaps? She was too young to be his mother.

"This is my house," Agnesa agreed. "I am Agnesa di— Rienzi."

"And recently wed." The woman's tone was teasing but kind. "I should have been more neighborly and called to welcome you. I am Laura di Crescia. You have been here, what? Three months?"

"Almost four." Agnesa blushed. "We came directly from our wedding."

"Then I wish you joy." Laura di Crescia had a sympathetic smile. "But I should not keep you standing in this sun. Suora, you look—" She stopped to peer at the nun's face. "Dear *suora*, you're not well."

Horicula began to flutter and assure the stranger that she

was only a little warm and required a little water to make her sound as a nut once more.

The neighbor disagreed. "I don't think so. Your color is not good. You must go inside at once and lie down for at least an hour." She made a shooing gesture with her hand. "Go inside. We have met, we'll speak again."

Now that her neighbor had commented on it, Agnesa realized that the redness of her companion's face had given way to a gray pallor. She bit her lip. Giani was at the gate, holding it for them as Agnesa led Horicula toward the house. Another three steps, then Suora Horicula crumpled beside her with a soughing sound.

Agnesa dropped to her knees in the dusty street, patting Horicula's hand, which was cold to her touch despite the heat of the day. Giani still held the gate, his mouth and eyes wide. "Get help!" Agnesa snapped. The boy hesitated, as if unsure she was empowered to give the orders, then he released the gate and ran for the house.

The gate began to swing shut and would have slammed heavily into Agnesa where she knelt, but another hand stopped it. The woman, her neighbor Laura, called after Giani. "Bring a chair to carry her inside, and another man to help you. Have a jug of water brought—cool but not too cold." She turned back to Agnesa. "Are you well enough to stay here with her? You will be no help if you swoon."

Agnesa nodded.

"Good girl. There's no need to worry for her. We'll have your *nonna* healthy in no time."

Giani came back with Domiro, an older servant, who carried an oaken chair. In a matter of a few moments, under Laura's direction, Suora Horicula was raised to the chair where she lolled, limp but conscious, murmuring apologies for the trouble she was making. The men lifted the chair awkwardly and began to carry it toward the house with Agnesa on one side and Laura on the other. It seemed to take a long time for this procession to make its way into the house and thence to the solar, where Agnesa directed them. When the chair had been set down Laura asked again for drinking water, not too cold, and a basin of water and cloths. Domiro looked from Horicula to Laura to Agnesa, uncertain of who had the authority.

Agnesa said, "Do as she tells you!" Domiro hesitated. "For Saint Matteo's love, *now!*"

He hurried out.

Laura di Crescia had found a cushion on another chair and asked if she might use it to make the *suora* more comfortable.

"Of course, whatever will help her. I should send for a physician." Agnesa considered. "Do you know one?"

Her neighbor seemed amused. "Many. *I* am a physician, little neighbor. If you wish me to treat the *suora* it would be my privilege."

This was the physician who lived next door? A woman?

Suora Horicula shifted in her chair, muttering. Agnesa abandoned her doubts for now. "Please, help her."

"I will do my best. Ah, good." Domiro had returned with a stone bowl that sweated with the chill of the water it contained and with cloths over his arm. Behind him, Giani came with a clay pitcher and cup.

Laura poured a cup of water, then tested a drop on her wrist. "Good. Not too cold. We don't want to shock her. Little neighbor, if you can coax her to take a sip at a time, slowly?"

Agnesa drew up a stool at Horicula's side and put the cup to the old nun's lips. For her part Laura dipped a cloth into the water in the bowl and pressed it against the inside of Horicula's wrist. The old woman stirred a little, then sighed and settled back against the cushion.

"Should we put a cloth on her brow?"

The *medica* shook her head. "The skin is very thin at the wrist, and the blood close to the surface. As it flows beneath, it carries the cool throughout her body." Laura exchanged one cloth for another, wrung it out, and placed it on Horicula's other wrist.

The nun stirred again and smiled a small, weary smile. "So much fuss for a silly old woman."

"A silly old woman who is much loved," Laura said at the same moment that Agnesa assured her that no fuss was too great for her dear *suora*. Horicula's smile flickered, then disappeared. She tried to sit up.

"Dinner must be—"

Laura di Crescia shook her head. "Vanity is a sin, sister. Are you the only one who can talk to the cook or order the fish? Here is this sweet young woman who I see owes you the respect and love she would owe her beloved mother. Let her carry the burden of tonight's dinner while I see to making you well for the morrow."

Suora Horicula was dismayed. "Not vanity! Blessed Father forgive me if I am guilty of—"

Agnesa took the nun's hand in her own and kissed it. "Dearest *suora*, you must not be feeling well at all, not to notice when someone teases you. I will go talk at once to the cook. This woman is a physician, so you must listen to her." She kissed the hand in hers again. "Rest. It's all my fault for making you walk so far. Let me care for you as you do for me."

*   *   *   *

The cook was bewildered at first to have the mistress of the house, rather than her deputy, come down to discuss what would be served for dinner. Agnesa gathered after that all that was required of her was to agree to the plans the cook had already made. With that understanding, mistress and

cook parted. Agnesa returned to find Laura sitting at Suora
Horicula's side. The nun was asleep, snoring slightly.

"How is she?"

"Her heart is not strong, and she strained it. No, there is
no point in scolding yourself for not indulging a weakness
you did not suspect. No talk of fault, little neighbor. Instead, let us talk of what to do to return her to health. I have
a tonic I will send to you, to be brewed fresh each day with
honey and a little vinegar and taken before vespers. Beyond
that, plain food and not too much, water rather than wine,
and sleep. Sleep is the greatest physician save only God
Himself. If you can, keep her in bed for a few days. Say prayers
to Saint Anne and Saint Luke, and take as much of the
weight of the household from her shoulders as you can."

"I will." Agnesa said it with the weight of a holy vow.

"Now, while she sleeps, tell those young men to carry her
chair to her chamber. Is there a woman who can help you
put her to bed?" The physician looked Agnesa up and down.
"Don't try to do all yourself; your *suora* is more substantial
than she looks, and she might be hurt if you dropped her.
Put her to bed, and when she wakes, give her a little gruel,
then the tonic I spoke of. I will come back tomorrow to see
how she does." She rose.

"You're going?" Agnesa felt a flutter of panic.

"I am. She should do very well once she's abed, but if you
have need, which you will not, I think—" Laura tilted her
head in the direction of her house. "I am only next door.
Send for me at once. I am happy to have met you, little
neighbor, although I'm sorry it is under such circumstances."
Her bow was formal but her smile warm.

Agnesa watched her neighbor leave, then called Giani
and Domiro to carry the *suora* to her room. By the time a
boy arrived from the house next door with a leathern bag of
medicine, Horicula was in her shift and in her bed, a shawl

tucked around her shoulders. It felt blasphemous to remove her companion's wimple; Agnesa had never seen her without it. She left the coif that covered the old woman's sparse yellow-white hair.

Following the directions Laura had sent with the medicine, Agnesa sent to the kitchen for honey, hot water, and vinegar and mixed them with a measure of the musty, spicy powder from the bag. When Suora Horicula woke again she fed her the mixture by spoonful. Only then would she let her companion ask what had happened and how she came to be in her bed. Again the nun made noises of distress, but she was too tired and gray to rise from her bed. Agnesa promised to see to everything that must be seen to, kissed the nun's brow, and left Martia, the kitchen girl, to sit with her.

* * * *

By the time Cencio returned home that night, Agnesa had had her first taste of being truly the mistress of her own house. The servants, used to going to Suora Horicula for direction, hesitated when Agnesa gave her own orders. It was only when she lost her temper and demanded that they do what she asked immediately that they were shaken out of their anxiety and returned to work. From that moment, her stewardship of the house was not in doubt.

Laura di Crescia came, as she had promised, the next morning. By this time Suora Horicula was sitting up, propped against pillows and wrapped in shawls, threatening to rise and be about her work at any moment.

"Your color is much better, dear *suora*," the *medica* agreed. "But your pulse is still fast and soft, and your blood is cold. For a few days you'll let this good child repay your kindness and devotion over the years and manage the house while you mend, yes?"

Suora Horicula frowned and sank into the pillows

fingering her pectoral cross. "May I pray, *magistra?*" It was the closest Agnesa had ever heard her come to sarcasm.

"I hope you will, *suora*. And I hope you will add my work to your prayers."

It was not an olive branch, but it softened Horicula's frown. She closed her eyes and her lips began to move in prayer.

Laura led Agnesa from the room and onto the gallery overlooking the garden.

"Is she truly better?"

"She is, but—" Laura held a finger up as if to stop Agnesa from celebrating too early. "What I said before is true. Her humors are badly disordered. The medicine I sent you contains galangal, which is very hot and will help, but I can see the mixture is not right. I will send over more galangal; mix it with the powder I sent yesterday and continue to dose her. Does she take much water? Good. And is she hungry? You must insist that she eat, no matter what she says."

She looked out over the garden. "This is a lovely prospect; I can't see as much of my garden from my house as you can from yours." Laura smiled. "And you, little neighbor. How do you do?"

"I?" Agnesa blushed. "I am not ill."

"No, but you have had great responsibility thrust upon you—and I don't imagine your dear *suora* permitted you much responsibility before this. You slept well? Good. When Suora Horicula is recovered, you must make sure you retain the management of your household, for her sake and your own."

"My sake?"

"For your sake in particular. I hate to see a woman without occupation; she becomes restless, then idle, and then unhappy. Illness and mischief can be born from unhappiness."

"I hope to be happy," Agnesa said. "I have wanted more occupation, but Suora Hori—"

Laura's raised hand stopped her. "She's old and she's set in her ways. She has known you since you were a child? This illness of hers may be a blessing for both of you. Now, make sure you eat and sleep well yourself, little neighbor. I will call again tomorrow, but if you have need of me . . ."

"You are right next door." It was a comforting thought.

Chapter Eleven

Suora Horicula lay abed for a week, fretting over the state of the household and lamenting that her poor Agnesa should be saddled, even for a moment, with such responsibility. Her poor Agnesa, in fact, was enjoying holding the reins of her household. The servants came to her for their instructions, reminded her when chores like turning the grain or cleaning the dovecote were needful. She learned new things every day. When Agnesa suggested that she might keep these responsibilities even after Horicula was well again, the blood rose alarmingly to the old woman's face. Anxious for the old woman's health and jealous of her new authority, Agnesa called the *medica* for advice.

She called for lemon water sweetened with honey and a plate of sugared figs and brought Laura to the garden to sit in the shade of a tree. The physician nodded as Agnesa explained.

"I was afraid she would be stubborn."

Agnesa raised her eyebrows, mildly shocked.

"Little neighbor, your good *suora* is a woman, not a saint.

She has been useful all her life; perhaps she fears becoming useless to you now."

"Useless? How could she think it?"

"Every mother dreads the day when her child doesn't need her. I will have a word with Suora Horicula myself, but you must help her. Go to her for advice, ask as much as you can, let her feel you still need her."

Agnesa nodded. "You're very wise."

Laura di Crescia laughed. "Wise? Because I am a little older and much in the habit of observing people? Little neighbor, don't make a hero of me any more than you make a saint of Suora Horicula."

"I do think you're a sort of hero. To become a physician? Study at the Scuola? How proud your family must be."

The *medica* shrugged. "My family died years ago, when I was a child."

Agnesa could not imagine such a calamity. "All your family? But who took care of you? Were you taken in by nuns?" She imagined the *medica* as one of the row of quiet, studious convent girls she saw sometimes at mass.

"Nuns? No, although the woman who raised me was pious and chaste as any religious. I was apprenticed to a mountain healer. It was she who sent me to study in the city."

"Surely *she* is proud of you."

Again Laura shrugged. "I don't know. We had a falling out." Her voice was so cool that Agnesa was afraid to ask more.

"Was the study very hard? It must take years!" Her family had little truck with the scholars and physicians of the Scuola, but Agnesa knew a few women studied there. "Did you have to learn about the inside of bodies?" She shuddered. "How awful."

"It's not awful," the physician said. "It's fascinating. I found it so, anyway. And I had to learn a great deal—reading and ciphering and many other studies—before I got as far as the study of the insides of bodies."

Agnesa knew a little of ciphering and nothing at all of reading. She was awed.

"Don't look at me so!" Laura patted her hand, as if to take the sting from her words. "If you had been in my shoes you would have learned too. Enough of my education. How is yours progressing? Does your cook permit you to set foot in the kitchen? Mine doesn't."

They gossiped pleasantly for a while longer, going from Agnesa's present to her future. Agnesa spoke shyly of her hope for children, and her disappointment that none, yet, had been conceived.

"You've been wed what? Four months? You're young. I don't doubt you'll have many babies."

Cencio's father was beginning to doubt, Agnesa knew. When Luca di Rienzi visited, the old man poked into every corner of their house, seeking to be disappointed. He prodded Cencio and joked with Agnesa, asking bluntly for a grandchild. Luca had other sons, already he was a grandfather, but he wanted a child from this marriage. If Agnesa did not have a son, all of her father's property would pass to her cousins and, from Luca's point of view, the marriage would have accomplished nothing.

"The families." Agnesa gestured vaguely. "They want grandsons, both Cencio's papa and my own."

"Fretting about it is hardly the way to achieve that. Worry can impede conception as easily as some more physical cause. Would you like me to speak to them?"

Agnesa imagined, horrified, the result of such a conversation. She didn't doubt that Laura would be tactful, but Luca di Rienzi would not be. He would listen, his beaked nose rising higher with each word the physician spoke. Then he would give Cencio a tongue-lashing for letting a woman make excuses for him. Her own father might be more polite, but Agnesa doubted he would be more ready to listen.

"No, no, please. It will happen in its own time and as God wills," she said.

As if she had shared the vision in Agnesa's head, Laura smiled and nodded. "Probably wiser so, yes. In its own time, and as God wills."

*   *   *   *

God's will worked slowly. Even Cencio began to fret. "Are you eating properly? Is there something particular we should eat? Is one day more propitious than another?" Luca must be scolding Cencio at the warehouse where Agnesa could not see it, and the scolding accomplished nothing good. Some nights when they lay together her husband was like a bull in his thrusting, as if it were a matter of business that must be quickly resolved. Agnesa was left tender and bruised, and Cencio apologized with tears standing in his eyes.

They had been married for more than a year when Agnesa finally consulted the *medica* again.

"The test is simple," Laura said. "But are you certain you want to know?"

Agnesa nodded.

She was to take two clay pots of the same size, Laura told her. She was to put a measure of wheat bran into each. Then she must dampen the bran in one pot with Cencio's urine, and the other with her own. "Mark them so you know which is which. Then cover them with a cloth and let them sit for a ten-day or so. If one of them begins to stink and worms grow in it, that is the one in whom the defect lies."

"And if neither do?"

Laura smiled. "Then there is no fault in either, and you continue as you have done to bring a child into the world."

Agnesa followed the instructions faithfully. When on the tenth day she uncovered the pots there was little odor and no worms. She stood in the corner of her bedchamber with a pot in each hand, tears of gratitude rolling down her cheeks. When she had composed herself she sent a message to Laura: "The tidings are good!"

It was several days before the physician came to call. She apologized when she did come—"There is fever in the convent of Saint Giorgio. It's been running through the place like water through my fingers. I think they'll all live, with God's grace. Certainly they have been praying enough for Him to grant them all long life. But you! You have good news. Do you still have the pots?"

"No, I didn't think—" Agnesa was dismayed. Should she have kept the pots and sodden bran?

"No, I trust you to know what your eyes showed you. So now we know there is no serious impediment in either of you. There are treatments I could suggest to encourage conception, but really, you're young and healthy. Why not let nature and God do their work?"

"What would *you* do?"

"I?" The healer was still for a moment. "I will never have such a problem." Her voice was so cool that Agnesa felt a finger of ice run up her own spine. Then Laura smiled. "If I were you, though? I would wait a while. Pray. Lie with my husband. And if your father-in-law or your papa fret, tell them you have sought medical advice and there is no impediment save their impatience."

That night in their chamber Agnesa told Cencio what the physician had said. In the moonlit darkness he traced the line of her upper lip before kissing her. "Nothing wrong with me?"

"Nothing. Or with me."

He kissed her brow. "I never thought a woman as fair as my wife could be unfruitful. God wouldn't permit it!" He kissed her again. Agnesa sighed and settled beneath him, her hand snaking up to thread through his curls. His hand found her breast, his knee slid between her thighs, but he was gentle tonight and tender. Before they slept Agnesa murmured a prayer that a child should come from a night as sweet as this one.

In the morning Cencio went down to the warehouse with his head high and a swagger back in his step.

*   *   *   *

Laura di Crescia, busy as she must be, visited from time to time to look in on Suora Horicula and to share a cup of watered wine and gossip under the olive tree with Agnesa. Since her illness the old woman had become more willing to doze or knit while Agnesa gave instructions to the servants. When Laura called, the old woman sat with them, but she said little. She seemed to find the *medica*'s presence as comforting as Agnesa did.

Early on a summer's evening the three of them sat just so, with a dish of sugared almonds and pomegranate seeds between them. Agnesa took an almond, raised it to her lips, frowned.

"*Suora*, is it possible there is something wrong with these?" She put the almond back in the dish and offered it to the nun. Horicula took the dish, sniffed at it, took an almond and bit it cautiously, then shook her head.

"They seem wholesome enough to me, *tesora*."

Laura leaned forward to sniff at the plate. "I smell nothing wrong." Her mouth quirked up. "What do you smell, little neighbor?"

Agnesa felt a rise of bile in her throat. "They smell foul to me. Greasy and—" She swallowed.

"Has any other food smelled bad to you?"

"The bream we ate at dinner last night. But fish turns so easily, I thought perhaps it had not been properly spiced." Even with the dish of almonds moved away from her Agnesa's nausea did not abate. She pressed her hand to her throat as if she would push the sickness back down again.

Laura di Crescia was watching her with professional interest. "When were your last courses?"

Agnesa swallowed again, but the lump in her throat did not diminish. She did not like to discuss such things, as Suora Horicula still found them an occasion to lecture on Eve's sin. "I don't—" she began.

Behind her the old nun clucked. "The laundry. It's more than a month since your cloths were laundered. Almost two months. I had not thought of it until now."

"Two months?" Agnesa clenched her teeth on her nausea and looked from one woman to the other. "Might I—"

Laura nodded. "I think God has answered your prayers. I would like to examine you more fully to be sure, if you will let me."

Suora Horicula, still smiling, had begun to weep. She reached for Agnesa, but Agnesa pushed her away roughly and bent to vomit.

When she had finished she saw that a damp cloth and a cup of water had appeared beside her, although she could not remember hearing anyone send for them. She rinsed out her mouth, wiped her face, and allowed herself to be led indoors and up to her solar. There Laura took her pulse, looked at her eyes and the flesh of her gums, and sniffed her breath.

"A good strong pulse, clear eyes, and your breath—for all that has just passed—is healthy. Have your breasts been tender? Do you have headaches? Rashes or darkening here—" Laura made a gesture at her own breasts. "You show every sign of pregnancy, Agnesa. We must keep you strong and healthy so you can give your husband—and the fathers!— joy."

Agnesa murmured a prayer of thanks to Saint Margaret.

Then she began with a dozen questions. "What must I eat? What may I do? Should I—"

Laura laughed. "For the moment, do what you always do, eat what you always eat. Drink good clear water or fortifying wine. Sleep early. Be as active as you can. Beyond that, God and the Virgin give the body wisdom to see to its own care. Follow its dictates. *Suora?*" Laura turned to the nun, who hovered behind Agnesa like a warm, damp cloud. "You will call for me at once if anything unwholesome happens, bleeding or paleness or itching of the breast. I rely on you to be my eyes. Now, 'Nesa, I will send over a draught which should help with the nausea—that is, if your husband is pleased to have me continue to minister to so important a mother."

Her tone was light, but it was clear Laura was serious.

"How could he not be pleased? And *I* want—" Agnesa was suddenly shy. "If you will. Do physicians attend at childbeds? I want so much for you to help me."

"If your husband permits it, nothing would give me greater joy. With God's help you'll have a strong, lively son or a fair, merry daughter. The first of many, I don't doubt."

*   *   *   *

Cencio first wept at the news, then was shy and proud. They stayed up late into the night making plans, talking. Cencio put his hand on her belly as if it were a saint's relic, praying that God keep the baby and his beautiful wife safe. When at last they did sleep his hand stayed there, protecting the new life even as he slept. In the last few months Luca di Rienzi had made no secret of his disappointment with his younger son. He had suggested that Cencio's failure to get his wife with child was part of his general incapacity. "Let him say that now," Cencio murmured sleepily in the darkness. "Let him call me a loafer now."

Agnesa knew how hard Cencio had worked to learn and

help; she had assisted him as much as she could. Still, old Luca believed his son had no ambition, no head for business. The old man was contentious and bullying and could not respect a son who was not. Now, though, he was loudly pleased. He talked to his friends and Cencio's brothers as if the potency were something miraculous. Now there would be a son to inherit the money and property that marriage had brought together. He gave Cencio a clap on the shoulder and a purse of silver. Cencio's mother and his sisters Clauda and Ghibilia began to sew and embroider linen for the baby's cradle.

Uberto was no less delighted, but he was anxious as well. He paid for mass intentions for the safety of mother and child, and of thanksgiving. Before the wedding he had spoken of a quiverful of babies; now he fretted over Agnesa's health. He wanted to hire a physician himself, a famous one who was often called to the governor's palace. Agnesa had to use all her wiles to persuade him that she wanted the physician who lived next door.

"Of course a midwife, 'Nesa. But a medico to oversee her, too."

"Papa, Magistra Laura is a *medica*. Like Magistra Trotula in the old days, the queen of medicine for women. Laura not only studied at the Scuola, she's taught there! And she's a woman, so I need not blush to tell her what I might not tell a man. And she's our neighbor, only a step away if I need her. What could be better? More suitable?"

Uberto would not agree until he had met this neighbor-physician. Agnesa sent Domiro next door to ask if the *magistra* could spare a moment, and, before the bells of the duomo rang again, Laura arrived. She was grave as she greeted Uberto, made a formal examination of her patient, and then sat to talk. Agnesa watched her father be swayed, first by Laura's answers to his questions and anxieties, and then by the *medica*'s charm. She stayed long enough to drink a cup of watered wine, then left them.

"A clever woman, and a handsome one." Uberto watched appreciatively as Laura left. "A great waste that she's unwed."

Agnesa watched her father from the corner of her eye. "Papa, you're not thinking of courting my neighbor, are you?"

Uberto was abashed. "Don't be childish, 'Nesa. I'm long past the age of wanting a wife. Your blessed mother was enough for me!" He crossed himself piously. Agnesa did not tell him that she had known for years of the maids her father tumbled, the women he sometimes visited before returning home in the evening.

"Of course, Papa." She poured more wine into his cup and served him one of the seed cakes he liked.

Later she thought about the physician. She was not a beauty, no matter what her father said. She was so thin, and her manner was so—confident? powerful? She hadn't the high-browed, pale prettiness that Agnesa admired. But Laura was graceful and her dark eyes were clever. Not beautiful but elegant and admirable.

Assured that Cencio and Agnesa's father had both sanctioned her care, Laura made it her practice to look in upon her neighbor once a week, to check on Agnesa's health and to sit and gossip a while. She usually had a bit of advice, a new blend of herbs to prescribe, foods that she advised or advised against.

"The sickness is not likely to last long," she told Agnesa. "After it passes you'll likely feel very well, so long as you eat and drink sensibly and sleep soundly. Once the baby is born there will be very little sleep! Now, you may feel that one food or another is the thing you crave more than anything else. Indulge those feelings, especially in the craving of meat or green vegetables. On no account should you eat largely of raw fruit or drink unwatered wine. Goat's milk is good, especially if you find your teeth are becoming loose in your mouth . . ."

For the moment there was nothing that Agnesa craved but an end to the nausea, and when, sometime in her fourth month, it ceased to trouble her, she was filled with a sense of well-being and power.

"It's God's gift, that strength," Suora Horicula told her.

Laura agreed. "Soon you'll feel the baby quicken."

Cencio becan to tease Agnesa that every her sentence began, "Magistra Laura says . . ."

But Magistra Laura spoke sense. In honeyed afternoon sunlight she sat with Agnesa, talking as a friend and neighbor about the city and its folk, the visitors from foreign lands who were drawn to the Scuola or come to Salerno for the waters or the climate. Sometimes Agnesa talked about her childhood and her mother, who had never recovered from Agnesa's birth.

"It's why Papa is so anxious for me," she said. Her own anxiety was unspoken but real.

"You don't need to fret, 'Nesa. I have no fears on your account, and nor should you have."

Sometimes Agnesa asked about Laura's studies at the Scuola. To be surrounded by men, learning such things, seemed exciting and frightening to her. Rubbing shoulders with Jews and Arabs and foreigners. Was it terrifying to know such folk?

"Each Jew or foreigner I met was just one person, and, frankly, some of the old monks were more frightening!—particularly the ones who made trouble for the women who studied there. Not many, though; the Scuola is famously tolerant. And my first teacher was a monk. Fra Bruncio had a ready hand—" She rubbed the side of her jaw as if she could still feel the ghost of a blow. "But I believe he taught me as true as he would have taught a boy. At the Scuola, the people who can't adapt to differences among the students— and the faculty!—don't often last long."

Again it surprised Agnesa that scholars, religious men, could be prey to the same jealousy and ambition she knew plagued merchants and artisans.

"But the Arabs, are they frightening? Do they speak like devils?"

"Some of the Arabs are black as night, others might be from Salerno for all the difference I could see. None of them were particularly frightening, and many of them are very clever. Since I don't know how devils speak, I can't say. The language they do speak is very quick and harsh to my ears, and they write a strange script like knotted thread. I learned a very little of it."

The Jews too had their own writing, but that Laura couldn't read. "Only Latin and a little Arabic." As if that were not enough.

Sometimes in the dark of night when Cencio slept beside her, Agnesa lay wakeful, worrying. She would repeat all of Magistra Laura's learning to herself like a prayer: astronomy and mathematics, Latin and Arabic, anatomy and philosophy. Laura had delivered babies and cured the nuns of Saint Giorgio of tertian fever. Her stories swelled Agnesa's imagination, but it was her kindness that inspired her with faith. Comforted, she would turn on her side and sleep.

*   *   *   *

By her fifth month Agnesa felt as strong as a mountain bear. She laughed at Suora Horicula's fluttering pleas to take care of herself. "I've never felt so well. And I'll be a mother with a son and no time to coddle myself." When the nun attempted to reclaim some control of the household, Agnesa invited her to inventory the contents of the stillroom. Agnesa began to embroider a hanging for the wall above the carved cradle Uberto had given them. Every day it felt more real: she was preparing the house for her child.

As her belly swelled, Cencio lay beside her at night, whispering instructions to the baby on hunting and fishing. She lay propped on a pillow stuffed with mugwort and lavender for street dreams, and Cencio spoke singsong to the pale skin of her belly. "You will want to play with other boys your age, and you shall. But when Papa comes to take you hunting, leave them and come with me." He spoke of games and hunting, not the man's work he was doing at his father's warehouse. Agnesa, twisting his dark curls around her fingers, thought that in some ways Cencio was still a boy. He was coming to fatherhood, though, as she was coming to motherhood.

* * * *

When autumn came and the worst of the summer heat was over, Agnesa sat on the gallery in the mornings, stitching animals and stars on the cradle cloth. The breeze often brought the delicious scent of herbs from Laura di Crescia's garden, but on one morning the smell was particularly enticing. Agnesa did not recognize it. Not basil or mint, not thyme or rosemary. The scent was green, sharp as mustard. Suora Horicula could not tell her what it was—the old nun had no sense of smell. Agnesa felt as if she must have some of it, whatever it was, to eat at once. She went down to the kitchen.

"Green?" The cook was perplexed. "Something smells *green?*"

Agnesa nodded. "Dark green and sharp. If you send to market I'm sure they'll have—whatever it is."

"And how will I ask for this green stuff, mistress?"

Agnesa frowned. Why couldn't the cook simply know what it was she meant? "Come with me." She led him out to the kitchen garden. "Smell."

The cook stood with his hands on his hips, a heavy, elderly man with a short, bulbous nose that he raised like a hound scenting the air. "I smell—mistress, I smell what we have planted here, herbs and lettuces. Nothing sharp."

Agnesa only barely kept from stamping her foot as she might have when she was an unmarried girl. "Come," she said again. This time she led the cook upstairs to the gallery. The old man wheezed as he hurried behind her into this unfamiliar territory.

"Smell, now! What is that?"

The man made a show of sniffing deeply, twitching his mouth, sniffing again, and pondering. At last he told her he could not be sure. "Perhaps the physician's medical herbs. Perhaps rabe or broccoli or *bietola*. I tell you in truth and by Saint Martha, I can't be certain."

"Then when you send to market get some of each. I want greens today."

The cook, who was a grandfather and had been married and widowed, nodded. "Sometimes it takes a woman that way. I remember my old wife—" Talking to himself, the cook left the gallery for the kitchen, and Agnesa, teased by the sharp vegetable odor carried on the breeze, returned to her stitching.

At dinner that night the cook himself presented her with a dish of rabe braised with sardines and pine nuts and another of broccoli. Both were delicious, but neither had quite the sharp, bitter-green taste she craved. The old man sent to ask if his mistress was pleased with the dishes, and Agnesa replied that they were delicious but not quite what she had hoped for.

Later she took Cencio out on the gallery to see if he could identify the scent. "What is that?"

He shook his head. "I smell salt from the sea, and a little thyme. Or basil. I don't know plants, 'Nesa."

Again Agnesa wanted to stamp or scold. It was not Cencio's fault that he did not recognize what was teasing at her. Her stomach knotted at the smell; she felt she could nearly taste it, sharper now without the sun's sweetening warmth. When she tried to explain the craving, Cencio vowed that he would get her anything she wanted, if only she could tell him what the thing was. She slept with a knot in her belly that night.

In the morning she sent again for the cook. Again they went out to the gallery, and again the mistress and servant stood, scenting the air like hunting dogs. "*Bietola*, perhaps. I'll see if I can find some at the market." He went heavily away.

Agnesa was distracted all morning. She felt that she was withering for want of the green. What must the lack do to the baby?

A while after the bells for sext had run, Domiro appeared with a covered tray. "Cook sent it up, mistress." He put the tray on a table and backed away as if afraid that she would scold. Agnesa spared only a moment to wonder if her temper had become so dreadful in a mere day or two. Then she took the cloth from the tray and saw a bit of bread, some butter, and a plain salad of dark green leaves and bits of red stalk, sharp and mustardy. She sank into her chair, forgetting even to offer thanks before she ate, and put one of the green leaves on her tongue. It was sharp and peppery, not quite the taste she had wanted, but close. She took another bite, this time of a dark fan-shaped leaf with a remnant of dark red stalk.

The bitter, salty flavor burst in her mouth. Agnesa smiled and took another bite, ate and ate until the greens were gone and the gnawing, distracting desire was gone. Suora Horicula, who hovered in the doorway watching Agnesa eat, smiled broadly.

"There now. Isn't that better? Nothing more to fret for, is there?"

Chapter Twelve

It grew too chilly to sit out of doors. When next Laura came to visit, Agnesa greeted her in the solar, a long room with tall windows on to the gallery. They sat at one end by a fire in a brazier that kept the chill at bay. Suora Horicula was settled on the other side of the fire, already dozing over her embroidery.

Agnesa's anxiety must have been written on her face. As soon as she was seated Laura asked, "What worries you?"

Agnesa rested her hand on a light flutter in her rounding belly. "I have had a—a feeling, like moths inside me. Is all as it should be?" This was a part of womancraft of which Suora Horicula knew nothing. Worse, the old nun had become so anxious when Agnesa mentioned the sensation that it was necessary to reassure her, soothe her, and insist that there was nothing to fear. But, "Should I worry?" Agnesa asked.

"Worry?" Laura di Crescia laughed. "Rejoice! That's quickening, your baby moving inside you."

"Moving?" Agnesa pressed her hand more firmly against the flutter, as if she could feel the whole child. "I didn't know it would move before it was born."

"No one told you? No woman in your family?" She looked around her as if she expected to find it populated by aunts and cousins. "No one in Cencio's family?"

Agnesa shook her head.

"And the good *suora* would have no experience." The *medica* looked thoughtful. "You must think of me as a woman of your family, then. Ask me whatever comes into your head. You shouldn't be fretting—it is not good for mother or child."

"So the flutters are natural?"

"Natural, and a good sign. I would worry if you didn't feel some movement. I'll warn you, though. By the time the baby is born, you'll wish for a night's sleep unbroken by his poking and kicks. Now, have you other questions? How are you eating?"

"My appetite is good, although sometimes all I want is greens: cress and rabe and lettuce."

"I've said before, your babe knows what he wants. There's certainly no harm in cress if you don't eat it in excess. We use it after birth to tighten the womb."

"Tighten—" Agnesa went hot with anxiety. "Surely I should not be eating it then? No more cress—"

Laura held up a hand to stop the cascade of words. "Eat what you like, in moderation. Cress or *bietola* or any wholesome thing you want will do you no harm." She took Agnesa's wrist between her strong fingers, feeling for the pulse. "Now, will you tell the fathers that the baby has quickened?" She had taken to calling Luca and Uberto "the fathers," with comic emphasis and a smile that denied disrespect.

"I want to tell Cenci' first. Once I tell my papa and Cencio tells his, it will be everyone's news."

The *medica* released Agnesa's wrist. "A fine, strong pulse. You're healthy as a kid goat. As for the news, tell Cencio first and be guided by what he says. I don't see how keeping it a secret for a week goes against any duty you owe your fathers; they'll know soon enough."

"He'll want what I want." Agnesa was certain of this.

"Then the two of you are well matched. Not every young wife is so fortunate. I've seen girls your age married to old men, or men who ignore them, men who beat them or work them into sickness, then call me to restore them to health so they can work more. Your father must love you very much to marry you to a young, handsome fellow."

"Isn't he handsome?" Agnesa blushed. "Papa loves me—but he loves the Rienzi warehouses almost as much."

Laura looked uncomprehending. Agnesa, raised among the merchants of Salerno, could barely believe that the business of the Rienzis and Marinis were not the first concern of the whole city. "Luca di Rienzi sends his traders out to fill his warehouses. My papa owns ships. Marrying me and Cencio together, Papa allied with warehouses and old Luca with ships."

"Ahh." The *medica* nodded. "An excellent piece of business for the fathers and a stroke of good fortune for you and Cencio."

The baby fluttered again. Agnesa smiled fondly. "My greatest luck is that Luca keeps Cencio here in the city. His oldest brother is away most of the year, trading, and Paolo, the second son, was given to the church. Cenci' might have been sent to the governor as a soldier." Agnesa imagined Cencio as one of the hard, grizzled men of war she sometimes saw in the marketplace. Her father hired such men, veterans of the king's wars, to guard his ships. Would Cencio have become one such? What would it have been like, to marry such a man?

"Cencio's choice was church, trade, or war, then."

"What else is there?"

Laura laughed. Suora Horicula snorted in her sleep.

"Was that funny?" Agnesa was not certain if she should feel foolish or insulted.

"Funny only in a small way, 'Nesa, and I apologize. I was laughing at myself and at human nature. We know our own worlds, but there are other worlds, even in Salerno, and other work. Cencio might have been a lawyer, a farmer, a physician—" Laura mimed a bow. "He might have been an apothecary, a judge, a poet, a mathematician—"

"I don't think my father-in-law would have seen much benefit to a poet in the family! Cencio isn't a mathematician like the learned men at the *studia*, but he's good with numbers. Even Luca says so. It is part of why he keeps Cencio here in Salerno."

"Only part?"

Agnesa looked behind her to make sure that Suora Horicula slept still, then murmured, "Cenci's a terrible sailor. He has only to step aboard a ship and he turns green and pukes until he steps on land again. Luca disdains him for it, but I'm glad. It means I have my husband home beside me at night."

"A great comfort to you," Laura agreed. "So I will not attempt to suggest cures for seasickness."

"Oh, please don't! The ones who are good sailors are sent away to trade. Cenci's brother Antonio and my cousin—" Agnesa stopped, caught by a memory. "Do you know, we almost did have a physician in the family when I was small."

"Almost?"

"My cousin studied medicine for a time, then gave it up. My uncle wanted a contact at the Scuola, and he was not pleased. My cousin pled for days!"

"To give up medicine? If commerce was the sole reason your cousin studied physic, I'm not surprised he didn't find it pleasing."

"No one tells a child much, but I heard some gossip. There was a great row—my uncle isn't the sort of man to change his mind on his son's whim."

"But he relented in the end?"

Agnesa was matter-of-fact. "He'd found a family he wanted an alliance with, a shipbuilding family in Pozzuoli. So he married my cousin away from Salerno, and now Grazia's family builds his ships, and I don't doubt that serves my uncle better than knowing medicos at the Scuola."

A coal popped noisily in the brazier. Laura leaned over to stir the fire. "Pozzuoli? Where is that?"

Agnesa nodded. "North along the coast somewhere. Far enough that he's come back to Salerno only once since he wed. For which we thank God."

Suora Horicula snorted again. Agnesa turned, anticipating a scold, but the nun still slept.

Laura straightened up. "When did this happen? I wonder if I might have known your cousin."

"It must have been a dozen years ago. I was only a little girl, and Matteo has a flock of children; the eldest boy has ten years now."

Laura was watching the fire intently, as if the ashen red glow bespelled her.

"Did you know him, Laura? My cousin?"

"His name was Marini?"

"No—we're related through our mothers. Matteo di Sette. They're an old mercer family."

The *medica* looked up from the fire. "I think perhaps I did. Tall, dark hair, light eyes. He wore a palmer's brooch in his collar."

Agnesa clapped her hands, delighted. "He did! I had forgotten! How clever you are to remember it."

"Not at all. He stood out from the other students, but in the end it was right he left. He had no passion for medicine. And now he buys silk and spice and lives in Pozzuoli."

"It's a great comedown. When I was a girl I thought him very heroic, traveling to the Holy Land! Then, Grazia and Pozzuoli. I think it's sad."

"Is Pozzuoli so terrible?"

Agnesa looked again at Suora Horicula, then muttered, "No, but Grazia is!"

"Perhaps she suits him better than she would suit you," Laura suggested. "Now, how have you been sleeping?"

"Soundly as a nut, thank you."

The *medica* asked the questions she always asked, but beyond the excitement of quickening nothing had changed. Agnesa had abundant energy, she ate and slept well, her urine was clear, her eyes white.

"All things in moderation, 'Nesa," Laura reminded her when she took her leave. "Heed the cravings; it is not good for you or the baby to ignore them. Already your son knows what he wants."

She bent to kiss Agnesa's cheek, an unusual gesture. "Call upon me whenever you have need, little neighbor."

*   *   *   *

The cravings came and went, sometimes for berries and sometimes for mutton. Berries, despite the shortening of the days, could be had; they had stores of dried fruit that, soaked in wine or water, returned to their succulence and sat juicy and sweet on the tongue. Mutton was as easy to find as sheep on the hills. But as the days grew cooler and the feasts of Saint Luca and Saint Anna passed, the season for cress ended. Suora Horicula returned often from the market with her basket half-empty. Rabe and *bietola* were scarce. The craving for *bietola* in particular did not come often, but when it did, no matter what other foods were brought to table to tempt her, Agnesa was not satisfied. She hungered for the salty, nutty leaf. Sometimes the hunger was so strong she felt it would consume her; she could think of nothing but the echo of salty, bitter green upon her tongue.

"Can you be so stupid that you missed it?" she scolded Suora Horicula when the nun came home without. "You're laden like a pack mule with every other vile thing in the world, but the one thing I ask—"

She didn't recognize herself in the railing woman who spoke so; the Agnesa who lived within her was horrified to see tears stand in the old nun's eyes. Domiro, who went to market with the *suora*, stood irresolutely by as if he feared to defend her.

Cencio, when he returned home that night, tried to defend the *suora*.

"She's an old woman, *cara*. You know she tries her best for you—"

"How should I know that?" Agnesa heard someone, a possessing spirit that spoke with her voice, scream at him. "Was I there in the market, watching her search? I can't move from the house in my state. I ask for one thing and she fails me, and you just make excuses—"

"'Nesa, stop! Calm yourself. This anger isn't good for you or the baby." Cencio tried to put his arm around her shoulders, but Agnesa moved away.

"Do you know what it is like to have your guts churn for something you cannot have? Laura says it's dangerous to crave something this way. Dangerous for the baby! *He* wants greens, and I swear he'll tear me to bits if I do not have them."

"Won't something else do? Beets or squash or—"

Agnesa dropped onto a stool, hunched around her belly and her misery. "Nothing. I need *green. Bietola.* I swear to you, Cencio, I will die without it." She was not certain herself if the words were simple truth or exaggeration, but the gnawing in her belly frightened her.

Cencio left.

He did not return until after the bells had run for vespers. His hair was tousled and his clothes dusty. He approached Agnesa cautiously, as if she might fly at him or scream in the still night air. She was calmer now; the edge in her belly filled her with bleakness, and she was ashamed of Cencio's timidity with her.

"Where were you, Cenci'?"

"I tried, 'Nesa. I went to every market, asked at the waterfront. No one has rabe or *bietola*."

"You were looking all this time?" Tears stood in her eyes.

"I was. Are you feeling better now?" He sat beside her gingerly.

"No." She shook her head. "It can't be helped. I've prayed that the craving might end. Maybe Blessed Mary will hear me." She could not keep the hopelessness from her voice. "I am sorry I scolded you, Husband." Clumsily she slipped to her knees before him and bowed her head. "It was unworthy of a wife, and I beg forgiveness."

Cencio looked down at her for a moment, then pulled her back up to sit beside him. He held her close, so close she could feel his heart's steady rhythm against her cheek. Agnesa began to weep silently, caught between contrition and the gnawing in her belly. Cencio stroked her hair and murmured wordlessly to her. She tried to be comforted, but the tears still flowed and the shuddering in her body did not cease.

"'Nesa? Do you think it grows wild? Might I find it at the roadside or in the hills?"

"I don't know." Her voice was gravelly. She coughed. "I know it grows in gardens—it was the scent of it from the garden next door that first made me want it, as if it were speaking to me. Cenci', you could go next door to Laura and ask her for some." Agnesa sat up, all at once energized by the notion.

He shook his head. "The *medica*? At this hour? 'Nesa, it's the middle of the night."

"You would go out in the middle of the night to search the roadside, but not ask a neighbor? The bells for compline have not yet rung, it's not that late. Please, Cencio, ask her. She's a physician, she must be accustomed to sendings at every hour of the night."

He still hesitated.

"I really fear—I feel as though I would die without it."

Cencio pulled away. "Perhaps I can find some. In the hills?"

"Why not go to Magistra Laura?"

"It's the middle of the night. I—" He hung his head. "I feel—"

"Please, *tesoro.*" Agnesa touched his cheek. "Just ask."

*   *   *   *

Cencio was gone a long time. Agnesa told herself it was the waiting that made it seem so, but the quiet and the night drew around her like a cape; she felt muffled in them. Distantly the bells for compline rang, and still Cencio had not returned. Agnesa prayed, letting the familiar words entrance her.

At last she heard a heavy footfall outside her door.

"Cencio?"

He was begrimed, smudges of dust on his face and tunic, but in his arms, like a sheaf of lilies, there was *bietola,* the dark green leaves fanning from purple stalks. Agnesa could smell it from across the room. Her mouth watered.

Cencio looked at her anxiously as if she might spring across the room and tear the greens from his arms, but she did not. Agnesa took the *bietola* from him gently, with a murmur of thanks, and made her way to the kitchen. Cencio followed silently, watched as she dipped water into a pot and stirred up the fire. She trimmed the stems and brushed off the dirt; she could not help but nibble at bits of green leaf as she worked. When the water was boiling she dropped the *bietola* in and a bitter, sulfurous smell blossomed intoxicatingly. Agnesa heard the growl of her stomach and took the pot from the fire before the *bietola* was fully cooked, poured off the water, and dumped the greens onto a platter where they sent plumes of steam into the air.

At the first taste she felt as if a wave raced through her, rising up in response to the bitter, saline flavor of the vegetable, then ebbing as her body recognized what it had been yearning for. Agnesa ate the whole platterful in just a few bites, without taking the time after the first ecstatic taste to savor it. When it was gone she closed her eyes, panting slightly.

She opened her eyes and there was Cencio, exhausted, watching her.

"Thank you," Agnesa said again.

"Is it better?" His voice was hoarse.

"So much better. Thank you, Husband."

"You ate as if you were possessed," he said uneasily.

Agnesa nodded. "I did. But now I'm well. The baby is well." She held her arms out to him. "*Tesoro*, it is very late. Come to bed."

Cencio banked the fire; Agnesa left the platter and kettle to be dealt with in the morning. The *bietola* sat light on her stomach and her blood seemed to sing with ease, now the craving was satisfied. Cencio took her hand, she laid her head against his shoulder, and the two went up to bed.

* * * *

Cencio had torn his tunic, she saw the next morning. When they had risen and said their prayers, she took it from him to mend and made him put on another. "How did this happen?" she asked, looking at the rent along the seam at the shoulder. "Does your father have you carrying crates, like a slave?"

He ducked his head, embarrassed. "I must have caught it on something. Forgive me, 'Nesa."

She shook her head. "Forgive me, Husband. I'll mend it for you this morning. What sort of wife have you, to let your clothes get into such a state?"

In perfect charity, they went down to break their fast.

* * * *

Cencio's mother and sister often came to visit, each time bringing another piece of embroidered linen for the baby that must be admired and exclaimed over. Suora Horicula

sent for honey cakes—the Rienzi women had a sweet tooth—
and they sat and talked. Cencio's mother or his sister
Ghibilia would begin by asking solicitously how Agnesa did,
but shortly their conversation turned to the perils of childbirth, the charms that Agnesa must be sure to wear or have
about her, the miraculous assistance Saint Margaret of An-
tioch had provided to Ghibilia when her life was all but de-
spaired of. And the ordeal, the dreadful pain. "The lot of all
women since Eve," Suora Horicula murmured sententiously.

"Why do they tell me such things?" Agnesa asked Cencio
after a visit. "Every time they come! Are they trying to
frighten the wits from me?"

Cencio shook his head. "Mama loves—she loves her ailments, and Ghibi' takes after her. Perhaps they're trying to
share with you, be closer?"

"Perhaps. I don't admire the way they do it, then. And
your mother wants to send me a midwife. She didn't like it
when I said we already had a physician to attend me."

Cencio fiddled with the lacing on his boot. "Perhaps you
should talk with this midwife."

"But I have Magistra Laura to help me. If anyone can
bring me and the baby safe through the birth, surely she—"

"If it makes my mother happy, why not talk to the midwife? Perhaps you'll like *her* too."

Agnesa pursed her lips. "Why does everyone meddle so!
Even my father says—" She broke off. "Cenci', did your
mama talk to you about this? *Tesoro*, if it's a matter of obedi-
ence to her—I don't mean to scold—"

Cencio relaxed with a shake, like a cat. "Just talk to the
woman, 'Nesa. I know it would make my mother happier."

Agnesa met with the midwife, a short, round, very busy
woman who smelled of onion and fennel. She had a bossy,
condescending manner. Even her mildest advice sounded
like a scolding. Still, she asked many of the same questions

that Laura had asked, her hands were sure and gentle, and she announced that it did not appear that the medico had done her any harm.

"Harm? How would she?"

"She?" The midwife's eyebrows rose. "A woman passing herself off as a physician? You had much better have an experienced midwife, girl. The saints know what they teach them at that school, but it ain't medicine for living women. Now, I have two charms that are particularly efficacious in summoning angels to watch over your delivery. I can send them to you—"

Mindful of the feelings of Cencio's mother, Agnesa did not dismiss the midwife outright, but neither did she ask her to return. Suora Horicula, reading her charge's expression, began the process of easing the woman toward the door. "She's tired, as I'm sure you see," the nun said as she took the midwife's arm.

"There was nothing particular to dislike in her," Agnesa told Magistra Laura the next time the physician called on her. "But she was very eager to speak ill of you, and to sell me charms."

"I know nothing to harm you in a charm, and it may do you good," Laura said. "If your family prefers someone else attend you, please understand that I will not be hurt."

"But I want *you*." Agnesa was near tears with anxiety. "After all your help, your kindness!" It was not only Laura's treatment of Suora Horicula or herself; the physician had ministered to Domiro when he had the flux, and wrapped Cook's arm with cooling salve and bandages when he ran afoul of a wasp's nest and was stung many times. "Your kindness to me! I beg you won't abandon me!"

"Perhaps it were better if you let your family be your guide." Laura was gentle, but there was a new distance in her manner.

"Don't you wish to—I mean, I believed that you would deliver my baby, but perhaps you—" She tried to think of how to say it without giving offense. "Perhaps it is not the sort of work physicians do. Were you humoring me, being kind?"

Laura sniffed. "Listen to how we talk around each other. Birthing a child is not beneath this physician, child."

"Good, then." Agnesa poured a little juice into her visitor's cup. She had been near tears for a moment at the thought of losing Laura's help. "It was God's own fortune that brought us to live next door to you. You have been my friend in so many ways! I can't thank you enough for giving Cencio the *bietola* for me the other night. Truly, I felt I would die without it."

"My *bietola*." Laura looked blank for a moment. Then, "Ah, yes. *Bietola*."

"When I remembered you had some growing in your garden I was sure you would spare some for me. I'm sorry it was so late in the night—"

"I'm called for at all hours."

"You see, that's what I told Cencio." Agnesa felt light again, pleased as a child. "I think he's shy of you. He looked high and low, but in the end it was so simple. And when he brought the *bietola* I had to eat it at once. Cencio looked at me as if I were a madwoman, but you did say—these cravings are not sinister, are they?"

"No, no, unless you crave something dangerous." Laura was thoughtful. "Is there anything else that you crave?"

"For a while, berries. Then mutton. Now, only *bietola*— and cress and rabe and dark green lettuces too sometimes. But *bietola*, most powerfully. You did say I must indulge these feelings."

"Certainly you must. A craving for *bietola*—pregnancy is a cold state; such vegetables are related to mustard and are hot. It must be your body's way of regulating the humors."

"It must be?" Agnesa echoed.

"It makes sense. Not everything is yet known to us, little neighbor. None of my teachers have ever mentioned *bietola* by name, but the darker the color is in general, the greater the heat. Warm baths with mallow or fenugreek will also help. So." Laura rose and smoothed the fabric of her cotte. "I'm glad to see you so well. Continue so, and call on me if you have need. I'll be busy in the next month or so, but not so busy that I cannot counsel you."

Agnesa was not given to reading subtly the faces of the people around her, but there was something in the physician's expression that made her anxious, as if the *medica* were drawing away from her. "You'll visit as a friend, I hope!"

"When I may. But I will be busy." The *medica* looked out the window behind Agnesa at the twilight as it gathered. Then, recalling herself from somewhere far, she smiled. "When I may. But don't fear, 'Nesa. When the baby is born I'll be with you."

* * * *

Fall rolled into winter. As her belly grew Agnesa left the house only for confession and mass and to celebrate the holy days of Christmas and Epiphany. On a chilly, dreary afternoon when rain coursed in sighing streams over the tiled roof, Agnesa felt, for the first time in weeks, the familiar fingers of hunger, the craving returned. Cencio was at the warehouse, so she sent for Domiro. "Go next door and beg Magistra Laura for some *bietola*," she ordered.

The servant blinked. "*Bietola*, mistress?" He turned to look toward the door, as if to say, *On a day like this?*

Suora Horicula tsked. "Do as you're told, man! Go ask the healer for *bietola*."

"She'll understand," Agnesa added.

But Domiro returned, soaked to the skin, empty-handed. The physician was at the Scuola and the servants would not give anything away from the garden without her permission. Agnesa, feeling the familiar gnawing in her stomach, only nodded. "When the master returns, he'll go," she said.

"Don't you want it now?" Suora Horicula asked. "I will—"

"No, dear *suora*, stay inside, dry. It's not a desperate matter." Agnesa smiled. It seemed the heavier with child she became, the less desperate every matter became to her. "Cencio has been there before. He'll know who to speak to."

An hour later Cencio arrived home, water streaming off the boiled woolen cloak he wore. Agnesa lumbered from the solar where she had been mending linens to greet him.

"Don't touch me yet, 'Nesa," he warned. "I'm wet as water! I feel like shaking like a dog."

She laughed at him but held up a hand. "Before you shake yourself dry, Cencio—will you go beg Magistra Laura for some *bietola?*"

He looked dismayed. "I thought you were done with that—you had not asked for it in such a long time."

Suora Horicula, standing as always at Agnesa's shoulder, made a noise of disapproval. "With great respect, master, your good wife asks for very little. Who knows what harm might come to the baby if she is balked of this one small thing . . ."

Agnesa squeezed her eyes shut, frustrated. She did not like the *suora* scolding Cencio. But the longing for *bietola* was a hand squeezing upon her heart. "*Tesoro*, I've not asked for it of late, but today the craving was so strong! I sent Domiro earlier, but Laura was not there, and the servants—"

"You sent—Christ and Saint John." Cencio's gaze flashed back and forth. "But the servants—no, no. I'll go. You sit by the fire, 'Nesa. One of us is wet through. It should not be us both."

He picked up the heavy sodden cloak and pulled it over his head again, squeezing drops from his wet dark curls to roll down his brow. Agnesa blew him a kiss that he did not see; he was already at the door and facing the rain. She returned to her mending, sitting closer to the brazier.

Giani came a little while later to ask when she and the master would dine. Agnesa had lost track of time. "Your master went out," she said. "We'll wait to dine until he returns." Giani went back to the kitchen; Agnesa was now enough acquainted with the workings of her household to know that the delay would have the cook screaming at Giani, the unfortunate messenger. But what was she to do? Cencio had been gone a long time. Perhaps he and Laura were talking. Perhaps about her. Agnesa felt a pang of fear. Perhaps there was some problem that neither one would speak of to her. Was the baby well? Was she?

Before she could work herself into a state of true anxiety, Cencio returned. She rose to greet him for the second time that evening and found him shoving a bundle of greens at Domiro. "Take this to the kitchen and have it made up for your mistress's dinner," he ordered.

"Cencio!" He was wet and shivering. "*Caro*, did you leave your cloak at Laura's? No wonder you're so wet. Come." She held out a hand to him, but Cencio pulled away.

"No." He was adamant, almost yelling. "No," more quietly. "'Nesa, I'm soaked to the skin. Let me change my clothes. Have the *suora* take you down to dine, and I will join you shortly."

Agnesa nodded but pursed her lips. Something was amiss, but she could not divine what it was, unless Cencio was angry that she had sent him out into the rain. When he joined them at table and the prayer was said, she rose from her bench and clumsily got to her knees before her husband. He looked at her, confused, almost panicked, and begged her to get up.

"I beg your pardon, Husband," Agnesa said formally. "On

such a night, to send you into the rain? It was unworthy
of me."

Suora Horicula was watching with a smile of complacent
pride that her charge knew how and when to make such an
apology. But Cencio pulled Agnesa up, almost into his lap,
and buried his face in her neck. "I'm sorry, *tesora*," he murmured. "I'm sorry."

"No, no," she tried to say, but he stopped her words with
his finger on her lips.

"Eat, 'Nesa. You must keep your strength. Eat."

He pushed the dish of *bietola*, sauced and sprinkled with
pine nuts, toward her. The smell, green and bitter, rose up as
delicious as love. Agnesa took her seat at her husband's side
and they dined.

Chapter Thirteen

Agnesa did not think it possible that her belly could
grow any larger. She went through the house, slow and
ungainly, counting the linens for the cradle, the swaddling
and robes. Cencio's sisters came to visit often, always with
some new gift. Winter had fled early. The days were warm
and sea-scented, and the orange tree bloomed in the garden.
Agnesa was shriven every day, and prayed often for a safe
delivery, particularly after Ghibilia's lurid tales of the disas-
ters that could attend a birth. Magistra Laura assured her
more than once that all the signs were propitious, and Agnesa
clung to that and let her spirits rise.

But Cencio seemed weighed down. Agnesa thought, at first,
that the responsibilities of fatherhood must be frightening

him. Then she worried that he feared for her, that she might die or take some great harm in delivering his son. She told him often that she knew what a loving and generous father he would be because she knew what a good and loving husband he was. She reminded him that she was young and healthy, and further that their good neighbor had told her she should have no problems.

Even that did not relieve him. If anything, it seemed to make matters worse. She did not wish to worry him with questions, but she hated to see Cencio without his sweet good spirits, and when she was worried he fretted the more for her.

Once the winter rains had ended the weather became unusually warm. Agnesa spent much of her time in the garden, seeking breeze scented with orange blossom and thyme. She was sitting so one afternoon, her feet raised to give her some relief from their swelling, drinking water with lemon and cucumber and embroidering the collar of a new shirt for her husband. Cencio came out into the sunlight, the dust of the city still on him. For a moment his face lit with pleasure as it always had at his first sight of her. Then a shadow lowered over his face, as if something had leeched the joy from him. Agnesa felt she could not stand to have that loving regard taken from her.

She called. "Cenci', come sit with me."

He looked around him as if she might have meant some other Cencio di Rienzi. Then he came and dropped onto the bench, apologizing for his dirt. Agnesa took his hand in hers and reminded him that he was her lord and husband and nothing as meaningless as a little dust would cause her to forget that.

He smiled. That smile had become so rare; it gave her pleasure. In that pleasure she forgot her resolve not to pry. "There, you look like my Cencio. I wish I knew what was troubling you so. Are you worried for me? Magistra Laura says—"

Cencio turned his face away. "I wish to God and all His saints I had never heard of her."

"The *medica?*" Agnesa craned forward around the awkward bulk of her belly to look at her husband's face. "But—we are so lucky! To have her so close, and such a friend? The care I have had—"

Cencio's face was dull red. He did not look Agnesa in the face. "The care." He muttered. "Care and *bietola* and more *bietola*—" He was working himself into a fury that frightened Agnesa. "That learned bitch. I swear she put a spell on you."

"Cencio!" Agnesa pushed against the wall until she was on her feet. She circled around him, took his face in her hands, and turned it up to read it. "What are you saying, *tesoro?* Spells? Magistra Laura is a physician, a teacher, not a hedge-grannie selling love philters. She has given the most solicitous care to me and our baby—"

"*Not ours.*" Cencio twisted his face out of her hands and turned to the wall.

"Not . . ." Agnesa stepped away. The only sense she could make of what Cencio was saying was so outlandish it seemed impossible to her. "Cencio, did someone say—did Magistra Laura tell you this child is not yours?" Her legs were weak beneath her; she trembled with anger and fear. "I swear to you by every saint, by the Virgin Queen herself, I'm innocent of—" Agnesa's head buzzed, and despite the warmth of the afternoon her hands felt like ice. If Cencio could believe she was unfaithful, what might he do? She had heard tales of women beaten, thrown into the streets, killed by husbands who only suspected infidelity. She did not think he was capable of such things, but this grim, angry man was not the husband she knew. "Cencio, please tell me what you mean.

Who told you these lies? You are my only love. Husband, I beg you believe, this baby—" She put her hands on the heavy globe of her belly. "He is ours, Cencio, yours and mine. I could never—" She heard her voice, shrill, begging him. "Your baby, Cencio, I swear it."

"Not when he's born," he broke in. "Then you lose me or lose him. She's sworn it. Me or the baby."

He began to weep.

Agnesa had never seen a man cry before, not this way, with bitter, hoarse sobs. Shocked, she wiped her own tears, sat beside her husband, took his clenched hand in both of hers, and stroked it until it opened and clasped hers. Gradually his weeping slowed and he leaned against her, exhausted. His head rested on hers, her head on his shoulder.

"There, you see?" she whispered. "We were made for each other. We fit. There is nothing so terrible that you and I can't face it together. For God's love, Cenci', talk to me. Tell me what you mean."

And he told her.

Almost three months before, when her desire for *bietola* had been so strong, Cencio had taken *bietola* from Laura di Crescia's garden. Stolen it.

"You said you would die if you could not have *bietola* at once. There was no other place to find it. Your *physician* . . ." What bitterness in one word. "She had said we must indulge you, give you what you fancied because the baby must need it. You were in such a state, don't you remember? How was I to know if you would truly die?"

He had climbed the wall—he gestured to the orange tree beside them. "See, if I step there, it's only another step or two to scale the fence." He had gathered *bietola* from the garden. "Not so much, just a little. No one knew. So the next time you begged for it and there was none to be had it seemed easy."

"Why did you not ask her, as I told you to?"

He bit his lip like a wayward apprentice. "I don't know. The first time it was so late, and I feared to disturb her. She always frightened me a little. The second time—how could I tell her I'd taken it the first time? It seemed simpler—"

Agnesa stared at him. "Simpler to steal from a neighbor?"

"It was only *bietola*, not gold. How would she even miss it?"

"And then what happened?" Creeping into Laura's garden like a thief on her account. Agnesa was queasy.

"And then she caught me. I offered to pay her, tried to explain what had happened, but she would not listen. Said as a woman alone she could not tolerate men creeping through her garden. Said as a *medica* she could not permit anyone to steal her material. She said she could report me to the court. You would be shamed. My father—'Nesa, you know what my father is. He would cast me off. You and the baby might die for lack of bread while I was driven from Salerno. I could have my hand cut off for stealing."

For a bundle of greens? How could Laura be so cruel? Agnesa could hardly imagine her calm, steady neighbor threatening their lives in such a way. The *medica* had said nothing of this to Agnesa in the month since she had caught Cencio. *I thanked her for the* bietola, she remembered. *Is that how she knew?*

"She said she would offer me one hope," Cencio was saying. Agnesa had barely been listening, caught in her own thoughts. "One choice. She would forget all, see that you had all the *bietola* in her garden if you liked it, and I would be safe. All she wants is the baby." He spoke faster now. "We will have another, we could have a dozen more. She has no man, no way to get a child of her own. This way—"

"*My baby.*" Agnesa leaned against the wall, shuddering with cold in the warm sun. The scent of orange blossom oppressed her. *I will never want that scent again,* she thought. *I'll have someone cut the tree down. Perhaps that will end this nightmare and I can forget it, Cencio can forget it, and everything will return to the way it was this morning.*

A gray, sour mist closed around her. She heard echoes of Cencio's voice and Suora Horicula's, from the house behind her, repeating like struck brass in her ears, until the mist and the sound swallowed her.

*   *   *   *

She came back to herself, still in the midst of a dreadful clamor. Cencio was saying her name, the *suora* was screeching and crying for someone to fetch the *medica.* Even the birds overhead were clacking and fussing. Agnesa's head sang and the stone bench beneath her was warm and rough and hard. She opened her eyes and saw Cencio bent over her, his face white, his eyes huge and fearful. She said nothing. She *wanted* him to be fearful.

Then, abruptly, she had no stomach for punishment, or for lying on the warm stone bench watching her husband's contrition.

She pushed herself up to sit, shaking off Cencio's help and the *suora*'s fluttering. Like a lumbering bear, Agnesa got to her feet.

"Sit, sit!" Suora Horicula urged. "You're not well, 'Nesa. Do you want some water? Wine? Is there—" She paused delicately. "Have you *pain?*"

Pain? Her heart was breaking and she felt a lump on her forehead where she had hit her head. The pangs the *suora* feared had not begun.

"I am going to my room," she said. Her voice seemed very loud. Slowly she stepped away from the *suora* and her husband, passed into the house, went up the steps to her chamber, and closed the door.

The beautiful cradle her father had sent them, the dark

wood carved into arches and ogees until it looked like a flower-decked cathedral, waited in the corner. She sat on the bed and wept until all her tears were gone. Then she felt hollow, empty of everything but grief and the baby her husband had sold for his freedom.

At last, as tired as if it were midnight, she dozed.

* * * *

It was still light when she woke, the clear and green light of a spring evening. The door to her chamber was still closed. Agnesa thought she heard quiet voices outside the room, but she was not ready to speak to Cencio yet, and to whom else could she speak of what he had done? Agnesa sat up, washed her face, and, used to occupation, took up another bit of embroidery and began to stitch as she thought.

Could she stay in this house? Where would she go if she did not? Her father would surely be horrified by what Cencio had done, but for a woman to leave her husband was a very grave thing: in law she was his. And Papa had so wanted this marriage to wed his fortune to Luca di Rienzi's. If she left this house there would be no secret, she would have to tell her father, and—what would he do? What would Luca di Rienzi do to the son he so often derided? Disown him? Have him beaten? Killed? She didn't want that.

What did she want?

A fat tear rolled down her chin. She wanted all of this never to have happened. She wanted to love her husband as she had that morning. She wanted to trust the woman she had thought was her friend and her physician. She wanted to be a girl again and not know how weak and cruel the world was.

If Cencio came forward, confessed his crime, and made Laura di Crescia's part known, perhaps the law would not be so harsh. The court or the governor, someone would understand. The *magistra* would be punished. Agnesa could keep her child. But Cencio's weakness would be known by everyone.

He had done it for her.

She had told him she would die if she could not have *bietola*. The physician had said she must be humored in her cravings. *When I begged him to find* bietola *for me, what could he do?* She recalled the hollow, unceasing yearning she had felt and had to admit that she had truly believed she would die without the taste of *bietola*, particularly the sharp, earthy, green-and-purple *bietola* that Cencio had brought from Laura's garden. He had gone there for her. It was as much her fault as his.

She kept stitching, although the work was not as careful as what she had done that morning. The red and yellow yarn felt coarse under her fingers, and a stubborn fleck of blood on the collar refused to be entirely washed away. What did it matter, if she was making bands for some other woman's child. When the light faded she put the work away carefully, said her prayers, and lay down to sleep again.

She woke in the dark, alone. Cencio had not come to their bed; had she driven him from the house? Agnesa rose, used the pot, then tiptoed to the door. When she opened it there was her husband, slumped against the wall in the flagged hallway, fast asleep. His mouth gaped open, his head lolled, and in the rushlight she saw salt tracks on his cheek. The dry tracery of tears made the hard knot in her breast loosen. He looked like a boy because he was a boy. He had meant for the best because he loved her. The villain, the evil Agnesa had never imagined, was Laura di Crescia, who meant to take her baby.

Agnesa brushed the trace of salt on Cencio's face with her thumb, gently. His lashes, long and dark, fluttered. He woke and looked at her, mute, expecting anger. Instead she smiled a small smile and held her hand out to him. Her husband rose and, handfast, they went to say their prayers and go to bed.

*   *   *   *

"But I will not have *her*," she told Cencio in the morning. They had gone to hear mass but did not take communion; their souls were too heavy with sins they had not confessed. The day was chilly and clouds stood off the coast, threatening unseasonable rain. "This city is full of midwives and physicians. If she is not at the birth, Laura cannot take our baby."

Cencio nodded, but his face was full of doubt. "She'll find a way," he insisted. "She's a devil."

They walked up from the duomo with Suora Horicula behind them, too occupied with her own puffing steps to listen. At the gate to their house Cencio kissed Agnesa's hand and said good-bye; he must go down to the warehouse. "Take care of your mistress," he told the fat old *suora*. "If anything changes—" He blushed. "Send for me at once." He turned back to Agnesa. "You'll be all right if I go?"

"So long as you come back to me." This morning she felt older than Cencio, years older, and it was easy to tell him what he needed to hear. "Say a prayer for me and go with an easy mind, Husband."

In the afternoon, when she sat on the gallery out of the sun and away from the cloying odor of orange blossom, Cencio's sister Clauda came to visit. Agnesa sent for cucumber water and honeyed nuts and the four of them, Clauda, Agnesa, and their companions, Suora Horicula and Hilaria, Clauda's elderly cousin, sat and gossiped quietly. Clauda, with two children and her body swelling with a third, loved to give advice and was far more cheerful than her morbid sister Ghibilia.

"Of course you must be shriven every day, but I would not worry. You're young and healthy. Although today you are looking pale and tired. You should eat figs to thicken your blood."

Agnesa sipped her water and nodded. When Clauda had finished with what she should be eating she started in on what she would need for the baby, a subject worn threadbare by Clauda and Ghibilia over the last months. When at last she and Hilaria rose to go, Agnesa stood and felt the dizziness of the day before. She grasped the back of the chair in which she had been sitting and kept her feet, but she had spilled her water.

No, she had not. The cup, half-full, was still on the little table with the brazen bowl of nuts. Her skirts were wet. Suora Horicula had escorted the visitors out of the house. Waiting for her to return, Agnesa was struck with pain. She closed her eyes and it was gone in a moment. Then it returned, this time so awful and devouring it seemed foolish to call it pain. She doubled up.

"Agnesa!" Suora Horicula was at her elbow at once, bustling, supporting her. She turned to call for Domiro. "Get the *medica!*"

Agnesa stumbled, but the *suora* kept her on her feet. "No."

"Yes, *tesora*. Come, we'll make you comfortable."

"No." Agnesa could not explain what she wanted, or, rather, what she did not want. The first pains, and another which struck as they reached her room, seemed to take her brain as well as her breath.

The *suora* cleaned her and changed her into a fresh shift like a child. By the time Agnesa was abed someone was at the door, not a midwife but the priest come to hear her confession. The man looked as if he had rather be anywhere else when Suora Horicula left him alone with Agnesa, but he suffered her to make her confession and be absolved. She did not know if her soul was lightened by the relief of its burden of anger. She had all she could do to make the responses

properly and turn her thoughts to God when another pain
struck.

The priest left. Suora Horicula brought her a cup of tea,
which she could barely drink, a flowery, dark brew that
made her sleepy. The pain continued to ripple through her
belly, but the drink took off the edge, made her feel lighter
and loose. She closed her eyes and, between the pangs,
dozed.

*   *   *   *

There was a noise in the room, a tumble of voices, and
someone was moaning. Agnesa fought her way out of thick,
sticky sleep and realized that it was she who moaned, and
the voices were arguing over what to do. Her eyes seemed
glued together. When she got them open she saw Cencio,
Suora Horicula, and a small, wizened woman in dusty brown,
each talking over the other, hands waving. She wanted to
shriek at them, tell them to go away if they would not help
her. And Cencio should not be there, surely that was bad
luck.

Another wave of pain broke over her. She closed her
eyes, and when the pain ebbed a little someone—she did not
look to see who—held a cup to her lips and she drank grate-
fully of that same thick, sweet-scented infusion, which soon
bore her back into her troubled doze.

"She can't keep laboring so," the midwife was saying. "She's
exhausted, even with the sedative. The baby is not lying
properly and it won't move for me. Perhaps a surgeon—"

Cencio and Suora Horicula exclaimed in horror.

Agnesa roused herself a little from the sticky, dozy place
where the pain was with her but muffled, trying to remember who this old woman was. Where was her *medica*? Laura
had promised to bring her through the birth, yet here was
an apple-faced old woman speaking of knives.

"Laura," she said. "Get Laura."

Cencio's face was as white as holiday flour. He leaned over her. "The *magistra*? Are you sure?"

"Get her, Cenci'." Agnesa turned, trying to find a way that the pain did not make her want to scream. "Get her. She promised me that all would be well."

Still Cencio hesitated, and Agnesa could not remember why.

"Get her for me. Please, Cenci'. I'm scared."

Cencio snapped an order; he was holding her hand. She felt very tired.

"The *medica* is coming, beloved. 'Nesa, don't die. Please, God, Saint Margaret, don't let her die." There were tears on his cheek. They should remind her of something.

Another pain shot through her, the worst yet. Her body went back and forward as if it were trying to break her in half the way a branch worn with bending will snap. She tasted brass in her mouth. She might die, and the child—she had almost forgotten that it was a baby that brought her to this pass—the child would die too. Cencio would be left alone. That was why he was so pale and frightened. When the pain ebbed for a moment Agnesa felt some pity for him.

"Agnesa, why did they not call me at once? Poor girl."

It was the *medica*. Laura di Crescia's voice was cool and sweet as water. Agnesa opened her eyes; when had she closed them again? She looked up at the *medica*'s fine-boned face, calm and unworried. Laura put her cool hand on Agnesa's brow, then touched her wrist, then felt the hard, rippling dome of her belly.

There was a stir of activity with physician and patient at its center. The brown-robed crone was banished, Cencio sent to order things—broth and hot water and blankets—with the *suora* in his wake. When the bustle stopped, Agnesa was given sips of cool water. Then, in the silence that had fallen when they were left alone, she told Agnesa what would happen.

"The babe is turned a little across the mouth of the womb and must be righted. And he has torn you in his hurry to be born. So first I will wash off the stains of every other endeavor of this day. Then I will help you deliver this child. Then I will stitch you up so you'll take no lasting harm." She smiled as if she were Agnesa's own mother, warmly and with reassurance. "And you will help me, yes?"

"Yes." Her voice sounded feeble to Agnesa's ears.

Laura washed her hands, saying three *Aves* as she did. Then she had Agnesa roll on one side and began a series of manipulations, moving her one side to the other, pressing on her belly as if she could divine the shape of the child within. Thrice she did this as the pain struck. Agnesa felt stupid, as if her mind was being shaken in the same quake. She was slow in following the *magistra*'s directions, turning, sitting up, lying again. Laura made little noises of satisfaction or displeasure as she worked, until finally she stood back, examining her patient's belly as if it were a piece of weaving and she was looking for flaws. She wiped Agnesa's face with a damp cloth.

"I think we have done what was needed. In a little while you will push." She helped Agnesa to sit against the wall, propped up with pillows, then she washed her hands again, praying as she did.

When the next pain struck Laura told Agnesa she must push. Now the pain was fierce, but it had a different quality, as if there were somewhere for the pain to go, a path to follow. "Cry out if you need, but push," Laura said. Agnesa did both, pushing hard and feeling something as deep and terrifying as the parting of the seas for Moses.

Then she heard a baby cry.

Agnesa closed her eyes and said a prayer of thanks to

Saint Margaret. She was so numbed by the pain she had already met and conquered that she barely noticed the delivery of the afterbirth, the sting of the needle and fine flax thread as Laura repaired her torn flesh. She lay back on pillows damp with her sweat and closed her eyes. By the time she had the wit to wonder where her newborn child was, someone was placing the baby, swaddled in linen, at her side. She regarded her child, the cause of all this laboring, and found the baby watching her in turn, regarding her with gray eyes as if the business of life were very serious. It had a damp cross traced in oil on its forehead, and the remnant of some white, waxy stuff in the crease of its nose.

"Go," she heard Laura say to someone. Suora Horicula? "I need to talk with my patient privately. Just a few words."

She washed her hands again, this time in silence.

Agnesa turned to regard her baby; it yawned broadly, then began to move its lips in and out.

"It's a girl," Laura said, "I believe you have taken no lasting harm. Next time it will be easier for you. Now, you must listen to me."

Exhausted and still groggy from the sedative tea, Agnesa knew it was important, what the *medica* was saying, but she could not remember why. At first what she said made no sense, nor could she understand why Laura was telling her this tale.

"When I was a student I fell in love. I was seduced and abandoned by another student, a man not sufficiently interested in medicine or, as I learned to my sorrow, in me. He got me with child before he left, although he did not know it. I lost the child and with it my hope of ever having another."

Laura took Agnesa's daughter in her arms and rocked her absently. "My mistress, the healer I told you of? She cast me out when she found what had happened; she placed a great importance on chastity, more than ever I knew. I might have died, but I did not. I survived. I kept my secret, finished my studies and was examined, and became a physician. I prospered. I thought I had put all these sorrows behind me." Laura rubbed her thumb across the baby's cheek. "Until I met you."

Agnesa was no longer drowsy. She could not look away from the physician. "Me?"

Laura spoke as if she had heard no question. "Not at first, of course. At first you were just my neighbor, a sweet little girl playing at marriage. I did not see God's hand in it until you told me about your cousin, the one who once studied at the Scuola."

Agnesa felt heat rising to her face. She knew what Laura meant to tell her.

"Your cousin Matteo, who lives in Pozzuoli. When you spoke of it, it seemed as if God were whispering something to me, but so quietly I could not make sense of it.

"You told me that Cencio had asked me for some of my *bietola* and even then I did not see it. Not until I caught him in the rain, stealing from my garden. Then—it was as if Saint Margaret had spoken for me. Even then, to be sure that this was what God willed, I promised Him that if the child were a boy I would leave him with you. Only if the baby were a girl would I take her, for the child I lost, and the mistress, and the love. I prayed for you, 'Nesa. I prayed that it would be a boy, but He has decided. I wanted you to know the truth. You'll have other children, 'Nesa. Boys, no doubt, to give your father and Cencio's the heirs they crave. But this child, this girl is mine. I claim her in justice's name."

Agnesa shook her head and reached to take her baby back. Laura shook her head as at a naughty child.

"I won't raise her up here, so close to you. I don't wish to be cruel. I've been making arrangements to move, from this house and this city." She smiled with a kindness that was as awful as anything Agnesa could imagine. "I've arranged for you and Cencio to take all the greens you want from my garden. You'll need to build up your strength, and greens are good for the blood." She brushed a kiss upon the baby's brow and looked back at Agnesa. It was as if she spoke to them both. "Sleep now, daughter."

Tears ran down Agnesa's face. She could not think of a word to say, a word to soften Laura's heart or a word of condemnation. Laura had a claim at law against Cencio and a greater claim against Agnesa's own handsome, irresponsible cousin. And the baby was a girl child. She did not think that Luca di Rienzi or even her father would fight for a girl child, not when both wanted a son to knit their fortunes and property together. Making all public would expose Cencio as a thief. Shame, punishment . . .

Laura was wrapping the corner of her gray cloak around the baby when Cencio entered the room, his gaze all for his wife. Laura said a few words to him that Agnesa did not hear, then, more loudly, "I will send a servant to fetch away my basket. Good-bye, Agnesa."

Then she was gone, and the baby with her. Cencio could not meet Agnesa's eye. He sank into a chair with his face in his hands, guilt in the arch of his back and the silent, despairing shudders of his shoulders. Agnesa, guiltier than he, lay still, unable to tell her husband that the fault was not really his, that it was her family that had brought this on them.

The room smelled of blood and woe. Agnesa was tired but far from sleep. It felt to her that sleep would never come again.

Part III
THE CHILD

Chapter Fourteen

B ietela di Crescia knelt on the seat of the carriage, peering out at the seaside bustle of the city where she had been born. They were riding up the hill from the harbor, past the market and many new people and things. It was plain to her that this place was different from Naples, where she had lived before now; Bieta wanted to see how different and why different.

The wheels of the carriage juddered, the carriage shook, and Bieta was bounced backward into Mama's lap.

"Bieta, sit like a young lady! You're going to bump your head and get a goose's egg, and all my arnica is packed away until we reach the new house." Behind their carriage a wagon filled with books and utensils, chests of powders and vials of oils, and Bieta's bed and Mama's desk, all watched over by Giulita, Mama's housekeeper, rattled and lumbered. Bieta liked the important sound of their progress; the creaks and rattles warned folk to clear a path for them. She got back on her knees at the window in time to see a bearded man in a pointed hat scurrying out of their way.

Mama patted the seat. "Come, sweet. Sit with me. There will be time enough to see all of Salerno. Just not now."

"But now is when I want to see it!" Bieta laughed and shook her head and pointed a plump finger out the window.

"I see horses, Mama! And a woman with a basket of fish on her head! And a priest and another priest and another, and goats." The sight of goats made her think of milk, which made her think of dinner. "I'm hungry."

"We're almost there, *bambola*, and we'll dine as soon as Giulita can contrive it. You'll want to explore a little while Mama and Giulita unpack."

Bieta nodded, her attention still on the street. They had been traveling for days. It was very exciting, but it would be good to be in their own home. When she was a baby Mama had gone to Naples as a physician to Avvocato Rocco's sickly daughter Nina, who was always too sour and tired to play. When Nina died in the spring Mama decided it was time to return to Salerno. In Naples they had had an apartment in Rocco's house, but here they would have a whole house of their own, and Mama would be a teacher at the school. Bieta had been promised a room of her own, for studying. "Will Tomo be there?" Tomo was the fat cat that had prowled the halls of their apartment in Naples.

"You know Tomo had to stay in Naples, sweet. But we'll find a new cat. A good Salernitan cat." Mama smoothed Bieta's flyaway yellow curls from her forehead; Bieta thought she would know her mother's hands anywhere, their gentleness and strength. Mama's hands were always red with washing and washing, paying her tithe to the Queen of Heaven, she called it, but they were soft with lotion Mama made in her workroom. Bieta let her head drop into Mama's hand for a moment, then a man in bright livery rode by and she was distracted again.

The carriage turned a corner, rattled a few yards, and stopped.

"The street is too narrow for our carriage. We'll walk from here," Mama said. The driver came to hand Mama from the carriage; she gathered her skirts in one hand and let him lift her down. Then he swung Bieta up in a circle and planted her at her mother's side. Bieta laughed and looked up at Mama to share her delight, but Mama was already starting up the steep street toward a gate on the left. Bieta ran and caught her at the gateway, looking at the walled courtyard to a house of plaster and creamy stone. It was not a large house as Rocco's had been, but it was not a cottage either. It had two stories, and a deep gallery ran along the upper floor, shading narrow windows from sun and rain There was a shed on the right for the animals—Mama often needed fresh milk or animal urine for medicines. Above the courtyard wall Bieta saw high walls and towers round and square, some with sharp peaked roofs.

"Mama, is that a church? Is it the cathedral?"

Mama laughed. "No, sweet. That is the Scuola Medicina. Someday you'll study there too, just like Mama."

Bieta nodded.

"Has Saint Luke sent us another healer?" A man's voice echoed from the courtyard walls. A stocky, powerful-looking monk, a little taller than Mama and with his shaved pate gleaming in the sunlight, stood at the gate, smiling. It was someone Mama knew, for she hurried forward to bow to the monk and greet him. The monk gave her the kiss of peace, then stood to look at her.

"You've prospered, Magistra Laura. Naples agreed with you. But you've put on no flesh! Still thin as a rail. And who is this?"

"This is my daughter. Bieta, come meet Father Anselmo."

Bieta went forward, eyes down, shy. When she reached Mama's side and looked up the man was smiling down at her in the friendliest way. Bieta gave her best bow and said, "Bless me, Father."

The monk put his hand on Bieta's head. "God's blessing on you, daughter. Although it looks as if God already holds you in his hand. Are you a good girl? Do you say your prayers?"

Bieta nodded. It was the sort of question adults always asked. Of course she said her prayers, how not?

"I'm glad to hear it. Do you like your new home? And do you wish to study medicine like your mother?"

Again Bieta nodded; this time she held up a finger on which a cut had scabbed and was healing. "I fixed that all myself." She was very proud of it. "When I cut myself I put spiderweb on it, just like Mama does!"

Father Anselmo chuckled. "Already an excellent practitioner. So you want to explore your new home, little *medica*?"

Bieta glanced at Mama for permission, bowed again to the priest, and ran to look at the shed where the goats would live.

"She's a pretty child," she heard the monk say. "And as clever as her mother, I don't doubt. You were wed in Naples? Where is her father?"

"There is no father. I adopted her, as I was adopted." Bieta stopped listening. She knew the story of her adoption, how Mama had taken her from parents who could not keep her. It was more interesting to explore the shed. Especially when she saw the short, whisking tail of a gray kitten darting in and out of the straw. Bieta set herself to wooing him and even forgot that she was hungry.

* * * *

The first few days in the new house were as exciting as a fair. Giulita stood in the middle of the great room directing porters to put this chair *here* and carry that bed *there*. Behind her back one of the porters called her "the general," but he did not seem to be angry. Giulita was not much older than Mama, with black brows and brown eyes and a spot above her mouth. Bieta had noticed before that men always seemed to like her, but Giulita was a widow and said she was happy that way. "One man was enough for me," she said. "I have all the family I need." She saw that the linen press was filled with linens, that baskets of kitchenware were carried to the kitchen, and that material and equipment for Mama's workroom were dispatched upstairs.

Mama let Bieta help her to put away the tools and pots and boxes and jars, using every label as a reading lesson.

"Each of those shapes joins with other shapes to make words, sweet. When you can read words, there is no secret in God's world you cannot unlock!"

Bieta was not certain what these secrets were that God kept so carefully hidden, and she wondered if it was safe to go unlocking them. She arranged the mortars with their pestles and tried to make out the names chalked on the jars, happy to make Mama smile.

*   *   *   *

Life in Salerno was very different from the way they had lived in Naples, when Mama had been at the call only of Rocco and his family. Once everything was in its proper place, Mama began to leave the house for hours at a time to work in the hospice where the poor and sick came for help. She began to offer lectures. At first only one or two students came; sitting upstairs Bieta could hear Mama's voice echoing in the big room below her. More students would come, Mama said confidently, although Giulita had a little tuck of worry between her brows and clicked her tongue when she discussed dinner with the cook. When Mama was lecturing Bieta was to stay out of the way, to play or work in the garden behind the house, or to help Giulita and learn housekeeping skills. Sometimes she sat in the shed, which now held two goats, and visited Pido, the kitten who was soon a half-grown cat. Pido grew sleek and round on a steady diet of mice and milk; he would permit himself to be pulled into Bieta's lap and petted for a short time before he disappeared into the roof at the back of the shed. At other times Bieta stood in the corner of the gallery nearest the courtyard wall, from

which she could see the busy street below. Black-robed
monks and nuns walked, heads down, among richly dressed
physicians and unkempt students. Here and there were the
hunched, miserable forms of the sick, rich or poor, making
for the hospice. From what Bieta could see, all of Salerno
was built around the Scuola.

One cool morning when Giulita was scolding the cook and
Mama was at the hospice, Bieta went up to her corner of the
gallery. She stood on tiptoe to grab at the stone rail and pull
herself up until her toes found purchase and she could half-
stand against the rail, watching people come and go below.
Two monks were stopped beside her wall; looking down Bieta
could see the circles of their tonsured heads—the fat man
needed to shave soon. He was very tall and very large; he had
a basket of oranges under his arm. The other monk was
equally tall and very thin, with a nose that bent sharply downward like the blade of an axe. And while the fat monk moved
and fidgeted so that his shadow was soft and gray, the thin
one was very still; his shadow was knife-edged and dark.

"If they bring knowledge to us, that's a blessing," the fat
monk was saying. "If they take knowledge away to the bet-
terment of the sick, isn't that what the school is meant for?"

The thin monk shook his head. "Let them tend to children, or the birthing of babies. But the ones who seek to
become physicians—mixing with men, inquiring into mysteries they are not suited to—"

"Ranulphus, many of these women are already nursing
the sick before they came here. They want only to learn the
best, most modern methods and understanding. Would you
deny a man in the fields treatment for summer ague? And do
you want to go out to those fields yourself and treat the fellow?" The fat man coughed. "If a trained woman can help
him, why should she not? The tradition—"

"Women have no place at the Scuola," Fra Ranulphus

said. His voice was as cold as stream water. "Let them train each other. Let them study among themselves. And your farmer in the field should seek out a proper medico—"

"And if there is none nearby? Should he seek out a quack or a hedge-witch to tend to him?"

"This is beside the point." The thin man looked upward, at Bieta's house. She leaned back to stay out of his gaze. "Letting her give lectures! Bad enough to have examined her and declared her fit to practice medicine, a peasant girl from the mountains. I don't mean to question Father Anselmo's judgment—"

The fat man chuckled. "I thought that was what you were doing."

The thin man ignored that. "He has always had a soft spot for her, from the beginning. I was there, I saw. When she left Salerno we should not have permitted her to return. And Father Anselmo wrote to invite her—"

Bieta hopped off the railing, scraping the heel of her hand on the stone. Did "her" mean Mama? She licked the scrape. That thin man did not like Mama. It did not sound as if he liked Father Anselmo very much either. Bieta liked Father Anselmo, who always had a friendly word for Mama and Bieta when they met in the street. She thought she might like the tall, fat man who had been talking with Fra Ranulphus; he had the same tone to his voice that said he was prepared to like everything and everyone if he were given only half a chance.

Bieta did not like the thin man who disliked her mama.

At dinner that noon, when Mama had returned to the house and they sat with Giulita eating a stew of *fagioli* and leeks and fennel, Bieta asked about Fra Ranulphus.

"Holy Margaret and Mary, Daughter, where did you hear that name?"

Bieta repeated the conversation she had overheard. She

was a good mimic and recalled almost every word. By the time she was done Giulita and Mama were staring at her without pretending to eat. After a moment's silence Mama shook her head.

"One who listens to other people talking rarely hears anything good, Daughter."

Who else was there to listen to?

"As for Fra Ranulphus, he's second to Father Anselmo at the Scuola. He has always been against women studying medicine, *bambola*. But Father Anselmo has stood our friend. When it is your turn to study—"

"Then I'll ask Father Anselmo and not Fra Ranulphus." Bieta straightened her back. "Fra Ranulphus is a bad man."

"Bietela Maria!" Giulita reached across the table to rap Bieta's knuckles. "Fra Ranulphus is a man of God!"

Bieta pursed her lips. Her eyes felt full of tears. She turned to Mama.

"You will always treat the faculty of the Scuola with respect." Mama was stern. "Do you understand? Priest or no, friend or foe, you will be respectful."

Bieta nodded, looking into her lap. She was confused. *He is not a good man,* she thought. *He is an angry man, and he doesn't like my mama.* Why shouldn't she say so? But she could tell that arguing the point would get her a slap. So she would be respectful, as Mama asked, but, "Mama? What *is* 'faculty'?"

She did not understand why Mama laughed and even Giulita smiled, but it was enough. The anger that Fra Ranulphus had brought to their table was gone.

* * * *

When they had lived in Salerno for more than a year, and Pido had become a large, rangy cat with a swaggering step, Mama announced that Bieta knew her letters and must begin real lessons, in Latin and ciphering. "You'll start earlier than I did and be far cleverer."

They sat in the garden behind the kitchen. Bieta was cuddled into the crook of Mama's arm, feeling the steady thud of her heart against her own cheek. She could not imagine being as wise as Mama, let alone being cleverer. The thought of sitting still at a table all day made her wiggle with frustration.

"Won't Giulita need me to help her?" Bieta put the end of her yellow braid in her mouth and chewed on the tail.

Mama pulled the hair out of Bieta's mouth with one finger. "Are you so eager to sweep and sew? When she called you this morning to help her fold the linens you didn't appear so concerned."

Bieta wriggled to sit up and look at Mama. She was smiling, which made Bieta smile too.

"I'm not sending you away to the convent! I'm so selfish that when I come home I want to see your sweet face. So your teacher will come here, and you'll help Giulita, and you'll have a patch here in the garden to grow your own crop, and there will be time to run and to play with your poppet." Mama touched Bieta's nose with a quick, gentle finger. "I don't want you becoming pale and weak from too much study. I'll tell your teacher no more than an hour or two for now, sweet."

The next morning an elderly woman with whiskers and three teeth, wearing a pectoral cross that thumped against her brown robes when she walked, came to begin Bieta's lessons. Suora Luina was a lay sister, living outside the convent and supporting herself by teaching the daughters of merchants who wished them to own a little learning. After Mama's brisk encouragement, the old nun's style of teaching was a shock. "I expect you to do your work," she scolded Bieta. "Do you expect me to congratulate you when you do? I do not dole out idle praise like sweetmeats." The sister expected Bieta to sit utterly still for the two hours of her lessons, to do her work without encouragement, and to suffer a slap when she made a mistake. The first time the nun struck Bieta she went crying, first to Giulita, then to Mama. Both told her the same thing: she was now a scholar, she must learn to please her teacher.

"Think, sweet. What does the sister want from you?"

Bieta could not imagine what the old woman wanted. Her tears splashed onto Mama's sleeve.

"She wants you to do your work. She wants you to respect her. These are not difficult tasks, *bambola*. When she sees that you can do these things—and I know you can—she will treat you more gently."

Bieta doubted it, but it was true that as time went on and she showed diligence in her work, Suora Luina slapped less. She never praised Bieta to her face, but from time to time Mama told her the teacher had spoken well of her work. That had to suffice. It was much better to have Mama's praise, anyway.

Sometimes when the old nun had gone for the day Bieta and Giulita went to the market or climbed into the hills to find flowers and herbs that could not be grown in their own garden. Other days, when Mama took Giulita with her to assist at a birth or sickbed, Bieta was left on her own to run off the energy she had to contain during her lessons. It was not permitted that she leave the courtyard on her own. Mama did not want Bieta to go anywhere without herself or Giulita. But the world beyond the gate of the courtyard was so interesting. Bieta would never have broken the rule had she not found the gap between the wall at the rear of the garden and the wall that fronted the alley. It was irresistible. Bieta peeked through, then leaned forward until she was standing on the street itself. After the first time, when she merely stood in the shadow of the wall and waited to be struck down for her disobedience, Bieta grew bolder. She ventured to the end of the end of the quiet alley to the busier street that ran alongside of their house. Scholars and priests and patients came and went, servants brought parcels and carts, carried tuns and chairs and baskets and bales. Bieta made up stories about the people and things she saw. On the days when sitting still at her lesson was difficult, knowing she could escape the closeness of the house made it easier to behave.

She didn't do it when Mama was home, though. Mama talked to her and listened to her answers, told her stories about the sick she cared for and the students she was teaching, and let Bieta watch and help in the workroom where she made simples and salves. Sometimes, for no reason at all, Mama would draw Bieta into an embrace so tight and fierce it made her squeal, and say, "My daughter! *Mine!*" as if someone might contest it. Bieta squeezed back and said, "My mama! *Mine!*"

* * * *

Students came twice a week to hear Mama lecture on women's anatomy and illnesses; other times some came for less formal discussion, which made the large chamber below Mama's bedroom ring with voices. When there were students in the house, Bieta was to spend her time in her own chamber or helping Giulita, who regarded the students with suspicion. When they had first come to Salerno there were very few students; many men did not see the point of understanding women's ailments, Mama said. Some were afraid they would be taken for midwives or surgeons, and some did not want to listen to a woman lecture. Bieta did not understand why anyone would dislike to be taught by her mother, who had a clear, firm voice, rarely scolded, and never slapped.

Bieta knew Giulita worried about the household accounts. No matter how often Mama told her that a reputation must be built, she looked at the students waiting for a lecture to begin and muttered under her breath about poverty and no bread to eat. It was not that bad, even Bieta knew that. In addition to her students Mama had patients who paid her. "The students will come," Mama told Giulita. "It will happen."

They had been in Salerno almost two years when, on a sunny afternoon when Bieta sat working sums on her slate and scuffing the toe of her shoe against the stone floor, a man on horseback clattered into the courtyard. Bieta did her work on the gallery, and at once put down her slate to look down. The man wore bright livery of yellow and green, and strode to the door like a lord or a soldier, pounding on the door, shouting for the *medica*. Bieta hung over the rail, frankly listening. This must be very important business. When Giulita greeted the man Bieta heard the words "sick" and "mother" and "commandant" before Mama arrived to speak to the man.

"It's a matter of urgency," the man said. "You must come at once. She woke with great pain in the, in the, the—the womanly parts. Will you come by carriage or ride back with me?"

"Behind you on that great beast? I will come on foot, and be there shortly."

"My master said—"

"I must gather what I need." Mama's voice was cool. "Should I come unprepared and be no use to the lady? I keep no carriage, and I will reach the general's house faster on foot. Tell them I'm coming. Make sure there is hot water, and if the lady pisses, retain the urine."

The liveried man spun around, spitting up dust under his feet, and was mounted and gone in an instant. At once Bieta heard a rush in the workroom that gave on to the gallery: Mama and Giulita gathering supplies she might need. Bieta watched from the doorway.

"May I come, Mama?"

Mama looked up from the basket before her. "No, sweet.

This is the important mother of an important man. Giulita comes with me. You must stay here and—" Her eyes were knowing. "Finish the sums that Suora Luina set you."

Bieta sighed, kissed her mother, and returned to the gallery and her stool and table. Only a short time later Mama and Giulita left. Their linen wimples glared white in the sun, and the basket Giulita carried was heavy with jars and packets.

At noon Bieta was summoned to the kitchen to eat dinner with the cook, Mica, and Marco. Afterward she went to tend the plot in the garden where she had planted *cavolini* and peppers and her namesake, *bietola*. It seemed the mice were enjoying the plants more than she would. When she had watered and weeded and played a while along the garden wall, searching for bugs to examine, Bieta returned to the house and took up her Latin, reading a fable Suora Luina had set her.

Mama and Giulita had not returned by suppertime. Bieta ate millet porridge in the kitchen and afterward sat up a little while, playing with her poppet in the corner of the gallery. When the sun had disappeared and the house was in shadow, Mica came to make sure Bieta said her prayers and went to bed.

Some time in the darkest part of the night she was wakened by a commotion in the front of the house, the sound of a wagon and voices. Mama and Giulita had returned. Bieta sighed happily and slept again.

"It was a triumph!" Giulita crowed the next morning. "The lady was in the hands of the angels and your mama brought her back! And the commandant! So grateful, almost weeping with joy. He sent us home in his own carriage, paid the fee I set him without caviling, and begged your mama to be the regular physician to his household!"

"To the women in his household," Mama corrected. "I don't think Maro imagines *he* will ever need physic. Still, he has a mother, a wife, two sisters, and any number of serving women in the household, so that should keep me busy. But most importantly, I was able to ease the lady's pain. It was a good night's work."

"What was wrong with the lady?"

"Her womb had turned and was pressing against her bladder, causing stones. Very painful. I had to treat the stones and right her womb, but the old dame was sleeping comfortably when we left her."

Within a few days it seemed that word of Magistra Laura di Crescia's providential cure had spread everywhere. General Maro was the commandant of the bishop's guards, a man as important in Salerno as Avvocato Rocco had been in Naples. Fra Anselmo himself came to congratulate Mama on her success; the general had the ear of the governor. "You bring the Scuola credit, and yourself, with such a success."

Success calls to success. The number of students who came for lectures, or for the less formal discussions, grew steadily. In a month, another bench had to be brought in. A month after that, Marco was sent to order stools from a joiner, to accommodate all the students. The clamor during discussions— the rumble of men's voices, the fluting of Mama's voice, or the sound of an occasional female student—filled the house. More people came to ask Mama to physic them, and she had to hire another manservant to stock the stillroom and negotiate her fees in Giulita's stead. The crease of worry between Giulita's brows relaxed.

It made Bieta happy that the people of Salerno valued her mama, even if her absences were filled with Giulita's lessons in housekeeping and Suora Luina's in Latin.

Not everyone was so pleased. From time to time, when she sat on the gallery with her slate or a book, Bieta saw a figure like a crow in the glare of midday, framed in the courtyard gate. Fra Ranulphus stopped to stare into their courtyard, scowling. Bieta did not know if he was looking for Mama or if he was angered by her increasing success. Twice Bieta saw him speaking with richly dressed men, physicians like Mama. They pointed at the house, gestured among themselves, frowned, and shook their heads. Once a medico spat at the house, and Fra Ranulphus smiled sourly. Bieta, watching, had to be mindful of her promise to Mama that she would respect the members of the Scuola. It was hard to keep her temper and return to her work.

It was harder still to meet the monk face to face. They met him one afternoon, returning from mass. Mama bowed to him, then Giulita, and finally Bieta, who asked for his blessing as she had been taught to do. Fra Ranulphus paused, looking at her coldly, before he extended his long-fingered hand over Bieta's head and murmured a blessing. Bieta, mindful that she must not shame her mother no matter what the monk did, bobbed her head. It felt wrong to thank him for a blessing so unwillingly given. The monk walked on, and Mama smiled at Bieta.

"That was very well done, sweet. I'm proud of you."

Bieta put her hand into Mama's, shamed by the praise. She might have behaved properly, but it had not been heartfelt. Fra Ranulphus did not like Mama and would do her a bad turn if he could. Bieta resolved to watch out for him; she must never give him cause to make trouble for her mama.

Chapter Fifteen

Tibalt knew the streets and alleys nearest Salerno's harbor as he knew the lines of his mother's face or his father's strong fisherman's hands. He knew the smell of salt and hemp and charcoal, the rough cries of voices in a dozen languages, the grit of sand under his feet when he helped his father and uncle unload the day's catch. He knew the way from the harbor to his house, past the great merchant warehouses, taverns, and brothels; he knew the way to the market where his mother sold the fish his father brought in. Beyond that, what did a fisherman's son need to know?

He was splicing rope and daydreaming in the shade of his father's boat when Erno came pelting along the shingle, yelling for him. Erno was his brother's friend, and Tibalt thought him both stupid and a troublemaker, but there was no question that his distress now was real.

"Tibo!" He gasped, bent double with his hands on his knees. "Drea. You must—" Erno took a long shuddering breath. "Come. You have to come. Drea's—" Another breath. "He's hurt."

Tibalt tossed the rope into the boat. "Where?"

"I don't know," Erno said. "I mean, I know where, I think. But I can't tell you." He turned to look up the hill in the direction of the duomo.

"You know where, you *think*?" Tibalt wanted to shake the boy. "What happened, Erno?"

"I. We. We were—"

Tibalt took Erno's arm and propelled him away from the

shingle. "Take me there. And talk. You'd better be able to find him."

Erno started in the direction of the market. "We were just—there was a fat monk at the market, and Drea found a thistle." He grinned. "We put it under the blanket on his mule's back—"

"And then you ran," Tibalt said baldly.

Erno reddened. "Not until we'd seen him climb on and—we didn't mean any harm. Who'd have thought the man could run so fast? I thought we'd got away, lost him past the market, but there he was again. We tried to climb into a garden, but Drea fell, and . . ." He stopped.

"And you left him. Hurt? In the middle of the street?"

"There was another boy who saw him fall, and he said he'd stay with him. I came to find you." A whine crept into Erno's tone. "What would you have had me do?"

Tibalt sighed. He would have had his younger brother stay at the stall in the market with their mother. He would have hoped that Andrea never became friends with Erno. And he would have had them both think twice before playing a prank on a monk. "All right, Erno. I'm glad you found me. But where *are* we going?"

"It's not too far from the market." They trudged through streets glaring with midday sun. Away from the harbor there was less breeze than Tibalt was used to. He felt sweat run along his sides, and his feet hurt—he had not thought to put his shoes back on. The farther they went, the less he knew. They were north of the cathedral, he thought. Surrounded by blank walls. If Erno quit him how would he ever find his way back to the waterfront?

"There!" Erno pointed down a narrow, dusty street.

Tibalt saw Andrea lying on his side, the back of his too-short tunic covered with dust and muck. Another boy knelt by him with his back to Tibalt.

"Is he another of your troublemaking friends?"

Erno shook his head. "I don't know him. He heard Drea cry out and came to help."

Tibalt raised his voice. "Drea!"

The other boy turned at the sound of Tibalt's voice. He was slight and fair, wearing a tunic and leggings that were of good quality but well worn and a too-large cap pulled down about his ears.

"His leg is broken," the boy said.

Tibalt was at Drea's side in an instant. "Idiot," he said, but gently. "What have you done to yourself?"

Drea smiled wanly. "Tibo, I fell." His face and hands were scraped raw, as if he had slid down the face of the wall before he fell. His skin was pale under the ruddy tan, and despite the heat of the day his hand was cold. When he moved he gasped and the pallor increased.

"I told you, don't move until we can bind that leg," the other boy said. "You'll only hurt yourself more." He turned to Tibalt. "You're his brother?"

Tibalt nodded. "How do you know the leg—"

"My mother's a *medica*. I know a broken leg when I see it."

"Can you fix it?" That was Erno, lingering at the end of the street, his voice watery.

"I, fix it? He needs a surgeon to set the bone."

Tibalt thought. "Can you bind it so he can get home?"

"I can, if you can find some cord and some wood: two pieces this long." The boy held out his fingers to show the length he wanted. "But you must take him to the surgeon as soon as you may, or it will heal crooked and the leg will be of little use to him."

Tibalt turned back to Erno. "Go get what he needs," he told him curtly. He hoped Erno was feeling properly guilty. "Go *now*."

Erno ran with comical urgency.

The other boy was talking to Drea, murmuring about his pulse and his skin as he touched his wrist and looked at his eyes.

"What is your name?" he asked.

"Andrea. Son of Egino, the fisherman." Drea was breathing rapidly.

"Where do you live?"

Tibalt was impatient. "We live south of the harbor—"

The boy rounded on him, his eyes fierce. "Hush." His voice was low, as if he did not want Drea to hear. "I was trying to see if his wits were addled in the fall." He turned back to Tibalt's brother. "How did you fall?"

"I was climbing—" Drea began.

"No, I mean, how did you fall and how did you land?"

"What has that to do with anything?" Tibalt muttered.

"The surgeon may ask. I can see that there's a broken bone here—" He pointed to Drea's left leg. There was something wrong with it, Tibalt could see that. It made him feel a little sick. "But I don't want to touch the ankle in case there is a break there as well. I don't know if he bruised anything inside him. I wish I had a cloak."

Tibalt stared at him. *Is this boy is crazy? It's hot. Why does he want a cloak?*

"A fall can knock the humors all askew," the boy continued. "See how pale he is? He must be kept warm."

If the boy's mother was a *medica* perhaps he knew things. Tibalt pulled at the laces of his own tunic and tugged it over his head. He handed it to the boy, who draped it over Drea.

His brother opened his eyes. "Tibo," he said. "I fell."

"I can see that, monkey. What a stupid thing to do. Imagine the scold Mama will give you!" He smiled. "This fellow here is going to set your leg for you—"

"Not I!" The fellow sounded alarmed. "I'll splint it— make a brace so you can move him. But you *must* get him to a surgeon. I'm just a—I'm only a student, I know nothing yet about bones."

"You keep saying take him to a surgeon, but I don't know a bonesetter, and I have no coin for one. My mother—"

"Take him to the hospice at the Scuola," the boy interrupted. "They won't charge you."

"The what?"

The boy sat back on his heels and stared at Tibalt as if he had just asked who the king or the pope might be. "The Scuola. The school of medicine." He pointed to a cluster of towers barely visible above the walls of the next street. "The hospice where they treat the indig—" He stumbled over the word. "The poor."

Tibalt bristled at being called poor, but he had just said he had no money for a bonesetter. "Where is this place?"

"I can show you. But not until we've straightened the leg and splinted it. He won't like that."

"You mean it will hurt."

The boy nodded. There was something odd about him, Tibalt thought. Still, he spoke with confidence, and certainly knew more than Tibalt himself did. He put a hand on his brother's shoulder. "Drea, this fellow means to help you, but it will hurt. You'll have to bear it and do as he says."

The boy looked surprised. Before Tibalt could ask why, Erno pelted up with a length of coarse rope and some wood: the handle of a short broom and a fresh-sawn tree branch.

"You." The boy nodded at Erno. "You stay near and hand me what I ask for. And you," to Tibalt. "If you'll stay by his head? Help me to roll him onto his back, then keep him still."

It was an awful business. Just rolling Drea onto his back made him whimper. When the boy straightened the leg, Drea, white as new milk, fainted.

"Probably the best thing," the boy said. He aligned the wood on either side of Drea's leg and lashed it there. When it was done Erno ran to vomit in the shade of a tree. Tibalt felt dizzy himself. The boy, however, seemed satisfied.

"That's all I can do. Now we get him to the hospice."

They had no stretcher. Between them the three boys took turns making a seat for Drea with their hands and carrying the boy through the streets toward that nest of towers and spires that Tibalt had seen all his life and never heard named. The boy seemed shocked.

"You really don't know of the Scuola? It's famous!"

"Not in the harbor it isn't." Tibalt felt defensive.

"Well, and I suppose I don't know much about the harbor," the boy said reasonably.

Drea lolled against Tibalt's shoulder, sticky with sweat; the tunic the boy had draped over him kept dropping into the dust. Every time they changed hands and reseated him, Drea clenched his teeth, but didn't faint again.

When they were in the shadow of one of the spired buildings, "I'll leave you here," the boy said. "Across the street and through that archway you'll find help." He had begun to look around anxiously, now they were so near to the medical school.

"Don't want to be seen with our like?" Again Tibalt felt defensive.

For the first time, the boy grinned. "I don't want to be seen, that's for sure, but it has nothing to do with you."

Tibalt thought, then returned the smile. "Runaway? Should be at work? At your studies?"

The boy nodded. "Something like that. Don't mention me to them."

"Well, brother, if you ever need a friend, ask for me: Tibalt, son of the fisherman Egino."

"He's the prince of the harbor!" Drea said groggily. It was an old, stupid joke between them.

"Call on me, or on Andrea, my idiot brother." Drea grinned weakly.

"I'm—I'm Marco di Crescia," the boy said gruffly. "Now take your brother in, for the love of God, before he swoons again."

*   *   *   *

By the time the monks and students at the hospice had done with Drea the sun was low. Tibalt knew his mother would be worried. He sent Erno off to the market to tell her what had happened, with the threat that if Erno didn't return to help bring Andrea home, he, Tibalt, would cut off his ear for fish bait. Erno ran and was back in time to help, with a borrowed wheelbarrow. They loaded Drea into it like a hundredweight of *tonno* and made their way back to the harbor, navigating mostly by guess. Tibalt resolved to learn the whole of the city so he would never get lost again. It appeared even a fisherman's son needed to know more of Salerno than he had thought.

If he expected his father to be angry that he had left work undone, Tibalt was wrong. Egino helped him to bring Drea into the house and settled him on a pallet that had already been laid on the floor of the front room. The monks had given Drea some drug that made him dozy as a cat, but from time to time a shudder of pain went through him. Their mother waited until he was settled on the pallet before she displaced Tibalt at his side and began to fuss over him, scolding all the while.

Egino took his seat on a stool against the wall next to Nonno, Tibalt's grandfather, who snored by the fire.

"I'm glad *one* of my sons wasn't up to mischief today. Your brother should be thanking you for taking care of him, boy." He nodded toward a pile of rope ends by the door. "I

brought your work home for you. As for you, Andrea—"
He raised his fist in a gesture of mock anger. "Do you
think we have nothing more to do than sit and fret over
your useless—"

"Leave him be, 'Gino," his mother said. "The boy has
been punished enough for one day. But if I ever hear of your
being so foolish again—"

"Sibela, I leave your son to you." Egino winked at Tibalt.
"And you, Erno, go to your own home. I'm sure your mother
wants you."

Erno left. Tibalt suspected he was pleased to have escaped
a scolding.

"Now, I want to know what happened. Everything that
happened." Sibela stood over Drea with her arms folded.
Drea looked at Tibalt imploringly.

"He fell," Tibalt began. "They were climbing . . . trees. A
tree. And he fell." He went on with the story. What need to
tell his parents exactly how Drea had been hurt? As his
mother said, Drea had been punished enough for one day.

"And this boy who helped you, he's a student at the medical school?" Egino asked when Tibalt reached that part of
the tale. "Did you learn his name?"

Drea spoke. "Benno? Was that it, Tibo?"

"Marco."

"Marco di Crescia. His mother's a *medica*."

Egino's eyebrows rose. "His mother? Well." He cuffed
Drea gently on the shoulder. "Saint Andrew was watching
out for you, boy. I'd like to thank your helper—or his family. Tibo, in the morning you'll go back to the medical school
and ask after them. I'll send them the best of tomorrow's
catch."

"'Gino, not the whole of it! What will I sell?" Sibela was
only half-serious.

"I'll save a basket of mullet for the stall, mother." Egino

put his arm around Sibela's waist. "Now, do you intend to feed your family tonight?"

Tibalt settled against the wall, picked up two pieces of rope, and began to splice them to the accustomed sound of his parents' fond bickering.

*   *   *   *

It was not hard to learn of a woman physician at the medical school; there were not many. "Di Crescia? Magistra Laura styles herself so. What do you want with her, boy?" The clerk-monk who spoke to Tibalt outside the hospice peered at him. "You don't look like her usual sort of patient."

Tibalt blushed. So Marco's mother only treated wealthy patients. "Her son helped my brother."

The monk shook his head. "Not Magistra Laura. She has a daughter, a pretty, modest little girl who means to follow in her mother's path."

"But I met the son. He helped—"

"I don't know who you met, boy. I've never heard of a son, and Magistra Laura is a very virtuous woman and not the sort to have sons lying about loose. I think this boy, whoever he was, played a trick on you."

Tibalt could make no sense of it. Why lie to strangers? But the boy had hinted that he had run from his studies. Perhaps he'd only give the first name that came to mind. Tibalt went to the market to tell his mother he could not find the boy.

Drea, stuck abed, could do no work. Egino set Tibalt to helping his mother at the market as he had done when he was younger. He did not have to rise before dawn with his father; instead he pulled the barrow laden with the day's catch up the hill to the market and helped Sibela put the catch out, helped her take the fish he had slit open and cleaned and salted and hang them above the table where the sun and breeze would dry them. When the day was done and the market closing, he helped her take down the stall and load the barrow again.

"You're a comfort, Tibo. Drea's a good boy, but not as steady as you."

That was no secret. Tibalt was happy to make his mother's life easier, but he yearned to be back on the water with his father, feeling the salt rime on his skin, throwing and pulling the nets until his shoulders ached and his hands blistered. When his leg wasn't paining him, Drea was now splicing rope and mending nets, which had been Tibalt's work in the afternoons when the boat returned to the harbor. Drea was bored and in pain, but *serves him right*, Tibalt thought. The surgeon had told him Drea must not walk on the leg for the length of two months. Until then Tibalt was stuck ashore.

*   *   *   *

Rigo the baker had bartered three good loaves for four large mullet, cleaned and ready for the pan. When they had sold the day's catch Sibela sent Tibalt to the other end of the market to deliver the fish and fetch the bread. "I'll meet you at home," she told him, and took up the handles of the barrow herself. Tibalt threaded his way through the midday crowd, past the butcher's stalls and the greengrocers and olive pressers and fruit sellers, to the area near the duomo where the yeasty scent of bread announced the baker's stalls. Rigo, a knotty old man with one milky eye and the scars of years of burns on his forearms, took the fish and slid it under his table before he handed the bread to Tibalt. It smelled so good Tibalt's stomach clenched with hunger. He wanted to tear off the end of one loaf now. If he did, Sibela would clout him until his ears rang.

He made his way through the crowd like a fish swimming against the tide, until he encountered a crowd that he could

not push through. Tibalt could hear a voice at the center of
the throng. A magician, perhaps, or a storyteller. People
came and went; when a clump of people to his left moved
on, Tibalt finally saw the man in the center. It was a brown
monk, standing on a stool and speaking in a high, scolding
voice. He had his eyes closed and his hands raised ecstati-
cally as if he was reaching for something sent to him by
God.

". . . dominion over them, as he has dominion over the
animals and all the world," he was saying. "The time of rev-
elation is upon us. God above man, man above woman. Holy
scripture says, *If they will learn any thing, let them ask their husbands at home: for it is a shame for women to speak!* How much
more shame that they pretend to the work of men!"

A round-faced grande dame to Tibalt's right snorted and
walked away.

What the monk was saying made no sense to Tibalt.
What sort of work did he mean? Tending a stall in the market as his mother did? If men were farming or fishing or
making shoes, who else was to do the work of selling?

". . . *the whoredom of a woman may be known in her haughty
looks and eyelids.* Women who pretend to learning, going
among men, holy men, like whores! *If thy daughter be shame-
less, keep her in straitly, lest she abuse herself through overmuch
liberty.* Brothers, surely God will not suffer long these
abominations . . ." the monk went on. He was young, bald,
with pocked and mottled skin. "This city harbors them! *Let
the women learn in silence with all subjection. But suffer not a
woman to teach, nor to usurp authority over the man, but to be in
silence.* . . . A woman who helps the sick, whose gentle touch
and care give succor to a man hurt or ailing in his shop or
vineyard, God and His saints love such a woman if she be
silent. But *these*—" The monk's finger pointed as if an abomi-

nation of womanhood stood before him, but his eyes were still closed. Bits of saliva flew with each word. "Demons . . . take on the seeming of women in disputation, spouting Latin like parrots . . . whores sent to trouble the hearts of men . . . call down a punishment on this city—"

Tibalt shrugged and turned away. The crowd had gathered behind him, and he had to push his way through. He was shoved into the shoulder of a youth who was craning his neck to see the speaker. Tibalt almost dropped one of the loaves in his arms; he meant to scold the boy until he realized that it was Marco, the one who had helped Drea.

". . . offering tainted knowledge . . ." the monk droned on.

"Hey! I want a word with you," Tibalt began. Then he saw that Marco's face was ashen, his fists clenched, and tears stood in his eyes. All this for a half-mad preacher in the market? But the boy's mother was a *medica*. That was how he'd known how to help Drea.

"Come away from this, brother," he said more gently. "It can't do you any good to hear this fellow maundering away."

Marco looked at Tibalt without recognition. "What?"

"Come. Come. My mother wants to thank you for the help you gave my brother. And this fellow?" Tibalt let a note of contempt creep into his voice. "He'd make his point better if half the women in here weren't working themselves. He'll not convince anyone that way. Don't pay him any mind."

He would have pulled on Marco's arm to make him follow, but Tibalt's arms were still full of bread. After a moment the boy turned his back on the crowd and followed Tibalt away. He seemed stunned by the fury of the monk's attack.

"So angry," he muttered. "I don't want anyone to hate me that way."

"Why would they?" Tibalt asked. "He doesn't know what he's talking about." He steered them to the edge of the market and south. "Looks half-mad, if you ask me."

Marco did not seem comforted. "I know some monks, some physicians, even, resist women studying at the Scuola, but . . . parrots? whores? If you knew how hard my mother works to care for the sick, how gentle, how learned she is!"

Tibalt shrugged. "She taught you enough to help my brother. That's proof enough for me." Then, "But I have a bone to pick with you. You said your name was Marco, didn't you? Marco di Crescia? And your mother's a *medica*. But when I asked at the hospice they said the only *magistra* there of that name has a daughter, not a son—"

That had turned the boy's attention. He blushed. "Why did you ask?! I told you not to mention me—"

"I didn't mean to get you in trouble." Tibalt paused to shift the loaves in his arms until they were more comfortably seated. "But my mother wanted to thank you. My father wanted to send you a basket of fish. And I couldn't find you. The monk I talked to said it was your sister who was studying medicine. What happened, did you run away once too often?"

The boy's blush had receded. He looked around him and grinned at Tibalt. "Something like that. My mother wants my sister to study all the time. She says she'll be a greater *medica* than Mama herself, as great as Trotula. I think my sister feels a little oppressed by such expectation."

* * * *

"What's Trotula?" The boy looked at Tibalt as he had when Tibalt had asked what the Scuola was. "Magistra Trotula di Ruggiero was a teacher and physician. She's famous. She wrote books!"

Books! Was Trotula the *medica* the monk had been preaching against? "Perhaps, if your mother and this Trotula are already practicing physic your sister won't need—"

The boy laughed, a clear, high chime of amusement. "Magistra Trotula lived, oh, a hundred years ago. Maybe more. And Mama would tell you there's room in Salerno for more than one *medica*. There are others. A few. It just—it would be dreadful to be so hated . . ." Marco's voice trembled. The amusement of a moment before was gone. In its place only bleakness.

Tibalt wanted to cheer the fellow up. "I'll tell you what you must do. Come along now to my house. I told you: my mother wants to thank you for helping Drea, and Drea himself will too. And if you're hungry, my mother's fish stew is the best in Salerno. And you can believe she'll feed you, boy."

Marco looked around him. Did he think he was being pursued? "I'd like to . . ."

"Then do it. Are you afraid someone will see you in our neighborhood? I promise you, no one you know is likely to be there. Or are you late for an engagement, *signore?*" Tibalt made the best bow the bread in his arms would permit.

"I'm nobody's lord, thank you." Marco sighed. "And I'm always late for something. Look, I'll come to your house and meet your mama. I want to see how your brother's leg is doing. But you must promise me never to try to find my mother! You can't imagine the trouble I would be in if—"

"Surely she'd like to hear that you helped my brother, wouldn't she?" They rounded a corner onto the street that led down to the shingle. A breeze, sharp and briny, swept up from the harbor.

"She might like that I'd helped. But not as much as she'd dislike to hear that I was gone from my home." The boy shook his head comically, then put both his hands to his head to settle his cap. "Promise me. Or I'll turn around now."

"And listen to that monk preaching again? I promise, brother. Here, take one of these—" Tibalt pointed at the loaves in his arms with his chin. Marco pulled one of them out of his arms and clutched it to himself, getting a dusting of meal all down the front of his tunic. "Now, we go down this way, parallel with the waterfront. If you look down that way you can see our boat—" Again he pointed with his chin. "The mid-sized one with the double-ended hull and red striped sail."

Marco looked down the street toward the shingle. "Which? What's a double-ended hull?"

Now it was Tibalt's turn to be surprised. For the rest of the walk home Tibalt lectured his new friend on his abysmal ignorance in the matter of shipcraft, as if they had known each other forever.

Chapter Sixteen

Bieta followed the fisherman's son unquestioning, listening to the exotic language of boats and boatcraft. She should be at home reading Euclid's *Elements*. She should be attempting to read Avicenna's *Canon medicinae*, which Mama had given her the week before as if it were a length of Persian silk or a dish of candied almonds. She should be helping Giulita to mend the linens or weeding the garden. But the day was clear and sunny and the work would be there when she returned. Bieta had pulled on the cast-off tunic and hose she had worn before, braided her fair hair and bundled it into a cap, and set off for the market.

The market was always full of surprises: jugglers one day, an Arab with a lion cub on a chain another, and always the rich smells and colors that were antidote to a life spent mostly inside at her work. No one looked beyond the boy's clothes to see the *medica*'s daughter who sometimes accompanied Giulita to buy fish or flour. When she was small it had been enough for her to edge through the gap in the garden wall and walk to the edge of the street, hiding in the shadow of the wall. Then she'd grown bolder and explored the streets around her house, but carefully so as not to see anyone who might recognize her. Two years before, when she started taking on a woman's form, Bieta had realized it was no longer safe for her to wander about alone. Students and sailors and foreigners, soldiers on their way to the Holy Land: all these would be happy to take advantage of an unaccompanied young woman. She could not face abandoning her forays into the city; instead her boy-self had been born. Bieta had never given him a name until the day she had met Drea and his brother, and in a panic had given him the only name she could think of: Marco, for Mama's manservant.

Tibalt did not appear to doubt that Marco was Marco. He spoke of lateen rigging and rope splices with the same enthusiasm that Mama gave to discussion of the humors. Bieta wondered where, exactly, he was leading her, but she did not worry. There was something in him that inspired confidence.

". . . like to come see how the fish are caught?" he asked.

"I don't know that I could be away from my books so long," Bieta said gruffly. She imagined Mama's horror if she asked leave to sail on a fishing boat.

"How much do you have to study to be a healer?" Tibalt asked. And, "Just down this way, brother." He turned into a narrow street. The scent of salt and lavender and acacia mixed with woodsmoke; in looking around her Bieta forgot what Tibalt had asked.

"Is it a great deal?" he prompted.

"To be a healer? A great deal, but to be a physician, more than that, even. You can't study medicine until you've learned—not just mathematics and rhetoric, but music and astronomy and—"

"Music? What has that to—here we are." Tibalt stood at a door of rough-hewn dark wood. "Come in, brother." He went ahead of Bieta and held the door for her, announcing, "Mama! I've brought a visitor!"

Bieta pulled her cap firmly around her ears and followed. The room she entered was small and full of people, noise, and the smell of cooking. A cat wound around Bieta's ankle on its way out the door. A short, round-cheeked woman bent over a pot on the fire. On the far side of the brazier a toothless, smiling old man was being helped to a seat at a table by another man, sunburnt, broad, and powerful looking, with tightly curled graying hair. And, sitting on a stool near the table with his splinted leg extended and a basket of rope in his lap, was Andrea.

"Mama, this is Marco, the boy who helped us when Drea was hurt." Tibalt pushed Bieta a little farther into the room.

"My hero!" Drea cried. He started to rise; as quick as thought his mother's hand came down on his shoulder to push him back.

"Sit there, foolish boy." The woman turned, smiling. "Come in, come in! How can we thank you for what you did for my rascal boy? I'm Sibela; this is Drea's father, Egino—" She gestured toward the curly-haired man. "And that is Nonno." That was the old man. "Drea, of course, you know. You must eat with us. Tibo, the bread! Where are your wits?"

"Sit," Tibalt urged. But first Bieta knelt to examine Drea's leg. It had been set in a way she'd never seen before, extended straight out, rather than with the lower leg bent back and lashed to the upper.

"I've heard never of setting a leg this way," she told Drea. "What did the surgeon say?"

"Say? He told me to hold on and bite my lip, and that it

would hurt. He was right, too." Wincing, Drea shifted on the bench to make room.

"It's good you went to the hospice; they have the newest treatments there." She rose and, swept on a current of good-will, was seated next to Drea with the old man on his far side.

"My grandfather," Drea murmured for her benefit. "He was hit by a spar when he was my father's age and it knocked his wits a bit awry. He hasn't spoken since—but he listens very well. Don't you, Nonno?"

The old man smiled and mouthed something at Drea. He had a knife and a half-whittled peg in his hands and was working as he waited for his supper. Egino had seated him-self across from the old man and was watching his wife, smiling. The sleeves of his tunic were rolled to the elbows, and Bieta saw the strong muscles of his forearms, scars here and there long healed. She was suddenly aware that these people worked with their hands, earned their bread with sweat and hard labor, not pens and scrolls and theory as the medicos and students and monks did. If she ate with them now, would someone go hungry later?

"Perhaps I should go," she said uneasily.

"Go? And miss Mama's fish stew?" Andrea shook his head. "What's the matter, medico, isn't our fish fresh enough for you?"

She wasn't certain that he was joking. She did know bet-ter than to ask if they could afford to feed another mouth.

"I can't imagine any fish fresher," she said. "But surely I'm intruding. Your mother didn't know I was—"

"Intruding?" Sibela had been ladling stew into wooden bowls. Now she stood, one fist on her hip, pointing at Bieta with the outstretched ladle in a parody of fierceness. "In-truding? Never let me hear any more of that! We were in despair of finding you to give you our thanks. If it had not been for you, who knows if Andrea would walk again."

"No, Mama, I'd be slithering along the ground like the Great Serpent in Eden." Drea made a comic face. "Brother Marco, if you do not let our mother feed you she will weep all evening long and send baskets of bream to your door—" He ducked as Sibela aimed a blow at his head with the ladle.

Bieta felt a bubble of laughter rise in her throat. She could not imagine Mama and Giulita playing so, or so much laughter over a meal. "I don't want to make anyone weep! I'll stay, I'll stay, with thanks."

The table was small for six people. Bieta knocked knees with Tibalt, who sat across from her. She was aware also of Drea next to her, and Nonno on his far side. It felt odd to sit so near to so many men at once, with only Sibela there. They all thought she was a boy; there was no impropriety to it, beyond the huge impropriety of her going about Salerno in man's dress. Then Sibela put a wooden bowl before her, and the scent of fish and onion and coriander drove everything but hunger from her mind. Egino gave the grace, thanking God not only for their food but for the gift of a guest at their board. Then one of the long, dense loaves of bread was passed around the table, and knobby wooden spoons, and the meal began.

Bieta ate and laughed. At home they spoke of Mama's work or Giulita's or of Bieta's lessons. From time to time another teacher or physician would join them, and Bieta listened while they debated the propriety of dissection and whether the bishop would attempt to interfere with the curriculum this year. It was not that there was no laughter at home, but nothing like this. These folk were so lively. They did not seem to disapprove when Bieta was lively too.

When the meal was done Bieta helped Tibalt gather up the bowls for his mother to wash. Then she knelt again to look at the way the surgeon had wrapped Drea's leg with linen, making a handsome pattern. When she rose again Sibela was watching her.

"Marco, a word?"

Bieta looked to Tibalt and Drea, both of whom shrugged as if to say, *When Mama calls, you go.* She followed Sibela through a door into the back room, a long, narrow chamber furnished with pallets and a chest and, at the rear, one larger bed. Bieta thought of the small chamber she had all to herself for her sleep and study at home.

"Marco." Sibela stood behind her, hands on her hips. Her expression was very serious. "You know how greatly in your debt we are for the help you gave Andrea. It is difficult for me to ask this, but, *What are you playing at, girl?*"

Bieta's stomach jolted so suddenly she thought she might lose her dinner.

"Playing—" she began. Then she had to put her hand over her mouth.

Sibela's expression softened a little. "I think you mean no wickedness. And I think Tibalt and Andrea took you at your seeming. It took me a little time to see it myself. Can you tell me some wholesome reason for a girl of—what? thirteen? fourteen years?—to walk the streets of this city in the guise of a boy?"

"I *don't* mean any harm," Bieta began. "I only wanted to—" She licked her lips. How to explain to a woman who worked hard with her hands how exhausting, how same the days were when all she did was study. "I wanted to walk," she said at last. "I wanted to see the city a little. My mother is very busy."

"No matter how busy your mama is, I doubt she would want her pretty daughter wandering about with no one to protect her."

"You won't tell her." Bieta's voice shook.

To her surprise Sibela put her strong arms around her in a quick hug. "I must tell her, sweet. But I think—I think I may have a suggestion for her. I must say I don't think much of the sort of physic that keeps a growing girl inside all day!"

She steered Bieta back to the front room.

"Tibo, I'm taking our guest home," Sibela announced. "I want to thank her—*his* mother."

Bieta thanked Egino for the hospitality of his house. He returned her thanks gravely, then turned to his sons and told them to note what proper manners looked like. Both boys said good-bye, then; even old Nonno waved at her and grinned a gummy smile. Then she was tugged out the door with Sibela's square, firm hand tucked into her arm.

* * * *

Mama was in her workroom when they got home. Marco opened the door to them, and for a moment looked at Bieta and Sibela as if both were strangers. In the same moment that he recognized Bieta, Sibela asked to speak to the *medica*. Marco just stared, but Giulita, who had come to see who was at the door, dragged Bieta immediately up the stairs to change into proper clothes. They stopped long enough to rouse Mama from her work; she gave Bieta a look that said they would talk later and then hurried down the stairs. Bieta heard her greet Sibela in her calm, kind physician's voice. "How may I be of service to you, sister?"

The last thing Bieta heard was Sibela suggesting that perhaps she could be of service to Magistra Laura. Then she was shut into her own chamber with Giulita helping her out of her boy's clothes, not at all gently, and scolding all the while. When she had been restored to her proper self Giulita gave her a pile of linens to hem.

"Do not stir from this room until you're sent for." Bieta sat by the window to catch the last of the light and took up the first sheet. She wondered if she would be permitted any supper that night. A good thing that she had eaten dinner with Sibela's family.

She sat hemming with the tiny, careful stitches Giulita had taught her, until the light was gone and she could not see to work. Then all she could do was wait in the gloom, listening to voices from the kitchen below her, Mama and Guilita and Cook and Marco and Mica sitting down to their supper. A little time later she heard Giulita on the stair, then in her own chamber next door saying her prayers.

There was a knock at her door.

"Bieta." Mama stood in the doorway. The light behind her from the sconce in the hall shadowed her face and made her look tall and forbidding. "I trust you have been thinking."

Unable to see her mother's expression, Bieta nodded. "Yes, Mama." She attempted to make her voice as calm and cool as her mother's.

"Good. Come and talk with me." Mama led the way across the hall to her workroom. The big room, lined with shelves stocked with jars and bowls and packets and drawers, smelled of spice and dust. It was lit by candles in sticks almost as tall as Mama herself. Mama took the high-backed chair by the worktable and motioned Bieta to the stool nearby. The silence between them seemed to go on for a very long time. Finally Mama spoke. "Do you know what would be said if you were found dressed as a boy? About you, but also about me? How it would reflect on this household? Without the respect of my colleagues I can't teach. Without the blessing of the church I cannot even work my trade. And you! You want to be a physician. You know that it is not an easy thing, and for a woman it is that much harder than for a man. If you were caught in such unseemly dress it would likely be the end of all our plans, all your work for nothing. All of this for what? *A walk?* If you want to take a walk, why not ask Marco or Anna to go out with you?"

Bieta looked at her mother, open-mouthed. She licked her lips, shrugged, shook her head. "I didn't—would they have let me?"

They stared at each other, mother and daughter, for so

long that Bieta could count the beats of her heart: ten, twelve, fifteen. Then Mama's shoulders shook. She put her hands to her face. Was she crying? No, she was laughing and holding her arms out to Bieta to gather her in. Bieta sat on her mother's lap, an uneasy fit as she was nearly as tall as Mama now. She was jostled by her mother's gasps of laughter until she began to giggle herself.

When they had both quieted, Mama, after smoothing Bieta's hair from her brow in an old-accustomed gesture, had released her to sit on the stool again, said, "Giulita expects me to beat you. Perhaps I should, so you would remember the danger of what you did, to yourself and to all of us. But the woman who brought you home told me some things. How did she find you?"

Bieta explained. She stammered, her voice caught. She managed well enough to explain how she had helped Sibela's son; for a moment she thought Mama might be distracted by the new fashion of bone setting she had seen that night.

But, no. "But you left your studies then, and today. Those weren't the first times, were they? How often, Bieta? For how long?"

Head down, Bieta admitted, "Years. But not often, Mama." Not as often as she had wished. "I'm sorry, Mama. I didn't dress as a boy until a few years ago. When I knew it wasn't safe to walk out as a girl alone."

"You took that much thought, at least. For years?" Mama shook her head. "That makes it my fault as well as yours. I thought I was giving you a gift, the chance to study without distraction. When I was a girl I worked so hard I never seemed to stop. I thought I was giving you what I didn't have myself." She sighed. "That woman, the boy's mother, says you need more activity than you get studying and working the garden. A chance to run off the hours of study, she said.

When you were a child I knew you needed to run and play, but now?" *Still a child?* her voice asked.

Bieta flushed. "I'm sorry, Mama. I won't ever do it again."

"No, you will not. Not in the seeming of a boy. From now until Saint Domnio's feast you will go no farther than the garden or the gate except to go to mass, and always with Giulita or me. Or both of us."

Bieta counted the Sundays between now and the saint's feast day. Seven weeks. "I understand." Her voice was a whisper.

"After that, the fishwife, that boy's mother—"

"Sibela, Mama."

"Sibela had a suggestion. You know I lived in the hills when I was your age and came into the city for my lessons. And my mistress arranged that I should have a child from the community to accompany me, keep me safe. This is what you must have, a page, to make it clear that your family will not suffer you to be molested. So the fishwife suggested that once he can walk again her son might make a suitable page. It will take until midsummer for his leg to heal strong enough, then he will be at your service. It comes at a good time, too. I had meant to tell you that I spoke last week to a teacher of harmonics. He'll take you as his student, but he's an old man and you must go to him."

"Harmonics?" Bieta's excitement at the idea of exploring Salerno with Drea as her companion was damped by the idea of another subject to study. "Mama, can't I wait until I understand geometry better?"

"Are you having trouble with Euclid, sweet? Can I help you? Isach says you have been progressing nicely." Isach was one of Mama's students, who meant to curry favor with her by tutoring her daughter. Mama spoke sometimes of the beauty of mathematics, the way it made sense of the world, but very little of what Isach said to Bieta gave her any idea of beauty or sense.

She shrugged.

"It is work, I know, Daughter. We all have our work, even the fat Salernitan ladies worried about turning the grain and pickling lemons. You want to do good in your life? You want to be a healer?"

"Of course, Mama."

"Go, then." Mama rose from her chair. "Say your prayers and to bed, sweet." She smiled. "If Giulita asks you, tell her I cuffed you a few times. It doesn't do for her to think I am too easy, and she would not understand what we have said to each other. She's old-fashioned. Now, to your bed!"

*   *   *   *

The weeks until Saint Domnio's feast seemed endless. Bieta had given her promise that she would not sneak out again, but the idea of the freedom to walk the streets of the city was tantalizing. The days grew longer and warmer. She worked her way through *Elements* doggedly; the Avicenna, which at least had to do with medicine, was interesting, but there were so many things to remember. And Giulita was meting out her own punishment for Bieta's offenses; her every spare moment was filled with mending. In the long evenings Mama sat with her, asking questions about *Canon medicinae* or talking about an interesting case, while Bieta polished or sewed.

On Saint Dominio's feast, after mass, Bieta finished the reading she had set herself and was almost done with the geometry work Isach had given her when Marco appeared in her doorway.

"There's a boy at the gate. Asking for you." Marco looked doubtful.

"My page." Bieta nodded as if her heart was not bound-

ing with joy. "Tell him I'll come down shortly." She finished
the problem, put her slate and scroll away, and went down to
meet Drea. He was using a stick to walk and he limped, but
he was able to keep up with her. As they walked down the
slope of her street toward the market, he kept glancing at her
sideways as if trying to catch sight of the boy she had played.

"A *lady*." He was all admiration. "And here I thought ladies were mild, gentle things who stayed home eating sweets
and—"

"Like your mother?"

"Mama? Mama's not a lady, she's—" Whatever it was, it
appeared Drea had no word for it. "But you! You had us
properly fooled, didn't you? Me and Tibalt and Papa, too.
Only Mama saw."

"Your mama is a very clever woman," Bieta said.

"Oh, Mama's a wonder." He seemed as pleased as Bieta
to be strolling in the afternoon air. "What sort of name is
Bieta?"

She grinned. "It's my own. In my family we're all named
for plants we may use or be nourished by. Mama is named
for the laurel, her mistress for cress, and I for *bietola*."

"*Bietola?*" Drea shook his head. "Why not name you for
beets or onion?"

"Mama says the woman who gave me birth was partial to
bietola, so—"

"Bieta. It's pretty enough, anyway. Where are we going,
then?"

"To thank your mama. After that? I don't know. The
harbor?"

Drea frowned. "I don't think the harbor is a place for a
girl," he began.

"If I were still Marco you wouldn't say no."

"If you were still Marco I wouldn't know you were a

girl—and Mama wouldn't have threatened to bone me like a flounder if I took you anywhere unseemly." He grinned. "She'd do it, too. Mama took a shine to you."

Bieta smiled. "I like her too. Perhaps not the harbor. *Today.* I can't be out all afternoon. Maybe there are jugglers in the market?"

They passed an ale shop where two Northern-fair soldiers were quarreling with a man with skin as dark as a sloe-plum; all three were shouting in incomprehensible languages. Above them, two women hung out an upstairs window, their naked breasts glowing red in the sunlight. *What might have caused that?* Bieta wondered. Rouge. They were prostitutes.

Drea blushed and urged her along the street.

"I've seen women like that before, you know," Bieta told him. "They come to the hospice, and we see them at mass—decently dressed, of course."

"Mama would skin me like a mule if she—"

Bieta rolled her eyes. "I'm not a child. I'm older than you are."

"Oh, yes. You're a respectable old *nonna.* It's why you were sneaking out dressed like a boy—"

They bickered until they reached the market. Here Drea was greeted, teased, clearly a favorite, known as well as she was at the Scuola. He dodged between the stalls and shoppers, leaving Bieta to follow as best she could. She lost him once behind an enormously fat man in a leather apron carrying a basket of salami, only to have Drea dodge back around the sausage maker, grab her hand, and pull her forward. He did not let her go again until they were at Sibela's stall.

"I've brought her, Mama!" he announced with the air of one presenting a prize.

Sibela wiped her hands on a cloth hung from her belt and stepped forward to embrace Bieta. She smelled strongly of fish; Bieta's nose wrinkled, but she returned the older woman's hug.

"This is what you look like in your real self?" Sibela picked up the tail of Bieta's braid, which hung long enough for her to sit on. "Why hide such a head of hair under a boy's cap, I ask you?"

A thin man in rich red and yellow livery pushed forward to negotiate the purchase of dried cod. When he had gone Sibela turned back to them.

"I am in your debt," Bieta said. She bowed formally. "For talking to my mother. I was afraid—"

"Did she beat you?" Drea was avid. His mother cuffed him.

"It's turned out well, sweet. You owe me no thanks. Though I think well of you for it. See, Drea? This is how gentlefolk behave." Sibela cuffed Drea once more with rough affection. "I expect to have you dine with us from time to time if your gracious mother permits it. But now I have fish to sell, and I'm sure the *magistra* did not intend you to add fishmongering to your education. Run along, children. Andrea, you be mindful of all I told you!"

He ducked his head in acknowledgment and the two of them left.

Two stalls along Bieta stopped. "What did she tell you?"

"I told you: Not to let you go anywhere there might be danger. To guard your tender gaze so you don't see anything unsuitable. That you're a fragile flower . . ." His voice climbed into a mocking falsetto.

This time it was Bieta who cuffed him. "I've seen anatomy charts in my mother's workroom! I can't think of anything more unsuitable than that!"

They stopped to watch as a man shuffled a bean under a cup, hiding it so that no one could tell where it was. They watched a pair of boys younger than Drea vault and tumble, imperiling the fruit stands on either side of them. The green-grocers had fresh sage and mint and basil; the tanner had goatskins freshly tanned, smelling faintly of piss. The color of the market seemed brighter for Bieta's freedom to enjoy it.

When the bells of the duomo rang for none Drea reminded her that it was time to return home.

"Next time the harbor. I know the market, I've been coming to the market for years. I want to see *new* things!"

"Mama will murder me," Drea said under his breath, but loud enough to hear.

Just past the duomo, as they argued over the places they might explore, they turned onto the street that would take them back to the Scuola and Bieta's house. A tall monk stood in the center of the street, blocking their way. He stood still, looking toward the market; it did not seem he noticed them. With a bad taste in her mouth, Bieta realized that it was Fra Ranulphus—*Father* Ranulphus, now. Mama said he had been ordained.

Drea had been walking backward, facing her. Before Bieta could stop him he bumped into the priest. There was a flurry as Drea untangled himself from the monk's robes and backed away. "Your pardon, brother." He smiled and bowed and would have continued onward, but Father Ranulphus grabbed Drea's arm.

"Is this your respect for the church, boy?"

Bieta could see how tightly the priest was gripping Drea's arm. His knuckles were white, and Drea's eyes widened with surprise and pain.

"No, brother. I'm sorry, brother. Your pardon, I beg."

Father Ranulphus looked down at Drea. He did not move, nor did he release him.

Bieta spoke. "He meant no harm, truly, Father." She bowed to the priest. Ranulphus looked down at her as if his cat had suddenly spoken.

Finally, "*You* are the daughter of Laura di Crescia." Surely he knew she was; she had met him many times before. Father Ranulphus's words sounded like an accusation.

"Yes, Father." Bieta kept her eyes down and her voice meek.

"You are not at your studies?"

"I came out—" She permitted herself a small untruth. "I came to do an errand, Father. Now I am returning to my books."

The answer did not appear to please the monk.

"Your mother has you studying hard?"

"Yes, Father. Mathematics and rhetoric. I am to begin to study harmonics next week."

That answer pleased him no more than the last. His frown deepened. "What do you understand of mathematics, girl? Had you not better be learning to stitch or do some useful thing?"

"I'm reading Euclid," Bieta said. "And Avicenna."

"To what end? A trained ape may run its finger up and down a page. A physician must understand what he's reading."

"Yes, Father." Bieta pressed her lips together to keep anything less respectful from escaping.

"Your mother means you to study at the Scuola." Father Ranulphus shook his head. "We'll see. It will not be easy, no matter who your mother is or how she has indulged you. Be ready, girl. "

Bieta tilted her chin up. "I will, Father. I pray God will support me—"

"If you would please God, girl, you'd do some more womanly thing." Ranulphus waved his hand vaguely. "Not playing at reading."

Drea was watching all this with his mouth open like a codfish. "Will you pardon us, Father? I am expected home."

The priest was still holding Drea's arm. Bieta looked at

his hand. After a moment Father Ranulphus recalled himself and took the hand away. "Go, then."

The priest turned away, but Bieta, moved by some malicious spirit, called to him. "Your blessing, Father? For us both?"

Father Ranulphus could not refuse. He stretched his hand above her hand. "God be with you." He waved toward Drea. "And you as well, boy." He turned away.

Bieta and Drea stared after him.

"Who in the name of Saint Dionysius's slumber is *that*?"

"Father Ranulphus. He's second to the Superior of the Scuola. He doesn't like women scholars."

"It don't seem he likes the sons of fishermen any better." Drea rubbed his arm.

Bieta's hands had fisted as she spoke to the priest. Now she shook them to loosen the tension.

"He's a grim fellow, isn't he?" Drea stared at the priest's retreating form. "Looked as though he thought he was blessing a *calamaro*."

Bieta giggled. "*You* are the *calamaro*. I—you heard him—I'm an ape!"

"Come then, Magistra Ape. I'll take you back to your circus."

Chapter Seventeen

Some days, when Egino's boat returned early and Tibalt had wheeled a barrow piled with bream, mullet, and one-eyed sole up the hill to the market, he joined his brother and the physician's daughter. There was no formality be-

tween Drea and Laura di Crescia; his brother wore no livery
and was as like to lead as follow decorously behind. Tibalt,
who came only as a friend, liked Bieta; she was a curious
mix of authority and curiosity, courage and ignorance.
Pretty, too, now she was dressed properly and wore her long
golden braid down. How had he ever believed she was a boy?

Tides flowed and the seasons changed. Tibalt grew taller
than his father, and Sibela spoke sometimes of the day when
he would have a wife of his own. Bieta di Crescia, with her
yellow hair and frank manner, was growing too. Her studies
grew more demanding; Drea was always busy escorting Bieta
to lessons, but time for their wandering walks had diminished. Tibalt could see the day coming when she would slip
away from them as a friend and they would see her no more.
He dreaded that day. If he were honest with himself, when
Tibalt daydreamed, standing in the bow of his father's boat
and casting nets out, it was of Bieta. Which was foolish. She
was the physician's daughter and was meant to be a *medica*
herself. He was a fisherman. His brother was her page.

None of this kept Tibalt from joining Drea when he
could, or sometimes using his authority as the elder to dismiss him altogether. At such times Drea smirked as he walked
away, but Bieta did not seem to notice it.

At winter's end, when Drea had been acting as Bieta's page
for almost three years, Tibalt saw a change come over her.
She was as friendly to Drea and to Tibalt as she had ever
been, but there was such heaviness in her step and worry in
her eyes. Her lips pursed and there was a crease between her
brows. Drea noticed but did not ask what the matter was;
that he left for Tibalt.

"Are you sad?" They walked along a high southern street
overlooking the harbor, enjoying the clash of winter's breeze
and the returning warmth of the sun. Great clouds scudded
along the horizon, and the trees around them hinted at

green. "With each day you look more troubled. Is your work so hard?"

"Hard?" The crease between her brows deepened, then relaxed. "No, my work is no harder than usual."

Drea, on her other side, laughed. "So it's no harder than, say, moving a mountain or squeezing lead from an apple."

"Oh, yes," Bieta teased back. "No harder than to ram some new notion into your thick skull, gudgeon."

They would have begun to bicker as they often did, but Tibalt interrupted.

"I mean it, Bieta. Something is wrong. What is it?"

"How do you know—" She stopped. "You always seem to know, Tibo. How do you do that?"

He would not be distracted. "What is it?"

She pursed her lips. "A dear friend of our house is dying. The Superior of the Scuola, Father Anselmo. I've known him since I was small, and Mama has known him since she was *my* age."

Drea and Tibalt crossed themselves. "The medicos can't save him?"

Bieta shook her head. "Even the best of them can't stay death forever. They've tried; Father Anselmo is much loved. Now the members of the Scuola want only to make his last hours easy."

"What is he dying of?" Drea took a short stick from his pocket and began to whittle at it. Tibalt wanted to clout his brother, who didn't seem to notice Bieta's distress.

"He has the chancre in his belly. Mama says every remedy has been tried, every strategy exhausted. His humors grow daily more deranged, his eyes are yellow with bile—" Bieta's voice broke. "Mama says he shows great grace."

Now Drea looked chastened. "I am sorry." More thoughtfully, "What will happen at the Scuola?"

"The Scuola will go on as ever. That's what Mama says. It's older than Father Anselmo and will outlast him and us and every other person now living. But it will be different. The new Superior . . ." Something in her voice suggested to Tibalt that this was part of her worry. It was someone she did not like.

"You know who it will be?"

"Father Ranulphus." Bieta spoke the name as if it were a hundredweight dropped from a height.

Drea cast aside his half-whittled peg. "That scarecrow monk who almost broke my arm?"

"The same." Bieta recalled herself. "He's is a good and holy man." It sounded like a lesson recited. "He has worked hard for the Scuola, and—"

"And he called you an ape," Drea finished.

Tibalt felt an outrage out of proportion to the priest's offense. "An ape?"

"That was a long time ago." Bieta shrugged, as if the matter had ceased to trouble her. "Father Ranulphus is a very . . . traditional scholar. He doesn't feel that women should study here, not even the nuns who come to take learning back to their houses."

Drea added, "He called Bieta an ape who could read, and—"

She rolled her eyes. "No, he said that any ape could read, but a physician must understand. And he's right—"

"Apes can read?" Drea raised his eyes, mock-astonished. Tibalt felt an unbrotherly urge to knock Drea to the ground and make him eat the dust. Couldn't he see this was important to Bieta?

"Physicians *must* understand, idiot." She turned back to Tibalt. "Giulita is afraid that Father Ranulphus could make it hard for Mama to teach, but Mama says no. The tradition is too old; he can't stop a woman who is practicing or teaching

without grave cause. But." Her voice dropped. "He could
make it harder for new women to become students."

"Like you."

That was the crux of it.

"You needn't worry," Tibalt told her. "With all you know?
And all that Magistra Laura has already taught you? You're
practically a *medica* now!"

"Hardly." But she smiled at Tibalt, and it was as if the sun
rose again. "And if I do not get to Ser Bonamio's rooms for
my astronomy lesson, I won't be a *medica* at all."

They turned their steps back in the direction of the Scuola
and their conversation became more general. Tibalt had carried Bieta's book and slate. When they reached Ser Bonamio's
he returned them to her.

"Thank you, Tibo. I'll see you another time." Bieta
turned to Drea, already hunkering down against the wall to
wait. "You I'll see when Ser Bonamio is done with me."

Tibalt watched her go up the short stairs to the tutor's
rooms. As soon as she was out of earshot Drea started in.

"*You're practically a medica now,*" he repeated in a honey-
sweet falsetto. "*Oh, Bieta . . .*"

Tibalt swung a fist at his brother's head.

"I'm sorry, I'm sorry!" Drea made a game of putting
his arms around his head. "Your pardon, Brother! Don't
hurt me."

Tibalt slid down the wall until he sat next to his brother.
"I won't hurt you, but not because you don't deserve it, sprat.
Mama wouldn't care for me to knock your head off, even
when you deserve it."

Drea took a new twig from his pocket and began to whittle. They used pegs to fix the boat; those they did not use
could always be traded in the harbor. "What are you going
to do?" he asked after a while.

"Do?"

"About Bieta."

Tibalt shrugged. "What's to do? She'll be a physician in another few years. I'll still be a fisherman."

"Not just any fisherman! Tibalt, prince of the harbor!"

"Not the sort of prince for a girl like Bieta."

"Anyway, you'll wed sometime. Mama's been looking for a girl for you," Drea pointed out.

"I hope she's not looking very hard. Papa needs me working with him and—"

"And you've set your heart on a girl you can't have. Why do you come walking with us, Tibo? Surely that's more hurt than pleasure for you?"

Tibalt examined his square, callused hands. "Is it so obvious?"

Drea skinned the thin bark off the twig in his hand. "It is to me. I don't know that Bieta sees it, but she's all for her studies and wouldn't see the Angel Gabriel come to call her to supper."

"You'll keep your mouth shut."

"Oh, yes." Drea grinned. "I have no wish to wake with my mouth sewn closed with fishing line."

Tibalt got to his feet and swatted the dust from the back of his tunic. "See that you don't. I should go help Mama take down the stall. See you at home, Brother."

* * * *

Father Anselmo lingered for some months. When Tibalt saw Bieta he asked after the priest; the news was never good. Finally, one day when he had gone to help Sibela pack up the stall for the night, Bieta and Drea appeared. She had been crying, Tibalt saw at once. Sibela hugged her without asking the matter; it was Drea who muttered, "The blessed old priest has died at last. The scarecrow runs the Scuola now."

"Andrea! Go home until you learn some mastery over your tongue!" Sibela put a pile of baskets into his arms and pushed him unceremoniously on his way. "Pardon, sweet. You know that sometimes Drea's sense of humor gets in the way of his sense. Tibo, my love, will you take Bieta home?"

"Of course."

Sibela gave Bieta another hug. "I grieve for your loss, child. Tibo will see you safely home. And you must come take your supper with us some time," she reminded her. Every time Bieta saw her Sibela made the invitation. It was only rarely that her mama let her go. "Run along, run along. Tibo, I'll see you later."

As they made their way through the crowds Tibalt kept his hand near, but not on, Bieta's elbow, so he could help her if need arose. He was not her page; he need not walk a pace behind her.

"I'm sorry for your loss."

Bieta smiled, a small, watery smile. "Thank you. He was such a very good man, and a good friend to our household. I thought—" She stopped and began again. "I hoped he would be at the Scuola when it came time for me to enter into study."

"This other fellow?"

"Father Ranulphus. There's so much to learn. Even with hours of studying, there are some things for which I have little ability. I can't see what some of it has to do with healing."

"Then why learn it? Why not just learn the healing part?"

She shook her head. "To study at the Scuola you must have learned the other things first—rhetoric and mathematics and geometry and music and poetry and astronomy—"

"What have they to do with fixing sick people's ills? Music? Do you whistle the fever from a man? Or poetry? It makes no sense."

The smile Bieta gave Tibalt was wide and grateful. It warmed him until he felt his face flush. Then a shadow came over her face. "Not the singing sort of music—I study the mathematics of intervals between notes in—" She broke off.

"I could tell you what they tell me: music and geometry and dialectic and rhetoric are the basis of all learning." She was mimicking someone, but Tibalt did not know who. "The real answer is that without mastering those subjects I won't be admitted to study at the Scuola."

"But not every healer studies there. There are a few who live near us who I swear can't read any more than I can."

"Healers, not physicians. My mother was trained by a mountain healer, a very skilled midwife and herbalist. But without training at the Scuola she would never have been a physician. And physicians are better learned, more respected."

"Richer?"

Bieta pushed him away. "Physicians know the most. And what would I do else? It's what Mama has meant for me since I was small, to follow in her footsteps as she followed in her mother's. Should I marry and run some fat old merchant's household as Giulita does for Mama, or—"

"You don't mean to marry?"

"I never think of it. There's no reason I couldn't. There are even some couples where both man and wife were medicos. The physicians who are monks don't of course. And Mama never did, but there's no reason I—one—could not."

"No reason." Tibalt's throat was dry. "You say your mama has meant you to be a physician since you were small; but is it what you want, Bieta? You're fretting yourself sick—"

"It's natural I should worry. I don't have Mama's gifts! She started much later than I, worked far harder. She's told me often. She expects me to do better than she did! I should work harder than I do."

"Harder? Are there that many hours in a day?" Tibalt tried to speak lightly. They had reached a crossroad. To the right a stepped and dusty path led up toward the hillside. Tibalt had never been that far from the harbor, but the green hills looked inviting. To the left lay the broader street that would take them to the Scuola and Laura di Crescia's house. He wanted to take Bieta's hand and explore the hills, walk away from the school and the harbor. "Will it please you if you break your brain with studying?" He heard anger in his voice and was dismayed. Bieta heard it too, and took a step down the street that led to her home.

"If you're going to scold me, Tibo, I'll go home alone."

"No. No, don't do that. I worry for you. I think you'll be a great healer, but not if you torment yourself with all this other stuff, stars and music and poetry!" Daringly, he reached for Bieta's hand and turned it palm up, as if to read something written there. "If the power of healing lies here"—he shook the hand he held—"and here"—he touched her brow—"then why do you need the rest of it?"

She drew her hand out of his. "I told you. You don't understand."

"Of course I don't. I'm just a fisherman and a fisherman's son. I can't be expected to understand."

This time it was Tibalt who stepped away. His shoulders were rigid. He had let himself become too angry, and he had let Bieta see it, and now she was watching him with astonishment and concern.

"All this because I am studying astronomy?"

Tibalt looked away long enough to take three deep breaths and control his wayward temper.

"I don't want to quarrel with you," she told him. "You're the best friend I have." It was cold comfort. "Besides, if you leave me here I'll probably get lost and never find my way home." This, despite the fact that the spires and towers of the medical school were visible behind her, rising above the meaner dwellings and shops nearby.

Tibalt grinned. "Liar. Three words ago you wanted to

walk home on your own. Turn around, take a few steps, and you're there."

"I don't *know* that." She returned his smile.

"If you don't, you need to make some room in your head for useful knowledge."

"And knowing how to splint Drea's leg wasn't useful?" She fell into step beside him.

"That was useful," he allowed. "But what good is reading and all the rest if you can't find your way from one place to another?"

"When I'm a wealthy physician I'll hire someone to guide me," she said. "Or I'll be carried through the streets in a chair—"

"A gilded chair, with pages fore and aft to blow a horn and clear the way. And a lion on a chain, or an elephant, to guard you."

When they reached the gate of Magistra Laura's house the imagined entourage had swelled to include Cathayan acrobats and Arab swordsmen, and Bieta was laughing. At the gate Tibalt swept Bieta a grand bow and took his leave. He watched her cross the courtyard and enter the house. When he looked up he saw someone else watching, a spare, slender woman, her pale face framed by the white wimple. Tibalt bowed toward the house again and left.

* * * *

He did not seek out Drea and Bieta for weeks after. The argument with Bieta had brought him too close to announcing his feelings. There was no point to that, even if Bieta was kind. He confined himself to his work, to helping his mother, to working in the lengthening evenings on repairs of the sails, then of the boat itself. He thought that his father suspected he was working off some feeling, but it was not Egino's way to ask.

Easter neared and the farmers were absent from the marketplace, readying their fields, then planting. Tibalt had gone up to the market to help his mother at the stall; there were some bream left today, and Sibela stopped to buy onions and fennel with which to cook them. At home, Tibalt had rinsed the market baskets and put them out to dry and was about to fetch wood for the brazier when someone knocked at the door.

The woman who stood there was as slender as a knife, meticulously tidy in her dress. He had never met her, but he recognized Magistra Laura di Crescia, Bieta's mother.

The *medica* had never come to their house before. Had she brought Bieta with her? Tibalt looked past Magistra Laura's shoulder to see. Bieta was not there, only a manservant leaning against the wall of the house across the road.

"May I come in?" She had a low, firm voice, cool and full of authority.

He bowed belatedly and welcomed her, giving her the chair with the back that was Nonno's.

"Are you come to speak with my mother? She'll be home very soon."

"No. I want to speak with you." The *medica* looked around the room, taking in every detail. The earthen floor, the brazier, the kettles stacked nearby, the table and benches made by Egino and Nonno. She turned back to Tibalt and smiled.

"This is a pleasant place."

He was surprised. He had expected a judgment, criticism. "Thank you."

He waited

"I see you sometimes with my daughter Bieta," she said at last. "When your brother should be with her. Or sometimes with both of them."

Did she mean to scold Drea for leaving Bieta in his care?

"Once my brother felt ill, and another time my mother sent him home. I didn't want to abandon her to walk home on her own, but Bieta's safe with me."

"I'm sure she is. And of course, you chat as you walk?"

He nodded. He was perplexed. What could this woman want?

"You know that my daughter is studying to join the Scuola and become a physician." Not a question, but Tibalt nodded again. "It is a hard study—I remember it very well. Bieta has many advantages I did not have; my mistress was poor, and I lived in the hills above the city." She indicated with a tilt of her chin which hills those were. "Bieta lives comfortably, has only so much work as to make a useful change for her mind and to keep her hands busy, and at your mother's suggestion she has exercise in walking to and from her lessons. Still, she struggles."

She looked at Tibalt, but he could think of nothing to say.

"Lately she has been questioning our plans. Questioning her desire to study at the Scuola, a desire she has held since she was small. I ask myself where these questions come from." Laura put up a hand as if to forestall an answer. "The work is hard. The benefit of some of it she does not yet see. I understand that—I couldn't see the point of mathematics until my tutor made it clear to me. So perhaps I will have to find her teachers who better help her make the connection between what she studies now and what she will study later."

She stopped for a moment. "May I have some water? The walk here has parched my throat."

Tibalt rose and dipped some water from the cistern into a wooden cup. The hand that offered the cup to the *medica* seemed to belong to someone else.

"Thank you." She went on. "Certain things have changed at the Scuola of late. What was a difficult preparation has now become harder. Bieta questions whether she will be able to study at the Scuola. She fears that all our planning has been for naught. *She is wrong.*" The *medica* looked at him fiercely. "Do you understand?"

Tibalt felt his heart thudding in his chest: five, six, seven, eight. Why did he feel so panicked? "Of course, *magistra*," he said. "I know she fears that Father Ranul—"

"The Superior will make stringent requirements. She will meet them. She can do this—so long as no one undermines her confidence or her resolve."

"I would never—"

The *medica* raised her hand again. "I have been a physician for many years, longer than you or my daughter have been alive. I have some skill at reading faces, young man. You fancy that you love my daughter."

Tibalt went still. There was nothing he could think to say, to deny or agree.

"If you do love her you'll leave her alone. Do not make her question what she's doing. I do not think Bieta knows of your feelings—she's very young in some ways—and I do not want her confused by them. I have some experience of the love of young men. I almost lost *my* confidence and *my* resolve, but that man showed me his true colors. I took some hurt before he was done with me. I will not permit that to happen to my daughter. I will not let you seduce her from her studies or our plans. If you care for her in the least, you will understand why I say this, and you will agree. After today, you will not see her again, nor will your brother. My housekeeper will take up the task of attending Bieta to her lessons. Do we have an understanding?"

It was as if there were stones in his throat. He could not speak.

"Do you understand?"

He nodded.

Laura di Crescia got to her feet. "Good. I will tell your brother this evening that his services are no longer needed. Surely your father will welcome more help? Please give my respect to your mother."

At the door she turned and said, "Thank you, both of you boys, for your friendship for my daughter. I know she valued it."

Then she was gone. Tibalt sat with the taste of dust in his mouth.

When he heard his mother's step outside Tibalt roused himself and went to fetch the kindling. He did not want to face his mother's too-sharp gaze. Not yet. He went out through the back of the house, brought back an armful of sticks and kindling, and then muttered something about fetching more, took the small axe, and left.

The house was full when he returned near sunset. Nonno sat in his accustomed chair, dozing over a half-whittled peg. Drea and Egino had a net stretched out between them and were repairing a tear. Sibela had her back to the door and was cleaning up her cooking. They had eaten already, but a bowl stood covered by the fire.

Tibalt put his bundled kindling and firewood in a pile near the brazier without saying anything. Sibela swung around to hand him the bowl. Her face was thoughtful. Tibalt put a bit of stewed fennel out of the stew and chewed on it.

"You missed my news, Tibo." Drea looked up from the net. "I'm to learn to fish at last."

Tibalt nodded over his bowl. "About time, Brother. You can't be a *page* all your life."

Sibela dropped the kettle she had been scrubbing. It clattered. "Saint Monica and her sons! What is going on between you two? It's as if you had a language you were speaking that I don't know. The *medica* has decided that her daughter is too old to be attended by a boy nearly her age. That's her right. And it's long past time for Drea to be learning his proper trade."

Drea nodded. "No one is arguing, Mama."

"I know that! Don't you think I know that? But there's something between the two of you—"

Egino put the net down and pulled Sibela to him. "Leave them be, mother. They're men grown, old enough to have a secret if they wish it. You come sit and tell me why the mullet and sole sold today and the bream did not."

Sibela rolled her eyes, sat on the bench beside Egino, and began to speak of fish. Tibalt caught his father's nod, almost imperceptible, and returned it with gratitude.

* * * *

For a month or more Tibalt found excuses to go to the market, wheeling the day's catch to the stall, fetching baskets and poles of half-dried fish home again afterward. He hoped to see Bieta, even at a distance, and twice he did. The first time she was with a dark, purposeful woman with a high folded headdress and a deep willow basket, and both of them were peering at the sheaves of fresh greens on a grocer's table. Bieta looked up just as Tibalt meant to look away, caught his eye, and smiled. He felt that smile's warmth to his toes but only nodded and looked away. When he looked back she was gone.

The next time he saw her, Bieta was crossing the square in front of the duomo, talking with her attendant. They must be going to Ser Bonamio's, Tibalt thought. Bieta would be studying the stars. This time she did not see him. He watched until she went around the corner of a stone house and was lost to him. Then he turned back to the market. He was teasing himself with these sights of her. It would make him dour and bitter if he kept at it. Their lives were different, meant to be different. She would be a *medica*, he would be the prince of the harbor.

He shouldered his baskets and turned away.

Chapter Eighteen

Giulita was no better pleased to become Bieta's escort than Bieta was to have her. Mama gave no explanation for the change; Bieta worried for days that she had somehow offended Drea or his family. Why else break off an arrangement of several years' standing? Giulita, her brow as black as a storm on the horizon, insisted they do the marketing first, then stalked beside Bieta to lessons with Ser Bonamio or Fra Idigio, the elderly tutor of harmonics. Bieta often took her lessons with baskets of onions and *bietola* at her ankles while Giulita sat nearby, darning. Giulita worried that the household would fall apart in her absence, yet she moved slow as syrup through the streets, and she would not consider sending Marco, or the cook's daughter Anna, to go in her stead.

"The *magistra* has given me my instructions. Hurry, girl, or you'll be late to your lesson."

Unleavened by Drea's company, Bieta's days seemed flat and dull. She ached to explore as she had been able to do with Drea and his brother. She missed the sights of the harbor, the ships standing at anchor, laden with oil and grain meant for foreign lands; the fishing boats lined in neat rows on the shingle, sails furled and lashed, the canvas pink and gold in the sunset; drunken sailors and shifty-eyed dicers on the fringe of the harbor; and rowboats plying to and from the ships, carrying sailors and merchants and visitors come to Salerno for their health. Sometimes the memories struck her with a physical pang. It took all her discipline to return to her work.

If Mama or Giulita noticed her restlessness they said nothing. Mama was much taken up with lectures and her practice; in addition to General Maro's household she was now physician to many of the wives and daughters of important men in town. In the evenings she reviewed arithmetic and geometry with Bieta, or talked about new methods of treatment under discussion at the Scuola, or reviewed the diagnostic properties of urine. When, as sometimes happened, Mama was called from the house, Giulita had mending or spinning for Bieta to do until it was time for prayers and bed.

If she had never had Drea's company, perhaps she would not miss it so now, but she had and she did. She missed his brother Tibalt too. She had seen him less, but liked him quite as well for different reasons. Drea was giddy and funny; Tibalt was warm, steady, thoughtful. Sometimes in her dreams she saw his smile.

On a day when Giulita was more than usually cross, they set out for Bieta's lesson with Fra Idigio, who lived in the monastery of Saint Sophia. But first they must go out of their way to the market for something or other and walk about and inspect everything. The market had once been Bieta's delight. Now it felt like punishment as they dragged from stall to stall. It was a shock, then, when she saw Tibalt across the square, half-hidden in the crowd, watching her. It was such joy to see him that she wanted to laugh; had Giulita not been next to her, haggling over the price of a cask of oil, she would have pushed her way across to him. She raised a hand to wave, but a man in a leathern apron walked in front of her, and when she looked again Tibalt was gone.

She turned away, worried. Did Tibalt and his family blame her for Drea's dismissal? She would probably never know.

"Good day, Bieta."

Like a conjuror's assistant Tibalt was beside her. He was smiling, but his eyes were wary.

"Tibo!" Bieta barely knew which question to ask first, and the bubble of questions and pleasure made her feel awkward. "Tibo?"

He looked to the side, at Giulita. "I shouldn't speak to you."

"Why not? Tibalt!"

He shook his head.

Bieta dropped her voice to a murmur. "If you won't talk to me here, now, come to the garden wall of my house this evening. I'll watch for you from the gallery. There is so much I want to—"

A change in his expression told her Giulita had finished her business. He lingered just long enough to nod before he turned away and the crowd closed around his absence. Bieta turned back to Giulita, who was instructing the olive seller where to send the oil. With Giulita's errand done, they could turn back toward Saint Sophia's for her lesson. It was hard to care about the mathematics of pitch. Fra Idigio lamented her stupidity and threatened to beat her if she did not pay attention. The old man was hobbling worse than usual; Bieta thought his bad temper came in part from arthritic pain and might have recommended arrogon, but she doubted he'd listen to advice from her. Mama paid him well, and the old man kept teaching, but Bieta suspected he disliked her as much as she disliked him.

Home after the lesson Bieta went up to the gallery with her scrolls and tried to study, all the while with one eye on the street below. She saw him from a distance, a brown partridge among the scholar crows, and waved until he saw her.

The smile that broke across his face was its own reward. Bieta held up a finger to let him know to wait, and darted into the house and down to the garden. Squeezing through the gap in the wall whence she had once escaped to adventure in the city, she waved again. Tibalt looked right, then left, then came to her.

Bieta could not stop her words from tumbling out pell-mell. "I have a thousand questions! Why did Drea stop escorting me without a word? How is he? Is he fishing with you now? And your mother and father and Nonno, how are they? And you! I could hardly believe it when I saw you today. How are you? I've missed you so!"

His smile warmed her. "We're all well. Drea seems to have found the making of a fisherman somewhere inside him; who'd have thought it?" He looked toward the house. "I shouldn't keep you from your studies."

"A plague on my studies! I don't see you for months and all you can talk about is my work? Tibo!" She looked up at him; had he always been so tall? "Tell me how you are."

"Oh, well enough."

"*Well enough?* Everything is well enough. Maybe it doesn't matter to you . . ."

"What doesn't matter?" He looked puzzled. More than that: lost.

"It's only—there's no one else I can tell how much I'm coming to hate—"

"Hate what?"

She stopped. The feeling had been growing in her, but it was hard to put it into words. "I hate running to make myself into someone I cannot be. I'm not brilliant like Mama. I don't care about the movement of the stars or the mathematics of intervals. I can't learn it."

Tibalt shook his head. "Bieta, you're clever enough to learn anything. Why give up when you're so close to—"

Bieta shook her head, seeking words that would explain something she had never before questioned. "The more I study, the farther it seems to carry me from being a healer— and from other things. *People.* Like your family." Bieta looked down at the weeds that had forced their way through a crack in the stucco wall. "Drea. And you. Have *you* missed me at all?"

"I shouldn't say it." He was looking at her, trying to read her as if she were a chart of the stars. "Yes. I've missed you very much."

Bieta smiled. "Why shouldn't you say that? It was exactly what I needed to hear."

"Because I'm a fisherman and you're a scholar. Because I must not distract you from your work."

"You're sounding like Mama."

He said nothing. In that silence an idea came to Bieta. Her voice shook with the enormity of it. "Tibo, did my mother send Drea away? Did she think that would *help* me with my studies?" His frown was her answer. "If I were not distracted by friends? I never went to lessons with other girls, never had any way to befriend or be befriended. Now girls my age are studying to be wives and mothers, and all I have is *geometry.* I hadn't any friends, only you and Drea—" Her voice broke.

Tibalt reached a hand to her, then stopped himself. Then pulled her close so that she could weep into his shoulder. So close to him, she could smell the dust and salt in his brown tunic, the ever-present odor of fish and the sea, and a strong warm scent that was his own. The cloth under her cheek was rough. When she had no more tears to cry, she looked up to apologize to Tibalt. His face was very close to hers, so close it made her dizzy. She closed her eyes.

Tibalt murmured something before he kissed her. His lips were gentle and tasted of salt.

"What did you say?" When she could speak again.

"I said forgive me. Bieta, I mustn't take advantage of you. Your mother is right about your studies."

"But she's wrong about *me*." As if Tibalt's kiss had loosened something in her, Bieta felt suddenly stronger, her thoughts clearer. "I owe Mama all the duty in the world, and all the love. *Most* of the love." She blushed but did not look away from Tibalt. "But not that duty nor that love is enough to make a scholar out of me."

"You must talk to her." Bieta was still in Tibalt's arms. He looked away toward the house.

"About my studies or this?" She put a hand up to turn his face back to her.

"About your studies. Bieta, I'm still a fisherman and you're still the daughter of a physician. We have no business together, and I should never have kissed you."

"I'm glad you did."

He did not smile back at her.

"I'll talk to Mama about my studies. Perhaps I can be a midwife's apprentice, as she was. I'd like that. And then, when she's accustomed to that I can tell her—" She looked up. "We can tell her. If you do want." She paused. "Perhaps you don't want."

"Don't want? I've wanted nothing else for—" He gave up trying to calculate the time and kissed her again, with a firmness that was almost angry. "Bieta, she's your mother. You *must* honor her wishes. She won't want me—"

Bieta tilted her chin up. "First I will talk to her about my studies. In the end it will all be well, I promise. When she sees I'm in earnest. Mama has always listened to me. She'll understand, I know she will."

Tibalt nodded but did not look convinced. Bieta was certain. While they had talked the sun had dropped behind the towers of the school. The street was full of shadows and it was growing cool. Bieta reluctantly left Tibalt, squeezed back through the wall, and returned to her work.

* * * *

When Bieta asked her mother for time to talk after supper, Laura nodded absently. Mama picked at her food as she always did when she was thinking; tonight she was preparing notes for a new lecture. When the meal was over and Giulita had gone to scold the cook about something, Laura started up to her workroom. Bieta stopped her.

"May we talk now, Mama?"

Mama shook herself from her abstraction. "I'm sorry, *tesora*. I was wrapped up in my own thoughts. What is it? Will you come upstairs with me where we can sit?"

In the workroom Bieta sat at her mother's knee and explained all, confident that Laura would understand and agree, if not at once, then soon. But as she spoke she watched her mother's face grow more and more still, until Laura di Crescia looked like an ancient statue in which only the eyes lived.

"Not be a physician," she said at last. "Your lifetime's ambition, gone." Laura smiled crookedly. "Sweet, it's only now that the work is difficult. When you're at the Scuola it will be—"

"Mama, I will never be at the Scuola! I can barely do the work that Fra Idigio sets me. Half the time I'm wrong, and his explanations make no sense to me. I can remember any number of herbs and treatments; let me study with a midwife and heal that way. I'm not meant for the Scuola. If I tried, Father Ranulphus will count my failure against you as well as me."

At the priest's name Mama scowled. "He will not keep you out if your work is—"

"But it can't be. That is what I'm trying to say. Not good enough for him, not good enough for the Scuola. Mama, Fra

Idigio and Ser Bonamio will tell you I try. I am clever enough, but I'm not you, Mama."

If she hoped the flattery would soothe her mother's distress Bieta was wrong.

"Where did these ideas come from, Bieta? All your life you have worked happily toward your goal, and now—" Laura snapped her strong fingers, her hands red from her repeated washing. "Who?" She leaned forward to look into Bieta's eyes, to read what she wanted to know. "Who gave you the idea that you cannot do the work? Who persuaded you that you should give up your goal?"

"No one!" Bieta flushed. Her heart beat loudly in her ears. After a moment Laura sat back.

"That boy, the fisherman's son. He encouraged this foolishness, didn't he? Have you seen him since I sent his brother away? I told him to let you be. I know what young men want. He shall not get it. I will not have you distracted from your studies or hurt as I was."

"As you were?" Bieta stared at her mother. It had been Mama who sent Drea away, and warned Tibalt away from her. But the rest? Who could have hurt Mama? "Surely your mistress, Crescia—"

"Do not speak to me of her. It's no thanks to her that I persevered and became a *medica*. She abandoned me, after I had already been abandoned . . . I will never abandon you, sweet. But you must do as I say. You'll finish your studies and become a *medica*. Then you will never need to look to a man for your life. You'll forget that boy and it will be better so. You'll thank me." She extended a hand as if to stroke Bieta's hair, but Bieta rocked back, away. "You're upset now. Go to bed. You'll feel better in the morning. In the morning you'll see that I'm right."

Laura took up a pen and turned to her desk, a clear gesture of dismissal.

Bieta left her. Her head felt as if it were filled with bees, buzzing and buzzing. She crossed the hall to her own chamber and sat upon the bed. A sharp bit of straw had worked through the ticking and scratched her hand so that she bled. Absently Bieta pressed a bit of spiderweb to the injury. It was easy to heal the little things, she thought. How to heal the great ones, the mortal wounds?

She did not say her prayers. She sat, thinking, until at last sleep overcame her and she stretched out on the bed. Her dreams were dark and furious.

*   *   *   *

General Maro's daughter, who had married only last year, was heavily pregnant. It was no surprise to anyone when a liveried page from his household rode into the courtyard the next morning as if purposed by imps and gasped that his lady had taken to her bed and was screaming. Laura washed her hands and sent Marco for the basket she kept for birthings. "I will be right behind you," she told the page, who was quivering, beads of sweat rolling down his temples. "Go tell your master. They always think it's the first baby in the world," Laura said to Giulita. Bieta, who had not spoken since she woke, watched her mother go in silence.

When Laura was gone with Marco in her wake, Giulita trudged off to some errand. Bieta returned to her chamber and looked at the scrolls on her table, but she could not think of the stars today. Tibalt would be fishing now, there would be no chance to talk to him, to tell him what had happened, until after noon. When the bells of the duomo rang for sext Bieta was already gone from the house, dressed in the boy's clothes she had not worn for several years. She had grown, nothing fit as it ought, but the cap would still cover her coiled braid, and her tunic, belted low about her hips, gave her something closer to a boy's silhouette.

She passed unremarked on her way toward the harbor.

Still, Bieta felt vulnerable. She had not left the house unaccompanied for years, and she had grown tall and womanly
in that time. When she reached the street that ringed the
harbor she stopped, peering down to the shingle. Egino's
boat was there, already emptied of its catch, and Drea and
Egino were lashing the sails and stowing what they would
not take home with them. Tibalt must be on his way to meet
Sibela at the market. Bieta started uphill again.

She saw him at last, standing by Sibela's stall, talking
with a one-eyed old man with the carriage of a soldier. How
could she get him away? If Sibela saw her it would be as bad
as being caught by Laura.

"Help a poor boy, brother?" The ragamuffin at her elbow
looked up at her with such angelic pathos that Bieta at once
felt for her purse. Her hand closed around a bony wrist.

"Let me go!"

"I will, if you'll do me a favor. See that fellow there?" She
pointed to Tibalt.

"What, the old grandsire?" The boy was being deliberately troublesome.

"No, the man he's talking to. Tell him someone's waiting
to talk with him."

"Someone?"

"*Someone.* Go now, and I won't have your hand chopped
off for thieving." She gave him a push and he ran off, moving in the crowd like an eel among mullet.

Tibalt was there a moment later, his fingers tight on her
arm as he all but dragged her out of the market toward a
quieter side street.

"What are you doing? This isn't safe for you. Bieta, for the
love of all the saints, what—"

"Shh!" She pressed a finger against his lips. "I spoke with
my mother last night. She will not relent. I must be a *medica*
even if it kills me."

Tibalt's face fell. He looked away. "Then I won't see you again."

"No! I've thought of something." She took a deep breath. "If we were wed—"

"Married? Jesu save us. The heat has turned your brain."

"It's not so hot, and my brain is fine. Listen, Tibo. Isn't the authority of a husband greater even than that of a parent? If we were wed my mother would have to accept it. Once she has accepted it, the rest will come. She'll be angry for a while, but then . . ."

For a moment Tibalt's eyes were full of light. "We could . . ." Then the light faded. "Bieta, what would we do, go to the duomo and ask the bishop to wed us? You're the daughter of a well-known *medica*. The priest would want her consent."

"We'll go to a chapel, or a church near the harbor. They might know you, but they won't know me." The more she talked, the more she persuaded herself that the thing could be done, and the more her own certainty carried him. "Please, Tibo."

When he asked, "Which church could we go to?" she knew she had carried him. A great tension in her gave way. Bieta had to fight to keep from laughing.

*   *   *   *

They married in a tiny chapel on the southern outskirts of the city. Bieta had rebelted her tunic to hang long, and taken off the cap, but the priest who wed them seemed more eager to return to his nap than to ask questions. First they were shriven, then they were married; when the priest asked Bieta about her parents she told him, with perfect truth, that she was an orphan.

When they left, handfast, it was to return Bieta to her home.

"Now that we have done this mad, crazy thing, we have to plan what comes next. Your mother will be angry."

"When she's used to the idea—"

"She could still go to the bishop, have the marriage annulled. Bieta, we *must* go carefully."

"What if the marriage were consummated?"

"Bieta, for the love of God!" Tibalt blushed. "Listen. I have thought of nothing else for—forever." The street was quiet. He pulled her against the wall and kissed her urgently. "Don't say such things to me. I am not made of stone."

He pushed her away, but Bieta stepped close to him again. "I'm not stone either, Tibo. I know we must be careful. Come to me tonight, after the bell for compline. To the wall. Husband."

"I must be mad," he said.

* * * *

When the household had gone to sleep Bieta stole down and led her husband silently up the stairs in the dark, like two children exploring a cellar. Her door was barely closed when Tibalt pulled her to him and kissed her with a fever that caught her too. She barely knew when her robes were cast off or how the two of them reached the bed. If she had brought him to her, now he was the leader, his strong, callused hands on her shoulders, her waist, her belly. Their words of love were whispered. Bieta wanted to shout them. Tibalt's feverish desire was more powerful because he was so gentle with her, as if she were fragile. It was Bieta who grasped him tightly, pounding his shoulders as her desire spent itself.

When they could speak again Tibalt had news.

"There's a ship sails for Sicily tomorrow night. I know Dasso, the captain. He'll take us with him." He lay with Bieta pillowed on his shoulder, his fingers tracing her chin and brow as if they were something marvelous. "He leaves with the tide, late. I'll come for you a little after vespers. You can get away?"

Bieta kissed his shoulder. "I will." She felt his heart beating, strong and regular, and the warmth of his skin under her cheek. They drowsed a little and when they woke they made love again, slowly this time. His skin tasted like his scent, salty and warm. His hands on her breasts and belly were strong. At the last she bit his shoulder to keep from crying out.

It was still dark when they crept from the room again, again handfast, and she took him to the wall. Bieta did not feel like a child any more.

"Tomorrow night, after vespers," he reminded her.

"Tomorrow night, after vespers."

Back in her room Bieta drifted into an intoxicated sleep.

* * * *

Laura had gone from the house when Bieta woke. "Gone to see the general's daughter," Giulita said. "Break your fast, child, then to your books. That heathen will be here after sext."

That heathen was Saul di Parma, the Jewish mathematician who had succeeded Isach as Bieta's tutor. When Saul came they sat on the gallery, hoping to catch the midday breezes, and Bieta nodded and scribbled as he explained, again, the principles of geometry that still troubled her. He was patient and soft-spoken; out of liking for the tutor Bieta tried to attend him, but her thoughts were too busy to admit mathematics. When he left, Bieta sat in the shadow of the tiled gallery, looking out at the glaring dazzle of Salerno in the afternoon. In the distance muezzins called from the mosques, summoning the Muslim faithful to worship. Would she miss all this? There would be sun in Sicily, and bells and song. Tibalt would be with her.

* * * *

Laura found Bieta on the gallery. Her cheeks were flushed; she looked oddly willful, not an expression Bieta associated with her mother.

"How does Maro's daughter?"

"Brought to bed last evening of a fine boy, and this morn-ing sitting up and giving suck. She'll do well—and the gen-eral is delighted to have a boy in his family at last."

Bieta looked out over the rail of the gallery. "That's good."

"It is." Laura sat beside her. "Daughter, I need to tell you something."

Bieta felt tiny hairs on her neck prickle.

"I asked the general to help me. You will not like it, but someday you'll see that it is for the best. For you and for the boy—"

"What did you do?"

Laura raised her chin. "I told the general about that boy. Maro is the father of girls, he understands that I will not let you waste your talent—"

"*What did you do?*"

"He's to be taken up by the general's men. They'll make a soldier of him and send him—somewhere."

Bieta stared at Laura, speechless.

"He was talking of what he owed me, not in money but in gratitude. He asked if ever there were a way to repay my loy-alty after all these years, and I knew there was. Without distraction you'll find your way, Bieta. I have no doubt of it. And the boy, he'll have a trade, he'll prosper, find a girl better suited to him. It will be the making of him." She stopped. "Speak, for God's love. I know you don't like it, but some-day you—"

"Do not say you mean it for the best for Tibalt." Bieta was on her feet, gripping the stone railing so hard her fingers hurt. "At least be that honest."

"If you'll have it so. I did it for you, for your good."

"Sold the general's goodwill to buy exile for Tibalt."

The flush on Laura's cheeks spread. "I would do it again, to save you."

"Save me?"

"From the error you were about to make. From the mistakes I made in my own young days, which cost me dearly."

"*When?*"

"When? When I was a student. I—"

Bieta interrupted. "When will the general's men go for Tibalt?"

"I don't know. In the next day or so. I didn't think it was so urgent that he needed—Bieta, promise me." Laura came to stand beside Bieta but did not touch her. "You must promise me not to warn him. Give me your word."

"I can't." The words fell as hard as pebbles.

"You'll defy me? If I must keep you locked away until I know that that boy is gone and he can't influence you any more, I will."

On the street below was sound and movement. From downstairs, Giulita's voice rose as she lamented some small fault. One of the goats in the shed *maaaa*ed sleepily. Only on the gallery everything was still, frozen.

At last, "Do what you will," Bieta said.

"Then go to your room," Laura said coldly. But a moment later, as Bieta turned to go, Laura reached a hand to her. "Bieta. Daughter, don't let there be this anger between us. You know I mean only—"

"Do what you will," Bieta said again, and left.

In her room Bieta sat on the bed, clenching and unclenching her hands, trying to wring some of the anger and fear out of her. She must leave now and get to Tibalt before the general's men could do so. She thought: If she went down the stairs and out through the front gate she would be seen and stopped. If she tried to leave by the kitchen, likely the same. She went and looked out the window at the narrow gap in the wall. Sat and thought, then began to gather some clothes into a bundle; she pulled out again her suit of boy's clothes. As she put them on the bell rang for none. The cook was in the garden cutting rosemary, talking over his shoulder at someone in the house, Anna or Marco or Giulita. It was not yet safe to leave.

She sat, looking at the rolls of parchment and scraps of paper on the chest, listening to the sounds of the household. When she heard nothing more from the garden she looked out and saw that it was empty, but to be safe she waited more. Finally Bieta thought it was safe, as safe as it could be. She uncovered her bed and remade it over a roll of winter robes meant to suggest someone sleeping. At the last, she took up her knife and sawed through her long braid, leaving her hair at chin length. It was strange to move her head and feel it so light. All that weight was in the yellow braid in her hand, more than an ell long. Bieta tucked the braid carefully into the sheets so that most of it lay atop them. From the door it would seem that she was asleep. Until someone came to wake her, no one would know that she was gone.

For the first time her cap fit properly over the spill of her hair. Bieta looked around her room, at the faded poppet Giulita had made for her when she was small, the chart of stars on the wall, the unlit lamps. This was farewell to her life here. Leaving meant commandments broken and years of penance. Who had the greater claim on her loyalty, mother or husband? Laura had forced her.

She took up the sheets she had twisted and knotted together and looped one around the foot of her bedstead, praying that her knots would hold. At last, her stomach roiling with anxiety, she tossed the sheets out the window and began to climb down. It was clumsy, easier to imagine than to do. Even wearing a short tunic kirtled up, Bieta got tangled in a flapping edge of sheet and in her own clothes. The wall was rough against her knuckles and knees. The garden below was in shadow and she could not see what she was climbing into. She was halfway down when the sheets dropped by an arm's length, then caught again. She bit her lip to keep a scream in, swinging like a pendulum. Then the sheet tore with a harsh rasp, dropping Bieta on her back. She struggled for breath. Her hands and chin were scraped and her shoulders sore.

Panting, she crouched and ran to the rear of the garden, to the gap in the wall. By the time she had squeezed through she had added to the scrapes on her hands. Her clothes were dusty and ripped, the better to add to the role she played.

The sun was setting, making golden Salerno an autumnal maze. At a trot, Bieta started for the harbor.

Chapter Nineteen

Word went through the market and down to the waterfront: soldiers were asking for Egino's older son. Three times as he brought the day's catch up to the stall, Tibalt was stopped by acquaintances in the marketplace.

"What have you done, boy? Word is that Maro himself, the bishop's commandant, is looking for you." Distracted by the memory of the night past and the frightening, exciting prospect of a life with Bieta, Tibalt could not make sense of the warnings and was inclined to ignore them. Sibela, who knew nothing of what he planned, was not so sanguine.

"Soldiers asking for you? They've confused you with someone else, I don't doubt it, but that won't matter to them.

Tibo, pay attention! The notice of important men rarely leads to anything good. You go home at once, do you hear me? Father will find out what the matter is. Until then—"

"Go home." He went, but not to Egino's house. Surely that was the first place such soldiers would look. Instead Tibalt went to the chapel where he and Bieta had married, and prayed for the success of their elopement. The chapel was cool and fragrant with incense. He had slept little the night before, risen early to fish with his father; after a while Tibalt dozed and dreamed of his new wife.

When he woke again the dozy priest stood before the altar, celebrating the vespers mass. The sonorous Latin echoed against whitewashed walls. Tibalt genuflected and crept from the chapel. He pulled his cap down low over his face and made for Bieta's house carefully, watching for soldiers. Why would they want him? He had done nothing to earn the interest of anyone—except to marry the *medica*'s daughter. But that made no sense. Why would the bishop's commandant care who married whom in this town? It was getting dark now; if he were late, would Bieta still be waiting for him? Tibalt walked faster, looking right and left at every corner. By the time he reached the *magistra*'s house he was sweating despite the breeze.

Bieta was not there.

Tibalt waited, trying to look as if he were casually loafing, cleaning his nails with the point of his knife and watching the street through slitted eyes. His heart beat faster and harder. Where was she? Had Bieta thought better of coming with him? Had Laura persuaded her against him?

He waited until he couldn't bear to wait longer. There was no movement from the house, no lights, no voices. Tibalt pushed through the narrow break in the wall, almost stuck twice before he was through. Before, Bieta had been his guide;

now he had to find his way on his own, in the dark, into a house bigger than any other he had ever been in. He found the stairs and went warily up, flattening himself against the wall at each sound. On the landing he looked around him; four doors, and he could not remember which one Bieta had taken him through: left or right.

He gambled, opened the door to the right, stepped in. To the dark he whispered, "Bieta?"

From the corner of the room he heard a creaking, as if someone had settled in a chair. "Bieta," he whispered again. "The boat leaves with the tide and there are men watching for me. Will you come?"

"You're too late." The voice was no whisper, a woman's, as cold as stream water and hard. "She's gone. You'd as well go back out the window, boy."

From the darkened corner of the room a figure appeared, a short, slender woman in dove gray. Her wimple and coif lay crumpled at her feet as if she had cast them off. Her hair, red shot with wiry gray, hung about her like a veil. Her eyes were dark, circled, red-rimmed.

"Magistra Laura." He was glad that his voice did not shake. "Where is Bieta?"

"Didn't you hear me, boy? Gone. Left me. Left everything I hoped for. God and His Son forgive her. I never will." The *medica* moved farther into the light; she had something in her hand. Tibalt realized with horror that it was a braid, more than an ell of fair hair that curled at its end: Bieta's hair.

"What did you do?"

"I?" The magistra raised her head and looked at him directly. Her eyes were not mad but deep with rage. "I did nothing. I did nothing but raise her and love her and plan for her and hope for her. And this—" She flicked the braid like a whip. "This is what she left for me." She flicked the braid again. "Why are you here? I thought she was with you."

Involuntarily Tibalt said, "She was to meet me—"

Laura's brows rose. "And she didn't? Perhaps she played us both false, then. Perhaps the little slut has more than one lover—"

"God's love, don't you know her better than that? Your own daughter?" Tibalt stepped back

"My daughter? My daughter died in my womb. Bieta is the cursed child of a cursed line, and may God give her the pain she deserves. You—" The *medica* seemed to speak to herself, not to him. "Took her from me. She had talent, you know. She could have been as great a physician as any in Salerno, but you, fish boy, you seduced my daughter away from me, lured her with the promise of pleasure. She'll find out soon enough how fast that fades. She'll learn men lie. All of you lie."

On the last word she lashed at him again with the braid, striking hard. The snap of the plaited hair raised a welt on his cheek. Tibalt stepped away, feeling something, shelves or a cabinet, against his back. When the *medica* struck him again he grabbed for the braid and pulled it from her. Behind him something rocked, fell from the shelf, and knocked his cap off. A clay pot. Then another fell, and then a rain of pots. He was dusted with bits of flowers and leaves and a cold, thick syrup that rolled down his forehead and burned like fire.

Tibalt dropped the braid. Trying to wipe the sticky stuff away he instead swiped it into his eyes. The pain increased fourfold.

"Don't touch it!" The harridan who had attacked him was suddenly a physician again. "Don't get more of it in your eyes. It's spurge."

Tibalt stood still, his hands fisted against the need to rub his burning face. After a moment he felt a hand on his shoulder, pushing him onto a stool and pressing a wet rag into his hands.

"Wipe your hands. Don't touch anything."

She began to dab carefully at his face with another cloth. Water rolled down his cheeks and soaked into the collar of his shirt. She dabbed at his brow, around his nose, gingerly at his eyes. It burned like Saint Polycarp's fire. Tibalt tried to open his eyes, but the spurge sap stung viciously. He clenched his teeth to keep from crying out with the pain.

"Giulita! I need you! Bring milk!" the *medica* called. To Tibalt she said, "It's the only thing will loosen the sap when it begins to stick so. Sit still." Her fury had disappeared like the sun behind clouds. Now she was a healer, her hands sure, her voice steady and dispassionate.

Even with his eyes shut the pain made him feel weak. The *medica* began to clear the sap from his cheeks, then she worked on his eyes. The pain lessened a little, enough so Tibalt could think. From the gallery a nightingale sounded a few notes, reminding him that time was passing: Dasso's ship would sail with the tide, with or without Tibalt or Bieta. He must leave, he must find her, but the *medica* was working on him still, wrapping his eyes with a bandage. From being the villain who had taken her daughter, he had somehow become the physician's patient.

His eyelids fluttered against the cloth of the bandage.

"Keep your eyes closed," Laura ordered. "For a few days keep the bandage on. When you do take it off, flush your eyes with clean water. That is as much help as I can give you. Giulita!"

He heard footsteps from the direction of the doorway.

"Tell Marco to take this fellow—wherever he needs to go."

"*Magistra*—" Tibalt began. "Bieta—"

"Don't speak her name." The *medica*'s voice was fierce again. "There are men looking for you—General Maro means to make you a soldier, get you away from Salerno and my daughter. If that doesn't suit you, boy, *go*."

Tibalt felt the itchy burn across his scalp and face where the sap had been, and nothing else. The *medica* was gone.

"Your honor?" A man's voice at his elbow. "Mistress said to take you where you would go."

"My name is Tibalt," he said. "I'm nobody's honor." He stood, with the fellow's help. Dizzy, weak, nauseated, but on his feet. "To the harbor," he said. "A ship owned by a fellow called Dasso."

It was a long walk from Laura's house to the harbor. Marco did not chat, and Tibalt, blindfolded and weak as a kit, had to spend his attention on keeping his feet as they went down the stairs. He knew when they left the *medica*'s house by the sudden coolness of the air and the dust and stones under his feet. He thought they walked downhill, but it was some time before he could tell they had reached the harbor.

His guide started and stopped, each time causing Tibalt to lose his balance. When he finally asked what was amiss, Marco complained that he saw no names on the boats moored in the harbor.

Tibalt was startled into a laugh that made his skin hurt. "Show me a sailor who can read! You'll need to ask someone. Hurry, Dasso's ship sails soon."

Perhaps to pay him back for laughing the man shoved Tibalt to sit on a barrel and left him. He was almost ready to call out when he heard someone approach.

"Tibalt?" It was old Iano, who watched the boats at night. "Holy Mother, what's come to you? Christ Jesu, boy, let me take you home."

Tibalt shook his head, a mistake that set his head spinning and made him want to puke. "I need to find Dasso." And hope to God that Bieta was with him.

"Dasso?" The old man paused to cough and spit. "Sailed

at the tide, boy, a little after the bell for last prayers. Thought I saw your brother aboard her."

Drea? Tibalt reached in the direction of Iano's voice. He wanted to shake the old man. "Was there another boy with him, a boy with fair hair?"

"I don't know. I only *thought* I saw Drea, don't ask me about anyone else. But look, boy, surely—"

"Iano, I need to get away from Salerno now, tonight."

"Tide's turned, won't be anyone sailing until morn. You can wait 'til then, can't you?" The old man sounded fretful, as if this were more trouble than he could handle. "I'll get you up to your family."

Tibalt thought. Shock and pain and the turmoil of the last hours made it difficult. Finally, "Take me home, then."

Egino met them at the door. "God's bones, what happened to you? Dasso couldn't hold against the tide. He took that girl with him, and your brother insisted he go with her, to keep her safe."

Tibalt loosed a long, gusty sigh. "Thank God, both of them?" He put his hand on his forehead, then pulled it away, surprised by the pain. "I need to follow them."

"You need," Egino said firmly, "to come inside, tell me what has happened to you, and make a plan. There's no ship that leaves the harbor until tomorrow—"

"That's too late." Tibalt tripped over the doorsill and almost went sprawling.

Egino steadied him. "I can row you down the coast, away from Salerno. But first—"

"First you tell us what happened," Sibela said. "And eat something." He felt his mother's hands on his shoulders, pressing him down on a bench. She pressed a cup of water into his hand and urged him to talk. In a few sentences he explained the confusion that had led him to Magistra Laura's house, the accident with the spurge.

"Accident?" Egino was doubtful.

Tibalt thought of the physician's fury as she drove him back into the cabinet. She had not meant him to be burned with spurge, though. And she had done her best to repair the damage.

"But your eyes?"

"By the *medica*'s handiwork and God's grace, I'll mend. I need to keep the bandage on for a few days."

"A few days." Egino was quiet. "I've friends in Agropoli, south along the coast. I could take you there until I come for you again."

"Come for me? Papa, I'm sought in Salerno. You couldn't bring me home."

"In a few days perhaps the general's attention will have moved to someone else. If not, we'll find you another ship to Sicily."

"Father, I can't let you——"

Egino growled. "I am head of this family and you will not tell me what I can or can't do, boy——"

"And I did not raise a living son to cast him off at the first time of trouble." Sibela had been silent until now. "I'll put some food in a basket for you—enough for a few days. Perhaps you may stay on the beach at Agropoli, as you wanted to do when you were a boy." From her voice Sibela was near tears.

There was no use in arguing with his parents. Within an hour Egino was carrying a basket of provisions and Tibalt had a blanket, a knife, some rope, all rolled together securely. Sibela blessed him, kissed him gently on one reddened cheek, and sent him off with a prayer. Egino led his son through the streets back to the harbor; somehow they put Egino's boat into the water.

"You rest now, boy. There will be time to fret in the

morning." Egino unshipped the oars and began to row the boat out to where he could raise his sail.

* * * *

Tibalt woke when the sun was high; he could feel the warmth on his face. The boat was bobbing with the tide and he could hear his father snoring. Tibalt groped around him until he found a jug, uncorked it, spilling some of the contents when a wave made the boat lurch. When he brought the jug to his lips he was pleasantly surprised to taste, not water, but his mother's sweet ale. He drank sparingly; who knew how long it would have to last.

For a time that seemed long to him, Tibalt thought, lulled by the motion of the boat and the warmth of the sun on his arm and shoulder. They were going east and south, his father had said, and the sun was hottest on the left, shoulder and brow, so it was not yet noon. How long until he could take off the bandages and see again? A bead of sweat rolled down under the wrapping and slid past his ear. A few days. The *medica* had said he must rinse his eyes with clean water, so not until they were ashore again.

Egino coughed, wheezed, woke, and spat over the side. "I slept," he said unnecessarily. "Eeeh. You're beyond the city's reach now, but we're not halfway there yet. Are you hungry? Your mother packed some dried fish and cheese. I hope the sun hasn't ruined it." He pressed a bit of bread into his son's hand. "I can't be gone from the city long, Tibo. I'm going to have to leave you, but when I get home I'll find out what we must do to get you to Sicily."

"You're certain Bieta was on that ship? I will not go to Sicily without her."

"Your brother and that girl were on the ship. I saw them. But I'm damned if I know what's so important about—"

"She's my wife."

Tibalt heard his father drop an oar, swear, and resume rowing.

"Married without my leave? I ought to drop you over the side myself. Married the physician's daughter? Reaching above yourself, aren't you?"

"Bieta says Magistra Laura was a peasant girl and made her own fortune. Bieta is no different from—"

"Don't be a fool, boy. She's different because her mother has the ear of important people. Has it occurred to you that the *medica* might have had something to do with those men seeking you in the market?"

"She all but told me she had. But she also treated my eyes when she had no reason to love me."

"Listen, Tibo. I am still your father: you'll do as I say. I will put you off on the shingle near Agropoli; I used to have friends there. If we find them, that's where you'll stay until I come for you. When I hear that Drea and your . . . wife . . . are safe, I'll tell you. If we can get her back, I'll bring her to you. But I tell you as your father, until then you are not to search for her. Do you hear? Promise me, on your life. I do not want to have to tell your mother she raised you to manhood only to lose you because your cock got tangled in your common sense."

He would not argue with his father. In time, when the shock of all this news had worn away, Egino would soften toward Bieta.

"Where are we?" Egino muttered to himself.

Tibalt sniffed the air. "About a mile off the coast, heading southeast."

He was startled when Egino cuffed him, but it was not a hard buffet, more affectionate than disapproving. "Don't seek to show me how clever you are, Tibo. That I know. Ah. Those rocks there mean I've got another ten hours at least, steady rowing, even with the wind at our back. I can't row that long. Perhaps in the morning . . ." He seemed lost in his calculations.

"I can row, Father. If you be my eyes, I can be your arms."

Egino scoffed, but Tibalt insisted they try. Shortly he was plying the oars in the gentle swell of a placid sea.

"So you're wed, are you? How did that happen? Whose idea was it, and what meal-brained cleric wed you?"

To the rhythm of his rowing Tibalt told Egino how he came to be married.

* * * *

Tibalt rowed until his shoulders ached; they let the boat drift while they ate, then Egino took up the oars and Tibalt rested and said his prayers and thought. In memory he saw Bieta's mother, her haunted fury, the pain in her eyes. What had she said? That Bietela was the cursed child of a cursed line, not her daughter at all. She had been raving, half-mad. Before last night he had thought her enraged by the thwarting of her plan for Bieta. Last night he had seen love and hurt in the healer's eyes: she saw in him the beginning of her own loneliness.

"Poor woman."

"What, the *medica*? You're too kind. They're not supposed to use their position for favors, are they? Them at the Scuola? Let it be known what she did and I don't doubt there'll be trouble for her. She may have the governor's ear, but so do others. I won't rest—"

"Papa." Tibalt fumbled for his father's hand. "Don't waste your time in vengeance."

"Not vengeance. I want my son back, by Christ! Your mother wants her son back. I don't care what happens to the old witch *or* the girl, sweet as she may be, except you love her. You and Andrea are our hope, and now you're both tangled up with this mess." Egino chuckled. "If she's punished, that *medica*, that's just an unexpected bounty."

Tibalt knew better than to argue with Egino. Still, as the boat continued along the coast he thought about the *medica* as often he thought about her daughter.

* * * *

Night fell. The air was cool, the breeze had stiffened and was sweeping them in toward the coast. Tibalt had taken another turn at the oars; now Egino was rowing, singing a wordless song under his breath as he went. Tibalt thought they had changed their direction, but he was not sure; the scent on the breeze was more green than salt, he thought he smelled earth. The bandage on his face itched; carefully he rubbed the skin around the edges, but that only made it hurt and didn't stop the itching.

"Leave it alone, boy," Egino muttered. "We'll be ashore in a bit."

Shortly after, he felt the boat sway. Egino had jumped out into the spray to pull the prow of the boat onto the shingle. The boat juddered on the pebbly sand; Tibalt caught at the side of the hull to keep his balance. Then Egino's hand was on his wrist, signaling him to climb over the side into the salty water. Together they pulled the boat up onto the shore where the tide could not draw it away.

"Now, boy." Egino led Tibalt farther up the shore. "You rest here." He put Tibalt's hand on the trunk of a tree. "I'll bring up the basket from the boat."

* * * *

The sun was high and hot when Tibalt woke, alone. He calmed his first panic with the thought that his father would not have left him without a word. Feeling about him he discovered that Egino had left the basket and ale jug resting on the roots of the tree. He ate a slice of cold fried porridge and sipped at the ale, but saved the rest of the provisions for later.

"Tibalt!" His father's voice startled him, and Tibalt choked on his ale. "I've found them, my friends."

Tibalt was led up a steep pathway. Blinded by the bandages, Tibalt could only hear his father's friends: a man and woman, elderly. Egino introduced him to Marizo and his wife, Clara, who welcomed Tibalt effusively and promised to keep him safe at their farm until Egino returned.

Before he left, Egino took his son aside. "Do what you can to help them. They're old and childless; when that bandage comes off and you can see again, you may be a great help." He turned from his son and said to the people nearby, "He won't be here long. I'll be back soon to bring him home."

Egino embraced his son. Tibalt, wishing he could look upon his father's face, returned the embrace and sent his love to his mother. "Pray for me," he asked.

"Always, Tibo. Do you so for us too."

Tibalt was left, blind, in the care of strangers.

* * * *

Tibalt spent the first few days of his exile attempting to help and, in the main, making a terrible job of it. Marizo grew grapes on the hill, and fruit, and next to the house there was a garden of beans and peppers and onions. Beside the cottage there was a shed in which Clara kept goats; she spun their hair into yarn that she dyed and wove; the cottage was almost always filled with the smell of damp goat hair. Clara was small, barely came up to Tibalt's breast, and his impression was that she was scrawny and anxious. She was uneasy having a stranger in her house: he could hear it in her voice and sense it in the way she fluttered about her work. Tibalt set about courting her favor, offering to wind her wool, to feel his way to the woodpile or spring to carry wood or water for her. She warmed to him; by the end of his fifth day there she was calling him "dear son" and chattering to him as she went about her work. She must be lonely, with Marizo in the field all day and no children to keep her company.

Marizo seemed to enjoy the company of another man. At some point Egino had rendered him aid—what, neither man would say—and Marizo said more than once that he was pleased to be able to repay his debt by helping Tibalt. When he went down to the shore to bring in his nets he led Tibalt down behind him, saying he was glad of his guest's expertise. Tibalt doubted he was much help in his current state, but as he learned to navigate the path he was happy to help by carrying whatever Marizo would part with.

On his fifth morning there Clara took the bandages from Tibalt's eyes. Her indrawn breath told him, before he opened his eyes, that the skin there was ugly to look on. He put his hand up to feel but found no deep scars.

"Open your eyes, dear son."

Slowly and fearfully Tibalt did. Through the right eye he saw light and shadows. Through the left, nothing. He shut them again. Opened just the right, closed it, opened it again. The light inside the cottage was not bright, he was not dazzled. He could make out some shapes, see movement. Tibalt bit the inside of his cheek, trying to keep his anxiety to himself.

"You must wash your eyes out," Clara suggested. "A little clear water will help." He heard her dipping water from the cistern into a bowl, which she pressed into his hands. The *medica* had said to rinse his eyes when the bandage came off. The water was pleasantly cool on his skin. He wiped his face on his sleeve and tried opening his right eye again. It seemed to him that the shadows were a little clearer now. He smiled at the hovering shadow that was Clara.

"And the other eye?" she asked.

Tibalt opened the left, keeping his hand over the right eye. He saw only darkness. He shook his head.

Clara's short, square hand stroked his cheek. "It will take a little time, Tibalt. That's all."

He took his hand away and blinked both eyes vigorously. The left one stayed stubbornly occluded; the sight in the right was hardly good, but it was something. He tried not to despair, not to curse God.

"Time," he agreed. "It will take time. But now perhaps I can be of some real help to you, mother. Have you wood that needs chopping? Goats to milk? Beans to sort?"

The old woman ruffled his hair as if he were a child. "So eager to go to work. Go outside, now you can see something of where you are, and get your bearings before you try to fetch and carry for me. The wood and the goats and the beans will wait."

So he did.

* * * *

A month had given way to two when Egino returned. The sight in Tibalt's left eye had grown no clearer, but the right had improved to where he could make out shapes, animals, and people. He knew Clara by her quick, anxious movements, and Marizo by his rolling gait, as if the land moved beneath him like the deck of a ship. Tibalt came to realize how much he had relied upon his sight for even the littlest things. The day he whittled a peg to repair Clara's stool without cutting himself or ruining the work, he felt a triumph all out of scale to the chore. His days were spent learning to do again skills he had carried since boyhood.

His nights were filled with dreams of Bieta.

When Egino returned, Tibalt knew at once. He got to his feet, careless of the stool that fell away behind him.

"Father!"

He did not run, but walked to meet Egino and embraced him. They spoke one over the other.

"What news, Father?"

"Your eyes, Tibo. Can you see?"

Because his was the briefer tale Tibalt answered first,

telling his father of what he had gained in one eye and what he had not in the other. He felt his father grow still. Anger, he thought. But Tibalt had thought again and again of the night in Magistra Laura's workroom. "It was an accident, Father."

"That's as may be," Egino growled. "The witch got what was coming to her, anyway."

Tibalt felt cold. "What happened? You—"

"I did nothing. God saw to it all, God and one of the priests at the Scuola. The Superior of the Scuola made complaint against the *medica* and they took away the old witch's license to practice—they take the matter of misusing influence seriously, more seriously than the monks take matters of simony, it seems."

Tibalt nodded, but this was not what he wanted to know. "And Bieta, Father? She and Drea reached Sicily safe? I've dreamed—"

"I'm thirsty, boy," Egino interrupted. "I need water before I can talk any more. And a place to sit."

Half-blind he might be, but Tibalt knew the tone of his father's voice and his heart froze. "Will what you have to tell me be any easier to hear after you've had a cup of ale, Father?"

"Christ Jesu. Tibo, if I could tell you anything else I would." His father put an arm around Tibalt's shoulders and led him toward a tree. "I need to sit, I do."

When they were settled in the shade Egino sighed, gustily. "Your brother reached home almost a month ago. There's no easy way to say this. Dasso's ship went down. Some of the crew survived, and Drea, praise God, was among them. He did his best for your wife: lashed her to a spar so she would not drown, and held on to it as long as he could. He came to shore down the coast—not so far south as we are here—and searched for her, but . . ."

Tibalt was still as the becalmed sea. "It isn't possible," he said at last. "I would have felt it if she died. Wouldn't I? She might still live."

"Tibo." Egino spoke very gently. "Your brother searched up and down the coast, asking for her. He found bodies of sailors he knew. We think the girl came loose of the spar and her clothes carried her under. I'm sorry, boy."

Tibalt sat stiffly. He could not weep. When Clara called them in to eat he rose and brought his father into the cottage. They ate fish soup and dark bread and talked quietly. Egino told his hosts only that it was safe now for Tibalt to return to his home. Of what had happened to Bieta he said nothing.

When they were done eating Egino thanked his hosts and went outside to let Tibalt say his good-byes in private. But when Tibalt emerged from the cottage he shook his head. "Father, I'm staying."

"Don't be stupid, boy. I told you: the bishop and his commandant called off their search. You have the freedom of the city again."

"If Bieta's not there— No, I'm better off here. I know my way about. There are no ghosts haunting me."

"And your mother and I?"

Tibalt reached for his father's hand and felt his way up to the older man's shoulder. He kissed Egino on the brow. "I love you, Father. I am your dutiful son. If you insist that I go back to Salerno with you, I will. But I beg you not to. I have no life in Salerno any more."

Egino wept, but did not insist.

Chapter Twenty

Bieta woke with dust in her nose. No, not dust, sand. She lay facedown, draped over something hard. She was somewhere far warmer than her mother's cool, pleasant house. For a few moments, eyes still shut, she tried to remember. They had quarreled. She had escaped from the house and made her way to the harbor and found Drea, who had brought her to Dasso's ship and—what then? Where was she now?

She tried to turn but could not. Opening her eyes she saw that she was tied to something: a wooden spar. That was what she was lying on. She was on a beach. The warmth was the sun on her back, and it was not only the rope around her waist that made it hard to move; she was stiff with salt and sand. Her short hair flew every which way in salty locks; she was missing one boot, and her arm hurt. She was not in Salerno; one glance along the shore showed no sign of the harbor or the city itself, not even in the distance. The beach was not familiar. What had happened?

She managed with clumsy fingers to find an end to the rope, puzzle out the knots, and at last free herself from the spar. She sat up, stretching, examining herself. A cut on her right forearm had bled, then scabbed over messily. Vaguely she thought, *I shall have to clean out the dirt and sand.* But that was for later. She tried again to remember: She had left Laura's house by the window. She was gone before the time she and Tibalt had arranged to meet and she had gone to the harbor to find him there. Her belly warmed at the thought of him, the memory of his scent and his touch. *Her husband.* Then a new memory: Andrea had seen her, told her his brother must be hiding from the general's men. Tibalt had told Drea about their marriage, sworn him to secrecy; now Drea felt responsible for Bieta until Tibalt arrived. He had taken her aboard Dasso's ship to wait as the moon rose over the harbor and the tide turned. Still Tibalt had not come.

"You know Tibo," Drea had said airily. "He'll find a way to get here. If he can't, he'll meet us in Sicily." He spoke as if Sicily were a town smaller than Salerno where anyone might be found. Andrea had wrapped a blanket around her and found her a place to sit on the deck, out of the way of the sailors who raised the lateen sails and cast off from the quay. She did not see Salerno slip away and vanish on the horizon; her face was turned away, toward Sicily and the future and Tibalt.

How had she come to this beach? Cautiously Bieta got to her feet. Her head ached and swam a little with the movement, and the white sunlight hurt her eyes, but her legs were sound. She could stand and walk. To her right down the beach there was wreckage: spars, splinters, shreds of rope twined in seaweed. The ship, broken up. Had they been attacked? Shipwrecked? Why couldn't she remember? The longer she stood the more Bieta's head hurt. She turned to her left and saw more flotsam and seaweed and something else, a sodden lump of fabric and meat she knew must be a human form. One of the sailors. She edged closer, thinking perhaps he was alive, until she saw the deep slash that had opened his belly and chest. Had his body not come to rest on its side the gulls would already have been at him. She crossed herself and murmured a prayer. There was nothing to do for him. When she looked down the shore she saw three more bodies. Bieta murmured a prayer and went to look.

Two of the men were dead without a mark. Drowned. Neither one was Tibalt's brother. She went a little farther along, to the third man, a short, round, sunburnt fellow with

a halo of gray curls and beard, lying on his back with arms
outflung. He was breathing.

Bieta sank to her knees and shook the man. "Uncle! Uncle,
wake up." His head rolled to one side and she saw a nasty
swelling on the side of his head, a wound, a little dried blood
in the silvery curls. She did not shake him again, lest she open
the wound, but instead pinched him hard. The sailor moaned
but did not wake.

She sat down heavily in the sand beside him. Her own
head hurt and she felt sick. She needed water; the sailor
would need water when he woke, but she could not summon
the energy to look for it. Bieta put her head on her knees and
wept, wondering what else she could do.

* * * *

She dozed, then woke again. The sun was lower now and her
headache was less. The man she sat beside was still breathing. Bieta said a prayer to Saint Margaret and the Virgin and
rose to look for water. By the time the sun met the western
horizon she had found a stream that emptied into the sea
and, walking along it, reached a point where there was no
salt, only the coldest, sweetest water she could remember
tasting. Thirst slaked, she realized how hungry she was.
Nothing for that but to find help, or find a way to keep the
sailor and herself alive until help arrived. She clung to the
idea that Tibalt would find her, if only she could stay alive. If
only—she realized with a pang—he had got safe away from
Salerno. She tried to weave reeds into a cup, but they were
sparse and too dry to work with. Finally she cupped her
hands and brought water back to the sailor that way. He still
slept, and she had had no luck in waking him, so she wet his
lips and tongue with the water and splashed the rest on the
wound on his head, to try to clean it.

Then she looked for something to eat. She had lived in
the city all her life; what she knew of plants was which

would heal or harm. This close to the sea there was little
growing, just scrub and weeds. She had no idea if any of it
was edible. Bieta went back up along the stream, reasoning
that where there was water there must, sooner or later, be
trees or plants, something edible. What she found was a
bush heavy with berries, but they were not a berry she knew,
and, her mother's daughter, she had a healthy respect for the
danger of eating a berry she could not identify. She held a
handful of berries in her hand, torn between caution and
hunger.

"You! Hoi!"

The voice came from beyond the bush, and startled her
badly. She dropped the berries and turned. A group of people,
a family, perhaps, stood at the rise of the hill, a rickety cart
tented over with rough cloth behind them. The man who
had called to her was swarthy and fine-featured like an Arab,
but he had a country accent and he wore the everyday tunic
and leggings of a farmer or artisan. Beside him were an elderly
woman, wrinkled as a dried grape, one eye milky with cataract, and a girl who looked to be about Bieta's age, but was as
dark and exotic as the man. He called to her again. "Are you
well, boy?"

Bieta thought for a moment. If she said she was alone, or
said she had been shipwrecked, who was to say these people
would not kill her or make her their slave? She had heard
such stories. But she was lost, who knew where, and hungry,
and there was the sailor who might be dying, or might live
with help.

"Uncle, I am not," she said at last. "I was on a ship that
went down on the way to Sicily. There's another—a sailor—on
the beach. And," she added plaintively, "I'm very hungry."

There followed such a sweeping up and solicitousness
that she could barely believe she had thought to doubt their
intentions. The girl turned back to the carriage long enough

to produce a piece of bread that she smeared with a paste of olives and cheese. She darted down the rise to offer it to Bietela. The old woman directed the man to find the sailor and bring him back at once.

The girl smiled shyly. "We was lookin' for a place to camp the night," she said. "Might 's well be here. But how'd you reach this shore? Sicily is a fair far way." She had an accent stronger than the man's; her voice was sweet and low-pitched.

"We had only just set out," Bieta began, but the old woman told the girl to hold her questions and light a fire. By the time the dark man returned with the sailor hung over his shoulder like a sack of grain, tinder and wood had been found and a spark lit from the firepot. The old woman began sprinkling millet into a pot and cutting onions for stew.

The berries were edible, sweet and seedy.

"Now, brother: tell us what happened to you." They had supped, and sat round the fire less for warmth than for its cheer; the night was balmy and the breeze that rattled the brush was gentle. Bieta, thinking the man spoke to the sailor, turned to see if he had wakened at last, but no, he still slept. "Oi, lad?" the man prodded, looking at her. She had forgotten: with her hair shorn and uncovered and in a short tunic, she looked like the boy she had pretended to be in Salerno. It was likely safer to continue so.

"I don't know, uncle," she told him. "I was sleeping on the deck of the ship, then I woke on the shore. As for my fellows, I was traveling with my . . ." She hesitated. "My brother Andrea. I don't know what has become of him."

"Only other'uns I saw was dead," the man said. He had told her his name was Alefri; the old woman he introduced only as Mother, and the girl was his wife, Alessia. "Where was you sailin' from?"

"Salerno."

"That's a good piece up the coast, son. We was there for Octave of Easter, though. Don't plan to go back that way for a time. Still, if you like it and 're willin' to work, you can travel along of us 'til we return to your home."

Bieta pursed her lips against tears that threatened to undo her imposture as a boy. She nodded, thankful. At least for tonight it seemed a good plan. Tomorrow, perhaps, she would have a new idea of how to find Andrea, reach Sicily, meet Tibalt. Tomorrow. Now, she yawned, unable to stop herself. "How is it you are so good to a stranger?" she asked.

Alefri shrugged. "We's travelers. Traders. Folk mostly mistrust us, so we try to trust first when we can. Beside, one scrawny half-grown boy and one half-dead grandfer sailor don't seem too great a hazard." He nudged the unconscious sailor with his foot. "Mother, is there anything you can do for the grandfer?"

"Yarrow and olive oil, if you have any, make a good poultice," Bieta began.

The old woman turned her milky eye toward her. "They do. That surprised you should know it, lad."

Bieta blushed. "I lived in Salerno. Everyone there knows a little medicine."

"I've heard." The old woman spat, then gestured Alessia toward the wagon. "Fetch out mortar and yarra', girl. You, lad: You're dead on your feet. Say your prayers and sleep now. Alefri, give the boy a cloak to cover hisself."

Bieta curled up in the woolen cloak Alefri had tossed to her, listening to the snap of the fire and the murmurs of the two women as they worked over the unconscious sailor. Weariness overtook her as she murmured her prayers, with a special one to the Virgin and Saint Margaret, who had taken the worst of her punishment for the sin of disobedience and left her alive to repent.

*   *   *   *

The sailor died three days later without recovering consciousness. Alessia and Nonna, as the old woman insisted Bieta call her, sewed him a shroud, and Alefri and Bieta buried him. The peddlers had stayed put while the sailor lived, but with the old man in the ground Alefri put the mule between the traces and pointed the wagon southward. Three of them walked alongside the wagon with the wizened old woman perched on the seat, twisting thread into lace that they would sell with Alefri's other goods. In the evenings when they had settled for the night, Alessia made lace too, or picked out pretty designs in colored wool. Alefri carved wooden bowls and cups with the figures of animals as handles. Bieta, taking up a knife, tried to learn the work, but it was not as simple as Alefri made it look.

When they came to a village or a town, Alefri folded back the heavy fabric of the wagon top and offered their wares for sale. They did not make much coin, but a good deal in trade: a bag of onions or two loaves of bread for a bowl; a bottle of oil for a length of Alessia's broidery work. It was not an easy living, but Alefri, when Bieta asked, said it suited him; he could not imagine staying in one place for longer than a fortnight. Casting about for some way to contribute to the peddler's stock, Bieta began to collect herbs and make possets and remedies to sell. She was careful to make only the simplest medicines. Her knowledge of such things was not deep; too, she did not wish to try something complex, only to be accused of practicing medicine without permission, or, far worse, of attempting witchcraft.

She had need of her own simples; daily she rose feeling wretched. As the day passed her stomach settled, but she sometimes had to dodge into the bushes along the path to vomit up the tea and porridge she had eaten only an hour before. Bieta had been traveling with the peddler's wagon for almost a six-week when she diagnosed her own condition: she was with child.

She was overwhelmed with joy and sorrow and fear. She wanted Tibalt fiercely, to tell him he was going to be a father and to watch her joy echo in his. She wanted Laura to comfort her and minister to her. She worried what would happen when her condition betrayed her to Alefri and Alessia and Nonna; would they cast her out? In prayers to Saint Margaret she wondered if the babe was a punishment for the sin of disobedience, for loving Tibalt and planning to escape with him, for that last awful scene with her mother. To be pregnant, playing a boy, miles from everyone she knew, among people who, for all their kindness, were still strangers—she redoubled her prayers to Saint Margaret and the Virgin, hoping for some unimaginable solution.

They had left Potenza behind them, heading east toward the coast. Alefri and Alessia, who had quarreled the night before, were at the front of the wagon and the rear, respectively; Alessia showed no sign of being submissive to her husband's will or opinions, and when they quarreled it was often her voice that was the loudest. Now, however, she trod mechanically behind the wagon, and when Bieta looked back she could see the girl glowering. Nonna, following Bieta's glance back, shook her head. "Girl's a fool, and my son wed for her pretty face, so he's a fool too. They's well-matched, eh?"

Bieta grinned. Her stomach had been settling of late, and it was easier to carry on a conversation with the old woman when she did not feel that she might have to turn to the side of the road to vomit at any second. "What were they quarreling about?"

Nonna shrugged. "Who knows? I don't pay 'em no heed in the night. Nor should you!" Indeed, many nights the couple indulged in vigorous noisy coupling where they lay on the far side of the wagon.

"Nor do I," Bieta said. It was impossible not to hear some of the noise, however, and it made her think of Tibalt. She felt blood rise to her cheeks and looked away.

". . . is you going to tell your secret?" the old woman was saying. Bieta shook herself from her reverie.

"Secrets, Nonna? What secrets could I have?"

The old woman leaned down from her seat in the wagon, bent almost double to mutter in Bieta's ear. "You's no boy, for one. Nor a virgin, neither. You been greensick since new moon time. Was the father a sailor on the ship that threw you to the sea?"

Bieta froze. Panic rippled through her. As Alessia passed her, her glowering lost in curiosity, Bieta moved forward, catching up with the wagon.

"How did you know?"

The old woman gave a high, delighted cackle. "Wi' six of me own? Yon Alefri was youngest, and one of only two as lived; his sister married a cooper in Taranto. I know the signs. But why play at being a boy? Woman can be shipwrecked as easily as man."

Bieta nodded. "We thought it would be safer aboard ship if no one else knew my sex. Then I woke on the beach, and there were the others, the sailors who drowned, and—"

Nonna nodded. "So where's your man? Drowned? Or—" She twisted her head round and looked at Bieta with shrewd sympathy. "Ain't there one?"

"We were wed," Bieta said. "And going to Sicily. But he didn't come, and the ship sailed without him. I don't know where he is now." Her voice dropped on the last words.

"Ahh." The old woman put her finger alongside her nose in a gesture of understanding. "Well, yours won't be the first child born to parents couldn't wait for the priest. You sure he meant to be on ship? There's men as'd think it a fine thing to get rid of a woman with a pouching belly by sending her off to another country."

"No." Bieta was firm. The idea was too foolish to consider. "Tibalt would not do such a thing. His brother was watching for me, which he would not have been if Tibalt's faith had been bad. Andrea—" She broke off. Andrea might have drowned like the sailors on the shore.

"None of that." The old woman wheezed, coughed, and spat, her usual response to emotion in the people around them. "You's part of our family now, at least until you find this Tiro? Tibo? Tibalt. Can't keep playing the boy, though. First thing to do is find proper clothes. I don't mind telling you I's shocked you been walking about so."

She turned around in her seat on the wagon, trusting Bieta to lead the mule while she rooted in a chest. She muttered to herself, holding bits of stuff up to her good eye, tsking, and returning them to the chest. Finally she produced a bundle of cloth: a robe of dark red wool, a shift, a length of dingy linen. "I'll stop and wait. You change. In the wagon, girl! Don't want to make the world a gift of the sight of you! They don't teach modesty in Salerno?"

Bieta looked back up the road, where Alefri and Alessia seemed to be reconciling, their heads together. "What will I tell them?"

"Tell 'em what you told me: we've heard worse, these chancy times. When you've a belly big enough to carry in a barrow it would be clear enough, so tell 'em now and they can get used to the notion. Rest of the world? We'll say you's my widowed daughter, travelin' wi' us 'til your time. Least then you can go be shriven when we reach a town, and go to mass as well."

Bieta clambered into the back of the wagon, drew the rough flap down, and put on the clothes Nonna had handed her. They were made for a shorter woman, and the knobs of her ankles were visible below the hem, but it was pleasure to put off the imposture and wear women's dress again. She tied the headcloth neatly and climbed down from the back of the wagon.

Alefri and his wife stood staring.

Bieta shook out the red gown and looked at her companions. "I have a story to tell," she said. "And I must start with my true name."

* * * *

They went over the mountains and down to the eastern coast, stopping in towns that were sometimes welcoming but more often wary of strangers. The sight of an old woman and an increasingly pregnant young woman seemed to allay some fears, and Alefri and Alessia were practiced at turning aside suspicion with a quick joke or a compliment. They were out of the mountains by the time winter fell, and turned first south, then north, to go along the coast, offering the embroidery and lacework and Alefri's carved bowls and cups and the herbs Bieta collected and hung to dry on the frame of the wagon. As her belly grew and walking for long miles became harder, sometimes Nonna would descend from the wagon and let Bieta take her place. Neither she, nor her son and his wife, ever seemed to begrudge her her place among them. Indeed, Alessia seemed wistfully curious about the pregnancy, laying her hands upon Bieta's belly to feel the baby's vigorous kicking.

When spring warmed the breezes and greened the hills and the Lenten season rose toward Holy Week, Bieta's pains began. Nonna, who seemed to know what was happening before Bieta did herself, had Alessia and Alefri make a bed for her inside the wagon where she could have privacy, then

sent the couple to the nearest town to say prayers for a safe
delivery. "And to get them out of the way," she admitted to
Bieta. "Birthing's no business for men, and 'Lessia would
drive me wild with her fuss."

Bieta labored for what seemed days, but the sky was still
light when her daughter was born. "Sibela," she said. For
Tibalt's mother. The babe did not cry, but looked about
her with calm curious eyes while Nonna cleaned her and put
her in Bieta's arms. The pains were still coming. "Afterbirth,"
Nonna said calmly. But perhaps a quarter of an hour later the
old woman uttered a plea that the Virgin bless her. "Comes
another 'un!"

The second baby was born quickly, as if she were in too
much of a hurry to do things properly. She emerged from the
womb screaming, outraged that so much was asked of her so
young. Then Nonna bathed the baby, swaddled her, and put
her with her sister in Bieta's arms. "Hope you're done," she
said. "Hadn't thought twins. What's this 'un to be named?"

Bieta had not considered twins either, and had only one
name ready for a girl child. Exhausted, she lay back on the
pallet looking at her dark-eyed, fair daughters. A name came
to her. "Filipa," she said.

Nonna nodded. "A good saint." She took a little water on
her thumb, drew a cross on Sibela's forehead, and named her.
Then she did the same for Filipa. "That'll keep 'em safe 'til
the priest christens 'em. Two daughters! Hope your Tibalt,
when you find 'em, likes girl children. Now drink, this, girl.
'Twill bring in your milk—you'll need it, sure!"

* * * *

The babies rode nestled together like kittens in a reed basket, in the wagon with Nonna. The old woman kept up an
almost ceaseless stream of observation and comment to
them; Bieta, recovered from the birth, went back to walking
beside the wagon, hunting for herbs at the roadside, learning

lacemaking from Nonna in the evenings. Alefri told her
they might reach Salerno in time for the feast of Saint Mat-
thew in September, and sometimes as she walked along the
grassy, rocky verge beside the wagon she imagined what it
would be like to walk through the city again, to bring her
daughters to the duomo to receive a blessing there, to smell
the sea and see the sunlight on Salerno's yellow stone buildings, the chalky stone of the cliffs that flanked the harbor,
the endless blue water. To find Tibalt alive and introduce
him to his daughters. When she prayed, the first thing she
asked the Blessed Mother and the saints was to guard her
love and bring her, and their children, safely home to him.

*   *   *   *

On a rainy afternoon the wagon crested the rise above the
city, and Bieta found herself looking down over the harbor,
with the square bulk of the duomo looming over the market
square. The ships in the harbor were slivers of white sail
against the choppy pewter sea, and the clustered stone towers
of the Scuola rose on the northern hills, all as she remembered. Alefri led the wagon down a stony road toward the city
with the women walking behind, shrouded in rough woolen
cloaks against the damp. At the duomo Bieta parted from
them. There were embraces but no tears; the peddlers were
too used to comings and goings to weep over them, and Bieta
was already looking ahead to where she must go. To Alessia,
who had confided only a fortnight before that she was, at last,
with child herself, she gave her especial love and prayers.
Then she took her daughters in their basket and entered the
duomo to make a prayer of thanks for her safe return.

The rain had stopped when she left the cathedral. She
walked down toward the harbor, with only her babies as attendants, to the narrow street where she had first met Egino
and his wife. Bieta had put her daughters in a sling before
her, and carried the basket with their small belongings and

her own. It had been a little more than a year, and yet everything seemed different, the houses seemed so close together.
The city hasn't changed, I have. But when she rapped at the
door to Egino and Sibela's house that sound was familiar to
her, and Sibela's answering voice brought tears to her eyes.

She pushed the door open.

* * * *

Sibela, once she was done weeping, had eyes only for her
granddaughters. She could not decide which one to hold
first, cooing and singing to them until her namesake, pre-
dictably, began squalling to eat. Bieta, swept up in telling
Tibalt's mother about the babies' birth and their travels, did
not ask about her husband yet, or Andrea. If she had to tell
Sibela that Andrea had drowned, she wanted Egino there
too. So she put little Sibela to her breast and was speaking of
crossing the mountains to reach the eastern coast when the
door opened again.

Egino entered and, behind him, Andrea. Sibela held the
infant Filipa up like a prize and cried, "Look! Look!" and
there was so much confusion, so many embraces and excla-
mations, that both babies began to cry and Bieta had to sit
and rock them until they quieted.

"I thought—I was afraid—I didn't know if you were alive or
not," she told Andrea. "I woke on the shore—what happened
to the ship?"

He sat beside her with Filipa on his knee, making faces at
the baby. "You don't remember? We struck something—
may have been wreckage, may have been a reef—and started
to take on water. You said you didn't swim so I tied you to a
spar. One of the sailors said he'd make sure we reached
shore—but he was struck in the head as he swam with us,
and the current swept me away." His voice was thick. "We
thought you were dead."

"I thought *you* were." She ignored the tears that were drying on her cheeks. "For a year I've prayed to Saint Christopher and Saint Margaret for your safety."

Again she told the story, as briefly as possible, of how she had lived for a year. At last, emboldened by the happiness of the faces around her, she asked.

"And Tibalt?" Her stomach clenched.

Sibela put her strong arms around her. "He lives, Daughter. Not here, but not so far away, either. Certainly not for one who has traveled as far as you."

Bieta rocked the infant Sibela as she wept. The fear she had carried for a year was suddenly gone.

When the worst of her tears had subsided, Egino began the story of what had happened to Tibalt: his confrontation with Laura and his blinding, the long flight down the coast to Agropoli. "Friends of mine there took him in. Even when he could, he didn't want to return—we thought you were dead."

Bieta sat quietly for a while, rocking her daughter. So much to take in. Her mother's part in all of it she could not fathom. Was it possible that Laura, who had given her life to healing, would cause pain deliberately? Whatever quarrel she had with her mother, Bieta could not believe that. "The general's men ceased to look for him?" she asked at last. "Did my mother—"

"The healer? Did *nothing*. One of the priests divined she'd set the general's men after my son. *He*—the priest—accused her of using influence with the general; seems he'd never trusted her." Egino smiled grimly. "The medicos at the Scuola met." He shrugged. "Cast her out of the school. She left the city, I think."

Bieta hid her face in baby Sibela's neck, smelling the clean, milky scent of her skin. She did not blame Egino for his vengeful satisfaction, but she was torn. Laura, who had loved her work and her position at the Scuola, had been cast out—for the first time in a year and more she felt pity. And curiosity. "Who was it made the accusation? Was it Father Ranulphus?"

Drea nodded. "The scowling priest who wrung my arm? Tall, with a face like a bad-tempered carp? I believe it. I know when your mother left the Scuola he was there at the gates, watching as if she might try to sneak back."

"He always wished her ill. All my life, when I saw him a cold finger ran down my spine. But do you know where she went, after?"

Egino spat into the fire. "Pardon me if I do not know or care."

"Egino!" Sibela frowned.

"No, I understand." Little Sibela, asleep in Bieta's arms, grunted, and her lips pursed in a dream of suckling. Bieta, looking at her and at Filipa, drowsing in her grandmother's arms, felt a pang of love like a physical force. Had Laura ever felt that love? It seemed to Bieta that losing her place at the Scuola must have hurt Laura more than losing her daughter.

"Tibalt lives," she said at last. "When can I see him?"

"We'll start tomorrow," Egino promised.

* * * *

The trip down the coast took two days under sail. It was hard for her, but Bieta left the twins with Sibela, whispering promises to the babies to bring their father home.

Coming ashore near Agropoli was, to Bieta, a ghost of waking on the beach where Alefri had found her. But here there were cliffs above the beach, and here she was safe with Tibalt's family, going to find her husband and bring him home. Andrea stayed with the boat while Egino, who had been here before, led her up the beach and along a path of tall, reedy grass, over a rise to a little farm that looked down on the sea and inward to a grassy hillside.

Tibalt sat on a stool by the farmhouse door, working something with his hands. Whittling, Bieta realized. Like Alefri.

His head came up. "Who comes?"

At the sound of his voice Bieta's strength leaked from her, she stumbled, and Egino caught her. "It's me, boy," the older man said.

"Father?" Tibalt sounded surprised. "Is anything wrong? Is Mother well? Who is that with you?"

Egino smiled and drew Bieta close. The skin on Tibalt's brow and cheek was scarred and red, and one eye stared sightless at her. He sat and watched as they drew closer.

"Father, who *is* that?" he asked.

Egino reached for Tibalt's hand and put Bieta's in it. The touch of his hand on hers gave Bieta back her strength, and she put her other arm around Tibalt's shoulder and wept, the tears falling on his scarred face as he looked up at her.

"Bieta?" His voice was hoarse.

"I brought you a wife, boy," Egino said.

Coda

SALERNO, 1250

The day was clear and sunny with a blustery wind when Bieta, wife of Tibalt the fisherman, set out to climb the path from the city to the hillside where her mother had lived as a child. Salerno was always changing; there were new houses on the roads up to the hills, some of them little more than shacks, others the property of merchants who wanted a home consonant with their dignity. The wind whipped the scent of the sea over the hills; even the trees shaped to the sides of the hills in its wake.

It had been seven years since Bieta had seen her mother: a magical number. For a long time, out of deference to her husband and her father-in-law, she had not inquired where Laura had gone, or if she still lived. But for months Bieta had wondered, then quietly asked questions. There was an old woman, a lay sister, living in the cottage in the hills where old Crescia had once lived, healing any who came to her.

This morning Bieta woke with the determination that, if Laura still lived, she would make peace with her. Her daughters Bella and Fila she brought with her. They ran up the hill before her, playing in the scrubby grass, calling to each other, their round legs flashing beneath the flutter of their skirts. It was difficult, on so clear and sunny a day, to resist putting down the basket she carried and playing with her daughters, but along with charity she must teach the twins manners.

The houses to the east were, most of them, small. There was a small church as well, to serve those who did not go to the duomo for mass. If what Bieta remembered was right, she should take the next turning to the west and follow the path to the old healer's cottage. She would not know for certain that Laura was there until she reached it, but Bieta could think of no other place her mother might have gone than back to the hills.

The path branched west. "Girls!" she called. "This way!" Up the hill the shattered bulk of the Castelo d'Arechi loomed. "Don't get your gowns dirty before you even meet your *nonna*."

"If she's our *nonna*, why have we never met her before?" Bella asked, all practicality.

"It's a long tale, sweet. A tale for another day."

"Why didn't Papa come?"

"He had to bring in the fish with your grandfather, like always." When Bieta had told Tibalt what she meant to do, he had been silent for a time, then nodded. "It's time there was peace," he agreed. "Tell her I can see again." His vision had only fully returned in the right eye, but it was enough. Tibalt could negotiate the harbor, take in the nets, do his work, see his daughters' flower-like faces smiling up at him.

They reached a gate set in a fence of rails. Beyond there was a small house of stone and plaster that extended back on the hill. A shed to one side had fallen in on itself, but the garden around the house was neatly planted and tended. Bieta opened the gate and shooed her daughters through it. Then, leaving them to wait there, she approached the house and knocked at the door.

"God be blessed," came in answer. The voice was her

mother's; Bieta felt a flush of joy and anxiety as she pushed
on the door.

"Mother?"

The woman who sat at the table was short, spare, bent. Her
fingers were twisted with age. But her expression was the same:
calm, curious, ready. In every memory of her mother but the
last, this was the expression she wore.

The old woman rose to her feet. "Bieta." The name came
out as a whisper.

"Yes, Mama."

Carefully, as if she might break something by doing it,
Laura reached out her hand to Bieta, who took it in her own.
For a moment the two women examined each other; Laura's
red brows were white, and her face, which had been smooth
and pale when she lived in the city, was creased and spotted
with age. One eye was filmed with cataract, but the other
was clear. The greatest shock, though, was that Laura wore
the habit of a lay sister; a pectoral cross hung on her breast.

"I had a good deal to make right with God," the healer
said, as if interpreting her daughter's surprise. "But you—
you look beautiful, Daughter. Happy. Did he find you?"

There was no question of who "he" was.

"I found him," Bieta said. "He told me to say he got his
sight back."

"Did he?" A subtle tension went out of Laura's face. "I
prayed for it. After that night—it was as if I woke from a
dream and saw all the wrong I had done, to him and to you.
I thought only to do right, to redress what was done to me.
After that night it barely mattered what they decided at the
Scuola; you were gone. I went to God to rail at Him, but—"
She shrugged and smiled, looking down at her habit. "When
I was done railing, God was still here. I hope someday to be
forgiven."

Gently Bieta took her mother in her arms. She looked fragile now, but Bieta could feel her strength nonetheless. "By me and by Tibalt, you are, Mama. And you, are you healing here?"

The older woman smiled. "Yes. In both senses. Sit, darling girl. Let me make you some tea, and you can tell me what happened to you and how you and Tibalt found each other."

"Yes, Mama. But first—" Bieta tugged at her mother's hand as impatiently as a child. "My daughters are outside. They want to meet their grandmother."